My Happy Ending
Part 2

Time Stands Still Book 4

A novel by Carlie Yates

Published by Cardinal Moon
This is a work of fiction. Names, characters, businesses, places, events, locales,
and incidents are either the products of the author's imagination or used in a
fictitious manner. Any resemblance to actual persons, living or dead, or actual
events is purely coincidental.

ISBN: 978-1-7332649-8-3

My Happy Ending
Part 2

CHAPTER 1

TALIA

In the fog between sleep and total consciousness, it is difficult to tell the difference between fantasy and reality. But this... oh, this must be heaven, or a step so close to it...

"You've got to quit doing this to me."

His voice was different... distant, fading in and out at times, but... different.

"I don't..." He sniffled as I felt warm, calloused fingers lightly touch my cheek. "I don't know if I can take seeing you like this anymore."

That's when I could pinpoint the difference in his voice.

He'd been crying.

No... no, no, don't cry. I'm okay. See? I just... I just can't open my eyes yet. But your touch, it feels so wonderful-- so soothing, so healing.

I felt his hand move to my hair, his fingers gently running through it.

"I was going to call you... did you know that? Fuck... no, you didn't, that was stupid."

That's not stupid...and... really? I was going to call you too. Except I was going to be a shit and wait until 2:35 in the morning. Paybacks, Warner. Paybacks.

"You know what's sad, though?"

Us. Like this.

"I didn't know what to say."

I felt the pillow shift beside my head, as if he were leaning down, or perhaps laying his head next to mine.

"How did this happen, Talli? How did we get here?"

I don't know… I mean, I have an idea, but maybe if we could just, you know… talk about it then…

His voice was much closer, his breath hot on my cheek.

Just stay this close, okay? Stay this close and make me feel safe. Loved.

"It hurts so much to see you like this, all these tubes, these wires. Your… your heart Talli? Did I…" I felt his fingers interlace with mine, his hand trembling. "Did I do this to you?" His voice cracked as he asked the question, and I felt myself struggle, fight to move, to say something.

It's just this stupid heart condition, I guess it got worse. They think the damage really happened when I had Elizabeth but didn't really surface…

It wasn't you, Jase. This physical break in my heart, it wasn't you.

"They said you… they said stress could…"

I felt his lips lightly brush up against my cheek.

"I'm sorry. I'm so… so sorry, I never meant for this to happen to you."

Oh…

To me.

Not you never meant to sleep with Bree, never meant to have a relationship with her. Just…

"When was the last time I kissed you, Talli? I mean… really kissed you?"

You can't even remember that? It was…

"Right before I left for Texas," he said, and I felt his fingertips touch my lips. "I remember that… it… was real, wasn't it?"

Of course it was real, damn it! You… you are it for me. And I was going to come to Texas, I really was…and you don't know it, but I was coming alone. Yeah, the kids were going to be with Linda, and I was going to surprise you, have the concierge let me into your room when you were gone, and...

And then Jack died, and it didn't happen.

And I'm sorry.

"I... I can see now."

You can?

"I can see that... that I've hurt you enough."

What are you saying, Jase?

"I... I won't fight you anymore. We've agreed, or... or I think we're going to agree for the kids' sake, but I... I just want you to be happy. And I won't stand in your way anymore."

What the hell are you talking about?

"I just wish you had been happy with me."

Oh, this must ... this must be some kind of a flashback, right? I remember this stupid conversation, the one where he tried dropping me off at Lisa's and...

And we didn't have kids then...

I felt his lips on my forehead, the odd sensation as a couple of his tears fell on my face.

"I'm going to get our kids back, Talli, I promise. You just... you fight, okay? You fight. For you, for them. Because I... they need you."

What the hell do you mean, get our kids back? Where the hell are they? Jase... Jase, where did you go? Don't leave! Don't... I'm... you're wrong, okay? You're so wrong, you have no idea. Don't go... there was so much going on, and... and even if I don't agree with everything they have to say, I'll tell you about it, okay? Don't go! Don't...

I gasped as I opened my eyes, the light hurting my head.

"Well, hello there, Talia."

It was Jase... just a different one.

"Brooks?"

"Yeah, in the absence of your cardiologist who isn't back from the Cayman Islands yet, they actually called me."

"You're... you work pediatrics," I stammered, squinting up at him.

"Well, judging by your chart you've been acting like a child about this, so it's rather fitting isn't it?" He winked and grinned at me before pulling up a chair. "How are you feeling?"

"I hurt," was all I could say, unable to find other words to explain, my hand coming up to remove the tubing from my nose.

"No...no, don't. You inhaled some smoke; I want you to leave that on. Besides." He lifted up a monitor, showing my oxygen absorption rate to be 96. "Don't argue with me."

Smoke? What the hell happened?

"You went into atrial fibrillation," he said, leaning in slightly. "They shocked your heart back into rhythm on the scene."

"On the scene," I repeated, racking my brain to remember the events leading up to it.

"And while that has brought you back here," he continued, holding one hand out as if to display the room, "unfortunately, it hasn't eliminated the problem."

I glanced over at the machine, where my heart was beating a steady rhythm...just a very fast one.

"Dr. Mendez," I began, trying to gather my thoughts, "he said... cardiac ablation."

"And he's right, but..."

"I can't do that, Jase," I said, shaking my head. "I can't take all that time, not... not yet."

"Would you quit interrupting me? Damn, I'm not your husband," he said with a smirk. "He's right about the ablation, however...shut it, Talli... he wanted to do the maze. I think we can do this through catheterization."

"Really?" I asked, feeling just a little bit of relief. "So... outpatient, then?"

"No," he replied. "No, I'd still want you here for a day, possibly two, but... what the hell are you shaking your head for now?"

"I can't do that," I said. "Not... not yet."

"Why the hell not?"

Because I have no more paid leave left. Because I can't even afford September's rent, and I have no one to ask to help... I just can't go to Jase for this. Because our children can't be with him yet, and...

Our children...

"Where are my kids?"

Brooks blinked a couple of times, a frown on his face. "I'm not...

sure. With Jase?"

"Are they?" I asked quickly, placing a hand on his arm. "I have to know."

"Talli, you have got to…"

"If you want me to calm down, you tell me where the hell my kids are."

He took a deep breath and nodded. "Jase's just down the hall."

"And the kids?"

"I'll go get Jase. But you and I aren't through talking, got it?"

"Yeah," I said, absentmindedly chewing on my thumbnail. But didn't Brooks just say that maybe the kids were with Jase? He has to be lying, because they wouldn't be down the hall with him. Maybe… maybe they were with Linda or Jackie or Sondra or…

"Hi."

I was stunned silent at the sight of Jase in front of me, his hair more tousled than usual, his shirt only half tucked in. His eyes were swollen slightly, red rimmed, and I wondered in a brief moment of hysteria what had happened to make him look this way.

"Oh no…" I began, but he held his hand up, shaking his head.

"They're okay."

His voice sounded strained, rough.

"Are they with Linda?" I asked, and he shook his head, staying close to the door. "Where…" My voice trailed off as his eyes dropped to the floor. "Jase, talk to me."

"I'm going to get them back," he said, his eyes locked with mine once more. "I called Rebecca, and… and she's working on it."

Wait a minute… he'd… he'd said that earlier, hadn't he?

"What do you mean back?" I asked. His eyes were pained as he looked at the machines hooked up to me, the heart rate increasing once more.

"Talli, please… calm… I can't stay…"

"Don't you walk out that door," I snapped. "Where are our babies?"

"They won't let me stay if… if that happens," he finished, gesturing to the machine.

Just hold my hand… please, just hold my hand, it would make me feel so much better…

"Please tell me," I sobbed, a tear escaping and trailing down my cheek.

"They took... they took them."

"They *who*?"

"We don't have any relatives that live here."

"They have you."

He winced at my words, shoving his hands into his pockets. "I'm not allowed to have them, Talli."

Oh fuck...

What have I done?

"But Rebecca, she's waking up any judge who will listen, and... and she's trying to fix this, okay?"

"I've got to get out of here," I said, sitting up abruptly and swinging my legs over to the side. The room immediately began to spin.

"Hey... hey, just..." He was beside me suddenly, his hands lightly touching my shoulders but his fingers outstretched, as if touching me were the last thing he wanted to do. "You're in no shape to just leave."

"They took..." I closed my eyes against the wave of nausea, leaning sideways down into the pillow.

"What... happened?"

He wasn't touching me anymore. He'd moved back, his hands back in his pockets as he stared down at me.

"There was... there was the alarm, and..."

"Your heart, Talli. What's..." He licked his lips, almost acting afraid to ask. "What's wrong?"

"Atrial fibrillation," I replied. "It's just... well, that's what happened there, and they shocked it back."

"Shocked it?" he repeated, biting his lip as I nodded. "Is it... a... fluke, or..."

"It's been bothering me for a while," I said, watching his face as my words registered, waiting for the anger to flash in his eyes.

There was none.

Only a profound sadness.

"How long?" His question was so quiet I barely heard it. I thought it over, wanting to be completely honest with him.

"Em's party," I replied. "I think... I think that's what happened."

6

"Why..." He took a deep breath and looked away, leaving the question unfinished.

But I already knew the rest of it.

"I..."

I didn't know how to tell you. I didn't think you'd care. You were already trying to say I was on drugs, trying to take the kids away. You were with Bree, what did it matter if something was wrong with me?

The silence was deafening as it stretched on, only the beeping of the machines filling the air.

How did it come to this?

"I should have," I finally said, and he lifted his eyes from the floor.

"What are they saying now?" he asked, and I took in a quivering breath.

"I need to have cardiac ablation," I answered. "But I can't..."

"You have to." His voice was strong, forceful when he said this.

"I... I have to get out of here, Jase. I can't..." I covered my mouth to stifle a sob before continuing. "One night. That's it, Jase. That's all they've ever spent without you... or... or me. One night."

"You let me worry about that."

"Are you fucking crazy?" I asked, and he shrugged.

"I've been called worse."

"I... I need to call Sherise. And I need to call..."

"You need to rest," he cut me off. "I'll... I'll fix this. You tell Brooks that you'll do the surgery."

"It's not..."

My voice trailed off as he narrowed his eyes, a muscle in his jaw twitching. "Don't make me be a dick about this, Talli."

Under any other circumstances I might scoff at him, tell him to bring his best he'd never beat me.

But not today.

"Not until our babies are back with you. If... if they won't give them back, then I say no. And I leave, and I get them, and..." I closed my eyes as another wave of nausea swept over me. When I opened them, he was standing by the door, swallowing repeatedly as he looked at me.

"Okay," he said softly. "Deal."

7

JASE

Silence is my enemy.

It cost me my marriage; it has at least temporarily cost me my children. And right now, it's costing me what's left of my mind.

As the minutes ticked away, the what ifs and should haves were eating away at my sanity. I sat in the darkness outside the hospital, the hard metal bench my only company as I watched the occasional car pass by on their way to the emergency department, or the parking garage. I wondered how many husbands were fretting over their wives, how many fathers were praying for their children to be safe, and to come home.

At least by that point I was fairly certain I'd cried all the tears I had.

My phone buzzed in my pocket and I pulled it out, squinting at the text from Rebecca.

Going to judge's chambers now.

My hands were shaking as I shot back my quick reply.

Thank you so much for this. If it helps, Jackie is picking my Nan up from the airport now.

I didn't know how much good it would do, if any at all. But they'd told me that because their custodial parent was incapacitated and there were no other relatives...besides me, of course... that the children were going to be placed in temporary emergency foster care.

Foster care.

With strangers.

For the first time I was almost thankful for the paparazzi. See, Rebecca explained to me how their stalking of the bowling alley had helped in more ways than one-- it showed that Talli accepted me in their lives, for one. And for two, they plastered my children's faces over every rag mag that would buy them. While that pissed me off to no end when it happened, the fact that they were now recognizable would help with my case that no foster family could possibly keep them safe. And if they wouldn't let me take them, then there was no shortage of people who could.

Especially my Nan.

My Mam who cried along with me, who promised to bring my

babies home.

Rebecca seemed very confident, though, that her presence, if needed at all, would only be temporary, and that I would be granted full custody until such time as Talli was able to care for them as well.

I want her to understand.

I want her to forgive me if it seems that I'm trying to take them away from her.

It had been fifteen minutes since I'd shot that text to Rebecca and had yet to see a reply, so I was truly hoping that she was in there making my case. She'd shot me a text earlier that said Sherise Adler didn't even show up herself and had sent one of her associates to iron out any details. Apparently conceding is not part of Ms. Adler's repertoire, not that I gave a damn.

One glance at my watch told me it was almost 11 pm. It had been nearly five hours since I felt my fragile existence begin to crumble even more. I looked up the side of the building, wondering if Talli was getting the rest she was ordered to, wishing that even if she was, she wanted my company.

I just didn't want to ask.

I just want her to be happy. I want her to smile as freely as she used to, laugh as if she didn't have a care in the world. I want that sparkle in her eyes, the blush in her cheeks when she's full of joy. I want her to enjoy life again, the way she used to, before... well, before it had all changed, and she'd become a shell of herself, only going through the motions, sacrificing her own happiness for everyone around her.

For me.

Since sitting around outside was only giving my mind license to wander into territory that it shouldn't right now, wishing for answers, longing to be that someone to her again, I decided it was time to either hunt down a damn good cup of coffee, or at least a vending machine with Dr. Pepper. Something told me this was going to be a long night.

One would think that I'd know where things were in this hospital, you know? My wife works here, my children were born here, I almost lost my girls here, before Talli and I were ever married. But do I know where the damn vending machines are? No. Apparently neither did the signs in the hallway, because somehow, I ended up down by the doctors entrance from their parking area.

"Fuck," I muttered, turning around, trying to find my way back. This damn place should have homing devices, I swear, and...

"Jase?"

I turned, startled that anyone was near. Dr. Stewart was walking behind me in the hallway, adjusting her glasses on her face.

"Hi," I said softly, a little uneasy. Talli worked closely with this woman, she had once saved Talli's life. This also meant that I was sure she saw me as the scum of the Earth. I stopped in my tracks, though, noting the look on her face was one of concern.

"I heard about the fire. I assume that's why you're here?"

"Yeah," I replied softly, shoving my shaking hands in my pockets.

"They said Emily's doing just fine, giving all the nurses her best saved smiles. I suppose it's a good thing that she's used to it here."

Emily's...here? She's here?! Observation... that's right...

"I... um..." I licked my lips, noting how dry they were, nearly over the edge. "From... daycare, right?"

"Well, I suppose," Dr. Stewart replied, an easy grin on her face. "It's probably more due to all the overnighters she's had to pull in that wing, that poor baby."

"Overnighters?" I asked, shocked back to the present.

"Oh, they were mostly for observation, when her croupe would become too much and her chest would begin to retract. They don't like to diagnose asthma too early with children, but I'm fairly certain that she does have it."

Oh God... Emmy... why didn't Talli...

No, she'd said... that she couldn't make it... and...

She hadn't lied to me. Talli... she wasn't making up... excuses, and...

"Is she okay?" I asked, my mind racing a million miles a minute, wanting so badly to go up and find our little girl.

"Haven't they...oh." She placed her hand on my arm soothingly. "Come with me. Let's find out."

I know I murmured my thanks but found myself unable to say much of anything else as I followed her to the elevators and up to the floor her office was on.

"I hope you don't mind," she said as she opened that back doorway, punching in the code to the alarm. "There's something I need from my office before I go to L and D. You know where Talli's office is, right? She always keeps Dr. Pepper in her mini fridge."

"Talli drinks..."

"She kept it there for you," Dr. Stewart cut me off. "Just in case you ever stopped by."

Which I hadn't. Not since I'd gotten off that damn tour.

But that small bit of information warmed my heart in ways I hadn't thought possible anymore.

"Thank you," I said softly, following her again down the back hall, pausing as she unlocked the door to Talli's office.

"She's good about having charts put away... but if anything's out, no peeking. It would be my ass, and I'd hand yours to you on a platter."

"I... I wouldn't..."

No amount of charts could have pulled my eyes away from that bulletin board.

"I think the mini fridge is behind her desk," Dr. Stewart's voice filtered in from her office just across the hall.

That's... us...

Talli and me.

She kept that here? Up on this bulletin board? Even after... after everything?

I sunk into her chair, emitting a short laugh at how my knees felt they were up in my chest. I raised one shaky hand, removing the pin and pulling the picture from its spot, holding it in front of me. When was this taken? I know we were on a vacation of some kind...

"Just a sec and I'll have what I need."

We were so close, smiling, our arms around each other. She was tucked right up against me, and if I closed my eyes I could almost feel her there...

"Got it."

I jumped as Dr. Stewart entered the room, quickly pinning the picture back up on her bulletin board.

"Sorry," I muttered, turning to reach into her mini fridge. I'll be damned... right there, beside her Diet Pepsi were six cans of Dr. Pepper.

For me.

"I made a quick call. Emily's sleeping soundly. If you'd like, I can sneak you up there."

"Would you?" I asked quickly, turning around, genuinely touched by her kindness and concern.

"Of course," she said, leaning in to take a better look at the picture I had been holding. "I know it's hard to imagine, but there are many, many families in your situation. I've had to help more husbands than you would know get through this. She misses you, you know. I can see it. We all can."

"Somehow I doubt that," I said, beginning to stand, but faltering when she continued.

"Postpartum depression doesn't just affect the mother; it effects the entire family. And many marriages don't survive, especially those who don't seek counseling."

"I'm sorry, what?"

"I know I can talk about this with you... I... just checked," she said, holding a file in her hand. "She'd signed a form long ago allowing me to discuss all aspects of her care, her diagnosis, everything with you. She never changed it. Not even with the pending divorce."

"Post...partum depression?" I repeated the words, trying to wrap my head around it, wanting a full explanation, but almost afraid to ask.

"After Emily was born," Dr. Stewart continued, sitting on the edge of Talli's immaculate desk, "there was a definite... change in her."

Yes... yes, there was.

"Some people call it the baby blues, and sometimes it's very mild and passes on its own. Just the anxiety, irritability, the crying... those are all normal reactions, hormones fluctuating along with getting to know this new member of your family. But postpartum depression is much more serious."

I accepted the pamphlet she placed in my trembling hand, tears that I had thought were long gone resurfacing.

"This is a disease, Jase. It is real, and it interferes with everyone's lives, and can do irreparable damage to a couple's relationship if left untreated, or if the father if left in the dark, and doesn't understand what is going on."

"I... I don't... are you sure?"

"May I ask you a few questions? To help me understand a little more of how deep this has gone?"

"I..." I swallowed over the lump in my throat, licking my lips again, "I suppose. Yeah, s...sure."

"With mothers suffering from this, there tends to be difficulty bonding with the baby. I remember her saying that Em was a Daddy's girl, but I need to know what sort of effort she put forth."

"She was so tired," I tried explaining. "I mean, she... sometimes she was too tired to get up, so... so I did. It was..."

Exhausting. Frustrating. A catalyst for more than one argument.

"...fine, I guess."

"Fine," she said, one eyebrow raised. "Is that normal for her, that kind of behavior? Did it happen after the other children?"

"No," I replied. "I just..." I looked down, shrugging. "I thought it was an excuse."

"An excuse for what, Jase?"

I felt the heat creep up in my cheeks, the bile in my throat as I had to voice it out loud, no matter how much it hurt. "To be alone. Or to not be...with me. But she was fine, you know? I mean... she really tried, before I..."

Before I left her to deal with this. Alone.

How did I not see?

"There is a noted deterioration here about... October, I believe. Of last year. That's when you went on tour, isn't it?"

Without looking up, I nodded.

"Those are some of the classic signs, Jase. And... what about... her outlook?"

I looked up briefly, confused.

"On life, Jase. Did she find any... joy? In... well, in anything?"

"She was just..." I took in a quivering breath, my voice thick with emotion. "She was unhappy. Just... unhappy. No matter what, no matter who, no matter when, and I..."

I just accepted it. Instead of questioning it, I accepted it.

"Many mothers who suffer from this also have a lack of sex drive," she rattled on, "lack of motivation, severe mood swings, their irritability becomes very intense. They are...well, they seem to be a completely different person."

I covered my face, stifling a sob, chastising myself as everything began to sink in. How could I have been so blind? It isn't as if I'd never heard of postpartum depression before; I knew it existed. How could I not see this?

"This is where I need your help, Jase."

I wiped my eyes hastily as I looked up at Dr. Stewart. "I don't know what I could do to help," I scoffed. "Hell, I've already failed her. I... I turned on her, I... I abandoned her. I never should have left; I should have seen this... I..."

"Jase, stop," she said softly. "You shouldn't beat yourself up over this."

"I... I just..."

I took it personal. She... she didn't want to be with me.

And I never questioned why. I just... well, it hurt, so I pulled away. And the more she pushed, the more I pulled.

Until I ran.

Right into someone else's arms.

"She has adamantly refused any form of medication," Dr. Stewart continued. "No mood stabilizers, nothing for depression, nothing for anxiety."

"She wouldn't..." I took a deep breath, trying to calm myself. "She always swore there's no way in hell she'd take anything like that again."

"But I really think she needs it, and I feel that perhaps... if you could talk with her about it?"

I laughed softly, wiping my eyes for what had to be the millionth time that night. "You don't know..."

"I know her rather well."

"No, I mean... *why*. I know there was stuff in the tabloids, but..." I took a shuddering breath, swearing at myself yet again. "She was very proud that she stayed clean for so long. And... and then I..."

"Please, don't blame yourself."

"But so much of this... is..."

"Jase, you can't..."

"This whole mess? With the kids? It's because all that shit about the drugs was brought up again," I blurted out. "And I should have known better, you know? So if I walk in there and tell her that she should take medication that she's sworn off for life, do you know what she's going to think?"

"I... I see what you're saying. And I have to admit that ever since she agreed to counseling, she's come... well, she's coming around. A lot."

And I'm sure Paul is there to help her every step of the way.

"Jase... I know this is a lot to process. Just...if you need to talk, please don't hesitate to call me, okay?"

I nodded, sniffling slightly as I looked down at the pamphlets in my hand.

"There's a plethora of information out there. It would help... probably everyone involved, if you educated yourself on the subject."

I nodded once more, knowing beyond a shadow of any doubt before all of this was over I would be an expert on the subject.

"I have a couple of nurses willing to help get you in with Emily. Would you like to give her a kiss goodnight?"

Holy hell would I ever!

But... but...

"Give me a few minutes, okay?" I stood, pulling her into a hug that she didn't expect. "Thank you... so much," I sobbed before pulling back and wiping my eyes once more.

"You're welcome," she said softly. "Go, pull yourself together. Meet me by the pediatric wing in, say, a half hour?"

"Absolutely... absolutely."

My mind was reeling with all of this information, my own self-loathing tearing me to shreds as I walked down that hallway. I knew I needed to get myself together before I made my way to see Emily, if she woke up to see me this way it might upset her. Unless she just decided to take my hat off my head and chew on it...

But right then...

Right then there was something I needed to do.

Something I should have done months ago.

MY HAPPY ENDING

CHAPTER 2

TALIA

It's amazing. One day you pay attention. Then the next day comes, and the next...

Days turn into a week, then a few weeks, then a month, and then two... All gone, all unnoticed.

Until you stop.

Something makes you just... stop.

I was lying there in that hospital bed trying to pinpoint the exact moment my eyes had begun to open, to see my surroundings, to see the shambles my life had become.

Scratch that... forget my life for just one moment...

The children. Their lives had been ripped to shreds by circumstances that were completely out of their control.

Slowly, over these last small handful of weeks, little by little I stopped merely existing. I opened my eyes to my surroundings, our surroundings, I opened my eyes to the person that I had become.

Or the lack of person, if that makes any sense.

As I laid there in my hospital bed, scowling at that silent phone knowing that Jaden should have called me back by now, it kind of occurred to me that there are literally chunks of my life that are just... missing. Gone, poof, nonexistent. But they couldn't be, since here we were in August, nearing September, so obviously life had gone on.

When had I become so cold-hearted, though?

When had sleeping become more important than intimacy?

When had smiles become uncommon?

When did I stop laughing?

When did I stop *feeling*?

Why did I use all of those as defense mechanisms, and against what?

I don't have the answers to those questions. I don't know if I ever will. All I know was that one day... one day, I just looked in the mirror, and there was this... this... *stranger* staring back at me. She had dark circles and...and frown lines, and all she wore was black or gray, or sometimes brown. Her hair screamed 'mom' or 'work'. Her eyes had no sparkle, no life to them. The girl who at one time had the world at her fingertips had let it all slip away.

And all that was left was this shell.

This shell that had gone through the motions of what once was my life, ripping every bit of hope and joy from it and leaving the depths of despair in its place.

The despair that she hadn't allowed herself to feel.

The despair that suddenly, out of the blue, had a vice grip on my heart.

And I could *feel* it.

I felt it with every fiber of my being. I felt the hurt, the pain, the anger coursing through my veins. And I embraced it, with open arms, weeping not only for everything that I had lost, but because now I knew.

Now I could live.

Simply feeling wasn't going to be good enough, though; I knew that, and I wasn't going to bullshit myself into thinking otherwise. But it was a start, a push in the right direction.

And then...

Then *this* happened.

And I didn't know whether to laugh or to cry, to be thankful that I could feel the pain of our children being taken away or pray for the oblivion, the emotionless zombie that could look at this through cold, dead eyes and just... cope.

I curled over on my side, looking out the window at the night sky, sighing as sleep eluded me once more. This was part of the problem with the zombie disappearing. Now my mind wouldn't stop working, wouldn't give me any peace. I needed reassurance, I needed to know that my children were okay, that they were going to be with their father. Because until that happened...

I bit the inside of my lip as once again my heart began to race.

Calm, cool, collected. Calm, cool, collected. You hear that?! Calm, cool, COLLECTED...

"Talli?"

I opened my eyes, glancing over my shoulder as Jase Brooks entered my room.

"I just finished my rounds," he said, pulling a chair up closer and sitting down. "So... I want to talk with you, okay?"

I nodded, turning towards him and swallowing over the lump in my throat.

"We've already done everything we can do. Shocking your heart brought you back, but it didn't fix the problem. Your cardiac medications aren't fixing the problem. You already know what it's going to take."

"Did you know," I cut him off, "that right now I don't even have a place to live? Not that it was destroyed by fire, but the entire building is closed until the repairs are made. Did you know that?"

He sighed, leaning forward and resting is elbows on his knees. "Yeah, I heard that."

"But you know, that's almost like a blessing, since... since I couldn't make..." My voice trailed off as shame overtook me, unable to voice that I couldn't pay my rent anyhow. "So my insurance might pay for a hotel room, until I can go back home. God, I hate hotel rooms," I said with a shudder. "And... and it's no place for my children to live, but... but right now they're not even with me so that doesn't matter."

"But they will be if..."

"I don't have weeks, Jase. I don't. I can't take the time off work, I can't take the time away from them."

"If you don't take these weeks, you are essentially giving them up, giving them away. Because it won't take much more before you won't be here at all."

I was silent, his words sinking in.

I knew they were true. I knew, above every other cardiologist on this planet, Dr. Jase Brooks would not bullshit me in any way, shape, or form.

That didn't calm my immediate fears.

"Nobody's called me," I continued, curling up slightly. "If someone would just call and tell me, let me know where they're at, tell me that they're going back to Jase, then…"

Brooks scratched the back of his head. "I had your phone shut off about an hour ago. I wanted you to rest."

I licked my lips, one eyebrow raised as I glared at him. "I could kick your ass for that, you know?"

"Jase's here," he said, his eyes narrowing as if he were trying to convey some message to me. "He hasn't left. And you know the moment he hears anything, he'll let you know."

Jase… was still here?

"No…" My eyes fell for a brief moment, before I raised them again. "No, I didn't know. What about Emily?"

"Then I'm sorry, the last thing I meant to do was cause any more worry. And Emily… well, she's the same as when you asked about her an hour ago, and she's just a couple of floors away. Tell you what," he said, standing up. "I'm going ahead and ordering that surgery for… have you eaten anything in the past couple of hours?"

"I don't want to eat, but…"

"I'll have them schedule it for eleven in the morning. And let's get technical here, it's not even surgery. You can even be awake for it if you want. But no eating, no drinking, no Starbucks, no Diet Pepsi."

"But… my kids, Jase. The children."

Brooks looked over his shoulder, smirking at me. "You've been married to him for how many years? He'll have them back long before then."

He had so much faith.

When had mine wavered?

Oh, right.

That's when.

I glared at the television that was on CNN, some entertainment news of some sort, where Bree was telling a reporter how Jase was just beside himself.

21

I'm sure he is, bitch.

I picked up my phone, dialing Jaden's number quickly, needing something... someone to calm my ass down.

Oh...wow...

I... I hadn't called someone for *that* in... how long?

"I swear I tried to call you," was how she answered the phone.

"I know, Brooks just informed me that he had my incoming calls stopped. Stupid fucker."

I heard her stifle what sounded to be like a half-laugh, half-sob. "You work in a hospital, Talli, you know how it works."

"Yeah, yeah, likely story. You know, if you were here, I'd have you break me the hell out so I could find Bree Hamilton and rip her extensions out of her bleached blonde head. Did you see that bitch on tv tonight?"

"Yeah," she said, and that time I knew I heard her sniffle. "Yeah, I did."

"My kids are god knows where and that bitch goes to the paparazzi to flaunt her relationship with my husband? I could just fucking kill her!"

"Talli, I..."

"And why the hell are you crying?"

"I'm just so happy. I mean I'm sad... because... because this shouldn't be happening, but... do you... can you hear yourself?"

"Um... yeah. And I think that if I don't keep my voice down everyone on this floor will hear me, too. Oh! Brooks scheduled that thingy for eleven tomorrow morning, but if the kids aren't with Jase by then he can kiss my ass, and... what?"

I couldn't continue as she sobbed and I heard Pete in the background asking what was wrong, what else had happened.

"Listen, don't sweat you not being here, okay?" I said, suddenly feeling guilty for dumping all of this on her. "You stay put, take care of he-who-has-yet-to-be-named and yourself. I'm fine; don't..."

"...worry about you, oh fuck, Talli, I've missed you."

I blinked several times at her answer. "Um... you just saw me, what... a couple days ago?"

"And... and I did see you, I saw glimpses of you, and... what happened? Where did my best friend go, and… and what brought her back?"

I bit my bottom lip as I contemplated not if, but how I should tell her. "Talli?"

But right then I was unable to say anything.

My eyes were fixated on a figure filling my doorway, his kaleidoscope eyes a stormy gray as he held me captive with his gaze.

"Talli, what…"

"I'll call you back, okay?" I finally said, not waiting for her answer as I put the receiver back on its cradle.

My breath caught in my throat as he stepped in, his eyes swimming, his jaw set.

"Oh fuck, is something wrong with the kids?" I asked in a rush, sitting up a little straighter.

He shook his head no, staying silent as he began to slowly walk towards me.

"Any news on them yet?" I asked, my stomach in knots even with the relief that nothing more was wrong.

At least not with them.

He shook his head again, pulling his hands out of his pockets as he continued walking closer.

"See?" I said, gesturing towards the monitor. "Normal. Completely. And if they don't pull their heads out of their asses, then they can just wait. And I'll walk out of here… and…"

My voice faltered as he reached my bed, sitting on the edge of it, so close I could feel him trembling.

"…and I'll go get our babies," I continued, my voice not quite as strong, his presence making every nerve ending come to life. "And then we'll… we'll fix this, and they can stay with you while…"

My eyes slid shut as his hand caressed the side of my face.

It was heaven…

I felt his arms encircle me, pulling me close…

Holding me to him.

Just…

Holding me.

Slowly, tentatively, so afraid, so unsure, I wrapped my arms around him, afraid to touch him, the monitor giving the pounding of my heart away. I felt his hands open wide, his grip tightening ever so slightly.

I buried my face in his chest, my hands caressing his back slightly before grabbing tightly.

Holding him.

Holding onto him for dear life.

The way I've wanted to.

The way I should have.

JASE

I didn't know what was driving me. It was nothing I could pinpoint, nothing I could put my finger on just then.

I just wanted to hold her.

The way I should have.

I barely registered what she was saying, the questions she was asking. I could only shake my head, not even form any words right then. My mind could only focus on that possibility, that sliver of hope. All I could think of was maybe…

Just…

Maybe.

She was so beautiful, no matter how pale, no matter how sad. I reached up, caressing the side of her face, just a little reassurance to myself that she was real, waiting for the flinch.

It never came.

She didn't cringe, she didn't move away.

I watched her eyes close slowly, her lips parting as she inhaled, and I knew… I knew exactly what was driving me.

It was love.

I was so frightened, so unsure as I pulled her into my arms, the way I should have every time I'd wanted to.

This… *this* was what I should have done when she'd said she was tired.

When she said she'd had a bad day.

When she looked so frazzled, so hurried, so upset when she would forget something.

When she pulled away... from... me...

She's not pulling away... oh... oh, god...

I felt her arms snake around me, barely touching, her ear resting against my chest where I held her, pulling her in just a little tighter as her pulse began to pick up speed.

Sssshhhh, baby, please... please calm down, please don't push...

I bit the inside of my lip, my eyes filling with tears as she pulled me closer, turning her face in to my chest.

Just like she used to.

I felt her shoulders began to shake, her tears soaking the front of my shirt as she clung to me, the pure raw emotion tangible... welcomed.

"They've never been with strangers..."

There was no disappointment, knowing her heart was breaking for our children. Only relief, only consolation.

"Rebecca was going in the judge's chambers. We're going to get them back soon, okay?"

"Are you sure?"

I smiled into her hair, a couple tears of my own dropping as I held her. "I... I'm sure. She's good. She's real good."

"I did not need to hear that."

I chuckled softly, a sob breaking through, and I held her just a little tighter. "I wouldn't know that, Talli. I don't need her husband to kick my ass." And with that, she let out a short laugh, too.

I had missed her... missed this... so much more than I had consciously thought.

"When... when you came in here... you... you scared me, and I thought that... something had... happened," she continued on, and I could feel her hands twisting in my shirt, just like they used to.

And slowly, she pulled back.

And without her I felt so empty.

And I felt her hand smooth the front of my shirt, just like she used to.

"What happened?" she asked, her voice barely registering over my heart that was hammering.

"I should have seen," I stammered, so afraid to continue, even more afraid to say nothing.

"But at the party…"

"Before," I cut her off, trying to stay on the subject, get out everything I had to say. "Before I left… on tour. I should have seen that something was wrong, but I was… I was too blinded, too complacent, too wrapped up in… in myself."

Her lower lip was trembling as she looked down at her hands, which were now twisting in her lap. I wanted so badly to look into those eyes as I told her this, but so afraid of rejection, of her pushing me away that instead I continued on.

"I… I saw Dr. Stewart, and… I'm… well, I'm refraining from the 'why didn't you tell me's right now, because I'm just so… ashamed. So full of guilt and… and I wanted to tell you that I'm sorry."

"You didn't do this, Jase," she said, her voice soft, shaking.

"But you're…" I wanted so badly to say that she was my wife, and I knew her better than anyone, but I obviously didn't, and… and she was in the process of…

"No, really… you… don't…"

"I do owe you an apology, Talli, because I should have been there. I should have seen it, and I should… I should have made you… get help. Made you talk to… to…"

"You know what they say about people in medical, right?" She let out a short laugh, brushing away her still-falling tears. "We're the worst patients. Constant…"

"Denial," I finished for her… no, *with* her.

With her.

She glanced up briefly, before looking back down at her hands. "I know I was difficult."

"Yeah, and then *this* happened… I'm kidding, I'm kidding." I held up my hands as she glared at me for one brief moment, before her trembling lips began to smile.

There's my girl…

"You don't…" I took a deep breath, knowing the gravity of what I was about to say, knowing the can of worms it could open and that it had the potential of being ugly. "You don't have to keep anything from me," I finally said in a rush. "Okay? And… and you don't have anything to be ashamed of, or… or… you didn't…" I licked my lips, feeling so very

26

awkward, hating that I was at a loss for words. "You didn't do anything wrong."

"That's not true," she sobbed, pulling back when I reached for her.

Fuck. Fuck, damn it... the walls, they're going back up.

"I told Dr. Stewart that it was a losing battle if she thought she'd get you to take the medication," I added, trying to keep the conversation going, praying she wouldn't shut down. "And... and you're going to get better, you're going to be happy again."

Even if it's without me.

"I can't think about that right now."

"You can't keep living in denial, Talli."

"I'm not living in denial, Jase," she snapped, her eyes angry.

It's okay, Talli. Just let it go. Just feel.

"Our children are... are with strangers, I'm stuck in the fucking hospital, Brooks has that... that thing that he thinks he's doing to my heart tomorrow..."

"He *is* going to."

"Not if the kids aren't with you."

"Talli..."

"Don't 'Talli' me, we made a deal."

"And right now, we're talking about your PPD."

"And do you know how sick I am of hearing about that?" she asked, exasperated, throwing her hands in the air.

"No, I wouldn't know. I've just heard about it in the past... oh, fifteen minutes? Ish?"

I regretted those words almost immediately as her eyes again fell to her hands.

"Talli, I..."

"I'm sorry," she interrupted me, her eyes locked with mine once more.

And I was frozen.

Stunned.

Heartbroken at the pain in her eyes.

"Don't be sorry," I said after the silence had lasted a beat too long. "Just get better. Be... happy."

But even as I said those words, I felt my own resolve begin to crumble, wanting more than anything to pull her into my arms again, tell her how much I loved her.

I couldn't do that.

I couldn't risk her pulling away even more than she already had, not with our truce of sorts so new, so fragile.

"Shift change," her nurse said as she walked in, a smile on her face as she pulled her cart in behind her. "Time for a vitals check."

And I took that as my cue, the perfect one, without an awkward transition.

"I should go," I said, standing up and walking towards the door, stopping as I realized I hadn't told her. "Dr. Stewart is taking me to see Emmy, give her a kiss goodnight."

Talia's mouth formed an 'o' and she placed her hand over her heart, making my own heart ache in return. "Give her a kiss from me, too?"

"Of course."

"And tell me how she's doing?"

"You know I will. Oh, and Talli?"

I knew she wouldn't be able to say anything as the nurse had place the thermometer in her mouth.

"This doesn't count," I said. As confusion settled over her features, I pointed to her nurse, then the clock, then held up five fingers for her.

This was *not* our five minutes.

As realization of what I was telling her settled in, she responded the only way she could.

She flipped me off.

I was an emotional wreck. A basket case, if you will.

I'd held her… I actually held her… so close to me, I could hear her heartbeat, smell the lingering smoke that overpowered the jasmine. All of the love, the confusion, the hurt, the frustration were boiling in my veins, threatening to consume me completely. I'd thought I'd be okay if I just… held her.

But I was wrong.

While it put a small band aid on the wounds we had inflicted on each other, it also succeeded in kicking down the wall I'd thought I had secured around my heart. I should have known it was too fragile to handle this.

No... I'm sure I knew. I just didn't care.

I'd do anything for her.

And then, I'd gone straight up and seen our baby, sleeping soundly in that metal crib, her butt up in the air. Her little mouth was opened slightly, just a trace of drool on the mattress below her head. Her freshly washed curls were soft to the touch as I gently ran my fingers through them, placing my hand on her back to feel the steady rise and fall of her chest with each breath.

I leaned down, placing a soft kiss on her cheek, biting my lip slightly as she squirmed, the sweet scent of baby shampoo enveloping my senses. They must have given her a bath, gotten that awful scent off of her, but somewhere I could still smell it. I thought for one brief almost hysterical moment that I was imagining things, or just had that severe case of Talli on the brain, until I saw it.

That small picture, crinkled, damaged, yellowed slightly, but held firmly in her chubby little hand.

And I lost it.

I folded, crumbled right beside that crib, trying to hold back, trying to stay as quiet as I could so Emily wouldn't be disturbed.

It was so cliché, seeing that picture in our baby's hand, as if she was holding on to the hope, the way I was so afraid to. I chastised myself over and over as I walked away from Emily, letting her sleep on, sneaking past the nurses who were ordered to keep me away.

I should have fought harder.

I should have seen what was going on.

I should have demanded that she talked to me. Then and now.

I should have really talked with her up in that hospital room, more than I did. I was afraid to, though... afraid that she'd put those walls back up, even more than she'd begun to. I was afraid that she would push me away, and I couldn't let that happen.

She needed me.

Whether or not she was willing to admit it.

I just had to make her see.

And help calm her fears…

I checked my phone, scowling that there were no missed calls, no texts from Rebecca. *This cannot be good*…

I was biting my thumbnail as I walked outside, my phone already up to my ear as I waited for the call to go through.

Fuck.

Fucking voicemail.

"Rebecca… it's Jase, and I… I'm going crazy here. Please call me back, I have to know what's going on, okay? It was, what, an hour… no, over an hour ago… please… please call me, and…"

"Daddy!"

That brand new cell phone slipped from my fingers, shattering into pieces at my feet as I turned towards the sound of Elizabeth's voice. There was no mistaking the outlines of our two oldest children as they took off running towards me.

Is this really… really happening?

I dropped to my knees, my arms outstretched for them, only accepting that this wasn't some sick figment of my imagination when they threw themselves at me, Michael joyful, Elizabeth sobbing.

"Daddy, we gets to come home!" Michael exclaimed.

Oh… I… I get to take them home…

My eyes slid shut as I bit back a sob, keeping myself strong for them-- our son, who didn't understand what had happened, and our oldest daughter, who understood all too well.

"Don't leave me 'gain…Daddy," Elizabeth stuttered through her sobs into my shoulder.

"Never, Baby Girl… never again," I murmured, holding them close, breathing them in.

"And… and Mommy? Daddy, is Mommy… dead?"

"Nooooo," I crooned, pushing them back slightly. "No, baby, she's right inside here…"

"Is she working?" Michael asked.

"No, baby, she's… she's getting better."

"I wanna see… I wanna see her," Elizabeth said, still sobbing, her bottom lip trembling. *Oh Baby Girl, you've probably been crying the whole time, haven't you?*

"I'll... I'll get you in there, okay?" I said, kissing her forehead softly, not knowing how but knowing it would happen.

They all needed it.

"D'you mean it?" she asked.

"With all of my heart."

"Can we hurry, Daddy?" Michael asked, his head a bit to the side. "I has to pee."

I laughed softly, tousling his hair and placing a kiss on his forehead. "Yeah, let's get you guys in there. But you have to be quiet, okay?"

"Easy there, Daddy," Rebecca said as she sauntered up, interrupting her conversation with my mom and Jackie to talk to me. "Are you so sure you can..."

I pulled her into my arms, cutting off her words as well as temporarily cutting off her air supply. "Thank you, Rebecca... I don't know what or how or..."

"Air..."

"But you did it, and they're back. And I can't thank you enough, and..."

"Air..."

"And I'll make this up to you, you know? And..."

"Jase," my Nan said, placing her hand on my arm, and I stepped back from Rebecca, grinning sheepishly.

"Sorry about that," I mumbled.

"No problem, no problem," Rebecca said with a grin.

"How are you?" Nan asked, pulling me into her arms.

"I... I have so much to tell you," I sobbed into her shoulder, before pulling myself together again, stepping back as Michael called out to me.

"Daddy, I has to pee!"

I smiled, placing my hand over my heart, trying to relay all of the love and appreciation I felt for them... all of them... before I ran after my kids, chasing them as they giggled their way into the hospital.

CHAPTER 3

TALIA

I t took less than five minutes of talking to my sister before I wished I'd never returned her call.

"So, I've been looking up airfare, and I can be there in two days, okay?" she was saying.

"No, that really isn't necessary, Lisa," I said, perhaps a bit quicker than I should have.

"What, you don't want me out there?"

No. Emphatically not. I suffered through weeks of torture after the accident, I can't go through that again.

"It's not that, Lisa. I just know that you have… things to do, and… and this isn't like the accident anyhow." I shrugged, even though she couldn't see me, as I played with a loose string on my blanket.

"Well, someone needs to take care of you."

"I am perfectly capable of taking care of myself, thank you," I replied as calmly as I could. "When I am released from this hospital, the worst I have to do is take it easy. If all goes the way Brooks thinks it will, I won't even need my cardiac meds anymore."

"I don't understand your aversion to medication."

"Really? Do you need a recap, oh she who is so quick to remind me I was a druggie?"

Oh, I'm gonna regret that one.

"You are so ungrateful, you know that?"

"How did this transform into *that* conversation?" I asked, becoming agitated.

"You know…"

"No, stop. Just… stop." I pushed my hair back out of my eyes with my free hand, wishing they would just let me get out of that bed to take a shower. "For years I have heard all of the lectures, all of the guilt trips, all of the 'everything is Talli's fault', and quite honestly I'm fucking tired of it."

"Well, I don't know where *this* is coming from," she huffed.

"Seriously? The whole family treated me like a pariah for most of my adult life, only coming around after I was married to a celebrity. No one fucking gave a damn that I turned my life around, the majority of them automatically assumed I was back on drugs when I initially got sick-- hell *you* tried to *give* the damn things to me, hello hypocrisy."

"Now you wait…"

"…one damn minute you ungrateful brat," I finished for her. "Right? Well, I'm sorry, Lisa, but I'm a big girl now and I learned how to do a lot of things on my own. I've lost my home that I couldn't afford to pay the rent for to begin with, I have to spend the next several weeks in a hotel room when I hate those damn things, and more than likely *without* my children. The last fucking thing I'm going to do in the midst of all of this is listen to what a horrible human being that I am and having the fact that I'm bound for hell shoved down my throat."

"Mrs. Warner," my nurse said as she walked in, eyeballing my heart rate on the machine, "I'm sorry, but you need to get some rest now."

"I don't know what the hell has gotten into you," Lisa was saying.

"Well, it certainly isn't mother's little helper," I snapped, rubbing my throbbing temple. Wow, was my head ever beginning to pound.

"We will continue this discussion when you have regained some sense."

"The problem with that statement is, I have regained my sense. You just don't like it."

"Mrs. Warner, I'm not going to be nice about this if I have to say it again." My nurse was standing by the wall jack, and as my mouth hung open in shock, she unplugged the phone, throwing the line into silence.

"Did you seriously…"

"No offense, ma'am, but I really don't care how pissed off you are at me right now. If Dr. Brooks comes in to perform the procedure and you've already keeled over because you didn't follow your instructions, he's going to be rather cranky. And I do not want to deal with a cranky Brooks tomorrow, or any other day for that matter. So, until further notice, no phone. You are to get sleep, and…"

"What if…"

"No one can call in right now," she cut me off before I could argue that Jase might need to reach me.

"Well, what if I need to reach him? I have no idea where my cell phone is, and…"

"Well, that's good because I'd take it from you."

My eyes narrowed as I looked at her. "Like hell you would."

"Try me," she said, placing a hand on her hip. "And before you come up with some witty reply, you might want to take to heart that I've been told that I'm a lot like you."

"Oh, great," I muttered, sulking.

"Now, we're going to turn off this television, and…"

"Ahem."

Both of us turned towards the doorway, my nurse becoming flustered while I sat there in a state of total confusion.

What the fuck was James Slade doing standing in my room? Mr. *Touring Band* who I hadn't seen since my wedding was just standing there. In my room.

"Excuse me… um… hi," he said, keeping his attention on my nurse. "I was wondering, could you help me? For… a moment? Please?"

"Um… what are… sure!" she readily agreed, barely waving at me as she followed James Slade out into the hallway.

I must be hallucinating.

"Coast clear?"

Jase's lawyer is sticking her head in, looking around.

"Good. You're awake."

Was I? Really?

"What the hell are…"

My words were cut off as Jase stepped in, holding Michael in one arm, his free hand securely holding onto Elizabeth's.

Oh... oh...

Elizabeth sobbed as she broke free, running and climbing up in my bed, clinging to me as she cried softly into my gown.

"Heeeeeeey," I said, holding her close, rubbing her back to try and calm her. "It's okay... it's over, it's okay."

"Hi, Mommy," Michael said, his voice barely over a whisper as Jase brought him closer. "Daddy said we hafta be quiet."

"Ohhhh, that's a good idea," I said, smiling through my threatening tears. I turned my smile to Jase then, patting the side of my bed.

I don't know why.

I just needed them... all of them... close.

"*You* weren't being quiet," Elizabeth finally choked out, sniffling loudly.

"You said bad words, Mommy," Michael scolded.

"Wow... um... I..." I stammered a bit, my face turning red, which judging by the smirk on Jase's face he found amusing. "This isn't funny."

"No, no. Of course not." He straightened up, sitting Michael on his lap facing me.

"Where's our Em?" Elizabeth asked.

"I already told you she's okay, do you doubt me?" Jase asked her, and I could smell the faintest trace of his body wash as he reached over and softly caressed the back of Elizabeth's head.

"Did you see her?" I asked, and he nodded. "Did you..."

"I gave her the kisses, I promise."

I nodded, the knot in my stomach lessening with the three of them there. "I... I can't believe..."

"I told you. Rebecca's good."

"She is... she... where did she go?" I asked, glancing around the room.

"Probably off to save James."

"Yeah, he came to get us with Daddy's lawyer friend, and I look awful!" Elizabeth sobbed, prompting Jase to roll his eyes.

"I see she hasn't gotten over her crush," he commented.

"A girl never gets over her first crush. Does she, Mommy?"

Elizabeth raised her head slightly, her tears clinging to her lashes, her blue eyes so earnest as she looked at me.

"No," I replied, my voice soft. "No, she does not."

I probably should not have said that.

"Mommy's first crush was *you*, Daddy," she said, turning those eyes to Jase. "She told me so."

Because that little snitch would take this time to spout off that little tidbit of information that I'm sure she'd been saving for a moment like this.

"Is that so?" he asked, but he wasn't looking at our daughter.

He was looking at me.

"Are they gonna fix your heart, Mommy?" Michael asked, saving me from the uncomfortable inquisition.

"Um… um… yes," I finally managed to say, noticing but not acknowledging the slight nod that Jase gave at my answer. "They found what's wrong with it, and they're going to fix it tomorrow."

"Will you die?"

I bit my lip at Elizabeth's question, not wanting to burden her with unnecessary worry with the risks of any procedure. "No, Baby Girl. They're just going to fix my heart."

"Hey…" Michael spoke up, sitting up a little straighter, "when they're done, maybe they can fix Daddy's, and Lizbeth's too, and they won't cry no more."

Jase bowed his head, his face unreadable, and I wondered if the tears had sprung to his eyes the way they had mine.

Out of the mouths of babes indeed.

"My heart's not broken, dummy," Elizabeth snapped.

"Baby Girl," Jase said before I got the chance to, and instead of the anger that used to course through my veins at the audacity of him thinking he could discipline her, I was instead warmed thoroughly by his tone. He sounded…

…*like their Dad.*

"I was crying cause I was sad, Daddy," she said, her bottom lip firmly stuck out.

"Why are you crying, Mommy?" Michael asked, and at first, I was confused until my hand reached up to my face feeling the moisture there.

"I… am crying because I'm happy," I answered honestly. "I am happy that you're all here."

Michael was obviously perplexed by my question, as he turned to Jase and shook his head. "Women."

"Tell me about it," Jase said, yelping as I swatted his leg. "Easy, Woman."

"I missed this," Elizabeth breathed, snuggling in to me.

So have I… more than any of you will know…

Once again, Jase was hiding his face, looking away as he placed a kiss on the back of Michael's head. We just sat there in silence, the four of us, missing our fifth but knowing she was okay. And for just one small moment, one brief second, although not whole, we were a family.

The way we should have been.

"Mommy needs her sleep," Jase said, his face still slightly hidden, but his sniffles were unmistakable. "So we need to get going."

"No, please just a little longer?" Elizabeth asked, her bottom lip sticking back out as Jase stood.

"It's okay… it's okay, Daddy's right. Tomorrow's a big day."

Elizabeth held me a little tighter, giving me a kiss on my cheek. "I'll miss you, Mommy."

"I'll miss you, too, but I'm so happy you're with Daddy," I said, holding her close.

"We get to go home!" Michael exclaimed happily.

"Yes, you do," Jase said, placing another kiss on Michael's cheek.

"I gots to give Mommy a kiss!" Michael said, and my heart overflowed with love. Jase leaned down so that Michael could wrap his arms around my neck, placing a kiss on my cheek. "I love you, Mommy."

"I love you too, Little Man," I said, returning his kiss and caressing the side of his face.

"Daddy, you too!" Elizabeth ordered. "Give Mommy a kiss, you always give Mommy kisses before you leave."

Now, that wasn't entirely true, but I wasn't going to argue with her right at that moment, especially not with the risk of being caught by the nurses.

But… a kiss?

I chanced a glance up at him, where his face was soft shade of pink.

I just...I couldn't put him on the spot like that.

"Baby, Mommy needs a shower in the worst..."

My words were cut off at the touch of his lips to my forehead, the soft scratch of his whiskers against my skin sending my heart fluttering.

I love him.

I just... love him.

"Hey, guys?"

The spell was broken as Rebecca stuck her head back in the room.

"You have company coming."

"Uh oh," Michael said, grinning sweetly.

"Come on," Jase said to Elizabeth, holding out his hand. "You'll see Mommy soon, I promise."

Somehow... even though they were gathering to leave... I didn't feel quite so alone.

"Hey, listen." Jase had turned to me. "I don't want you to worry, okay? You can call." He licked his lips, suddenly seeming shy. "Anytime."

Anytime?

I smiled weakly, the only way I could think of saying 'thank you' at that moment.

"And we do need to talk, but... don't worry about anything tonight."

I nodded again.

"So you sleep, okay?"

Yeah, like that's gonna happen.

"And we'll see you tomorrow."

"You will?"

Seriously? You find your voice, and that's what you say?

Oh... look at that smile on his face...

Yeah, I'd say it all over again.

"Oh, and Talli..." he began, without answering my question.

"This doesn't count. Yeah, yeah. I know."

He winked and my damn heart started running away from me again.

"'Til later, Mommy," Michael said, waving at me, and I choked back a sob. Wow, kids really do pick up on the little things, don't they?

"We love you, Mommy," Elizabeth added.

"I love you, too," I replied.

All of you.

JASE

"I don't know where to begin."

Jackie had taken Nan and the kids back to the house to settle in for the night and I was standing on the curb with Rebecca, where she was waiting for James to pick her up. She smiled softly at me.

"You begin by not screwing this up."

I chuckled in response, scratching the back of my neck. "Yeah, I'll... see... Rebecca," I said suddenly, something in that eavesdropped conversation popping into my head.

"Yeah?"

"Talli said she couldn't afford her condo. The child support should more than cover that."

"Do you not read your paperwork?" she scolded. "She didn't ask for anything during this period. She asked for child support to be awarded at the time of the divorce."

"You mean she's..." I stopped myself, choosing to bite my tongue and growl in frustration. "Damn it, those are my kids too. I promised her I would take care of her, and them, no matter what."

"Jase, you can only do what..."

"No." I stood up a little straighter, knowing what I was doing was right. "No, Rebecca, I... I'm going to get ahold of her landlord. I want her rent paid up through the end of the lease."

Rebecca gaped silently for a moment before regaining her composure. "I was going to ask if you'd lost your mind, but I'm beginning to think that's a given."

"Why?"

"You know that it's not going to count towards your child support, right? It will be considered a gift."

"She can consider it whatever the hell she wants, the point is that... well, I guess it's her home now, her and the kids, and she doesn't need to worry, you know?"

"Hell, Jase, you don't even know if..."

"Well, that's why I want to talk to him, or her... whomever, okay?

Because if they're going to remodel and bring the tenants back, then she…" I licked my lips, shrugging, shuffling my feet on the curb.

"You're a good person, Jase," Rebecca said softly, and a smile tugged at the corners of my mouth.

"Sometimes, maybe." I took a deep breath, looking over towards the garage.

"She'll understand the custody arrangement," Rebecca tried to reassure me. "It's an emergency situation, and once the doctors clear her, then the two of you can implement whatever custody and visitation arrangements that you come to. I'll call the mediator first thing tomorrow to reschedule."

"Thank you," I murmured, then laughed softly. "All I wanted was for her to get checked out, you know. I wanted to know she was okay."

"And she will be."

I smiled at the conviction in my lawyer's voice, so grateful for the day Kate had called her for me.

"Oh, before I forget," she said, "we're with the same cell company, right?"

"Yeah, but my phone is…"

"In pieces, yeah. Got it?"

"Got what?" I asked, confused.

"Your phone." She was rummaging through her bag before she pulled out a second cell phone. "This is just temporary, got it?" She handed it to me with a sigh. "Put your SIM card in there, so people can reach you until you replace yours."

"You have two cells?"

"I tend to live a bit of a double life, what can I say?" she said with a smirk. "But this way you can keep in touch with your grandmother if you need to, and Talli if she calls."

"I'll just be up with Em," I said with a light shrug. "Until they release her in the morning, then I'll take her home." I paused, biting my lower lip as my emotions threatened to get the best of me again. "Thank you, Rebecca."

"I'm telling you, sir… the best way to thank me is to not screw this up."

"How could I...okay, I won't finish that question," I said when I caught the glare she was throwing my way.

"Elizabeth calmed right down after seeing her mother," she commented.

"Yeah. I think James had a bit to do with that," I said, a grim smile on my face.

"Wow."

I blinked a couple times at her tone. "Wow, what?"

"You're not being replaced, Daddy. You'll always be number one to that little girl."

I shrugged slightly. "I'm not ready to share my little girl's affections yet. She's five."

"And very much like her mother, from everything you say, so she's going to be boy crazy."

We were silent for a little bit longer, the light breeze lifting the ends of her hair as she looked over at the parking garage, the headlights of an SUV clearly seen as James made his way to us.

"I'm sorry I interrupted your evening. I really did interrupt it too, didn't I?"

She smiled as she continued watching the approaching vehicle.

"Yes, but I forgive you."

I shook my head, grinning at her. "How will I ever thank you?"

"Right now, you'll just follow my advice and go spend the night with your daughter."

I pulled her into a warm embrace, rubbing her back as James pulled up beside us. I stepped back, smiling at her as she waved, almost shyly before climbing into the passenger seat and driving away.

Nan had readily agreed to take Elizabeth and Michael home, tuck them in and look after them until I brought Emily home the next day. Michael was so tired he could have cared less, and once Elizabeth understood that she was going home, to her bed and that I was going to stay with Emily, she was okay with it.

And I wasn't worried.

Not anymore.

These papers that I had with me said that no one was taking my children away. And I wouldn't use them to keep Talli away from them;

there was no way in hell I could do that.

Talli...

My steps faltered as I realized that I'd ended up on her floor, instead of Emily's.

I was right outside her door.

How the hell did I end up there?

Silently, I peeked in, not wanting to disturb her just in case she was...

Oh, she was sleeping.

The room only had the soft glow from the bathroom light being left on, just enough for me to get a good glimpse of her beautiful, peaceful face.

I'd almost forgotten how much I loved to watch her sleep.

She sighed, turning slightly, her curls fanning out on the pillow behind her, one lone curl falling across her face. My hands twitched involuntarily, wanting so badly to just reach out, gently push it back, and I swear I had every intention of staying frozen to that spot. I used the sound of approaching footsteps as a reason to step into her room, standing in the shadows as I continued to watch her, feeling the longing for her deep in my veins.

"I'm sorry," I whispered, even though in her slumber she couldn't hear me. "I'm so very sorry."

I stepped closer, so afraid of waking her, unwilling, unable to explain why I was there.

"I should have stayed at home."

My heart constricted as I remembered her saying that house had been a prison for her. If only she had told me, I would have done anything for her.

Anything.

Dr. Stewart had said she'd only recently begun to get the help she needed. Why had she waited so long? Had she simply refused the help, or had she not seen? What was it she had said? Something about... medical personnel being the worst patients. Denial. That's right, she'd been in denial.

I just can't think straight around her.

I wanted so badly to crawl in bed beside her, cradle her in my arms, let her know everything was going to be okay. Hell, to be completely honest, I almost did.

Just… almost.

Rebecca's words echoed in my head about not doing anything stupid, so I held myself back.

But not before I reached out, gently brushing that curl back out of her face. She scowled slightly, but slept on, a soft sigh escaping her lips.

"I'll be back in a few hours," I whispered, wondering in one moment of sleep deprivation how much she could hear. "I'll sneak Emmy in here for you."

I leaned in, so close I could feel the heat of her skin, but I refrained from leaving a kiss on her forehead.

Now wasn't the time.

"Oh, wow," I muttered, hearing Emily's screams as I rounded the corner. She must have woken up to an empty room, and I immediately felt guilty for not coming straight up here. I picked up my pace, walking swiftly down to that room where a nurse was trying in vain to console her. Emily was leaned back, her face a deep shade of red as she pushed against this stranger's chest, screaming with all of her might.

"Sssssh," the nurse said softly, only enraging my Princess even more.

"Heeeeey," I said, startling both of them. I was rewarded by my youngest daughter reaching for me, her chubby hands repeatedly opening and closing. "Come here, Emmy."

"Sir, I…"

I handed my papers to her as I took Emily into my arms, holding her as she clung to me, wiping her snot on my shirt. "Girl, that's gross."

Her bottom lip instantly began to quiver.

"Noooo, no, it's okay," I said, rubbing her back and kissing her tears away. "You can wipe all the snot on me you want to."

"I was just going to say that visiting hours are over," the nurse said softly.

"I'm no visitor," I corrected her as Emily sighed in my arms, snuggling in. "I'm her dad."

She smiled and nodded, motioning over to the recliner in the corner before leaving us in peace. I picked up the blanket from the crib, draping it across Emily to keep her warmer as I sat down in that chair.

"I don't know about you, but I'm really tired," I murmured, feeling the tension release from my limbs as she snuggled into me. "Did you know I used to put you to bed every night? Yeah... I did. I would hold you, and rock you, sing to you. Do you remember that?" I chuckled softly and added, "Of course you don't; you were so little. Kinda funny hearing me say that now, huh?"

She pushed herself up, her eyelids heavy as she stared at my face, almost as if she were daring me to leave her alone.

"I'm not going anywhere," I promised her.

With a big yawn, she laid her head back on my chest, her chubby hands fisted up in my shirt.

Just like Talli.

I placed a kiss in her curls before kicking the chair back, getting as comfortable as possible before sleep took hold, finally bringing this day to a close.

I never dreamed things could change so quickly in 24 short hours.

But this was nothing, not even a drop in the bucket when compared with what was to come.

CHAPTER 4

TALIA

I almost felt sorry for my nurse. Stressing the almost. I know I'm a difficult patient-- I'm a difficult person to begin with-- but is it too much to ask to have my phone back?

"Ma'am, it's going on 3 a.m. You don't need a phone, you need to go back to sleep."

"My name is not ma'am, and I want to know how my children are."

"They're probably asleep."

"You don't know Emily," I muttered, rubbing my temple. "Look, my youngest daughter is in the pediatric wing. Can you at least let me know how she's doing?"

"Of course. What's her name?"

"Emily. Emily Warner."

After she'd left the room, I growled in frustration, burying my face in the pillow I was holding in my hands. I had been sleeping, rather peacefully even, but had startled awake, my body knowing I was in a strange place.

And doesn't it figure it was 2:35?

I sunk back into my bed that I had raised to a sitting position, pouting. Maybe Emily gets her fear of being alone from me, although it wasn't quite a fear. It was more of an annoyance. There was so much going on, my mind was racing in five million directions, and I just needed to talk.

To just... talk.

And they wouldn't give me my damn phone back!

"I was just told that your daughter is sleeping soundly."

I jumped slightly at the sound of my nurse's voice, scoffing when her words finally sunk in. Sleeping soundly? In a hospital crib, by herself, no one else in the room?

"They said her Dad is with her, and they're asleep in the chair."

Is it possible to melt? I mean really, truly melt? Because if it is, I melted right on the spot. I smiled at her, murmuring my thanks for the news, still smiling after she left.

Yeah, it was a good thing I didn't have my phone. If his cell phone had been on in the hospital, I would have woken them up. And I didn't want to do that; I knew how cranky Emily could be.

I'll just let them sleep.

I wondered for a brief moment how it was that Emily turned to Jase so quickly, so easily. She wasn't the kind of child that warmed up to strangers, and she didn't have that trusting gene that many children have. Jase had pretty much been absent from her life since he'd left in October. Even when his mini-tour had come to an end, he'd still been busy, withdrawn.

Wrapped up in Bree.

But before he'd left...

Damn it, so much of that is a blur to me. It sucks to have pieces of my life-- of her life-- missing. I remember in the midst of an argument with Jase, screaming at him that he'd never been close with Emily. What was it he'd said to me?

Oh, right.

That I had selective memory.

I suppose in some ways he's right. It's equal parts frustrating and embarrassing, perhaps that was part of my motivation for keeping everything silent. The time for silence was officially over, though. There was only one person who could truly fill in all the blanks for those first three months of Emily's life.

I could only hope he wouldn't judge me when I finally got up the nerve to ask.

"Well, good morning." Paul walked in, and easy smile trying to cover that he obviously hadn't slept for shit. "Sorry I didn't make it here sooner."

I glanced at that slow-moving clock, groaning. It was only six a.m.

"How's Mary?" I asked, shifting uncomfortably.

"She's good. She's resting now, safe and secure in the guest room of my house."

I smiled softly, almost wishing my family was close so the children and I could stay with them. Just as quickly, I remembered my conversation with Lisa, shuddering at the thought of spending several weeks under her roof.

I'd already gone that route.

I wasn't about to go there again.

I'll put up with the anxiety that hotels bring out in me. And... and...

Oh, what about the kids?

"Earth to Talli." Paul waved his hand in front of my face and I frowned.

"Sorry, um... what were you saying?"

"I was apologizing."

"For what?" I asked, raising an eyebrow.

"Mary wasn't being malicious, just concerned."

"Oh, okay," I said, then shook my head slightly. "What?"

"She was the one who told the authorities about the visitation."

"Oh." I blinked several times, remembering the look on Jase's face, the look he'd tried so hard to hide from me.

"Rumor has it,"

"He has the children now," I interrupted Paul, shifting again. Damn, I couldn't get comfortable.

"Are you okay with that?"

"Of course I am," I said, a bit confused. "Oh, God... what other rumors are there?"

"I don't want you to worry."

"Too late. Spill."

"Talli, I don't want…"

"You brought it up, now spill."

"I know he stayed with Emily. I called to check on her."

"You did?" I asked, smiling for a brief moment.

"Did he tell you who was watching Elizabeth and Michael?"

I felt the blood drain from my face.

No.

No, he wouldn't.

"I mean, it could easily be a line of bullshit, but…"

"Could you do me a favor, please?" I asked quickly.

"Sure. Sure, anything."

"My nurse hijacked my phone. Can you go get me one?"

"Why did they hijack your phone?" he asked with a laugh.

"So I'd get some sleep, behold my success with that. But this is important."

He was still grinning as he assured me that he was going to acquire a phone for my room. The machine was giving away the speed of my hammering heart, and I leaned my head back, closing my eyes, willing it to slow down. To just… slow down…

I jumped as I felt fingertips on my face.

"What the…"

I faltered, my eyes adjusting to the light, expecting to ream Paul a new one for scaring me that way.

Only Paul wasn't there.

Jase stood beside my bed, in the same clothes he'd been wearing the night before, his hair in perfect disarray. Emily was on his arm, her hospital bracelet on her arm, but she seemed perfectly fine as she held on to Jase's cap, chewing on the bill of it.

"I didn't mean to wake you up," he said softly. "I was just sneaking her in… in case you were awake. They just released her."

"Thank you," I murmured, my voice soft as well. I wondered briefly if I had dreamt about Paul coming in before, until I spied the phone sitting back on my bed side table.

"What time is your surgery?" he asked, trying to act casual, but his cheeks were turning pink.

"Where are Elizabeth and Michael?" I asked.

"At home," he replied, seeming surprised that I would ask.

"Who's with them?" I asked, one eyebrow raised.

"Nan is. Why? Oh..." He sighed as one corner of his mouth lifted. "Have you so little faith in me?"

"Is that a rhetorical question, or do you really want an answer?" I asked, my automatic question for him when my response would either be obvious or a bit sly.

This time it was obvious.

He scowled slightly, and I waited for the anger, the venom to spew forth.

"I deserve that," he said.

Momentarily stunned silent, I glanced away, blinking back the sudden tears. I heard, rather than saw, him sit in the chair beside my bed, his tone even as he continued to speak.

"I... I'm not going to keep things from you. Not anymore."

I nodded my thanks, wishing I could believe him.

"I've been given emergency custody... full custody," he added. "This is just temporary, I swear to you, and... and I won't keep them from you. We won't have to deal with that center, okay? I just did what had to be done, so we could have our babies back."

I nodded again, unable to look at him right at that moment.

"That private school, the one we'd talked about, is that where you have Elizabeth enrolled for kindergarten?"

"Yeah," I managed to squeak out, wiping away a tear that had escaped.

"Talli... please don't... I'm not taking them from you."

"It's okay," I sniffed, drawing my knees up. "I understand, and it's... it's okay." I smiled as best I could through my tears. "They have a set schedule."

"And I'll stick to it, I promise."

I nodded again, choking back a sob. "It's... it's better right now, you know? We couldn't go back to the condo now anyways. Not... not yet."

"Where are..." He began the question, then stopped. I glanced over at him, where he was concentrating on something, I didn't know what, but a scowl was on his face.

"Well, Lisa was insisting that she was coming down here," I said, laughing softly through my tears. "I said hell no, though."

"Why?"

I blinked several times, glaring slightly. "Are you being serious?"

"You're... you're getting ready to..."

"Really, this is nothing. Nothing compared to what the first doctor wanted to do to me anyhow." I shuddered, recalling how I'd almost given in to having extensive open-heart surgery. "I'll be in here for a day or two, taking it easy for another day or two, then that's it. Good as new."

"Talli, you don't have to pretend."

"I'm not!" I insisted, reaching out and touching his knee, just a little touch like I used to when I would talk to him.

It almost seemed to burn.

I drew my hand back sharply, curling up a little more. "I'll be fine."

"Don't worry about you, right?" he asked with a sad smile.

One that I returned.

"Right."

Emily reached for me, and I gathered her close, kissing her forehead as she snuggled in to me.

Oh...

Oh, fuck...

How was I going to do this?

"It's... it's only until your doctor releases you."

"Six weeks," I squeaked out, the tears starting again. I was going to be without my children there... for six weeks... Not that they wouldn't be okay, because Jase would take good care of them. The best, even.

But they wouldn't be with me.

"Talli..."

"No, it's okay," I insisted, holding Emily just a little tighter. "The kids don't need to spend the next few weeks in a damn hotel anyhow, waiting for the building to reopen."

"Talli..."

"Please don't be upset with her...with Em," I said quickly, looking over at him. "She just doesn't like to be alone, not at nighttime."

Neither do I...

"Please don't cry," he said, his voice barely above a whisper.

"And... and try not to be short with Elizabeth and... and Michael. They just argue all the time, but that's just... that's just them, okay?"

I couldn't seem to stop my tears.

"And daycare...it's been really good for them. You should consider letting them still go, at least part time. And... and then they wouldn't bother you when you were trying to work, like they did when..."

"Talli," he said, his hand resting on my leg, and I fell silent.

My tears still fell as I looked at him, his gaze unwavering as he leaned just a little closer.

"I..." He licked his lips and I felt, as well as heard, my heart skip a tiny beat.

"You what?"

"I have an idea."

JASE

It's official; I've lost my fucking mind.

She was crying, though, and I'm an absolute sucker for it... for her. I can't handle her crying; I've never been able to. So what do I do?

Open mouth.

Insert foot.

"Stay with me."

"What?"

I cringed, realizing what I'd just said.

But I meant it.

"Stay... with, you know..." I licked my lips, shrugging as I looked sheepishly at her. "Me."

The more I thought about it, though, the more it made perfect sense.

Her mouth was gaping open slightly, her eyes narrowed as she looked at me, those big blue eyes still swimming with tears, and I knew this was the right thing to do.

"Talli," I began, speaking as quickly as I could, "think about it, okay? You don't want to be without the kids, they shouldn't be without you."

I'm going crazy without you.

"You need to recover, you need to get better... and not just... not just your heart, okay? Everything. *Everything.*"

I promised you the world, and... and I took it away. I thought you didn't love me anymore...

"You need to have peace of mind, you need to be able to work on... on you, on getting you better."

Give me this chance, let me make this up to you.

Or... or just tell me I'm fucking crazy, because I so obviously am...

Fuck, what if she says no?

"You can't do that if you're in a hotel...I'm sorry, I know you don't want to think about this, but you just... you don't like hotels, you don't like hotel rooms, that's just one of your quirks that are..."

So adorable... so missed...

"...well, they just are. How can you possibly get better if you're worried about... about... the sheets on the bed, or about the towels they're leaving, or who's coming in to clean up. Seriously, how long did it take you to get used to Linda?"

She almost smiled.

I took this as a good sign.

"And the kids... our babies... you need them. You need to be near them, because... because they bring out the best in you."

The way I wish I did

She blinked a couple times, her eyes widening at my last statement, but I was on a roll. I had to finish.

"And you won't have to worry, because... because I'll be there to... you know, help."

Her expression changed to one of skepticism at that.

I deserve that, too. I know I do.

"I... I can take care of them too, you know? So you can rest, and you don't have to worry about..."

Money, sleep, recovery...

"Well, you won't have to worry about Lisa coming, that's for damn sure. Eric might poke his head in from time to time, but Lisa? Yeah, I don't think she wants to come back to our..."

I faltered as her eyes dropped down to Emily.

"Just... think about it, okay? I... I promise that I won't be in your way, I promise I..."

I won't make it feel like a prison to you. I won't pressure you; I won't badger.

I'll just love you.

From afar if I have to.

"Just think about it?" I repeated softly, holding my breath as her eyes reached mine again.

She wasn't crying anymore.

She certainly didn't look happy, but... she wasn't crying.

That was a start, right?

"Oh, um..." I continued on with my nervous rambling, motioning over to the bags I sat down by her bed. "Jackie brought by some stuff. You'd left it... in... well, it's your shampoo, body wash, and stuff."

"Oh, thank you." She seemed to snap out of her daze, looking down at the bag, her arms still securely wrapped around our little girl.

"I don't have any clothes, and... and I think that the building is still off-limits. But... but Sondra and Linda both said they'd bring you something." My eyes narrowed as I looked over her. "A size smaller. Please tell me that's because you've been sick."

Her eyes widened again before just a hint of anger crossed her features. "My weight is my business."

"No! No, I mean... well, no I said just what I meant." I shrugged, remembering my promise to her, to myself. "You are too thin."

Way to go, Warner. Ask her to come stay with you, then start criticizing her.

Her lips were together in a thin line, her nostrils flared as she inhaled, some catty retort on her lips I'm sure. And I know what she would be referring to. Or who, I should say. For just a flash, I remembered the feel of Bree beneath me, and I knew I was right.

Talli was too thin.

"I'm not... I'm just concerned, okay?" I took a deep breath, knowing by her expression she was more pissed about the weight comment then she was letting on. Her jaw was set, one of those perfectly sculpted eyebrows raised as she fussed with Emily's shirt. "Talli..."

"Do you have to just... put down everything about me?" she asked, her eyes shooting daggers at me.

"I... I didn't mean to...I'm not putting you down, Talli." *Fuck, again with the foot and the mouth. They must be getting married today or something.*

"First, stuff I forgot, and then my weight, and…"

"Now you're putting words in my mouth. I just brought that to you because I thought you'd rather have your own shampoo and stuff instead of whatever they provide…do they even provide anything here?"

"Oh."

Just oh?

Bite your tongue, Warner. Don't fight. Not now.

"I'll ask Sondra, if you'd like," I reiterated the offer, hoping she wouldn't take offense to it this time. "I'm sure you don't want to wear hospital garb when you leave here, right?"

"I can call her," she said with a shrug, still picking at Emily's shirt until our baby girl fussed, pushing her hands away.

And a light bulb went off in my head.

"You're avoiding the subject."

"What?" she asked incredulously.

"You…" I pointed at her for effect, gauging her reaction. "You're picking a fight with me to avoid my question."

"Oh, please," she scoffed, but the blush in her cheeks gave her away.

Please tell me this means you're thinking about it…

"You do this all the time, Talli. You pick a fight to avoid answering my questions."

"And there you go, criticizing…"

"You're only proving my point, Talli."

"You just… it… hurts." She frowned, looking down again. "I can't live like… I can't be under a microscope, I can't have every little thing I say or do picked to pieces."

It was my turn to be silent, my turn for my mouth frozen in the opened position as she continued.

"I can't be, you know, afraid to… to forget things."

I didn't realize how much I'd hurt you… it had started so innocently, I swear.

"The kids and I, we have our own thing, our schedule, our… our way about doing things, and I can't… I just can't deal with everything I say and do with them being torn to pieces, thrown in my face."

What is she…

Oh...

Oh.

I had been that way. I had criticized every little thing, from play clothes to dinner, bedtimes to sleeping arrangements.

All of it.

"I..." I faltered for a moment, shame bringing a deep shade of crimson to my face. "I shouldn't have. That was wrong of me, and... and I won't do that again. I promise."

"That's a promise you'll never be able to keep."

My eyes slid shut at her words, feeling the depth of her hurt at my actions... and these... these had nothing to do with what I thought she'd have the most trouble with.

"I promise you," I said, opening my eyes, placing two fingers under her chin to lift her face to mine. "I promise you that I won't do that to you, ever again... if you can promise me to... to not think everything I'm saying is a personal attack on you. Because it's not, Talli, I swear it's not."

Two large tears spilled over her lashes, trailing down her cheeks, and I caught one of them with my fingertips, repressing the urge to just kiss her.

"What's... oh, sir, I'm sorry, but you can't bring small children up here."

I stayed there, staring into those beautiful eyes of hers, the nurse not deterring me in the least.

"What do you say, T?" I asked, my voice soft.

She suppressed a sob as she held Emily just a little closer. "You don't play fair."

"Damn straight I don't."

"We have to get her prepped... please, before the doctor comes in and I get in trouble."

Taking a chance, I placed my hand over hers, gently caressing it with my thumb.

Score.

Her heart rate picked up slightly, and I glanced down just long enough to confirm that her breathing had picked up as well.

You do the same thing to me...

"Wow, are you two in your own damn world, or what?"

Aren't we always?

"Sir, please... Dr. Brooks,"

"Won't do a damn thing to me," I said, still looking into Talli's eyes, still caressing the back of her hand. I leaned just a little closer, my voice barely above a whisper. "C'mon, T. What do you say?" I gave her my best smirk, matching her raised eyebrow with one of my own.

She opened her mouth, shutting it firmly before she said anything.

Please say yes... before I panic and change my mind... just say...

"I'll think about it."

I wonder if she saw the goosebumps spring up on my arms as her words cut through me.

"Fair enough," was all I said, sitting back and holding my hands out for Emily. Her bottom lip stuck out, her free hand wrapped in Talli's curls. "Come on, Princess. They're booting us out."

Talli placed a kiss on Emily's cheek, unwrapping herself from our daughter's embrace, holding back tears of her own as Em began to cry.

"Sir..."

"I know, I know, the cavalry's gonna come." I walked towards the door, trying not to let Em's tears get to me. I paused to take a look back at Talli, curled up in her bed, chewing on her thumbnail as she tried her hardest not to cry. "Talli?" She looked up at the sound of my voice, her resolve crumbling as Emily cried out, reaching for her.

"Okay," she said quickly.

"I'm sorry...what?" I asked, my heart so afraid to soar.

"I said okay, now get the hell out of here before I change my mind."

She said yes...she said yes...she said...

She's pointing towards the door

"Gone," I said with a wink and a smile, on cloud fucking nine...million as I walked out into that hall.

Only to come crashing down.

Oh, fuck.

She said yes.

What the hell do I do now?

CHAPTER 5

TALIA

I jumped as I felt a hand on my leg, and I peeked groggily through one eye. "Jase?" I asked, my throat a little scratchy. Holy shit was I ever thirsty.

"Yeah. Kinda." Dr. Brooks grinned as he looked over my stats. "Damn, I'm good."

I rolled my eyes but had to match him with a grin of my own. "So, it was a success?"

"I believe so, yeah." He sat down beside me, leaning forward and still grinning. "It's a bit early to say with a hundred percent certainty, but coming from where I was standing... I'll be saying 'I told you so' in roughly six weeks."

I groaned at his approximation of time, but he held up his hand.

"No, listen. You will feel so much better before this week is even up. I want to continue to monitor you for a couple of days in here before we release you, but you should be back at work by then. Or feel free to wait until Monday, whatever tickles your fancy. I hear for some unfathomable reason you just can't wait to get back to this place."

"Less than a week, huh?" I asked, and he nodded. "So..."

"No release from me until your six-week checkup."

"Damn," I muttered. "I really was wanting to stay awake, but I hardly got any sleep last night. Thank you for arranging the sedative."

"Not a problem," he replied. "I did have to go in a little deeper in the chamber than I had anticipated, but honestly there shouldn't be any difficulties from the surgery. You probably won't even need the cardiac medications that you've been on."

"Thank god."

"I figured you'd say as much." Dr. Brooks stood, stretching and crooking his neck from side to side. "You have a place to stay, once you're released, right?"

I felt the heat creeping up in my face as I recalled how I'd been pretty much cornered into that one. "Yeah... yeah, I do."

And I could almost kick Jase's ass over it.

Just... almost.

All of the arguments, even the one that we'd had in that hospital room this morning, came rushing over me, all distinct reminders of why this was such a horribly bad idea. I wasn't even thinking about what anyone else would say about our arrangement-- not our friends or family, not the whore, not the paparazzi. No, I was thinking about how much tension there had been, how I'd continuously walked on egg shells to not set him off, how I'd had to keep the kids out of his office and how they'd cry and he'd get angry, how he wouldn't even eat dinner with us as a family anymore.

How all of it hurt, immensely.

Why did I say yes? What the hell possessed me to?

But I already knew.

And it wasn't completely how Emily cried, reaching for me, and how I knew I couldn't make it several weeks without being a constant in her life.

No, it was about one little sentence.

"You need to be near them because... because they bring out the best in you."

He'd really said that. To *me*.

And like the sucker that I am, I fell for it. Hook, line, and sinker fell for it. Maybe because I wanted to, maybe because I wanted to believe he really felt that way, maybe because I wanted to believe that he had that kind of faith in me.

Because I'd been doubting myself for so long.

In the end, I have no one to blame for my insecurities other than myself. I'd fallen into this hole, and while I wasn't at the bottom of it anymore, I certainly wasn't very close to the top either. I was more clawing up the sides, my hands caked with the grime that this hell was covered in.

And just as soon as that thought entered my mind, I had to stifle a giggle.

I really need to get out more.

So… hospital. For another day or two. We'd already agreed we'd follow the rules and not bring the kids, but I was going to see them in a couple of days and could speak with them any time I wished. I couldn't spend all of that time on the phone, though. The cable here doesn't carry TV Land, which some people such as myself would consider blasphemous. The food sucks. All of my books were…

All of my books were at the house. Not the condo. The house.

I hadn't moved any of them.

What harm would it do to ask if Sondra could bring me a book or two when she dropped off some clothes? Clothes that I absolutely would pay for… somehow.

I have to admit, in that short span of time I'd memorized Jase's new home phone number, which was a good thing since I couldn't find my cell. I sank back into the pillows as I waited for someone to answer, feeling a sudden sense of panic as Nan's voice filled the line.

"Hello?"

Oh, great. My grandmother-in-law that surely knows all of our dirty laundry by now. Just… super.

"Um… hi."

Wow, you sound so smart Talli. Way to live up to your reputation.

"Oh, hello. Jase said you'd come out of the procedure with flying colors. I know the kids really want to speak with you."

"Thank you," I said, my mind working in overdrive, thinking among other things that of course my children wanted to talk to me, but I kept that to myself.

"They've been absolute angels. Even Em. And that sounds wrong, I'm sorry. They're angels. All of them."

I had to laugh. Only Nan would feel guilty about saying something negative regarding her great-granddaughter's behavior.

"Seriously, you can say it. She screamed bloody murder, threw her food on the floor..."

"Well, no and no. I think she's too exhausted to bother."

That's right; she was always exhausted after a night in the hospital.

"You really sound like you're doing well."

"Yeah, yeah... I... I feel pretty good."

"That's wonderful news. I'll go get the kids real quick, okay?"

"Sure."

Wow, that was weird.

One grandmother-in-law that probably knows more about my personal business than she should, the woman who raised the man I was in the midst of a very messy divorce with, and she's being nice to me?

Wait.

No, she doesn't think...

He doesn't think...

No, of course he doesn't think that. He knows better; I know that from our argument, when I'd agreed to stay there, in that house. There was nothing in the discussion, nothing in his demeanor that would make me suspect that he expected me there as his... wife.

Should I be relieved?

Because if I should... it's not working.

"Okay, so she was nice to you," Jaden said with a giggle when I had her on the phone later. "What's the big deal?"

"Are you serious, or are you having baby brain again today?" I asked, picking at my crappy hospital food. "Grandmother-in-law? I'm divorcing her grandson? I've been the biggest bitch in the world to him?"

"Hey," she cut me off, and I could tell she was enjoying her ice cream that she'd demanded from Pete, "he's lucky he's married to you. I would have chopped his damn balls off."

This elicited a rather loud response from her husband, who was voicing his opinion about the wrongness of threatening the manhood.

And I had to laugh.

Partly because it was damn funny to listen to them bicker back and forth, and partly because it reminded me so much of what used to be. Way back when... actually, not so long ago... when the both of us could take the teasing, before the simplest of comments set one or the other of us off because we would take it the wrong way.

"You only *think* you're in charge," she said to him, before returning her attention to me. "Sorry about that."

"Oh... don't apologize," I replied. "Please... please don't. Enjoy it, okay?" My voice wavered a little as I continued. "Because... there's going to be a time soon when sleep will be short, and tempers even shorter, and... and one of you will say something just like you did... and... and the other will..."

A sob broke through as I had my millionth mini meltdown of the day. I *hate* acting so girly. So, on top of going back into a house, into a situation that makes me edgy at best, I have to face it while pms'ing.

Just. Shoot me. Now.

Or bring me a Caramel Macchiato, one or the other.

Lucky for me, two days later when Jase arrived to pick me up, insisting that he be the one to do it, he came bearing a hot white and green cup bearing that Starbucks logo.

"A peace offering," he said, as he held it out. "Truce... at least... for now?"

He looked so earnest, his eyes almost kind as he held out the equivalent the Holy Grail to me at that moment.

"You're bribing me," I replied, one eyebrow raised.

"Well..." He looked down before glancing up with his eyes, his brows disappearing beneath his bangs. "Yes."

I took a deep breath, sighing in mock-defeat. "Fine, whatever."

He pulled his arm back when I reached for the cup.

"What the hell?"

"Say it."

I felt my heart fall to my feet, my stomach tie up in knots, and my palms begin to sweat as the first time he pulled this stunt on me played over in my mind.

"What?" I asked, my voice small, and about that time, his face turned nearly as red as my hair.

"Truce, I mean," he said, the smile no longer reaching his eyes. "Sorry..."

"No, um... sure." I attempted to smile, failing miserably and only accomplishing a slight grin. "Truce."

Our fingers brushed as I took the cup from his hands and a shiver passed straight through me.

And if I'm not mistaken, through him, too.

God, help me.

This is going to be the longest 'few short weeks' of my life.

JASE

She's going to kill me.

That was the first thought that ran through my head after I'd finished the masterpiece laid out before me. Elizabeth's bed was along one wall, her bookshelves neatly lined another, her toy box was neat and tidy, its lid closed just how Baby Girl liked it. Beside it, on the next wall, was Emily's crib. It was positioned just perfectly so that when Princess would open her eyes, she could see across the room where Elizabeth would be sleeping.

She could see that she wasn't alone.

I'd thought it was a fluke that she'd slept so well the previous night, until I'd spied Elizabeth sprawled out in the bed that Talli used to sleep in, and it just dawned on me. Elizabeth had cried when she knew I saw her in there, telling me she was sorry, she knew that Emily just wanted someone there. I'd calmed her down, told her not to cry… she wasn't in trouble. She, in fact, was a genius.

So now, I was going against Talia's wishes and putting our children in a room together. She'd insisted on all of them having separate rooms, not wanting anyone's space invaded the way hers had been her entire childhood. But she was just going to have to understand.

Emily didn't like to be alone, which she already knew.

Elizabeth wanted to help, wanted her sister in with her.

So, it was settled. The situation, that is… not my nerves.

"You're doing the right thing," Nan said, a reassuring hand on my shoulder as she glanced around the newly rearranged room. "Emily will sleep so much better now."

"I'd promised her that while she was here, I wouldn't trump her, you know? I would discuss big decisions with her."

"Well, she's not going to be here if you don't hurry and pick her up."

I glanced down at my watch, my heart pounding as I checked the time. I wasn't going to be late; I was just on my way to tempt fate, test it a little, see if I could right some of the wrongs I had dealt her.

"I'm just doing this to help her out," I said out loud, more to convince myself than my Nan, who gave me a knowing smile.

"You do what you need to do," she said, taking my hand in hers. I looked down at my shoes, unable to watch her as she continued. "You know I'm worried about you. I'm worried…" She placed her hand over my heart and the ground began to blur. "I'm worried that what's in here is going to overrule any amount of common sense that you have left. But love isn't about sense, is it?"

I shook my head no, not wanting to hear it, but knowing it had to be said.

"You two didn't get to this point overnight. No one does. I just hope you aren't setting yourself up for an even bigger fall."

"I'm not," I reassured her as best I could. "I just want to help."

And I hadn't told another soul about it, other than those in the immediate vicinity. Linda knew because the kids had told her excitedly that Talia was coming home. Jackie, of course, knew because Linda told him. Pete knew because Talli had told Jaden, and he'd been so…

Hell, I don't know what he'd been.

Other than he was the only person who agreed with me that it was the right thing to do. He didn't give me any lectures about being hurt, or about hurting the kids, or about common sense. He'd told me it was the smartest move I'd made in almost a year. I could have kissed him for it, but he was still back in Groves Point, where he would stay by Jaden's side until their baby was born. And he made me promise that we, the whole family, would be there if not before, then soon after his son arrived. And that's a promise I intend to keep.

But right at that moment, it was time to begin the process of healing the wounds from promises that I'd broken.

———————

Caramel Macchiato from Starbucks. Double shot. That was always her drink of choice. I'd known that about her before I'd been graced with her presence in Cleveland all those years ago. I had taken one to her when she'd been holed up in that hospital after the accident, and ever since then I'd just known when to bring her one. The familiarity of it all washed over me as the look on her face registered her surprise, and then delight.

So I can blame the mother of all stupid moves on familiarity.

Just as she reached for it, I pulled back, the words "Say it" escaping from my lips before I could stop myself.

Fuck.

"What?" she asked, although I barely heard her. The smile was no longer there, and her hand... her hand was trembling.

Fuck, fuck, FUCK, Warner...

"Truce, I mean," I tried in vain to recover, but I could feel myself blushing. "Sorry."

Just... great. You don't even have her in the car and you've already made the situation more uncomfortable than it would have been in the first place.

"No, um... sure." She grinned slightly, and my heart went out to her. "Truce."

I kept my eyes on her expression as I held the cup out for her, my breath catching as our fingers brushed together sending a tremor straight through me.

I love you, more than I thought was humanly possible... more than you'd ever believe...

"So, um," I said, shaking the feeling off, regaining my composure as best I could, "I pulled around to the employee entrance. Dr. Stewart said it was okay today, and... and we can get you out of here."

"Good," she said, a tight smile on her lips. "I... I want to go see the kids."

"Yeah, they're at h... at the house, with Nan," I rambled as I stood back so she could get in the dreaded wheelchair.

"Ms. Talli, you know what the doctor said about caffeine."

"Either one of you tries to take this from me I'll cut your damn arm off," Talli retorted quickly.

There's my girl.

"And you're damn lucky I agreed to let you put me in one of these things," she continued as I followed them down the hall, carrying her bag of assorted items I'd brought to her on my shoulder. "I could easily walk to the car, you know."

"But you won't," I said.

"Don't you start on me, you know damn good and well I could," she said, and I couldn't suppress my grin. She'd said those exact words to me on her way to the car after Emily was born.

About that time, she fell silent.

I think she remembered, too.

Sometimes the memory is a wonderful thing. It reminds us of the good times, of the happy occasions, of the simple joys in life that make it worth living. But sometimes… sometimes those memories can be bittersweet, when the hurt and anger are still so fresh that even the good times are painful to remember.

But the familiarity of it all…

The way she sunk down into the seat just so.

The way she seemed to remember at the last minute to buckle her seatbelt, and said that little "Oh" every time.

The way she'd close her eyes and sigh.

The way she would turn her head towards me, her eyes half closed as she watched my hands on the steering wheel. Always… she always did this.

I could feel those eyes on me as we drove in silence towards what was once our home. There was a time when silence between us was simple, comfortable, when we were secure in our love for one another.

That just wasn't the case anymore.

"This doesn't change anything."

Her voice caught me off guard, and I startled a bit before glancing over at her. "Hmm?" I asked, knowing what she'd said, not wanting to give away the hurt.

"This," she repeated, using her hands for emphasis. "This doesn't change anything."

Out of the corner of my eye I saw it. Just a tiny glimmer in one little glance, but I knew exactly what it was.

She was still wearing her rings.

I swallowed over the lump in my throat as she crossed her arms in front of her, nodding as I absentmindedly twisted my wedding band that was still on my left hand where she had placed it.

"You're right," I finally said, wanting to ease just a little bit of the tension. "I know."

"Good," she mumbled, reaching for the radio and changing it to her favorite station.

Just like she used to.

She was right.

As we drove on to the house, taking the same route, listening to the same songs, wearing the rings we'd given each other all those years ago, I knew she was right.

This didn't change anything.

I would love her forever.

I pulled into the garage, shutting off the engine but remaining still in that seat. There was something I hadn't told her, something she needed to know about the house she was walking in to.

"Talli, I…" I licked my lips, the nervousness overwhelming. Damn it, why did I wait so long?

"It's okay," she said with a soft smile. "I know that you redecorated. It's, you know… it's fine." She shrugged, still smiling but again it didn't reach her eyes.

"I just want you to understand…"

"I do, Jase." She opened up her car door, reaching towards the back seat for her bag.

"I've got that," I said, stopping her.

"Jase, come on…"

"No, I'm serious. I've got it." I picked up the small bag, taking it with me as I got out of the car slowly.

Please let her be telling the truth.

Oh, God… what if she hates it?

So what if she does? It's my house, right?

But… but…

"Mommy!"

She was bombarded with hugs and kisses from Elizabeth and Michael as soon as she walked through the side door. I slipped past them, placing her bag on the counter, trying to hide my shaking hands.

She's here. She's really here.

The last time she was here, she'd collapsed, and…

The kiss. Damn it, Warner, don't think about it. She's right behind you, your Nan's still here, you don't need to try and hide…

"Em's sharing a room with me now!"

"I'm sorry, what?" Talli asked, trying to keep her tone neutral, but I could feel her eyes on me.

"Em and Elizabeth share a room here," I said, as if it were the most natural thing in the world.

"And...and she didn't cry last night," Elizabeth added, her smile as wide as Talli's eyes when she saw...

"You lost a tooth!"

Elizabeth had lost her first tooth that morning and thought the world was coming to an absolute end. I didn't realize she wasn't aware that this was a natural thing for children, but once she heard about the tooth fairy and money, she was completely on board.

"Yep, and see? Daddy said there's one gonna come take its place!"

"Wow," was all Talli could say as she gathered our oldest child in her arms.

"And then the tooth fairy's gonna come, and I might get a *thousand dollars*!"

"Hey, whoa, I didn't say that," I corrected her.

"A girl can dream," Elizabeth replied with a shrug.

"Daddy gots us more clothes 'til we can get our stuff," Michael said, pulling on Talli's hand. "And he gots stuff for his house! Lots of stuff!"

"I can see," Talli said, her voice trailing off as she looked around. The kitchen appliances were the same, but the breakfast table and chairs were different, a little more modern. Her smile was tight as she followed Michael through the hallway towards the front of the house, which was now completely redone in black and white.

That's when I saw the change come over her.

When she looked around the empty walls where all of our family portraits had once been.

I watched her visibly swallow as she looked around, one corner of her mouth lifting in a wistful smile as she glanced at the corner that we always put the Christmas tree up in.

"Talli..."

"It looks nice," she cut me off. She had that same damn smile on her face, but I know her so well, too well sometimes.

"And we gots new dining room stuff, too," Michael said as he danced around at her feet. "And Daddy and... and Jackie are gonna go get your car, I heard 'em say it."

"Oh, thank you," she said, and I nodded.

"I know you don't like to be without it."

"But the keys…"

"The spare ones were here," I said, and she nodded slightly.

"Nana is changing Em's poopy butt," Elizabeth chimed in. "Wanna see our room, Mommy?"

Not that Talli had much of a choice since the children were already dragging her towards the stairs. I saw her glance down the hallway as she reached the landing, and I knew exactly what was crossing her mind.

I wondered briefly what she would say when she finally made her way down that hallway.

She has to understand.

She just… has to.

CHAPTER 6

TALIA

This must be what purgatory feels like. The perpetual hurt, the ache, the burning in your soul, all of your past wrongs being thrown into your face little by little, inch by excruciating inch.

This day, this whole entire day had been one instance after another, and there was nothing I could do to stop it. From his "Say it" all the way until I closed the door to the room I once shared with Emily, where I sank to the floor in a pool of tears, I had to live with the fact that he had been erasing me from his life.

Why did I think I could do this?

And the second I thought that, I'd wonder... why does it matter what he does with this house? I'd left. With good reason, too. I'd moved on with my life, with my existence. Why should he be any different? Why should he have to keep our furniture, our dishes, our pictures...

This is too much. This is just too much.

And I can't call in my reinforcements. My reinforcement was in Groves Point getting ready to have a child of her own. And she'd told me to have my guard up when I went to the house, but I wasn't prepared to see it.

I'm sure that Jase was wanting to tell me about putting Emily and Elizabeth together, and perhaps he should have before I heard it from Elizabeth. I don't know if I should be angry or happy about it, though. I know I've been very adamant from moment one when we'd discussed having a second child that I didn't want them sharing a room, regardless. I'd gone through hell with Anna going through everything I owned, eventually I changed my style from tomboy to… well, streetwalker to keep her the hell out of my clothes. I listened to weird music to keep her out of my cd's, read complex novels that she wouldn't steal, hung around people she loathed so she wouldn't try and out-friend me.

I didn't want that for my children.

Jase had once said that I needed to remember that Anna was a douche, and I'm sure he'd said it to make me laugh, which completely made me more at ease. That was when he'd played the psychobabble card about how our children were their own individual souls, would have their own wants and needs, and I didn't need to worry about them going through what I had with my own siblings. Because, as he so eloquently stated it, most of my siblings were douches anyhow.

I couldn't see Elizabeth being so cruel to Emily. She was so happy to be sharing a room, happier than Anna had ever been to be around me. And I knew that Emily hated to be alone, but…

But I did, too.

And it hit me as I sat alone in that darkened room on that floor, staring at that empty wall where her crib had once set, maybe it wasn't all about Emily after all. Perhaps I'd used it as an excuse, so that when I opened my eyes someone would be there with me.

But Em… that wasn't even all of my problems, all of my hurt.

No, this house…

This house that had been my home didn't have any semblance to the sanctuary it had once been to me. I know I'd spouted off about it being a prison, but damn it… that was after I'd seen him in bed with her.

Just down the hall from where I'm at now.

Our breakfast table, where we'd had coffee on chilly or rainy mornings was gone. Sure, it needed replaced, thank you to the many knicks and scratches, but those all had meaning to me, too. The huge gash that we'd tried to repair after Damien and Jase had nearly toppled the thing over in a tipsy wrestling match always made me smile and was one hell of a conversation piece. We'd repaired two of the chairs that had been broken over the years, but those, too, were gone.

I remembered standing beside the wall, watching Jase drink his coffee the morning I found out that Michael was on the way. We'd been trying, not for very long, but had made the conscious decision to have another baby. He was reading the morning paper, the entertainment section if I'm not mistaken, with the only sound being the light drizzle just outside that back door. As silently as I could, I walked up behind him, snaking my arms around him and placing a kiss in his hair. He jumped slightly, smiling over his shoulder at me.

"Hello, beautiful," he'd said, turning and pulling me onto his lap.

I miss him doing that.

I remember kissing on his neck, along his jaw line, up the outside of his ear as he sat there saying, "Uh huh... mmmm... okay, okay. I see where you're going with this..."

"Do you?" I asked, sitting back, smiling at him.

"Um... into my pants?" he asked, his eyebrows underneath his bangs.

I remembered giggling, snuggling into him and kissing his neck again. "I can get that whenever."

"So you think," he murmured, his coffee forgotten as he held me to him, rubbing his hands along my back.

And he'd made me cry with that one simple gesture.

And he forced me back until he could lift my chin, looking into my eyes with such love, such concern, his thumbs brushing away my tears. "Baby what's wrong?" he'd asked.

I miss him calling me baby...

And I'd told him nothing was wrong, that everything was right.

And when he'd held me to him, crying tears of joy, we'd bumped into the table, spilling the coffee all over it.

The table that was now gone.

It was stupid of me to be so damn sentimental over something as trivial as a breakfast table, right?

But that entryway, the great room... the day I'd packed up the U-Haul and left, I'd wanted to take a butcher knife to every single one of those family portraits, those ones that depicted the perfect, happy family. It ripped me apart to see the smiling faces shining down, knowing how he'd turned his back on that, on us. But now?

Now that they're gone?

I knew from the moment I saw him with Bree that his heart wasn't with me anymore. I'd resolved myself to that fact; I'd slowly begun to heal, putting my own life back together. But seeing this room, all of the pictures that had adorned those walls now gone, where he could bring her in without feeling the least bit guilty...

I buried my face in my hands, trying my hardest to keep the sobs as quiet as I could. It wasn't as if I didn't like the new furniture-- if I was perfectly honest with myself, I loved it-- but what about our memories, our Christmases in there?

Elizabeth's second Christmas, the first one that she spent at home, was spent videotaping her in awe over the tree with its colorful twinkling lights. I held the camera most of the day because she was such a Daddy's girl, and he was so wrapped up in her. He'd gotten past her birthday, we'd jumped that hurdle when he told me how he'd seen me, when he was finally convinced we weren't going to disappear on him. And he sat on that floor with her, taking in her expressions with complete love in his eyes, kissing away her tears when she didn't understand that the presents were supposed to be ripped open.

Would he put that Christmas tree up this year, in our spot, in with his new furniture, to make new memories with *her*?

I sniffled softly, recalling walking into the formal dining room for dinner that evening, thanking Nan for so generously cooking a meal for all of us when she was there visiting. And she'd been so nice to me, so gracious, so kind when she told me how well behaved the children were. And they were, which surprised the hell out of me. Emily didn't even throw her plate on the floor when she was done.

But it was so... different.

Where our last formal dining room set was darker wood, this was a more polished black almost lacquer finished tabletop, and the seats were padded, very comfortable but very... different. Gone were the place settings we'd used for when we'd had company over, and in its place were more modern dishes, square instead of round, which the kids found hilarious. Michael loved putting his fingerprints on the table to see them disappear almost immediately, and when I'd tried to tell him that he shouldn't mess up Daddy's new furniture, Jase had intervened and said it was okay, it was nothing that couldn't be cleaned up.

Just a few months ago, I would have loved this, would have adored this interaction. I craved it, wished for it, longed for it when Jase had been so short and impatient with the children, and with me. But tonight, when I was in the midst of sensory overload, when this was the first meal we'd sat down to as a family in ages, I almost burst into tears. Not the happy kind, either; the tears that were born of pure frustration, hurt, anger.

I wasn't needed here any more than I was wanted here.

Hell, he'd even gone and bought new patio furniture. The asshole had the audacity to go out and buy the same set that I'd wanted to get for us, but he'd said was unnecessary. Why let go of the old when it was perfectly fine and held so many memories... that's what he'd said to me.

But it was clear, so very clear, that it was out with the old and in with the new.

At least the fountain was still there, and it was still the same, calming me at the end of the day. I sat curled up in that amazingly comfortable chair, staring out at that fountain that he'd put out there for me, wondering how soon before it was going to be gone. Hopefully he'd at least leave it until my condo was ready. Nan had brought out her evening glass of wine and joined me, in silence, as she read her book in the dwindling light.

"I'll be leaving tomorrow," she said. "I don't want to impose."

"It's no imposition," I replied, not wanting to add if anyone was imposing it would be me.

"You kids need your own time, your own space."

"This isn't... my space," I said softly, and she nodded sympathetically.

"Nor is it mine."

I wasn't looking for any reassurance, so I wasn't disappointed when it never came. But neither did the chastising, or the comments about hurting her grandson. There were no words of disdain, no condescending remarks, no unwanted, unsolicited words of advice. Did it make the silence any easier? No; it actually made it more deafening, more unnerving. When I excused myself to help put the children to bed, she'd merely smiled, murmuring how she hoped to see me in the morning before she left.

The children were just as content with having Jase put them to bed as

74

they were with me, although the kisses and hugs put little Band-Aids on my bleeding heart. I told myself as they laid in their beds that I was doing this for them, but I didn't need to kid myself into thinking that it was for their benefit. They would do just fine without me.

I, on the other hand, was already lost. They were my anchors, keeping me sane. Without them, where would I be?

Other than...

Alone.

I couldn't walk down that damn hallway downstairs, I couldn't see what had become of the room he'd once so lovingly decorated for me. I couldn't wander around this house; my heart couldn't take anymore change that day. So I'd sat on that bed reading a book until I was certain that Elizabeth was asleep, taking a dollar out of my bag to place under her pillow.

And I saw Jase in the hallway.

And he looked so sweet, almost child-like as he was sneaking out of the room, motioning for me to be quiet as he pulled the door to where it was only open a small bit. "Is five overkill?" he asked in a whisper.

Well, yes. Yes, it most definitely was.

But I couldn't say it as I stuffed my dollar in the pocket of my jeans, wondering if he'd seen.

I merely smiled and shook my head.

"Is everything all right?"

He looked so happy.

It was tearing me apart.

"Yeah," I choked out with a shrug. "Yeah, I'm fine."

I looked past him, where the light was on in his office down the hall, just as it had been nearly every night. I longed to ask him what he was working on, who he was working with, what was going on in his world that made him smile like that, made him so happy when it was something I wanted so very badly.

But I couldn't ask.

I was too afraid of the answer.

"I'm just really tired."

"Understood," he said with a nod. "If you need anything, let me know okay?"

I'd nodded. I'd thanked him.

And then I'd fled back to this room, sinking to the floor, wishing he was there to hold me.

I lost track of time after I'd resigned myself to actually get into the bed, listening for his footsteps to come down the hall, to that bedroom that we used to share.

I must have drifted to sleep, though.

Because the footsteps never came.

JASE

She's home.

My whole family is home.

I admit she doesn't look very happy about being here, even when she's telling me how nice all of the changes look. I'll live with it, though, to watch her sit in that large black chair in the great room, looking for her book through the bag she'd brought home from the hospital. She looks absolutely amazing, even when she was so tired, her curls coming loose around her face.

I'm fairly certain she's upset with me for the dinner incident last night, when I said I didn't mind Michael putting his fingerprints on the table. I know I went overboard, overkill even when I was picking out the new dining room furniture, and it really wasn't as kid friendly as it should have been. But I liked it, it was as dark as my mood had been that day, and the chairs were comfortable. I suppose its best selling feature, though, had been the stark contrast to the old traditional set that I'd inherited from… someone I'd worked with back in the day, for the life of me I can't remember who. But, yeah… it was different.

Different was good.

Different was needed.

"Can I get you anything?" I asked Talli as she walked towards the kitchen.

"I'm just going to get some coffee," she murmured softly.

My heart fluttered as she brushed up against me in the hallway, mumbling her apologies, and I couldn't even tell her no apology was needed. All I could do was stand there, amazed at my luck, my fortune having taken such a drastic turn.

"Mommy! Daddy!"

Elizabeth sounded so excited as she bounded down the stairs. Talli rushed back towards where I stood, her eyes wide for a brief moment before she settled, realizing nothing was wrong. Our daughter stood before us, proudly displaying her five-dollar bill. Oh yeah. I'm good.

"I'm rich!"

I coughed to cover the laugh I was failing to stifle, grinning at the look Talli shot me before she put her arms around Elizabeth. "I still can't believe you lost a tooth."

"Yeah, I was talking to Michael and it *totally* flew out of my mouth," she giggled, crinkling up her nose. "It went in his cereal bowl and he cried."

"Oh."

It was Talli's turn to unsuccessfully stifle a laugh.

And my turn to attempt the look, which she rolled her eyes at. But she was grinning.

And that's a good start.

"Want some breakfast?" I asked them both, and Elizabeth excitedly began to babble about frozen waffles and lots of syrup as she grabbed my hand, dragging me into the kitchen that Talli was returning to for her coffee. "Eggos for you as well?"

"Hmm?" she asked, looking up from her spot where she was pouring about ten tons of creamer into her coffee. "No thanks. I'm good."

"Talli,"

"I'm good, Jase," she reiterated, her eyes boring into me.

Okay. I get it. She's grown accustomed to her life without me in it, and it was pretty much likewise for me. It had been so long since we'd been under the same roof and civil at the same time that I wasn't quite sure how to act, or react for that matter.

But I was determined to make this work.

"Mommy has fruit in the morning," Elizabeth announced, and I grinned. Did I have any around at the time? No. But that would be easily remedied when I was out taking Nan to the airport.

"Good morning, sweetheart," Nan said as she entered the kitchen area. "Sleep well?"

Hell no I hadn't, but it wasn't for lack of trying. She was here...

77

right here… but she hadn't been with me.

"Just fine," I lied, but my smile was genuine. I picked my cellphone up off the counter, grimacing as I saw how many text messages were awaiting me, how many missed calls I'd had, and who they were all from. Something told me that the news, although incomplete, had gotten out. To read, or not to read…

Or not to have a choice as Chris is calling and I really need to answer.

"I have to get this," I said apologetically, walking out of the kitchen and towards the stairs. "Gooood morning, Mr. Webber, how is your day so far?"

"Oh great," he said, his tone flat. "So it's true."

"Don't sound so happy, Chris."

"You two are just one big… headache, you know that?"

"I love you too," I replied.

"No, I am happy for you, I am. How soon do we release the statement, or have you not officially called off the divorce?"

I was silent as I unlocked the room to my office, quickly entering and shutting the door behind me. It gave me just enough time to compose myself, keep my voice from breaking.

"Jase… what is going on?"

"We're not… we haven't called off anything, Chris. She's just here until they open her condo back up, that's all."

"Yep, I was right. You'll be the death of me, the both of you will."

"Thanks, dude."

"Hey, at least I called first instead of getting the congratulatory fruit basket that my wife wanted me to pick up and bring over first thing this morning."

"Hell, I wish you would have. Talli would have some breakfast then," I said with a laugh that I so needed. I could hear Chris chuckling softly through the line.

"On the record," he said, all business once more, "as someone who works with you, I'm going to tell you that this wasn't one of your smartest moves. It can confuse your fans, make them feel like you're playing with her. On that same note, it can help redeem you a little in the eyes of those that see you as the villain."

"You know, not to sound rude, but… I really don't fucking care what others think."

"I know you don't," he said softly. "Not where she's concerned. But as your friend, I just want you to be careful."

"What's there to be careful about?" I asked defensively. "I'm just trying to help my w…" I stopped, pinching the bridge of my nose.

"That's exactly what I'm talking about, Jase. That's exactly what I'm talking about."

Not him, too. My heart was going to be just fine.

"Do I have to release a statement?" I asked.

"I think it would be best," Chris said, and I sighed heavily.

"Can it be completely smartass… like… I kidnapped her and drug her here against her will or something?"

Chris laughed at my question before saying, "No, I'm sorry but that won't work."

"Fine," I said, almost pouting. "But let me see the statement before it's released, okay?"

"Listen, we need to make this quick. It's all over *Celebrity Gossip*, it's getting picked up by other tabloids on the wire. We want to nip this in the bud, not make the situation any more uncomfortable than it must be."

I opened my mouth to protest, to say that it wasn't uncomfortable, but that would be a lie. I was comfortable, I was rather happy to tell the truth, but Talli? Not so much.

Not yet.

But she would be.

"Jason Michael Warner."

Oh, great. Even my best friend was into the full name thing today. I made sure my headset was positioned properly and I muted my radio to hear the whole conversation perfectly.

"Go ahead, Kate."

"What was one of the last damn things I said to you before I had to leave?"

"Don't drink myself into oblivion," I replied.

"Other than that."

"Don't go blind masturbating."

"Other than *that*."

"Stay away from the blonde twatbucket or you'll kill me dead, which by the way is redundant."

"Damn it, Jase!"

"All right, all right… the last thing you said was 'Don't do anything stupid'."

"And?" she asked, rather forcefully.

"This was not stupid, Kate."

"I beg to differ."

"This was *not* stupid!" I repeated. "The condo is out of commission, and Talli doesn't need to be recovering, or living for that matter in a hotel room."

"So she asked if she could stay with you?" Kate asked, and I could hear the clicking away of her keyboard.

"No, I asked her. I just… offered, Kate. That's it, I just offered her a place to stay while she recovered and said she could stay there until the condo was ready."

"By the way, I'm going to kick your ass for learning about this through the media."

"Well, answer your damn phone."

"Well, I was busy. And you should answer yours when I'm available."

"Ooo, play the high and mighty wedding planner card," I teased.

"Fuck you, Warner. At least I'm doing something productive."

"Ouch," I said with a laugh. "Damn, Kate, way to kick a guy when he's almost down."

"Almost… what do you mean almost?"

"Nothing. It's nothing."

"Bullshit! See, this? This is what I was talking about." The clicking of her keyboard had ceased and I could tell I now had her full attention.

"What?"

"You weren't thinking logically, Jase, you were thinking with your heart. Perhaps your dick too, but definitely your heart."

I was quiet as I turned down the street towards my house, the fruit from the store securely in the passenger seat beside me. I couldn't come up with a witty retort for Kate, because there was none.

She was right.

With the heart part, of course.

"I know this about you, I've always known this about you. You live by your heart. You always have. And when you make these life changing decisions, you don't think them through. You don't think about what's going to happen when that shoe drops, when that coach turns into a pumpkin... when that condo is ready for Talia and those children to move back into."

I hit the garage door opener, pulling in and putting the car in park. "I'm going to be fine, Kate. I'm a big boy, you know?" There was a double meaning to my words, that she immediately picked up on.

"I'm not here to stroke your ego, Warner."

I laughed as I shut off the engine, grabbing the bag of fruit as I climbed out. "I know, I know. We'll talk later, and maybe you'll get back on that supportive train before then. Listen, I'm home now."

"I do support you, Jase. I'm just... I'm worried."

"Yeah, I know," I said, reaching for the door. "I appreciate that, thank you."

"You're welcome. And Jase?"

"Yeah?"

She sighed before she said, "Be careful."

I was so tired of those words already. How could this have possibly been the wrong decision?

"Where's Nana, Daddy?" Michael asked as I walked in.

"I took her to the airport. She had to go home."

His bottom lip stuck out as he shuffled away.

"Hey, listen." I caught up with him, motioning for him to follow me to the kitchen. "Don't be sad, okay? Nana had to go back home, and..."

"That doesn't go in the fridge, Daddy. Mommy leaves that on the counter."

"Oh," I mumbled, looking around for a bowl to put the various pieces of fruit in. "Anyhow, when Aunt Jaden has her baby, we're all going out there, okay?"

"Okay. But what about Mommy?"

I looked down at him, tousling his hair softly. "She'll be coming, too."

"That would be fun. Can I have that?" he asked, pointing at a banana.

"Sure. Here." I peeled it, following him as he walked to sit at the kitchen table. I handed it to him as something just caught my attention out the corner of my eye.

I watched as Talli walked towards the kitchen, Emily on her hip slowly playing with her mother's curls. I felt my heart pick up pace the closer she got, the scent of jasmine filtering through as she placed our daughter in her highchair.

"Daddy gots some fruits for us," Michael attempted to say, his mouth just a little too full. I was about to correct him, tell him not to speak while he was eating, when Talli's voice made me weak in the knees.

"You did?"

She's speaking to me...

Of course, she's speaking to me. We're living together. Temporarily, but still living together.

Say something, damn it!

"I was looking for a bowl to put it in."

I cringed as she turned towards the bag of fruit, wanting to kick myself, feeling like that awkward teenager in that hospital waiting room all over again.

"He was gonna put it in the fridge," Michael piped up.

"Traitor," I whispered, then plastered a smile on my face as Talli turned our way, amusement etched in her features.

"I can take care of it, if you'd like."

Oh, I'd like. No, wait. Fruit. She's talking about the fruit.

"Sure! Sure, if you... if you would like. I bought it for you, you know."

She blinked a couple of times as I felt my face flame as red as her hair. *Smooth, Warner. Real smooth.*

"How much?"

"Just a bunch of bananas, some oranges, apples…"

"No, how much do I owe you?"

Why did that question make me want to cry?

"You don't," I replied with a shake of my head.

"Jase…"

"No, don't argue with me, not about this okay?"

I didn't mean to sound so forceful, I didn't mean to hurt her feelings, I didn't mean…

I didn't mean it the way she must have taken it.

She was silent as she kept her eyes downcast, placing the fruit in a bowl that she'd found in the first cupboard she opened, as if she'd been looking around the kitchen to see where everything was. She grabbed an orange along with the breakfast she'd pulled out for Emily, not even looking at me as she walked past.

"Talli…"

The phone was ringing yet again, interrupting just like it always used to. I sighed as Chris's name appeared on the display, knowing I had to take the call.

"I'm sorry."

"I know, you have to get the call," she replied, like she always did.

With a sigh I left the room, not taking the time to correct her and let her know the call wasn't what I was sorry for.

In hindsight, though, I should have.

CHAPTER 7

TALIA

His lips were like a whisper upon my skin, startling me awake. I could feel his hot breath on my neck as his lips teased me, open kisses stirring my soul. His whiskers tickled slightly, his teeth and tongue weakening any defenses that may have been up, any misgivings tugging at the back of my brain ceasing as he latched on where my pulse was hammering. I moaned deep in my throat as I felt his calloused fingertips on my torso, trailing down between my legs.

"Jase…"

It was a whispered plea that was silenced as his lips found mine, his tongue dancing gracefully with mine. Oh, how I missed this… the kisses, lush and full, building in passion the way only he could. I gasped against his lips, feeling his fingers reach inside my panties, separating my folds, stroking me.

"Oh…"

"I tried to stay away," I heard him whisper as he pushed a finger inside of me. Oh fuck… fuck, I can already feel my insides quivering as I whimper and moan, begging him for more.

"Don't stop…"

"I won't."

"Just… love me. Just love me…"

The alarm screaming my most hated song of all time caused me to jump, squeaking slightly before I ran a shaking hand through my hair.

Just a dream.

It had been just a dream.

That I could feel, and see, and touch, and kiss, and... oh hell, did I break out in a sweat?

I finally reached the radio, my hands shaking as I shut that stupid fucking song off.

"Fuck," I moaned, pressing my back against the wall and sliding to the floor.

I swear it was the best damn thing in the world that I was going to work today.

Every single nerve ending of mine was on absolute fire as I dug through the few clothes from the condo that I'd actually been able to get the smell out of, settling on a skirt set. "Damn it," I muttered, realizing the only pair of shoes I had to wear with those were my Manolos.

Fuck it.

I just needed a shower, fixed up, and out that damn door. Away from here, away from this house that just screamed 'Jase' at every turn, away from the memories, away from...

"Morning."

He was in his office? Again?

God, he looks good.

He smells good.

He...

"Morning," I managed weakly, my hand on the doorknob to the washroom.

Make that a cold shower.

But I never did turn that water to extreme cold; instead I let the hot water run over me as I moaned his name, hoping my self-served orgasm would carry me through another day.

The weekend had almost been excruciating it was so... peaceful. So calm. We were more like a family, no matter how distant I kept myself, then we had been in months. It was heaven and hell all wrapped up into one, and I just needed to clear my head.

And I needed him to not look me up and down when I walked into the kitchen.

"Coffee?" he asked, holding out my cup. He'd made my coffee exactly the way I'd wanted it, just like he used to every morning before I left for work when he was home. Well, before things had changed so drastically, and...

"Thank you," I said, trying to stay cordial, trying to stay occupied so he wouldn't see me pick up, then drop an orange.

"Here, let me..."

"I've got..."

Simultaneously we reached for it, our fingers brushing, and I was thankful for my jacket. Seriously, did my nipples have to stand at attention from just one touch? Oh, great. Self-service was of no help to me. I was still hot, bothered, and in danger of fucking up our still fragile truce.

"Here," he finally said, holding the orange out for me.

Ah, what the hell.

I took it from his hands, growing hot and damp at the way his eyes stayed on my hand, his breath quickening ever so slightly.

"I... oh hell, I'm going to be late," I said in a rush, even though it was a total lie.

"I moved my car; you have a straight shot out."

I stopped briefly, my hand on the doorknob to the garage as I looked over my shoulder in wonder. I remembered how he'd practically snapped my head off one morning, telling me if I couldn't maneuver around his car, I needed driving lessons.

I wondered if he remembered, too.

"Thank you," I said, and he smiled briefly.

Before he could tell me to have a good day, before he could omit the 'I love you', I hurried out to my car, taking the long way to the hospital to try and clear my head.

"You know what? I don't know what the hell I'm doing," I finally admitted. Problem was, I was most likely admitting it to the wrong person.

"What makes you say that, Talia?" Dr. Litton asked, peering over her glasses. Wow, I really hate when she does that, looking at me all shrink-like.

"It's not my home anymore," I replied, throwing my hands up. "It's his. I mean, I know that we're getting a divorce, but it's so uncomfortable there!"

"You just told me it was comfortable."

"It's both. It's complicated."

"So what is it that he's doing that's making you so uncomfortable?"

"He's being nice to me," I mumbled, sounding more like a pouting child.

"Pardon?"

"He's being nice to me! I mean, like extra nice, a hell of a lot nicer than he was before we split up, that's for damn sure."

"I see."

"Do you?" I asked, again holding my hands up. "Because I don't... I don't want his pity, I don't want to be handled with kid gloves, I don't..." I shrugged, my voice trailing off. "I don't want to be reminded."

"Of what, Talia?"

"You know... of... of... *stuff*."

"Define 'stuff' for me."

"'Oh, stop psycho-babbling, you know what I meant!" I snapped, stifling a sob with a whispered apology.

"It's okay; I understand. I just think it would help you tremendously, though, if you would say it."

"I don't..." I sobbed, wiping away my freely falling tears. "I don't want to see him that way. I don't want to... to feel, I don't want reminded why..."

"It's okay."

"...why I fell in love with him."

It was killing me inside, to look around and see what was once our home completely changed, see how much everything suited him, how he was so happy there. I didn't want to get comfortable, get complacent, feel the warmth that shouldn't be there. Hell, I was too afraid to walk down that hall, see what had become of what was once my room, half afraid to be crushed even further, half afraid that I would love it even more, that I would somehow delude myself that whenever he was in there, he would be thinking of me.

Because he just... wouldn't.

I held myself as aloof as I could, trying to come to grips with the face that he'd erased me and seemed... again, so happy with it.

Why the hell does it hurt to see him so happy?

No, I know why. I don't have to ask myself that question, I know. Because the man I vowed to love until the end of time was there, right in front of me, and his happiness was coming from elsewhere. His beautiful kaleidoscope eyes were dancing, and while they weren't carefree, they were kind. Because he was happy... happy with his life... without me. Which I already knew, I'd had it thrown in my face before when I opened that bedroom door, but now? To see him this content, this at peace?

It was absolutely killing me.

"Talia, you need to address these issues with him," Dr. Litton said, her voice full of authority. "As a matter of fact..."

"No. Absolutely not. I'm not in school; I'm not doing homework."

"By the next time I see you,"

"Did I stutter?" I asked, my voice rising. "Am I inaudible or something?"

"I want you to have discussed your issues with Jase."

"No."

"If you're not comfortable being there, you need to say so. And if need be, you must remove yourself from the situation."

Remove myself from the situation.

It would mean leaving my children behind.

Could I even think about doing that?

"Welcome back," Paul's smiling face was in the doorway of my office as he leaned against the frame.

"Wow, are you that bored that you would find yourself in an OB/Gyn office?" I teased.

"I am on a scheduled break, thank you," he replied, holding up a caramel macchiato for me. I blinked back my surprise, not wanting to hurt his feelings by telling him I didn't really want one at the moment.

"Thank you," I murmured, walking over to take the cup from him, blushing as he whistled long and low.

"Damn, Talli, you look phenomenal. Way to fuel the gossip."

"Oh, shut the hell up," I said, dragging him into my office by his arm and shutting the door. "Okay, I know the shit that's on *Celebrity Gossip.*"

"Yeah, so which is it? Are you passionately reuniting, or are you having to stomach him being with Bree right in front of you?" Paul asked teasingly, yelping as I slapped his arm hard. He was still laughing as he sat in a chair.

"Not that it's any of your business," I replied, "but... neither."

"Really?" he asked, seeming genuinely surprised.

"Yes, really," I said, sitting in my chair again, hiding my Diet Pepsi and sipping on the caramel macchiato. "We are most definitely not together, and he's at least trying to hide his... whatever it is he has with her." I scowled, wondering how many hours he'd spent on the phone with her when he was holed up in his office.

"I'm sorry that you have to go through this, especially now. Going through so much stress, on top of your recovery,"

"Oh hell, physically I feel great," I said with a wave of my hand, and it was the absolute truth. "I can't remember the last time I had this much energy. I just have no way to really... expend it. Is that the word I'm looking for?" I blushed fiercely as the words left my mouth, not knowing if he was catching on to where my mind was going, and he certainly didn't need to.

"Tell you what," he said, leaning forward slightly. "Come to dinner with me."

"Excuse me?" I asked a little too quickly.

"Did I stutter?" I could tell by the twinkle in his eye that he was in a rather playful, yet serious, mood. "Come to dinner with me some evening. Get out of the house for something other than work."

"As... friends," I stated, and he smiled.

"Of course."

I looked down at my hands, frowning as I turned my wedding rings around my finger easily. Could I do that, leave the children with Jase to go out for dinner with Paul? My first thought was no, hell no I couldn't. But my second thought was... why not? How many times was I left with the children while Jase traveled god knows where with her?

"What do you say?" Paul asked and I looked over at his smiling, friendly face.

What else could I say?

"I'll think about it."

JASE

It was inevitable.

Things were going so well, so smoothly that something was bound to give, bound to crack. Hell, perhaps things were only going well in my mind. Maybe I had just imagined that the past few days had been wonderful, bringing us—all of us—closer in ways I'd only hoped for.

But all it took was one day away, one day at that hospital, one day full of gossip and who knows what else, to have it all blow up in my face.

First, there was the phone call. The one from her that was rather short, telling me she would be late, she was going to dinner with a friend. As if I'm not supposed to know who the friend was, right? I suppose I didn't have the right to be upset. It wasn't supposed to hurt, but damn... seriously? The minute she gets out of the house, she runs to him. No wonder she dressed like that, wore those heels.

I couldn't say no. It isn't my place to say no. She needed a break. She deserved one. That break, though, was unceremoniously interrupted by the paparazzi. And it wasn't her fault, or his either.

It was mine.

Because I was the one in the limelight, it was my life they were picking apart, and that made Talli a target.

Was it bad of me to be oddly satisfied when it had happened? Hell, of course it was. But I felt vindicated, as if I was right, I knew her going out 'with a friend' was a bad idea.

I also knew by the way she kicked those shoes off her feet that she was in a mood, too. Her cheeks were flushed, her expression taut, her lips tightly closed as she walked past me into the kitchen, her eyes flickering over the contents of the refrigerator that she put her leftovers in-- her leftovers that probably hadn't even been touched-- before she shut it closed with a muttered curse.

"Why didn't you eat with us?" Michael asked innocently as he wandered into the kitchen. She glared at me as if I had put him up to it.

"I went out for dinner, with a friend," she said, stressing that last word for my benefit I'm sure.

"Who was your friend, Mommy?" he asked.

I narrowed my eyes as I looked at her, watching her expression, daring her to lie to our son.

"I was with Paul," she said as she shrugged out of her jacket.

"He's a doctor, right?" our son, Mr. Twenty Questions, continued as I silently watched, silently seethed.

"Yes, he is," she said, picking up an apple which apparently was going to be her dinner.

"So he's your work friend, like... like Bree is for Daddy."

I felt the heat creep up in my face just as Talia glared at me again, her eyes narrowed to little slits.

"No," she said, her voice full of venom that our son didn't need to hear, her eyes locked with mine. *"Nothing* like that."

Michael seemed confused by her sudden change and I smiled tightly at him.

"Little Man, why don't you go upstairs, watch that movie with your sisters?"

He shrugged at my suggestion, shuffling along like it was no big deal, leaving his mother and I in a battle of wills, staring each other down in the middle of the kitchen.

"Was that really necessary?" I finally broke the ice, and her eyebrow shot up.

"Is it necessary for every single bit of my life to be under a fucking microscope?" she replied, and that just set me the fuck off.

"You knew what you were in for before you ever fucking left Ohio,

Talia. You knew before we had children, before we married exactly what it could, and sometimes would, be like. You can't hold it over my head that your dinner with your boyfriend…"

"Do not patronize me, and don't put any words in my mouth," she hissed, stepping closer. "Paul is not my boyfriend, and even if he was not only would it not concern you, at least I waited."

"Here we fucking go," I said, throwing my hands up. "Things don't go your way, you bring up Bree."

"Our son brought her up, or did it not finally dawn on you everything they picked up on that whole damn time you were carrying on with her?"

"What the hell does that have to do with your mood tonight?"

"Everything!" she shouted. "Every damn thing, and if you can't see that then you're…"

"I'm what, Talli?" I stepped closer, a muscle in my jaw twitching as I glared down at her.

"You've always been blind when it came to her."

I know… I know I was, or maybe I was too focused on getting even sometimes, but damn… did she have to say that to me when I was so pissed off? Because of course I would open my big fucking mouth and say, "Once upon a time, I was blinded by you, too."

Fuck, that came out wrong.

But if I expected tears, I was surprised when her nostrils flared, her hands clenched in fists as she began to shake. "You… bastard."

"Is that the best you can do?"

"Why the *fuck* did you ask me to come here?" she demanded, her chest rising and falling with every deep, shuddering breath. "Did you think you were doing me some kind of favor, or were you just trying to keep tabs on me?"

"Jeezus, Talli, seriously?"

"Is it some kind of control issue with you? Or… or did you just want to prove to me how far you've come, how easy it was for you to move on?"

"Coming from the person who moved the fuck out!"

She opened her mouth to say something, but what the hell was she supposed to say other than the obvious?

It was my fault.

But instead of stopping while I was ahead, I had to push it, and the most ignorant slip came through.

"Your first day back to work, and you couldn't even come home for..."

"Home?" she cut me off, her voice piercing. "Home?! What the hell about this house is my home? You... you erased everything about me, everything having to do with me from this place!"

What?

"You," she continued, her finger pointed straight at me, "you wanted your perfect bachelor pad, no remnants of the person you left behind long before I left this fucking house!"

"Talli, I..." My voice was much softer now, my heart breaking not just for me, but for her as well.

She didn't get it.

She... she was wrong.

So wrong.

"Tell me you weren't purging this house, Jase."

But I couldn't say that.

I couldn't say it, because I *had* been.

"And you couldn't wait to shove this in my face!"

"That's not..." I couldn't finish my sentence, instead holding my hand out. "Come with me."

"Why?"

"Down the hall, Talli." I licked my lips, just now realizing she hadn't seen. "Come with me."

"Fuck you, Jase," she hissed. "You want to throw that room in my face?"

"Just... come with me."

"Go to hell."

"Talli,"

"No!" she yelled, her blue eyes flashing with anger. "So you can show me one more corner of this house that you've erased our lives from?"

At that point, it was useless to argue with her. I knew she wouldn't listen.

But that didn't mean I was done.

As she stood there in my face going on and on, I dipped down, hoisting her small frame up and over my shoulder easily, moving swiftly out of that kitchen towards that hallway.

"Jason Michael fucking Warner, put me down right fucking now!"

With her extensive use of fuck words, I knew she was on a roll with her little rant.

"Have you lost your fucking mind?"

Why yes… yes I have, thank you very much… and a lot of it has to do with the way my heart has been so wrapped up in you. See, I'd said once upon a time… but my once upon a time was still happening.

"You think you can bully me, push me around, toss me…"

I sat her down in the middle of that room…her room… the only place that in my darkest hour, my lowest point, my time of need held any peace for me.

"You're right, you know?" I finally said, my voice breaking slightly as she looked around in wonder. "You're absolutely right. I went through this house and I took out everything, *everything* I could, everything that was a reminder, and I purged it. I wiped it as clean as I fucking could. But not of *you*. Not… of you."

As she stood there surrounded by her pictures, her music, her books, her movies just the way she left them, my resolve began to crumble around me. All of the hurt, the anger, the frustration I had been dealing with, the belief that my wife didn't love me anymore, the hope that I had been wrong, the awful truth that hit me that night… I just couldn't handle that look of pity that was sure to come.

Because I was a fool.

I was such a fool to think she would see this house the way I'd intended her to.

I turned and walked away, out of that room, leaving her there, wishing she'd call out to me and knowing she wouldn't. I couldn't even man up enough to keep the tears away as I walked up the stairs towards what once was our room.

"Daddy?" Michael's voice was so soft I barely heard it.

"It's okay, Little Man," I said, sniffling slightly. "It's okay, go back in with your sisters."

I couldn't look at him, though, and let him see how broken I was. I don't care about all of the lectures, all of the 'it's okay for your children to see you cry' because damn it, they'd been through enough and I was supposed to be strong for them.

And I couldn't even be strong for me.

I closed the door to that bedroom, that one room in this house that needed changed above all others. There were no traces left. I didn't see it the way I had before, when I'd finally looked at it through Talli's eyes. There were no traces of the candles, the rose petals... hell, even the room had been rearranged so I wouldn't even think about it whenever I walked in. The different shades of blue were supposed to be so comforting, but most nights all I could think of was how they paled in comparison to those beautifully striking blue eyes that I longed for, that once looked at me with love.

I still couldn't sleep in here. It was so cold, so empty, so lonely without her.

With a shuddering sigh, I walked down the hallway and back to the office, resigning myself to another night on that pullout couch, hoping that tomorrow I would be strong enough.

CHAPTER 8

TALIA

I t's my room.

It's still… my room.

I must have looked like an idiot just standing there, staring. I could feel myself begin to shake, my lower lip trembling as his words filtered through.

"You're right, you know? You're absolutely right. I went through this house and I took out everything… *everything* I could, everything that was a reminder, and I purged it. I wiped it as clean as I could. But not of *you*. Not… of you."

I closed my eyes, two large tears dripping down my cheeks, my vocal cords apparently paralyzed for a brief moment. I wanted so badly to call out to him, but I just couldn't. I couldn't form so much as one syllable. I opened my eyes, turning around in a circle, my heart sinking as I realized he wasn't there anymore.

I knew I needed to talk with him. But first… first I needed to process this, to think, to… to…

I needed to cry.

And I did, as I looked back at that Italian leather sofa, the one I'd missed so badly, my blue knitted blanket thrown across the back of it.

I cried as I looked at my matching overstuffed rocker recliners that had a few of Emily's stuffed animals in each of them.

The pictures... all of the pictures on the wall, all of them were the same. There was the one from the hospital all those years ago, the one Lisa had snapped, that I hadn't seen until I was recuperating at her house after the accident. My parents, my mom and dad, were smiling from their perch, right next to a picture that we'd added of the children. Oh, that picture from Vegas, where I was shooting him one nasty mean look as he grinned so cheesily... is that even a word?

My books. They weren't even collecting dust; Linda must be cleaning this room; Jase would never keep up with it. Oh, all of my movies, my music... and the kids movies that were on the shelf where Elizabeth could reach them perfectly, a couple of the cases on the floor. I stifled a sob as I picked one of them up, remembering Jase's invitation to come back to this room to watch it with them just the night before. I'd been too afraid to, I hadn't wanted to see what he'd done with this.

But it was the same. Exactly the same.

And Bree had never once stepped one toe into this room. She'd stood in that doorway, smiling her sweet fake smile, asking if she could 'borrow' my husband for a bit, but never... *never* did she step over that threshold.

How could I have been so wrong?

I stepped out into the hallway, walking slowly towards the great room, pausing as I looked over the new furniture. If I closed my eyes, I could see it as it had been. Not just the Christmas decorations, either. No... no, I saw her. I saw Bree on the old loveseat, leaning up against Jase as she giggled over whatever it was on her phone that she was showing him.

But that was gone now.

Now I saw the black and white room, with small accents of red, where my children ran through in the morning discussing what they wanted to have for breakfast, or how they should pounce on Daddy if he was sleeping in... in...

Oh... in my room.

I wiped a few stray tears away as I shuffled slowly into the kitchen, looking over at the new breakfast table and chairs. How many times had I come home from the hospital only to find her there? But... not anymore.

Not anymore.

And the dining room, where she would sit opposite me, on the other side of Jase, laughing loudly at their tales of being on the road, or in the studio… tales I wouldn't find funny, and at times were inappropriate for my children's ears. Now I saw our family in those exuberant comfortable chairs enjoying slightly tense dinners. Tense but… uninterrupted. Untainted. Untarnished.

"Jase?" I called out, walking towards the stairs. I wiped my tears from my face, my hands trembling as I climbed the staircase, holding onto that railing as I stood at the top.

I still couldn't face *that* room.

"Daddy's… in his office," I heard Michael's voice, and I turned around to see him sitting a little too innocently on his bed.

"Thank you," I said with a slight sniffle, pausing to turn back towards him. "Were you jumping on your bed?"

"No," he said far too quickly, and I raised my eyebrow at him. "Not anymore I'm not 'cause I don't wanna get in trouble." He grinned at me, looking so much like Jase that it made my heart ache.

"Don't do it again," I said sternly, taking a deep breath as I looked down the hallway. Fuck it, there's nothing to be afraid of, right? What's he going to do besides tell me to go away? Or tell me he doesn't accept my apology? Or…

I laid my hand flat on that door, taking a few deep cleansing breaths before knocking. I didn't want to just barge in… no, the last time I'd done that…

Oh, the last time I'd done that, his arms had been around her. And he'd told me it was innocent, that he was just consoling her.

Innocent my ass.

It took less than a minute for him to open the door, his eyes, his expression showing he was upset, too. As I took in his appearance— really took it in—I saw the circles under his eyes, the slight reddening giving away that he'd been crying, too. He didn't appear angry anymore, just… sad.

So very sad.

"Can I come in?" I asked, my heart hammering in my chest. It would have been so easy for him to tell me to go to hell, perhaps he should have, but he nodded, stepping aside and opening the door wider to his sanctuary, letting me see it for the first time since I'd moved out.

Wow, it had changed.

He had a sofa in there, along the wall by the door. That was most definitely new. The cabinets were new, and the drawers probably didn't stick in them the way they did with his old one. He'd moved a guitar in here, on a stand on the far wall. It didn't seem to be more than a decoration, as if it were here as a reminder of what he should be doing.

Oh, reminders... She... she was gone from here, too.

He'd finally gotten rid of the desk that Chris had given him before I'd ever moved out there, the same desk I'd seen her sitting on countless times. The chair... no, the chair was the same. Why would he keep a broken chair? Unless he just replaced it with a new one, one that wouldn't sink to the floor without warning.

I blushed as I recalled exactly how we broke that chair.

And I blushed further as I saw black and white photos on his desk. "I'm sorry if I interrupted you... I can come..."

My voice trailed off as I felt his fingertips on my cheek, capturing a curl and tucking it behind my ear, just like he used to. I couldn't turn to look at him, I couldn't even move as he stepped a little closer, his voice soft and low.

"You weren't interrupting."

My face turned instinctively towards his voice, my breath catching in my throat as he stepped in even closer. "I... should have told you, about the house. I shouldn't have left it to you, I should have just said it."

My eyes slid shut before I opened them again, blinking back tears. "I'm... I'm sorry," I finally said, and I swear I almost heard a sob from him, but I couldn't move. "I'm so sorry. I just... I just assumed, and... don't. Don't say it."

"Take all my fun away," he said softly, and I couldn't help but laugh.

"I..." I took in another deep breath, "I'm being serious, you know."

"I know."

Luckily, he'd moved away, back closer to the desk. I was so close to just melting into his arms, and not for any other reason than to just cry. I could just see that, in all of its awkwardness. My eyes followed him as he sat behind that desk, shuffling through the photographs.

"I… I can come back some…"

"No… no…" He looked up, his eyes still so sad, so troubled as he said one little word that brought back so many memories… "Stay."

I wondered if he felt it too, that shiver as a memory flows through you.

I nodded, walking over to one of the chairs in front of his desk, sinking down into it. I glanced at the photos, my fingertips gently touching my lips as I realized what they were.

"Jaden took these," I said with wonder, seeing the photos for the first time. They'd been taken just this past April, and the kids… oh, they'd changed so much, even since then.

"You haven't seen them?" he asked, and I shook my head 'no'. For a moment it looked as if he were going to just hand the stack to me, but instead he stood, walking around to sit in the chair beside mine. He smiled warmly as he looked down at the first one. "I can't believe how much they've grown," he said, handing it to me. It was an 8 x 10 print of the three of them, Emily in the middle and holding on to Elizabeth's and Michael's hands, all three of them looking off in the distance, to the side of the camera.

"She wasn't even walking then," I commented, suddenly remembering what it was they were looking at. I smiled up at Jase, remembering the goofy faces he'd been making, and how they all looked at him like he was on crack.

"Yeah, she… what?" he asked, catching my expression. I shrugged it off, looking at the next on in his stack. It was one of Michael looking down at the ground, pouting.

"Oh, I love this," I said, picking the picture up to take a closer look. "He looks so much like you."

"I don't stick my lip out like that."

"You did when you were little; I've seen the proof." I smiled over at him, the smile fading as our eyes met, our earlier words spoken in anger still hanging in the air between us.

"I shouldn't have given you any grief over Paul," he said, and I felt a little piece of my heart die. "I don't have the right to."

I didn't say whether he was right or wrong, I only nodded. My hands were trembling slightly as he handed the next photograph to me, and I smiled wistfully. Elizabeth was looking up towards the sky, the wind catching her hair and pushing it in her beautiful face. There was something so real about it, so innocent, and yet she looked sad.

Just like Jase looked now.

"I shouldn't have brought her up," I said softly. "Again, you know. I... well, it's an easy out, something to point my finger at whenever... whenever something goes wrong."

He didn't look at me, he just kept staring at that picture of Elizabeth as I continued.

"But she wasn't the only problem. She wasn't even the start of it." I couldn't even believe the words had left my lips as I admitted it to him, out loud, for the first time.

"What was it, then?" he asked suddenly as he raised his eyes to mine. "What started it?"

I wish I had an answer for him. I wish I could tell him it was the drinking, or the yelling. I wish I could tell him it was the ignoring each other, or when he gave up on me. Truth is...

"I don't know."

And in the silence that followed, I stared into his eyes searching for something, anything that would give me the answer. But all I saw was the overwhelming sadness and guilt, the same feelings I had been dealing with.

Emily's crinkling diaper broke the spell as she ran into the room, giggling, playful, her curls bouncing on top of her head. I held out my hands to her, rather surprised when she bypassed me completely, burying her face in Jase's side.

"Hey."

"Don't feel slighted, Mommy," he said a bit playfully. "You don't do... this." He hoisted her up, flipping her upside down easily as she squealed with delight.

"Oh god, be careful!" I exclaimed, placing the photos on the desk and moving my hands beneath her quickly.

"We're always careful," he replied, standing up and holding onto her by her ankles. "You ready?"

"No!" I exclaimed.

"I wasn't asking you. Are you ready, Princess?"

Emily squealed once again as he began to swing her.

"Jase, quit!"

"Quit being such a party pooper. One…two…"

"Jase, what if she gets…"

"Three!" he said, setting her down on the sofa a lot easier than I expected, but immediately tickling her tummy, her laughter loud as he did so.

"Oh, you're going to be the death of me," I muttered, sinking back into the chair.

"Me next! Me next!" Michael was running into the room, his cheeks flushed with excitement, his big sister right behind him.

"And then me!" she added. "Oh, you gots the pictures out! Did you decide?"

"Not yet," Jase replied, hoisting Michael up into the air to give him his turn despite Emily's protests.

"Decide?" I asked, my head tilted slightly as I watched him swing our son, grimacing at what was sure to be an injury, breathing a sigh of relief when he was also safe on that couch, only screaming because he was being tickled.

"Pictures for the front… room thing," Jase said, crooking his finger at Elizabeth, who jumped into his arms and giggled with glee as he flipped her upside down.

"For the great room," I said, looking down at them again.

"Yeah, I wasn't… too good at deciding…"

"Please watch what you're doing," I said quickly as he began to swing Elizabeth.

"I'm fine, Mommy," she said between her giggles, screaming loudly when she was 'dropped' on the couch and tickled mercilessly.

"You were always the one who did that sort of thing," Jase finally said, turning towards me as he motioned to the children to get in a line before picking Emily up once more.

"Oh, you're making me nervous," I muttered, turning away from them even as he laughed.

"You could help," he said, and I looked over my shoulder at him like he was completely mad.

"Have you lost your mind? I'm not going to swing the…"

"The pictures, Talia." he said with a roll of his eyes, a smirk planted on his face.

"Oh." I straightened just a bit and added, "I knew that."

"Is that a yes or a no?" he asked just before he made Emily squeal so loud I thought my ears would bleed.

I looked down at the pictures, then back over at them… all of them, laughing, playing as if they hadn't a care in the world. Jase happened to glance at me at just the right time, raising his eyebrows slightly, gesturing with his head at the pictures.

I knew our conversation was far from over. I knew the hardest parts were yet to come. But I also knew that this was his way of waving that white flag once more.

Who was I to say no?

JASE

"Are you sure you don't mind?" Talli asked as she put the finishing touches on her hair, its messy bun looking absolutely adorable. I smiled wistfully, unable to count the number of times I'd watched her do this simple task.

"Positive," I replied. She was fixing her light makeup, wiping a smudge from under her eye as she stared into her small compact before snapping it shut and shoving it into her pocket. My smile faded as the memories of that hospital in Illinois crept into my mind.

"I swear this is the last night for this," she continued, grabbing a Diet Pepsi from the refrigerator. She turned to me with an easy smile. "This time around, anyhow."

I opened my mouth to ask what she had done for childcare during her on-call and rotation hours when we were living twenty-two minutes apart but decided against it. I knew it was my place to be concerned—they're my children, too—but I knew it was normally Linda when she'd been at the house, and I knew it hadn't been since she'd left. Paul had watched them before, but he was a doctor and couldn't do it all the time. Was it that hateful bitch that had seen to it my kids were kept from me that night?

I felt Talli's hand on my arm, burning straight to my soul, and I glanced at her again. Her eyes were so soft, so kind as she said, "This means so much. Thank you."

I couldn't tell her it was unnecessary to thank me, see. Because not so long ago, when she would get that call, or her pager would go off, I would be absolutely livid. I would protest about having to deal with Emily when I had just gotten home and was exhausted. I would snap at Elizabeth and Michael when they would have one of their arguments. And the moment Talia would get home, dark circles under her eyes, I would grab my keys and leave like some pouting child.

I wonder if that's what she was thinking of, too.

"I... I should have done this," I said, and her eyes dropped to the floor. "Before, I mean."

She took a deep breath, her head tilted slightly to the side. With the most incredibly sweet yet impish grin, she said, "You're right. You should have."

"Wow," I said with a laugh.

"There," she said, seeming satisfied. "Now I don't feel so guilty."

And that pretty much summed it up. Not this great big revelation, not this wonderful picture-perfect family. No, there was this underlying tension, this definite strain on our relationship that nostalgia over photographs couldn't heal. We did our best to be civil to each other, to not step over those unspoken boundaries again. But the boundaries were killing me slowly. This was my own personal hell, I'm sure. I loved her but I couldn't love her because I'd thrown that away, I wanted her with me, but I couldn't tell her she shouldn't be with Paul because I didn't have that right anymore. I couldn't long for her, ache for her, feel so very lonely even with her just down the hallway.

It was just like before.

Only worse.

Because now we were consciously trying to get along. I'd heard of the phrase about killing someone with kindness, I just never thought it could actually happen. But I swear, every time we said good night-- sweetly, nicely, nonchalantly, however it happened-- and went our separate ways towards opposite ends of the hall, my heart would die just a little more. And she would ask if I was going back into my office, and she would ask if I ever rested, and I didn't have the heart, or the balls, to tell her I slept in there. I didn't want her pity. No, it was much worse.

I wanted her love.

But I didn't have that anymore. More and more every passing day it seemed evident that what I wished for was reserved for someone else. More than once she'd let me know she was going to be late. I had promised I wouldn't ask, so I didn't, but that smile on her face, that spring in her step... there was no denying what was doing that to her, for her. It was wonderful to see her smile like that again, but damn it, it should be because of me. Because of us.

She would curl up in her papasan chair in her room, the kids playing around her, and giggle on the phone like a schoolgirl. I could tell when it was Jaden, with the obscenities that Pete and I would pass through them just like we always did, but it wasn't always Jaden.

It wasn't always a female she was on the phone with.

And she would get secretive. She would walk out of the room. She would talk more softly, tell the kids they were nosey when they would ask who it was on the phone.

I knew the drill.

I knew it because I'd played that game before.

I hated feeling like I needed to escape from my own house... no, it wasn't even my house I needed to escape from. It was my own head, and I hated it. I hated it almost as much as sitting at that kitchen table, the one I wanted new memories at, and going over our plans, our wishes.

Not for us, not for our future together.

No, we were making plans for the end of it, for parting ways, for our divorce, for our impending separation... and this one would be permanent.

So I wasn't in the best of moods when Kate finally called to tell me she was back.

"Warner, let me tell you, Europe was absolutely brilliant! Much better without Brooks."

"Good, good. I'm glad you had fun."

"Fun?" she asked with a breathy laugh. "Oh, honey, I was living it up in Italy!"

"So..."

"So what?"

"Tell me, dork." I sat in the recliner, smiling as Michael came up and gave me one of his spontaneous hugs he must have known I needed.

"Oh no."

"What?" I asked, alarmed. "What's wrong?"

"Exactly what I thought would be wrong," she said with a groan. "Oh, Jase... I love you, you know that I do, so I say this... from that part of me, okay? The part of me that knows you so well."

"What are you talking about?"

"I know you had the best of intentions, and who knows? Maybe you did the two of you and the kids a world of good by opening up your home to Talli."

Did I?

"But listen to you... oh, God, Jase. You are so lovesick, so... so heart sick."

"I was just..."

"No, no... it's time to stop lying to yourself, Jase. Especially when you can't lie to me, and I'm going to call your ass on it."

"Really, Evans?" I asked, picking at a thread on my shirt.

"Yeah, really. You wanted this to work, you wanted the two of you to get back together. And don't bother to argue with me because you know I'm right."

I shut my mouth as she continued, her words resonating around in my head.

"You wanted to show her what you had, how it could be if you two stayed together. You wanted her to... to tell you that she loves you, tell you that she doesn't want this divorce, tell you that..."

"Just stop, okay?" I said, my melancholy mood coming through.

"Where is she?"

"Work."

"I don't want to cause any problems, Jase, okay? I just... I think you need a friend."

I sighed as the kids ran out of the room, giggling about something that Elizabeth had been drawing. "I think you're right."

"I'm going to grab some ice cream, okay? What kind do the kids like?"

"No… no, I'm going to put them to bed soon," I said, glancing at the clock. "Elizabeth has school tomorrow, and the kids will be going to the daycare center for a few hours. I don't want them all cranky."

"Oh, listen to you, Mr. Responsible Daddy!"

I laughed, scratching the back of my neck. "Who woulda thought, huh?"

"Me."

I was silent for a moment, my hand still on the back of my neck, but still. "Wow."

"I'm being serious, Jase."

"I know… I know you are," I said, my voice still full of wonder. "Thanks."

"Don't mention it," she replied with a laugh. "So I'll be by in about an hour, with ice cream. Including that crap you like to eat."

"Awesome."

"And a movie."

"I already have the movie," I corrected her.

"Do you still watch it?"

I pondered her question for a moment before answering. "Not so much lately. But yeah, I watch it from time to time."

"And you still quote Penny?"

"How could I not? Kate Hudson's a goddess. No boobs, but still… a goddess."

"Oh lord," she groaned. "I'll be there in an hour."

It was wonderful to smile genuinely without the heartache associated with that lovely mediator appointment we had coming up in two days. Two fucking days. In two days I was going to sit in front of someone appointed by the court and tell them that yes, I wanted this over with, I wanted a divorce, I wanted to split the time with our kids, divide our assets, I wanted to be free.

But the price of freedom… it's so high. So very high.

"Do you remember," she began from her seat beside me in the media room, "when you and Debra went to go see this movie?"

"Debra?" I asked incredulously, laughing at her question. "Damn, Evans! Not... 'do you remember all the times we watched it'; not 'remember the time we snuck onto the football field and had a private viewing'; not 'remember when we had it playing to drown out the noise of...' OW!" I rubbed my arm where she had hit me rather hard.

"I'm trying to make a point here, dickhead."

"Oh, a point. This should be good." I grinned, taking a bite of my ice cream.

"Do you know how much that hurt?" she asked, and my smile faded.

"Not as much as the..."

"Sadie Hawkins dance, yeah. It took you awhile to top that one... well, other than you kissing Talli on our one month anniversary," she added with a wave of her hand, then grinned at me.

It was a smile I couldn't return.

"I'm sorry... that wasn't... my intention, that wasn't where I was going with this," she said softly.

"Where were you going, then?"

"I forgave you. It hurt so... so very much, but I forgave you."

I nodded, remembering all those years ago. "That you did, Evans. That you did."

"Have you asked her?"

"Huh?"

"For forgiveness, Jase? Have you asked for forgiveness?"

I blushed as I shook my head, focusing on my ice cream that was melting into a puddle of green soup. "No. And before you ask, no... I haven't told her that I want us to make this work. I haven't told her I lay awake at night wanting to walk down that hall and just... crawl in bed with her."

"I love you, but... T.M.I."

I laughed at her statement, nudging her softly. "Just to sleep, Kate. Just to sleep. Because I... I miss her... here." I crossed my arms in front of me, hoping she'd get what I was saying. Judging by the tears in her eyes, she did.

"So what happens, in two days?"

I sighed and shrugged. "I agree to the arrangements we've made for the kids."

"And when they leave?"

I had tried so hard to not think of that. I'd put my head in this… in this bubble, telling myself just what Kate had said. She was coming back to me. She would spend the time with me, the way we used to. I'd be the man she used to love, and… and she'd fall in love with me all over again. In a perfect world, in a fairy tale that's what would happen. But this wasn't a fairy tale. This was real life, and it was brutal. It was imperfect. It… it hurt.

"Jase…"

"Life goes on," I said sadly.

"What about the kids?"

My heart constricted slightly as I said, "I hope… I hope they can understand. I hope they aren't…"

"Confused? Hurt?"

"No, they know what happened with the condo. This… we didn't play the 'Mommy and Daddy are getting back together card'."

"That's good, that's good," she said, and I felt her hand run through my hair as I stared at the large screen in front of me. "But that doesn't stop the wishing."

"Don't I know it."

"So you didn't want to confuse them."

"Right."

"Why didn't…"

"Before you ask why I didn't put her up in another apartment, or something… truth is I didn't want to." I shrugged again as the words left me. "I honestly didn't want to."

"You wanted her here."

"Yeah."

"And you told her this."

"Kate, it's… it's complicated." I frowned slightly, my mood souring. "I thought you were coming over to cheer me up."

"I said I was coming over because you needed a friend, I didn't say anything about cheering you up. Jase, you need to… well you need to shit or get off the pot, basically. You need to tell her or let her go."

"What if I do tell her, and she says no?"

And there it was, out in the open. I had been rejected, pushed aside by her for so long that regardless of any diagnosis, regardless of any progress we had made, I was too afraid. Of pain, of more heartbreak, of... of the end.

All of this over a girl who wanted to love like it was never going to hurt.

Over a girl that I loved that fully, that completely.

A girl I loved enough to set her free.

And I knew the pain of that all too well.

As Kate put her arm around me, shifting so my head was on her shoulder, comforting me, she was also my reminder.

I had paid this price before.

CHAPTER 9

TALIA

It took less than two hours with the mediator for all custody and visitation issues to be completely settled. Hell, he'd even joked with us that most married couples don't get along as well as we do.

If he only knew.

"I'll present this to the judge, who will look over the matter and give the final ruling."

"Seriously?" I asked with a laugh. "We come up with what we feel is best for our children and someone else has to rule on it?"

"Such is the way with the law."

I rolled my eyes for the umpteen millionth time at that phrase, and Jase smirked at me mouthing the word "behave." Whatever. It was so difficult to behave when I felt so uneasy, so full of this anxiety that was continuing to build.

I felt Jase's hand on the small of my back as we left the conference room, and for a moment the world stood still. How many times had he touched me that way, so innocently? Sometimes... not so innocently. But today it wasn't being led through the crowd at our reception. It wasn't down the hallway of our home. It wasn't through the maze of people backstage at one of his concerts. It wasn't to a doctor's appointment, where he would come unglued when the kids needed their shots.

It was out of a conference room, where we were agreeing how to share our children.

"Are you all right?" he asked, his voice full of concern.

"Yeah, yeah," I replied with a wave of my hand, turning to look at him. "You didn't have to do that, you know... back in there."

"The emergency custody was only worded that way to keep them away from our kids," he said softly, close to my ear so others couldn't hear. "You are doing so well, Talli... so much better. It wouldn't be fair to keep them from you."

So just like that, even though technically Dr. Brooks hadn't signed off on my case, Jase was essentially handing me my walking papers. He was telling me I was free to go, take the children if I wanted. He wouldn't stop me.

Of course he wouldn't.

This must be driving him crazy. We've been there for three weeks now; he hasn't been able to live the way he had been. His friends haven't come over. Hell, even Chris has stayed away, and he's normally around sometimes to just give us grief.

But there wasn't an 'us' to give grief to. Just him, and me, and our separate lives that we were being forced to combine.

"Would you..." Wow, if I wasn't mistaken, I'd swear that Jase was blushing. "Um, want to get some lunch?"

"Lunch?" I asked, glancing at my watch. "Oh... hell! I have an appointment in less than an hour, back at the hospital!"

"Oh."

He sounded so nonchalant when he said it, as if it was so normal for the two of us to go grab something to eat after we'd put one more nail in the coffin that our marriage would be residing in. There wasn't even a hint of disappointment when I'd had to turn him down.

"But I'll see you at... at the house tonight, right?" I asked, trying to stay calm and casual myself.

"I kind of had plans," he said with a shrug.

"Kind of, or do?"

Way to go, Talli. Sounding like the jealous, bitter, cast aside wife when you're the one who filed for divorce. Way. To. Go.

"I do have plans," he said a little softer. "I can..."

"No, don't change them. Hell, I'm sure I'll see you eventually, right?" I didn't mean to sound as if it didn't matter, because it did. I just needed to get the hell out of there before I broke down sobbing in front of him.

"Yeah," he said as he began to walk away. "See ya."

'Oh look,' I thought as I stood there watching his form get smaller and smaller as he made his way down the hall, 'there goes my heart.'

"I'm sorry I'm late," I said in a rush, placing my hands on the counter as I tried to catch my breath.

"Not even ten minutes," the receptionist said with a smile. "Have a seat, we'll call you back shortly."

So there I was, back in Dr. Litton's office for the umpteenth time in the past couple of weeks. Damn, it was a good thing I got one hell of a discount with the hospital. I hate to use the term 'breakthrough', but it really did seem as if one had happened. And it all started with one innocent question that she asked, about my family... about my support system.

Support system.

Yeah, that made me laugh. Almost hysterically at first, which turned to sobs and tears and about a box of tissues later I had spilled my heart out onto the floor. And it wasn't just about the bullshit that had been going on forever it seemed, it was all the bullshit that had recently begun to happen.

Have you ever felt that you had to love someone, because they were family? Because that's how I was really beginning to feel about mine. My darling brother Jeff had decided that now-- now, during my divorce, now that my and Jase's names were being dragged through mud and any other filthy substance the press could conjure up-- it was time for the 'terrible three' as I began to call them to make their demands.

I'm a rather private person, I always had been. So the last thing I was going to do was explain to someone I rarely ever talked to about how I not only was going through a very public, very painful divorce, but was struggling to make ends meet with missing income and extra residual bills. I temporarily lost my home and am in that house with a man that I love watching him slip through my fingers again, so what does my darling brother Jeff do? Jeff, who has barely spoken to me throughout the years, has taken it upon himself to call on an almost daily basis. Does he just want to chat?

No. God no, because that means he was considering my feelings.

No, see he was telling me everything that I needed to be doing. Not for myself, or for my children, either.

Anna's having a baby and needs pretty much everything, which I'm supposed to provide because my husband is 'loaded'.

Shelly needs her house paid off or they're going to lose it, and since my husband and I make money while she doesn't work and her husband is too depressed to, I should pay it off. Oh, and their property taxes from now until eternity as well.

Jeff's car that he's failed to do regular preventive maintenance on is breaking down, but there's this awesome Dodge Charger that I should give him for a birthday present. Or just to shut him up and keep him from going to the press, or just to his friends that would go to the press.

And every time when I would tell him I couldn't, when I would try to explain without detail that things were rough for me, rough for the kids, he would tell me I owed him-- all of them-- for having to deal with me and my failures, and how I'd failed Mom.

He always brought her up.

I would leave the room when he called, not telling the kids who it was because they'd either want to talk to him, only to have him tell them that I should help my family. Seriously, they're children. What are they going to do? Oh, or my children would say "who's Uncle Jeff?" the way Michael had, which set Jeff right off. Hey, it's not my fault-- I was following the golden rule.

If you have nothing good to say, don't say anything at all.

I had plenty to say to Jeff, though. And the more I said 'no', the more I told him my honest feelings, the better I felt. Hell, I didn't even feel the guilt anymore.

"How does that make you feel?" Dr. Litton asked as I relayed the previous nights' verbal beat down that I have bestowed upon my brother.

"It was wonderful, but you really need to come up with a new line of questioning," I said as I picked at my fingernails. She actually laughed at me then, and I almost smiled.

"Hard day?"

"Yeah," I said with a shrug. "Watch the news?"

"If you call *Hollywood Insider* news," she replied.

"Oh, great. My shrink is watching a show my ex-boyfriend is a correspondent on," I groaned, then added a quick. "Sorry, no offense."

"None taken," she said. "So, tell me…"

"How I feel about it?" I finished for her, then shrugged. "I'm trying not to."

"I don't have to tell you that's a bad idea. You already know."

"Yeah, well," I sighed, rubbing my temple. "We go in there, agree how to divide our time with the children, then he asks me… to lunch? Seriously?"

"And how did that go?"

I scowled slightly. "It didn't. I was late for my appointment here."

"I see." She was silent for a moment before she asked, "Did you want to go?"

"I don't know," I said honestly. "I mean… yes, because I love spending time with him. But, no."

"Why not?"

"Because… because I love spending time with him."

"So you're torn."

"To say the very least."

She was shuffling her papers as she said, "I tell you what."

"Here we go with the homework again."

"But you're doing so well with your assignments, Talia," she said, almost teasingly. "Seriously, though… I want you to contemplate your true answer. Do you want more time with him? Now, before you interrupt me… just think about it. And if you find the answer is yes, then make it happen."

Make it happen.

Oh, much easier said than done. Hell, I even told him we could have dinner together, and he'd told me he had plans. I didn't have to ask who he had the plans with. For once, Bree's name didn't even pop up in my head. No, instead I remembered the kids telling me about Kate coming over and watching movies with Daddy while I was at work.

Kaitlyn Evans.

There was one name, one person who would never go away, would she? I should have known when his freedom was eminent, she'd be in the picture in a more prominent way. But, just like Jase had said about Paul, I had no right to question anymore. I couldn't very well go to Dr. Brooks and tell him to make his wife lay off, because hey! She wasn't his wife anymore. Their divorce had been final for a couple of weeks now, thank you hospital gossip for keeping me informed. And boy were their tongues ever wagging about the whole connection, their divorce and ours. I think that was an even hotter topic then all the talk about Jase with an up and coming starlet.

I was walking back to the staff parking lot, where I'd parked even though I'd only had an appointment that day, when a familiar set of footsteps fell in time with mine.

"Are you avoiding me?"

I turned, smiling as best I could at Paul. "No, of course not," I replied. "I really am sorry about that whole mess at dinner the other night."

"Don't sweat it," he said with an easy shrug. "I was kind of used to it, if you recall."

He would be used to it, especially having gone through a rather messy public divorce himself. I did recall.

"How are things at home? Any better?"

"It's not my home," I said quickly, looking down at my shoes. "It's just a… just a house."

"Have you had your five minutes?" he asked, and for just a brief moment I was confused. Then I remembered.

The five minutes that Jase had won in that game. The five minutes we never got because he said that it had to be alone. It had to be uninterrupted. It had to be all in one setting, not in small increments. So, between my job, the phone, the kids, and his 'plans', we never got those five minutes.

Hell, he hadn't even mentioned them in a while.

"No," I said softly. "It must not have been that important."

"Or he's just as afraid as you are."

"I am not afraid," I said quickly, rolling my eyes when he gave me his 'you're kidding me' look. He was rather good at that one, but I wasn't one of his children. "I'm a grown woman, what the hell is there to be afraid of?"

"For starters, more hurt."

I had nothing to say to that.

"If you want the five minutes, Talli, just ask him for it. I'm sure he'll comply."

I didn't want compliance, though. I wanted him to want that five minutes. I wanted him to still care enough to ask for it. So I stayed silent, no matter how much it was killing me inside.

"So, to change the subject, how about a rain check?"

"A what?"

"A rain check, for that dinner that was so rudely interrupted."

"Sure," I said with a soft smile. "Yeah, a rain check is fine with me. Just…"

"I'm not going to push it, I promise," he said, holding his hands up. "But I do have to get going. You work tomorrow?"

"Yeah, as far as I know I do," I replied.

"Good. I'll see you then."

I know I wasn't being a very good friend to him, and it wasn't as if I was intentionally blowing him off. I'd just had so many other things on my plate, on my mind, in my heart. I could feel the distant calling of those blues, and I was fighting it… oh, I was fighting it hard.

So when I was home that evening cleaning up the dinner dishes, wishing Jase had been there with us and I saw Jaden's number pop up on my cell phone screen, all I could wish for was a little bit of good news.

"Girl," I said as I answered, "quick. Make me smile."

"Well, I'm not a girl but…" Pete's voice trailed off and I looked at my phone like it had grown antlers or something. Pete never used Jaden's phone.

Oh…

OH!

"Is he here?" I asked quickly, perking up immediately.

"He's on his way."

I startled the children when I loudly, quickly fired questions. "Holy shit! Has she been admitted? How far apart are her contractions? Did they say how far dilated she was? How is she doing?"

"Whoa, slow down Aunt Talli," he said with a laugh. "You sound like me when she told me it was time… I forgot everything, I swear."

"Which is why you're on Jaden's phone."

"Right, and… um… yes, she's been admitted. They said it's going a little slow, but her water broke and she's between three and four. They did an epidural to help with the contractions because she couldn't really relax any, so she's trying to rest right now. What the hell is that commotion?"

"That's me trying to get everything pulled out and get us packed, that's what," I said as I rummaged for, and found, the duffel bags that I'd had stored in a hall closet.

"Good, I'm so glad you're all coming," he said with a sigh of relief. "She really wants you here. You're all welcome to stay at our place, or… Nan said you could stay with her, too. And there's also Mom. She's all moved in near here."

"That's sweet, but…"

"Don't argue. You can even split time between the two, and if you and my shithead brother can't get along then one's at one house and one's at the other."

I let out a slight laugh and said, "Hell, it seems our split has made us more amicable."

"Talli, I…"

"Oh, don't worry about it. We're adults, we will be on our best behavior while we're there. Just give Jaden a kiss for me and tell her we're on our way, okay?"

"I will."

I shot a text to Jase, asking him to call, as I made my way up the stairs towards the kids rooms.

"Whatcha doing, Mommy?" Elizabeth asked as she came up behind me.

"Packing."

"I don't wanna leave, you know."

I took a deep breath, refraining from having that argument with her, and instead said, "Oh, so you don't want to go see Jaden and Pete's baby? That's fine; I can call Linda and…"

"The baby?" Her big blue eyes were wide with excitement as I nodded. "I… I'll get my stuff, you get their stuff, and hurry! We gots a long way to go!"

I laughed at her, reminding her I'd be checking her bag for everything, not commenting when she said her daddy would buy anything she'd be missing.

That couldn't be further than the way I wanted her frame of mind to be.

But just like everything else that was bothering me right at that moment, I pushed it aside as I packed our things to head out to Missouri. It was time for some happiness.

JASE

The house was bustling with activity when I opened up the door leading in from the garage. The kids were still up, running around excitedly and giggling, minus Emily who was lying on the small loveseat in the great room fast asleep, clinging to her stuffed puppy and leaving a small puddle of drool on the cushion beneath her.

"Here, Princess," I said softly, reaching to pick her up, but I was quickly stopped by Talia.

"No… no, don't, just let her be. It's easier to just pick her up and go."

And… go?

I turned back to Talli, who was carrying two duffel bags into the kitchen area, and my heart dropped to my feet.

"You're packing?" I asked, my voice so small. I didn't remember any news or phone calls about the condo being ready, but truth was I hadn't been paying attention to anything of that nature. I'd been so wrapped up in my own head, watching her flourish the way I'd wanted her to, and yet it felt so bittersweet.

Because her happiness had nothing to do with me.

"Yes, I'm packing," she said, looking over her shoulder at me, confusion etched in her features.

"Oh."

"Did you need to get something to eat or anything?"

"Huh?" I asked. It was officially my turn to be confused.

"To eat. Did you eat, or do you need to?"

"I... ate already." And I wasn't lying; Kate and I had ordered pizza and just vegged all evening in front of the television. After I'd broke down over the damn courthouse thing and Talli not wanting to go to lunch, of course, but I blame that on my own stupidity.

"Good." She walked past me towards the stairs, seeming just a little hurried.

"So, um... this can wait until the morning."

"What can?" she asked, paused on the stairs as she turned to look at me.

"You... leaving. It can wait until morning, right?"

"Um... no." There she went again with that look on her face, but I wasn't able to question her right then.

Right at that moment I was too hurt.

She called back down the stairs asking something about messages, and I remembered then that my cell phone had been left in my car all night and was still there. As I was fishing in my pocket for my keys, Elizabeth ran past me, skidding to a halt in the kitchen before she opened one of the duffel bags and stuffed a Barbie into it.

"Whoa there, Baby Girl, be careful."

"We don't have time to be careful, Daddy!" she exclaimed excitedly before running past me again.

Okay, that didn't make any sense.

Elizabeth had said on more than one occasion that she didn't want to go back, she didn't want to leave the house. She'd said it was her home, and we just had to tell Mommy that they all had to stay.

If only it were that simple.

"Talli... what's going on?" I asked as she came back downstairs with Emily's diaper bag. She turned to look at me, her eyebrows furrowed together.

"I sent you voicemails and messages, Jase... did you not get them?"

"No," I said, turning towards the garage door so I could go out and get my phone.

"So you didn't get the tickets?"

"Tickets, what tickets?" I asked, trying to hide that my breath caught in my throat as she placed her hand on my arm.

"You ... oh, you don't know!" Her face lit up, her blue eyes dancing as she said, "Jaden's having the baby!"

"Seriously?" I asked, and she nodded. I could feel my smile all the way to my toes as the news sunk in. My baby brother was about to have a baby of his own.

"And... I'm so sorry, I just... the tickets..."

That's right. She'd left her credit cards here, for our joint accounts, when she'd moved out. I'd told her that it wasn't necessary, but she had insisted, and I couldn't force her to take them. I pulled my wallet out, handing her my card. "Here... I... um..."

"Go! Pack!"

So that answered that question. Hell, I hadn't had to pack for a trip that we were taking together since... well, ever. She'd always packed for me. But that was then, when we were together, when our lives were completely entwined with one another. I actually missed having to dig through her clothing to find my things, it was one of the million things that I loved about her. She'd never seen us as 'separate'.

But she certainly did now.

"Are you coming too, Daddy?" Michael asked as he pulled several of his Transformers out of his overflowing toybox.

"Yes but put those back. You can only take a few on the plane."

"Are you... and Mommy gonna do it, too?" he asked, following me into my bedroom. Thank God I didn't have anything in my mouth; I would have choked instantly.

"I'm sorry, what?"

"Have a baby," he said, climbing up on my bed, making himself comfortable.

"Um... no. No, we're not." I felt my face grow hot at his question, wondering how confused they must be, even though we'd sat them down and told them that this was just temporary.

"Why not? Is it cause Em cries all the time?"

"She doesn't cry all the time anymore," I reminded him. "But no, that's not the reason."

"Then why not?"

With a sigh I sat down, tousling his hair slightly. "Because Mommy and I aren't... together."

"Mommy says Jaden and Pete are having a baby 'cause they love each other."

"Yes, that's true," I said, knowing that at the tender age of three he was far too young to understand the rest of it.

"You love Mommy, right?"

"Yes, I do." There was no hesitation before my answer, because there was no question.

"And Mommy loves you, so…"

I placed a kiss on his forehead, returning to my task of packing for the trip, unwilling to correct him, wishing it were true.

"What's the verdict?" Talli asked from her seat in front of me. I turned my cell phone off, stuffing it in my pocket with a sigh. "What?"

"Just kidding. No baby yet, and the only person Pete has a problem with is me for not answering my phone."

"Quit leaving it in your car," she said with a shrug. "We wouldn't call to just interrupt." Her face turned a delicate shade of pink and she turned around quickly.

"I know you wouldn't."

"I want my raisins," Michael said, tugging on my sleeve.

"In a moment."

"Is my DS in Em's bag, Mommy?" Elizabeth asked from her seat beside Michael, and Talia handed it over the seat to her.

"No…no." That was Emily's addition as she was trying to go back to sleep in her carseat that we'd strapped into the seat beside Talia. Michael giggled, and Elizabeth piped up about how we should all be sitting together.

"We're fine," Talia said, holding her hand out to the other people in first class that had heard our oldest daughter's comment.

"I can sit with Em so you can be back here with Daddy," Elizabeth added. "She's just gonna sleep anyhow."

"Turn that off, Baby Girl, we're getting ready to take off," I said motioning to her DS, and Michael smiled excitedly.

"I love this part."

"Speak for yourself," I heard Talli mutter. I knew she despised take offs and landings almost as she did hotel rooms.

Oh…

Hotel rooms.

Shit.

"Hey," I said, scooting forward slightly. "What's the plan when we get there?"

She glanced back, and my stomach flipped at the color of her eyes. They were so bright… so very blue. So beautiful.

"Pete said we could stay at their house. Your Nan offered, too. Or your mom, if she doesn't mind. Or hotel, whichever."

"Hotel? I wouldn't dream of doing that to you," I said with a playful smirk, and she rolled those beautiful blue eyes of hers, returning my smirk with one of her own.

"I wanna see Nana," Michael spoke up, and Talli's eyes turned to him.

"So, Nana's?"

"We gots to go to Aunt Jaden's when the baby comes home, too." That declaration came from Elizabeth.

"I was lucky enough to get three days off, I can't promise you'll get a lot of time with them."

"You could have taken more time off," I said perhaps a little too quickly, without thinking, without remembering that she was Miss Independent now.

"No, I couldn't have," was all she said, turning around and facing forward as the stewardess came out to begin the little speech that I knew by heart.

"You say this, Daddy!" Michael exclaimed. "You and Kate, all the time!"

I felt my face grow hot as eyes turned on us, some of them sure to have heard and or seen the gossip. And the fact that Elizabeth and Michael were trying, and failing, to quote the airline stewardess as she was giving her speech wasn't helping any. I'm sure she was paid to smile and say how cute it was, but it made me feel uneasy.

That uneasy feeling stayed with me as we made our way to pick up the rental car, some helpful soul dragging a cart with our luggage beside us.

It was still there as we pulled up to Nan's house just as the sun began to rise.

"Still no?" Talia was saying as she spoke with Pete on her cell phone. "Good. I mean... not good, but... oh, hell, you know what I'm saying."

"Come on, sleepy heads," I said to Elizabeth and Michael, who were both conked out in their booster seats. "Let's go."

"Are we gonna see the baby now?" Elizabeth asked as she waited for me to pick Michael up before shimmying her way out of the back seat.

"No... no, I don't think the baby's here yet," I said, and Talia turned to me shaking her head. "Nope, no baby yet. Besides, you guys need some sleep."

"But I don't wanna sleep," she protested, her bottom lip stuck out as she shuffled along behind me. I glanced over my shoulder back at Talli, who was lifting a sleeping Emily from her car seat.

"I can get her," I called out to her.

"No, that's okay." She shut the door with her hip, both arms securely around Emily as she walked towards the door. Oh, the memories that brought back... with Elizabeth, with Michael, with Em, hell with a bag of groceries even.

And I was losing her.

"Are you gonna knock?" she asked with a half laugh.

"Hmm? Oh, yeah. Yeah." I knocked on the door, biting the inside of my lip, that uneasy sinking feeling weighing heavily.

"Kind of weird, isn't it?" Talli spoke my thoughts. I looked down at her, where she stared straight forward at the door.

"Just a little," I admitted.

"We can talk about it later," she said, "about if we should go elsewhere."

I scowled slightly saying, "We won't have to do that."

"No! I wanna stay with Nana!" Elizabeth pouted, her bottom lip sticking out.

I know that Talia wasn't going to argue with her, not right then when the kids needed rest so badly, but I also knew that she was wanting to get away. I likened this to me perhaps going to Ohio with her and...

Oh.

Ohio.

Sure, I had to think about that now. Now when we were getting ready to go help greet our new nephew as he came into this world. And it just hit me like a ton of bricks that I never once got to tell her I was sorry to hear about Jack's death, and how I would have been there if only she'd asked.

Which she obviously didn't want to.

"Knock again," she said softly.

"Talli…"

"I have to pee, sorry," she cut me off, and I stifled a laugh.

"Okay, knocking."

I raised my hand to the door only to have it fly open with my cousin Tom standing there looking like he'd just crawled out from under a rock. "Hey, dude… little dude… dudettes."

"Tommy!" Talia exclaimed, trying to keep her voice soft to not startle Emily. She put one arm around him and hugged before excusing herself to lay Em down.

"Hey," I said to him, giving him a one-armed hug myself. "What's up?"

"Oh, we were all kinda camped here waiting for some news," he replied. "Hey, Squirt."

"I'm not a squirt," Elizabeth mumbled, shuffling towards the stairs. "I want my bed." My Nan always had the kids' beds ready whenever we were coming into town, and today was no exception.

"Oh but you don't want to go to sleep," I teased her, but was only met with a growl.

"Women," Tom commented, shutting the door.

"Tell me about it. You look like hell."

"Thanks; I'll try and return the compliment after I've woke up." He yawned and stretched, dragging his feet as he made his way towards the kitchen. I walked up the stairs to put Michael in his bed, pausing as I looked in on the girls. Elizabeth had only taken her shoes off before climbing into her bed and was already fast asleep, and Emily was curled up on her side in her crib. My ass was definitely dragging, but the bed wasn't what was calling me.

Just one door over and I was laying Michael down in his bed, taking his shoes off as he continued to sleep. Once I'd pulled his covers up, he rolled onto his side, taking the blanket up and covering part of his face just like he always did. I was going to miss doing this, tucking him in.

"Is everything all right?"

I jumped at the sound of Talli's voice and I turned towards the doorway. The hall light was on behind her, casting that eerie glow around her that had once reminded me of how close she'd come to losing her life. Okay, so it still did, but I had to have my big boy pants on, my brave face. Nothing about her was supposed to affect me anymore.

"I just got a text from Pete," she said, continuing to talk softly. "He said it's almost time."

"I don't remember you taking this long," I commented, snapping out of my gaze and walking out into the hall with her. Her soft laughter caused the hair on my arms to stand straight up.

"I didn't."

"They were both pretty easy… the last two," I said. "Or, from where I was standing, they were."

"No, they hurt like a bitch, but…well, yeah." She grinned up at me. "They were easy."

We were stopped at the top of the stairs and I motioned for her to go on in front of me. She murmured her thanks, the soft scent of jasmine trailing behind her as she brushed up against me and began her descent. I stood there, momentarily stunned as I watched her, my body reacting in ways that vividly showed how easily I could push her up against the wall and bury myself in her.

Oh, great.

I was in one of those moods.

"Are you coming?"

And that question from her didn't help matters either.

Downstairs in the kitchen area, Tom was pulling out cups for us to have coffee, and Talia was standing on tiptoe to try and reach the creamer that was on one of the top shelves. I reached around her, easily grasping onto that bottle , my other hand on her hip to keep myself steady. It was a simple action, one I'd done so many times over the years, but one that today left my hands shaking.

"I'm staying put, so you can leave the kids with me," Tom was saying.

"Are you sure?" Talli asked.

"Yeah, I'm sure. Don't sweat it, at all. I wasn't going to head out to the hospital until the little squirt was here anyhow, but damn... those kids have the right idea, all curled up in bed."

"So you say as you're drinking your coffee," I muttered, smirking at him.

"That doesn't mean my ass is going to be out and about any time soon," he said, his big booming laugh filling the confines of the kitchen. "You two should go, though."

"That's very sweet, Tommy. Thank you."

"You do realize," he said to Talli after she'd spoken, "that you're about the only person who gets away with calling me that, right?"

"That's because I'm special," she replied.

Tom raised his cup of coffee, his smile genuine as he said, "Yes you are."

I couldn't agree more.

"Holy shit, I'm so glad you guys are here," Pete said in a rush, pulling me into a hug. "They're checking her, they think she's ready to push, and... I just feel..."

"I know, Pete," I said with a laugh, squeezing tightly. "I know. And it's nothing compared to when you actually see him."

"I'm so ready, but I'm so fucking scared," he continued, and I held on just a little longer.

"And it's completely normal. If it helps, I was the same way with all of mine. Well, except..."

"Yeah," he said, knowing I was talking about Elizabeth, knowing I still had a hard time with it. He stepped back, wiping his face with his trembling hands. "Talli went in to see her, right?"

"She made a beeline for that door the moment we rounded the corner."

"Good, good. Jaden's been asking for her. I think you've lost her til the baby is here."

"I don't think anyone could pry Talli out of there right now."

"I... I need to be getting back in there," he said with a short laugh. "Holy shit, I'm gonna be a dad!"

"You'll be a great one, Pete. I know it."

He merely grinned as he slipped back into the room, where Jaden was with my mom and Talli. I shuffled down to the waiting area, choosing a seat by the far wall just like I always did, and I settled down to wait for news. I leaned my head back onto the wall behind me, closing my eyes for just a brief moment, the memories of our son's birth surrounding me.

"I can't do this," she said, gasping as she laid her sweat covered head back against the pillow.

"Are you kidding me?" I asked, leaning down and taking her hand in mine. "This... this is so much easier than Baby Girl, right?"

"Wouldn't know," she replied. "I was dead at the time."

"Would you quit with that?" I asked, actually laughing softly. "Come on, baby... next contraction, he's going to be here."

"Are you sure?" she asked, panting. I glanced down to where Dr. Stewart was working to turn his tiny face just a little.

"Oh, I'm positive." I began to move, to place my hand back on her leg, but her whispered plea stopped me.

"Don't let go."

"Never, baby," I promised, placing a kiss on her damp forehead. "You ready?"

"Yeah... yeah, let's do this."

"Okay, Talli, let's go," Dr. Stewart said as the next contraction began to build. "Push!"

She raised up, bearing down as she pushed with all her might. She was squeezing the hell out of my hand, but I didn't mind. It was worth it. She was worth it. He... was worth it.

She gasped, falling back onto the pillows as one tiny squawk sounded. "Jase?"

"He's here, baby," I sobbed, raining kisses on her face. "He's here."

"Jase."

I jumped slightly, a smile touching my lips as Talli's beautiful face came into view. She was beaming, radiantly happy, two large tears tracing down her cheeks.

"He's here," she said, squeezing my hand. "And he's got a head full of dark hair, too. He looks so much like Jaden, and..." Her smile lit up the entire room, just like it always did. "Jase, you've got to see him. Come on."

I followed silently... or, I should say, was drug silently to Jaden's room, Talli's hand securely around mine. I could barely hear her voice above my pounding heart.

"She did so wonderful, Jase! She was exhausted, but I didn't hear one complaint from her. And believe me, I'm used to complaining. And... remember when Michael was born? How he just kinda squeaked and didn't cry anymore?" She turned to me, her cheeks flushed, her smile so warm and inviting.

"Yeah," I finally managed to say.

"Ethan did the same thing."

"Ethan?"

"Yeah, Dork. Our nephew." She giggled, opening the door to the room, dragging me in before I had a chance to respond. She immediately moved away, going to Jaden's side, leaving my hand empty even as my heart was full of love.

"Wow," I said as I took in all the hair on top of my nephew's head from his perch in his mother's arms.

"I know." Pete was beside me, sniffling slightly. "I know."

I pulled him into a warm embrace, rubbing his back as he let go of a little sob. "My baby brother is a dad," I said, choking back tears of my own.

"God, I hope I'm as good at this as you are," he said in a rush, and I let out a laugh.

"Ah, Pete... learn from my mistakes, okay? Don't fuck up the way I have. Just love them both, let it grow every day, and don't let go. Just... don't let go."

"Not even if hell froze over."

I pulled back, wiping my eyes and following him over to the other side of the bed, where I glanced down in wonder at my nephew. Talli was right; he did look just like Jaden. His dark eyes were open as he stared intently at his mother's face, and Jaden was beaming as she looked down at him.

"I'm gonna do right by you, you know," she whispered to him, and my heart jumped up in my throat.

I'd made that same declaration to my children, all of them. Hell, I'd made that declaration to Talia. I watched Talli's face as she blinked back her tears, and I knew she was thinking of the same thing: all the promises I'd made, only to break later.

How could she ever forgive me, when I couldn't forgive myself?

CHAPTER 10

TALIA

S he's a mom.

My best friend, my sister in law, my reinforcement, my rock… is a mom.

And she damn near broke my hand while she pushed to bring that little boy into this world, too. Oh, he was so gorgeous, from minute one. Jase was able to joke with Pete, tell him that Ethan was only that cute because he didn't look a damn thing like him, which was payback for Pete saying that about Emily. Which led to Jase reminding him how he'd gushed over Elizabeth and Michael, and then led to some lovely brotherly bickering that Jaden and I once again paid no attention to.

I was sitting on the side of the bed where she laid propped up to a sitting position, her newborn son in her arms. "Why Ethan?" I asked her softly, reaching out to touch his hair.

"Ethan Frome."

"The book?" I asked, and she nodded. "Jaden, it's so depressing."

"It was my dad's favorite," she said, tracing the side of Ethan's precious face with her fingertip. He instantly turned his face to the side, his mouth open like a little bird. Jaden never spoke of her father much, other than to tell me that he'd passed away when she was very young. I put my arm around her, giving her a little squeeze.

"It's perfect."

"How are you?" she asked, still mesmerized by her son's face.

"Oh, I'm fine; don't worry about me."

"I do worry, Talli. Although I gotta say…" She looked at me then, her tired eyes so sincere. "Your living arrangements agree with you."

I blushed slightly. "Not really," I mumbled. "But we're gonna do what's right by the kids, so…" I shrugged.

"So, what?"

"So I suppose that's it."

My eyes drifted to the far side of the room, where Jase and Pete were laughing as softly as the two of them could. His eyes were narrowed, the soft, faint laugh lines so endearing, making my heart ache, longing for simpler times.

"What are you doing?" he laughed, pushing my fingertips away.

"Just touching them," I replied, shifting slightly in the bed.

"Them?"

"Your laugh lines."

"Oh, way to say I'm getting old."

"No!" I said, curling myself into him, my body instantly responding to that skin-to-skin contact. "I love these." His eyes slid shut as I caressed the sides of his face, my fingertips tracing the soft laugh lines at the corners of his eyes. "They… they show me when you're happy."

"You make me happy." His eyes were a brilliant green when he opened them, a smile on his perfect lips. "All four of you."

"Three and a half," I said with a giggle that faded to a moan as his hands caressed me. He gently urged me onto my back, his hand coming to rest on my lower abdomen.

"I love that we're having another baby." His eyes were so vibrant, conveying his message, and I knew despite my misgivings he was telling the truth.

"You just love how completely fucking horned up it makes me," I teased and he laughed, placing a kiss on my forehead.

"That's one of the perks," he said, his kisses trailing down my face, along my jaw line, and down the side of my neck.

"You, sir," I moaned, "need… to… to not start… any…thing…"

"I can't finish?" he asked when I was unable to speak, his fingers pressing inside of me. I merely nodded as he laughed soft and low,

pulling my leg up as he slid inside of me. "You..." he breathed as he
began to move, "fuck, you should... know better..."

"What are you thinking about?" Jase's voice brought me back to the present. I glanced over at him, watching his hands as he eased the rental car out of its parking space. I knew I was blushing, I could feel it.

"Reminiscing," I replied honestly, although not adding any of the details.

"You too?" he asked, smiling wistfully. I turned my head away to hide the impish grin I could feel coming on. "What's this?" he asked, pinching my cheek slightly.

"Shut up," I muttered, giggling and swatting at his hand when he continued pinching my cheek.

"Ow, damn!" he laughed. "Abuser."

"I could do much worse."

"Why? What did I do to..."

I know he saw my change of expression, and his changed almost simultaneously. He returned his hand to the steering wheel, his fingers drumming along softly to the song on the radio. His cell phone was on the seat beside him, its screen lighting up when it began to buzz. He glanced down, silencing the call, but not before I saw who was calling.

Kaitlyn Evans.

I rolled my eyes, shaking my head as I looked out the side window, my annoyance growing. Why not answer it? Did he have something to hide? Hell, he'd been hiding things for this long, why stop now, right?

"What?" he asked, and I glanced over at him. "You rolled your eyes, Talli. What?"

"Nothing," I said with a shrug.

"Fuck... fine, Talli. Fine. You're right. It's nothing."

"Are you really going to start a fight with me?" I snapped.

"Who's starting a fight? I'm not the one rolling my fucking eyes at..."

"Just answer your damn phone," I cut him off as it began to buzz again, Kaitlyn's name on the display. He glanced down at his cell, scowling and muttering a curse.

"Don't fucking start on me," he said, his tone dark, reminiscent of the dozens of arguments we'd had over his discretions.

"I wouldn't fucking dream of it," I said through clenched teeth, silently seething the rest of the ride back to the house.

I was in a bad mood. Hell, that didn't even begin to describe it. Nothing was helping. Not talking to Jaden, not visiting with Tommy, not watching the children run around and playing with Beth, not the nap I'd taken. Obviously, I was destined to be in this mood, this awful state of mind when I rounded the corner, hearing Jase's booming laughter.

Wow, I was not in the mood to see him, or to hear...

"Evans, can you believe it? My pain in the ass little brother is a dad! Yeah... yeah, I spent some time earlier up there with them. He's really cute."

He spent time up there.

Not *we* spent time up there. Hell, no mention of me being in Groves Point at all.

"Yeah, I got in pretty early this morning.. Now? Um... no. Not such a good time right now."

I rolled my eyes, turning and walking away from him. Apparently, I wasn't quick enough because I could hear his voice as he rounded the corner, his conversation cutting abruptly short.

"I gotta go, okay? Yeah, I'll call you later."

How lovely. He doesn't say goodbye to her.

"Were you spying on me?"

I turned around, my eyes narrowed as I looked at him, spitting back my reply. "Get the hell over yourself, Jase. I heard your voice, I walked away."

"No, you stamped away loud enough for me to see what the hell was going on," he said, standing so close I could smell his body wash.

"Whatever," I muttered, shaking his hand off when he put it on my arm. I took the stairs two at a time back up to the room I would be in by myself, if I could handle staying under the same roof as...

"All right." He shut the door as he entered, his chest heaving, his eyes dark and angry. "I've had enough of you acting like a child."

"I'm not the one running around with something to hide, Jase. That would be you."

"What's there to hide? I was on the phone with one of my oldest friends."

"Whose call you couldn't answer when you were in the car with me."

"Because I didn't want you to overreact!"

"Who's overreacting, Jase?" I asked, holding my hands up. "Am I following you around, starting arguments?"

"No, you don't have the balls to argue with me, sweetheart."

"Oh, really? Well, let's have it, Mr. Warner. Last I checked, even as a woman I have more balls than you. I don't go sneaking around, I don't lie to you,"

"How am I lying to you? How am I sneaking around on you? Oh... OH. Of course."

Yeah, of course. The elephant in the fucking room, asshole.

"Just go, Jase. This is your grandmother's house, I don't feel like having this conversation with you now."

He scoffed at me saying, "A conversation is hardly the worst thing we've done in this house."

"And you think with your dick still, nice."

He came so close to me our chests touched with every breath, his teeth clenched as he said, "How the fuck would you know?"

"I walked in on..."

"You don't know what you saw."

"Oh, so it was the innocent friend you were consoling bullshit, you just happened to do it with no clothes in our bed."

"Since when had it been *our* bed, Talia?"

My eyes grew wide as I mustered up all of the control I could. "You were screwing around on me, and it's my fault?" I asked in hushed tones.

"You know so much about what was going on how, Talli?"

"Because I walked in on you fucking her, that's how."

"Like you fucking cared."

That was just it. That was the problem. I did care. I didn't just care, I was crushed.

"You have been completely indifferent towards me for so goddamn long, what was I supposed to do?"

"You just… gave up," I snapped, not correcting him, not telling him that indifferent was the last thing I had been. "You gave up on me, you gave up on *us*, you ran to the first thing that would spread her damn legs for you, and you're… you're doing it again."

"What do you mean, again?" he asked, leaning down slightly.

"Oh, what, were you screwing her this whole time, too?"

"You're fucking kidding me!" He stepped back, running his hand through his hair as I continued.

"Am I supposed to believe that you weren't? Bree was just a friend, remember? Bree was just someone you worked with, someone you wanted to help through a hard time, someone who would never take my place but she did, because you! You… you *let* her. You've said the same fucking thing about Kate for how many years now?"

He opened his mouth to say something, closing it and his eyes shut and he grabbed a fistful of his hair in the back.

Oh, hell no.

No, this fucker started it, he wasn't going to get off that easy.

"Say it."

I stepped closer to him, a muscle in his jaw twitching as he seemed to be fighting that inner demon, the one that brought him up here for this fight to begin with.

"Say it," I demanded a little more forcefully, my eyes watching Jase's face as he inhaled deeply, closing his eyes for one brief moment before he opened them, his gaze hard, unrelenting.

Fucking pussy.

I stepped up to him, pushing at him with both of my hands, using all my might. "Say it!"

A gasp escaped my lips as I was pushed roughly against the wall, strong hands holding me captive, unable to say a word as his mouth covered mine.

Hard.

Demanding.

Seeking.

Punishing.

And as his tongue caressed mine, I lost all coherent train of thought. I was just…

Lost.

JASE

"Say it."

Fuck, please, Talli… please don't come any closer. You don't want to hear what I have to say…

"Say it."

Oh God… oh God, oh God… Talli, I love you. I love you, I miss you, I want you

"Say it!"

One moment she was pushing me, and the next… the next I just snapped. It wasn't my intention to touch her, I swear I didn't mean to push her up against that wall. And in that second, that one split second, I didn't think at all.

I felt.

I acted.

Logic, common sense, and my heart be damned.

Those beautiful full pouting lips that called to me were suddenly beneath mine, and it was like a dam bursting forth. One touch, one kiss was never going to be enough. She was my drug, the one that I had craved for so long, the one I'd been denied, and I couldn't stop, I couldn't let go. Kiss after kiss I opened her up to me, pressing up against her, waiting to be pushed away even as she whimpered, fueling the desire that was already consuming me.

Just tell me to stop… just push me away… I'm not strong enough to stop on my own…

But she didn't stop me, even as she held herself back. Her quickened breaths only egged me on, each touch of lips punctuated with a moan or a sigh. I could feel her trembling beneath me as I held her captive, nibbling slightly on her lower lip, another soft gasp leaving her as my hips moved of their own accord, grinding up against hers. I couldn't help myself, couldn't stop myself, not even if I had wanted to… and as my tongue stroked against hers—fuck, how long had it been?—I could feel it. I could feel it within my very soul right as it happened.

She let go.

Oh... god...

She leaned forward, melting into me as our kiss reached a fevered pitch immediately, her hands wrapped in my shirt front, her breasts pressed up against my chest, driving me over that edge that I'd been teetering on for so long. There were no soft, gentle caresses, no words of love whispered as my hands trailed down, grasping at her hips tightly before frantically pulling at those damn yoga pants to get them the hell out of my way.

Just stop me, Talli... please... I never knew a love so strong could make me so weak

One touch and I was soaring, one kiss I was a man possessed, one moan I was in heaven.

The sound of her pants falling to her ankles with a small swoosh was only barely heard above my hammering heart, our heavy breathing, the cry that escaped her as I tore her panties from her body with one hand, roughly moving my fingers against her. Oh... she was so hot... so... so wet...

"Oh..." She whimpered as I pushed first one, then a second finger inside of her, moving within her as she writhed beneath me. Every response from her drove me on, pushing me forward, making me want her in a way I'd never wanted anyone before.

And I... I had to have her...

She moaned again as my fingers left her, matching me kiss for fevered kiss as I tried so desperately to get that damn belt undone with one hand, the other buried in the curls at the nape of her neck. There... there went the belt... and... and the button, and the fucking... zipper. The friction as I fought with the material, pushing it down just far enough was nothing... nothing compared to...

"Fuck," I moaned, the tip of my cock nestled between her legs, her wetness nearly my undoing. She... she wanted this, too... I could feel how much she wanted this, there was no denying her body's reaction. I rubbed up against her, leaning down to grasp the back of her thighs as I lifted her, slamming straight into her. Her cries were muffled as she buried her face into my shoulder, clinging to me as I thrust hard, over and over, one hand braced on the wall, losing what was left of my control.

I had no control with her.

I'd never had any control with her.

Is this really happening? Is she kissing me, moaning for me, wrapping her legs... oh...

Yes. Yes, she's here.

I was lost in her... her kisses, her moans, her sighs, her body... I held her as close as I could, as tight as I could, as if this, all of this, would make us whole again.

Because I needed her so desperately...

She was clinging to me, her walls beginning to contract around me, each thrust into her eliciting one of those breathy moans, the kind that I missed so badly, the kind that threatened to send me spiraling into the depths of insanity. She was close... I knew, I could tell, I could feel her body tensing up just like it used to, just like I wanted it to.

Let go, baby. Just let go... I'm here to catch you

Her nails dug in through the fabric of my shirt as she buried her face once more, her cries as she came driving me harder, faster. I pounded into her, feeling her juices wash over me again and again, then... then it hit me.

What was I doing?

Why was I doing this to her?

I love her, with all of my heart and soul, but this... this isn't love. This unbridled, blinding act of passion was something so far beyond my control, and I was hurting her. I knew I was hurting her... and not... not just physically... and I couldn't stop...

"Oh...fuck... oh...oh, oh fuck..." I began to moan, the words spilling out in broken syllables as I came, shooting so hard into her I swear she went over the edge again as well. "Oh God...baby... I... I..."

I couldn't finish that sentence as I kissed her, trying to pour what was left in me out to her, let her know I loved her. She just... she had to know how much I loved her as her walls caressed me, milking every last drop as we shuddered together.

It was heaven.

It was hell.

It was insurmountable pleasure.

It was unhinging pain.

Slowly I set her down, pulling myself from her, my hands on her shoulders. It was if she needed help standing, but I understood. My hands and legs were shaking just as hers were. I tried searching her face for something… anything… but she held her head down, her curls hiding her expression.

"Talli?"

With a broken sob, she shook my hands off.

What have I done…

"Talli, I…"

"Mommy?" Michael's voice sounded just outside our door, and I scrambled to get my pants pulled up as he pulled on the doorknob.

"Just a minute, Little Man," I called out to him, turning my gaze back to Talli as she sunk down, her trembling hands fumbling with her pants, her torn panties lying discarded to the side.

"Talli… I…"

"Don't," she said, her voice a strained plea, my heart shattering, my guilt as consuming as the passion, as the primal need that had driven me earlier.

"Please, just… Talli…"

She shot up quickly, without warning, stunning me as she pushed past me and hurried down the hall. I followed behind her, trying to catch her, but just like she used to, she bounded down those stairs and out that door so quickly I never had a chance.

"Talli, wait!" I called out to her, only then realizing she'd grabbed the keys to the rental car. She couldn't drive away, not now, not like this… all I could see was her losing control of the car, getting hurt, possibly even killed because…

God, because I was such a fucking idiot.

"Mommy, come here! See the picture I drew!"

Michael, none the wiser, was calling to her from the front door, and I prayed with everything in me that he didn't come outside, didn't see her like this.

"Stop!" I called out to her, nearly yelling even though I'd reached her, "Just… just stop."

I finally put my hands on her shoulders, turning her to face me, ready to pour my heart, my soul out right there, right then. I knew I shouldn't have touched her the way I did, I knew I should have had more self-control, I knew...

Oh... fuck...

She was cringing, wincing, cowering away from me as if I had... as if I had...

"Please don't," she cried, her sobs shaking her body. "Please don't."

I felt all the air leave my body as it hit me.

She... she hadn't wanted this at all. And I... I wasn't going to take no for an answer, and...

Oh god, what have I done?

I loosened my grip on her shoulders, the panic, the anxiety setting in, knowing how badly I'd hurt her. And I hadn't meant to...fuck, I hadn't meant to...

"I'm sorry," I said softly, tears stinging my eyes even as I felt hers fall on the tops of my feet. I backed up slowly, my heart hammering so hard, my palms sweating, the reality of what I'd done—what I hadn't meant to do—setting in. "I'm so... so sorry."

She was shaking, crying, hysterical, but I couldn't reach out to her. I couldn't touch her. I couldn't swear to her I'd never meant to hurt her, never meant for it to be like this. I had taken something that was so beautiful and tainted it, soiled it, ruined...

Please tell me I didn't ruin it.

"Talli, please... please look at me."

She only shook her head, backing away from me until she was up against the car. I was so afraid to go to her, afraid of her reaction, afraid that my own worst fears were about to be realized. I heard the front screen open, and soon Tommy's voice was booming, ringing in my ears.

"What the hell is going on?"

I hurt her... and I didn't mean to... and she's leaving... and...

I swear I didn't mean to.

I love her. If I had known, I would have stopped.

Wouldn't I?

I knew I didn't want to drag him, or anyone else, into this mess I'd made. I... I needed to fix this.

"It's nothing, Tom," I said, although my voice gave me away. "I got this."

"I have to get out of here."

My heart broke as Talli said those words through her tears, turning to that rental car once more. No… no, she can't leave. She… she has to stay here, or… or I'll go and…

Tom walked right over to her, putting his arm around her the way I obviously wasn't man enough to, murmuring something in her ear. I felt the hysteria begin to build, and I needed to talk with her.

I had to talk with her.

"Tom, I said…"

And if looks could kill, right then I would have been a dead man on my Nan's lawn. But he didn't get it. He didn't understand what had just happened, he didn't know what… what I had done, and…

And as she walked around to the passenger side of the car and I noticed the keys in Tom's hand, I felt a little bit of relief. I reached my hand out to him, saying softly, "Give me the keys, Tom."

"I don't know what you've done," he said, stepping close and keeping his voice low, "but right now, you're going to march your ass back in that house and you're going to calm the fuck down."

"Just give me the fucking keys, Tom, I need to talk with her."

"Not even if hell froze over."

"Tom, you don't… you don't understand," I said, feeling the anxiety build again, running my fingers through my hair, stunned silent as my body reacted to the smell of her.

She was under my skin.

What have I done?

"Hey, hand me the keys dude," Pete spoke up as he came outside. Hell, I hadn't even known he was there. Tom readily handed him the keys, and I grabbed Pete's arm.

"What the hell, Pete? Give me the fucking keys. Let me go talk to my wife."

"Yeah. Sounds familiar. Go chill the fuck out, Jase, lay off the fucking testosterone."

I felt my hand clench into a fist, but before I could even swing Tom was guiding me into the house, reminding me that my kids were still there, and that was the last thing they needed to see. I was a mess… a shaking mess, needing nothing more than to just tell her I didn't mean it...

I didn't mean it.

I didn't mean to... to... force her to...

I pulled out my cell phone, dialing her repeatedly, cursing each time it went to voicemail. I could hear the kids playing out back, the sounds of life going on all around me, but I was completely falling apart. "Fuck, just answer!" I slammed my phone down about the time Tom sat down at the table with me, handing me an open beer.

"Drink that, help calm your damn nerves."

"Fuck you, Tom," I muttered, but I drank it anyway. No beer was going to change what I had done.

"I don't know what the hell you two were arguing about, but I'm pretty fucking sure I can guess."

"Let's not and say you did," I said, staring at the bottle that half was already gone from.

"Man," he said with a sigh, "you two just need to have sex and get it over with."

"That's not funny," I snapped, my eyes shooting daggers at him.

"I wasn't meaning it to be." He took a drink of his beer, tilting his head to the side. "Want to talk about it?"

I glared down at my phone. "You're not the person I need to talk about it with. No offense."

"None taken," he said. "It's about damn time you realized that."

"I've known it for a long time, Tom. I just... I can't talk to someone who won't listen."

"Been there," he reminded me. "But at least you didn't come home to..."

His voice trailed off, but it wasn't necessary for him to finish. I knew exactly what he was talking about, when he'd come home on leave only to find his wife with someone else.

"You must hate me," I said softly.

"You're family; I'd never hate you. Not to say I didn't think you needed a swift kick in the ass, but... not hate."

"Tom, how..." I licked my lips, unsure of quite how to ask, but knowing I had to. "How did you react? How... how did you... feel when that happened?"

"I felt like I was dying inside," he said, and I could relate in my own way. "But react? That didn't happen right away."

"What do you mean?"

"It wasn't that it didn't hurt. It wasn't that I didn't want to kill them both at the time, it's just..." I looked up at that mountain of a man, the way he looked so sad, so forlorn, even after all these years. "I just knew it was over. I'd known it was over for a long time, that she didn't love me the way I loved her. I suppose that's why I just... walked away."

I sighed, emptying my beer in the next drink, my thoughts running rampant in my mind when I felt my phone buzz in my hand. I was excited for only a moment before I realized it was merely Pete, sending a text.

On our way to see Jaden.

I quickly shot back, *Is Talli okay?*

It didn't take long for his one-word answer. *No.*

Oh god...

He followed up just a quickly with *But she will be.*

I don't know how long I sat there, staring at his last text, wanting to believe it was true. Another part of me that was buried underneath the hurt, the pain, the confusion had no doubt she would be okay.

With everything in me, even if it meant walking away, I would make sure of it.

CHAPTER 11

TALIA

"Talli, wait!"

I could hear Jase calling out to me as I grabbed the keys to the rental car and ran out the front door. I couldn't face him, not right then; I couldn't stay in that house, I couldn't be anywhere near him.

I could hear Michael calling for me and I choked back a sob, the tears blinding as I fumbled with the keys. How hard could it possibly be to get the damn remote in my hand properly, to press a stupid little button? When your hands shake and you can't control it, you can't keep the tears away, you can't see you can't even think straight, it's pretty fucking hard.

"Stop… just… just stop."

I felt strong hands turn me and I froze, wincing, cringing, my head bowed as the sobs racked my body. "Please don't… please don't," was all I could manage to say. I felt his grip loosen as I opened my eyes, staring at his bare feet on the pavement of the driveway. In my near hysteria, only then did I realize I wasn't wearing any shoes either.

"I'm sorry," he choked out, stepping away from me. I gingerly touched my arms where bruises must have been beginning to form, from earlier up in the bedroom. I heard a muffled sob from him as I watched his feet back away. "I'm so... so sorry."

He's sorry.

He's sorry that for one shining moment I actually believed he wanted me, and it felt so right, so amazingly right in his arms... and the next...

Oh the next...

The next he was filling me completely, the way my body had been screaming for him to. Each stroke from him felt so good, so right, and I was over that edge before I knew what was happening.

I didn't want it to end.

But then I closed my eyes... and all I could see were rose petals. And candles. And... and... them. The two of them, in our bed. It was as if every single emotion I had kept bottled up, every memory that I'd pushed aside, everything that I'd denied myself the time to process, to feel then was hitting me now with the force of a hurricane. The front I'd put up for the sake of my children, for the sake of my own sanity, was crumbled at my feet, and the denial I had been telling myself that I didn't have was mocking me as reality set in. And even as I knew I couldn't escape it anymore, I couldn't run, I couldn't hide from the truth, I still felt that overwhelming sense of panic telling me to go.

Run.

Get the hell away from him before he can hurt me anymore.

"Talli, please... please look at me."

I shook my head, backing away until I felt the cool metal of the car behind me. I couldn't look at him, not right then. If I saw his eyes, if I saw the regret I would break.

It wasn't supposed to be like this.

No matter how much I wanted him, no matter how living under the same roof as him had been like being in a perpetual state of arousal, no matter how much I missed his hands, his lips, his body... it wasn't supposed to be like this. Where... where were the declarations of love? Where were the soft, tender touches? Where were the 'I'm sorry's then? Where were the 'it should have been you's? Where... where was all the romance that he had shown to her, when all I got was shoved up against a wall and...

"What the hell is going on?" Tommy asked as he ran outside.

"It's nothing, Tom. I got this," Jase said, his voice stronger but still wavering.

Nothing.

I'm... I'm *nothing*.

"I have to get out of here," I said, turning once again to the car, Tom's voice sounding in my ear over Jase's protests.

"Talli, you shouldn't drive like this. Come on..." The touch was much softer, even though it was a much bigger man who was putting his arm around my shoulder. "Come on, I'll drive."

"Tom, I said..."

Jase's voice trailed off... I don't know why he stopped or what stopped him, I was far too close to hysteria as Tommy took the keys from my hand, urging me around to the passenger side of the vehicle. I sat in the silence of the car, my knees drawn up, my bare feet on the seat. I had to get myself together, had to just... get away. Just calm down. Relax.

Think.

Not that thinking would help me very much, since my own thoughts were well over half of what was driving me insane. But I at least had to regain some semblance of control, some peace and calm before I could talk with him.

"And have him rip my heart out all over again," I said bitterly, out loud in that otherwise empty car.

Fuck... this, today, was *my* fault. All my fault. I couldn't help myself, and now... now that I'd thrown myself at him, now that I saw, now that I felt what he thought of me, I guess it was time to accept it. I wasn't enough for him. I was never going to be enough for him.

"Hey." I was startled when Pete was suddenly in the driver's seat, the keys jangling as he stuck them in the ignition.

"When did you get here?" I asked, my voice sounding like someone who was starring in one of those damn cold commercials.

"A little bit ago," he replied, starting the car and putting it into reverse. "Get your seatbelt on."

I almost snapped that he wasn't my keeper, but he certainly wasn't acting as if he were pissed off at me. I complied, my feet going to the floorboard as I pulled the buckle around and snapped it into place. Only then did Pete start the decent down the driveway.

"Where were you wanting to go?"

"Anywhere," I said, wiping away a tear. He nodded, his jaw set tight as he hit the gas, the car accelerating quickly as we drove down the road. We were silent as he drove, the houses passing by more and more quickly the further we drove. When we reached a stop sign towards the end of the plat, he paused, his breathing a little more labored than usual.

"Did he hurt you?" His voice was low, even, but he didn't turn his face to me. Instead he kept his eyes straight ahead on the open, empty road.

"What?"

"Like before... at his birthday party. Did he hurt you?"

I stifled a sob, wiping the freshly flowing tears, remembering that drunken outburst. "Not... not like that."

"Did he lay a hand on you, Talli? Because if he did..."

I was blushing, I know I was, when I stammered, "It's... well, it's..."

"Don't try and tell me it's nothing." He looked over at me then, looking over my disheveled appearance, my tear stained face. "That's not... nothing. Did he hurt you?"

I nodded, one hand over my heart. "Right here, Pete. Just right here, where it matters most."

His face softened and he reached out his hand, squeezing mine tightly. "I was really hoping, you know? Hoping that the whole... you being at his house and stuff would help, would heal some of the bullshit you two put each other through. You would get a chance to talk or take the chance because it was given to you. And then you'd see."

"See what?" I asked with a shrug. "What's left to see?"

"I can't speak for you, not right now," he said, still holding onto my hand. "But I can tell you what I know, what I've been told."

"Let me guess," I started with a halfhearted laugh, "I was a nag, I was... I was indifferent, I was inaccessible..."

"Were you?"

I blinked several times at his question, seriously contemplating my answer.

"Yes. I... I suppose that's how I acted, yes."

He only nodded without comment on my behavior, but he squeezed my hand extra tight before saying, "He loves you, Talli."

I could only shake my head, my eyes lowering to my lap. "That's not love, Pete."

"Really? Because last time I checked, when you love someone, logic is one of the first things that fly out the window."

"You don't... do those things. You don't... you don't turn to someone else."

"I did."

I narrowed my eyes as I raised them to him, ready to give him so much hell he wouldn't have an ass to sit on, but his next words stopped me.

"Remember Leah?"

"Ugh." I rolled my eyes and actually laughed. "Oh lord, Hurricane Leah. Who could forget her?"

"I was so in love with Jaden that I couldn't see straight. I couldn't think straight. I made myself the biggest fool for her, and... and the little voice in my head, the realization that she didn't love me back was just *devastating*."

"But she did love you," I reminded him.

"That wasn't something she was entirely sure of," he said softly, stunning me. I had always believed she loved him... always. "And I did the most awesomely stupid thing I could possibly do. I turned to someone else."

"You weren't married," I pointed out.

"True, but... we certainly wouldn't be married if she hadn't been able to forgive me."

"So I'm supposed to say 'hey, Jase, it's okay that you fucked someone else in our bed, I forgive you' and live happily ever after?"

He rolled his eyes, releasing my hand to gently knock on my head. "Where the hell is Talli, and would you mind letting her out for a little bit?"

"This is me," I mumbled, turning to face forward. "Like it or not."

"This is a shell of you," he retorted, leaving the stop sign behind and heading towards our unknown destination. "This isn't the girl who gets out the air horn to punish people who've had too much to drink."

"That was damn funny, though."

"Oh, it was hilarious," he said, his voice dripping with sarcasm, and I couldn't help but laugh. "Ah... see? There she is."

"But where was she months ago, right?" I asked out loud.

"Look, I'm not condoning my brother's actions. I never will. But Talli... just... just a year or two ago, you would have ripped Bree's hair out of her head before it ever got that far."

"She wouldn't have had a head for me to rip hair out of," I corrected him. "And I can't... I don't know, Pete. I just don't know. If I had the answers, I could give them to you. But I can't... I can't take the brunt of the responsibility for the whole Bree fiasco when I wasn't the one screwing around. But..."

"But what?"

I sighed, sinking even further into my seat as I tried to convey everything that was running around in my brain. "I know that our problems started before. I know we were fighting, more and more. I know that I pulled away from him. And that was before he ever met her."

"So... what happened? Today, I mean," he clarified, and I felt my face begin to flame, not only from the fact that I wasn't about to tell my brother in law what we'd just done in their mother's house, but from Jase's words.

His own words.

"Nothing," I said, taking a deep breath as the tears threatened again. "Nothing happened."

"Yeah, and I'm Mary fucking Poppins. Hey... listen. I got this awesome wife, see, and she's like the best listener ever."

"And she just had a baby, and I'm not burdening her with this."

"Fine, fine, but... that baby's pretty damn cute. And I think he could put a smile on your face."

I could feel the grin tugging at the corners of my mouth before he was even done. "I don't have any shoes on."

"We can stop and get you some. I can run in, right there, grab some flip flops or something for you. Come on. What do you say?"

I sniffled as I pushed my hair back behind my ears, glancing over to the store on the right. "Yeah, I guess."

"Good. Done."

I watched him walk up to that door, pulling his phone out to text before he'd even made it in the store. I wasn't naïve, I knew it was Jase he was sending the message to. Instead of the annoyance I might feel at any other time, I was happy he was keeping him informed. I pulled my phone from my pocket, glancing at the screen as I pulled up the missed calls. Wow. Ten of them. All from Jase. He must have dialed the number over and over and over. No voicemail, though. Perhaps he just didn't know what to say.

Like me.

Jaden, on the other hand, apparently had diarrhea of the mouth. She was in the middle of welcoming Pete back, telling him how much she missed him when her eyes glanced over to me.

"Holy shit, Talli, you got laid!"

"What?" I asked, blushing, pushing my hair back away from my freshly washed face.

"What?" Pete asked also, looking back at me. "Oh... shit."

"I don't know what you're talking about," I lied.

"Oh, bullshit. And it's about time too! Sit down, spill."

"I'm not..." I motioned towards Pete, who shook his head.

"Oh, hell no. I'm in on this girl talk. I do girl talk well."

"He does," Jaden agreed, then her face lit up as she smiled at me. "See? Don't you feel better now?"

"About Pete being good at..."

"Quit being facetious, you know what I'm talking about." She moved the small clear bassinette my nephew was sleeping soundly in and motioned to the chair beside her bed. I lowered myself slowly, wincing as I did so, and Pete groaned.

"God, maybe I shouldn't be in here."

"Fuck you, Pete," I said with a roll of my eyes.

"Didn't my brother just do that?" he teased, and then his eyes clouded over. "Oh..."

"Yeah." I sniffled again, begging the tears to stay away. "Oh."

"You're not supposed to be crying!" Jaden exclaimed. "You're supposed to be happy, ecstatic even! You two needed this."

"He hurt you," Pete said, ignoring Jaden's proclamation.

"Hurt?" she asked, then turned her attention back to me. "What does he mean, hurt?"

The message I tried to convey to Pete with my eyes must have hit their mark, because he stood and said, "Listen, I... I'm gonna take a walk, see if Dad made it in yet." He kissed Jaden's temple, whispering something into her ear, before he walked towards the door. "I'll be back," he said to the both of us. As he left, he shut the door behind him, the tears deciding right at that 'click' to just let go.

"What the hell did that asshole do to you?" Jaden asked as she moved to get out of bed.

"Oh... oh, I'm fine, don't..."

"Shut up," she muttered, kneeling beside me and pulling me in, letting me cry on her shoulder.

"I'm sorry, I shouldn't be..."

"Don't apologize, okay? Did you... really?" She leaned back slightly, looking me in the eye. "Did you sleep with him?"

"Oh, there was no sleeping involved. And yeah."

"Like today, between the time you left here and... and now?"

I nodded, wiping the tears hastily. "It just... it just happened. One minute I was yelling at him, and the next..." I shrugged. "The next it just..."

"You ended up on the bed, and..."

"No," I shook my head. "No, I ended up against the wall. Romantic, huh?"

"Oh, Talli... you don't want me to answer that, do you?" She smiled wistfully, pushing a stray curl out of my face. "Because my answer and yours aren't really going to be the same."

"You think banging up against the wall was romantic?" It was more of a statement then a question, and she rolled her eyes at me just like I knew she would.

"Talli, it wasn't... what are you doing? Right now?"

"Sitting in your hospital room feeling so very small."

"You're *feeling*," she emphasized the last word, holding my hands in hers. "You are feeling everything you should have felt this whole damn time, you… you remember now, don't you? How it felt, how the two of you felt together?"

"Well, obviously, since it was… hey!" I rubbed my arm where she swatted me. "What the hell was that for?"

"You don't get it, do you? The love you feel for him, the way it's just ruling your life even when you're 'not together'," she said, using air quotes for her last two words. "Just because you're hurting, both of you, that doesn't make the love go away. And… and you are two of the most passionate people I've ever met, and not just the whole two of you fucking like jackrabbits whenever you were together. Something was bound to give. And yeah, maybe in your eyes it didn't give in the right way, but don't you see?" Her own eyes were filling with tears as she took my hands in hers once more. "Do you remember now? Do you know now why he's worth fighting for, why the two of you, why your marriage is worth fighting for?"

"But what about…"

"Don't even say her name in front of my newborn son, I don't want his ears to bleed."

I laughed at her statement, my hands trembling as I pulled back.

"Well?"

"I don't know if I can," I replied honestly, my heart breaking at my own admission. "I don't know if I can get past it. Hell, right now… right now I need to…" My voice trailed off as I tried to form the words, but they just wouldn't come.

"Right now, you need to work on you."

"I love you, you know that?" I said with a laugh. "I love that you know me so well, even if I hate it sometimes."

"Yeah, I'm pretty awesome," she said, grinning, and like the best friend ever, she didn't bring his name up again the rest of the time I was there. I actually got to hold that precious baby in my arms for almost an hour before he started searching for something I just couldn't give him. Pete didn't even mention Jase's name on our ride back to Nan's house.

But I knew he'd be waiting for me.

And I knew where.

After I'd kissed Elizabeth, who didn't seem to know I was gone, and Michael, who was happy to see me but had long been consoled, and Emily, who was drowsy, falling asleep on the sofa, I made my way up the stairs to that room I'd run out of earlier. I wasn't surprised in the least to see the soft glow of the light from the bottom of the door, and even less surprised to see Jase sitting on that bed, his head lowered, his hands folded in front of him.

He didn't look up as I entered the room, the only evidence that he knew I was there was his breathing becoming more labored. I walked over to the bed, a fair amount of distance between us when I sat down. I was silent as well, taking in his appearance, wishing I could curl up against him... but knowing it wasn't the time to.

I wasn't sorry that I kissed him. I wasn't sorry it had turned to something more. Jaden was right; it had needed to happen. It's just that...

"I'm sorry," he finally said, his voice barely above a whisper. His hands were trembling as he rubbed them together, his eyes still on them. "I swear to you... I am so sorry." He swallowed, taking a deep shuddering breath as the light caught a tear as it fell down his cheek.

"Jase..."

"I shouldn't have, I should *never* have done that to you," he sobbed, interrupting me. "And I swear if you'd let me, I'd..." He raised his eyes to me then, the grief, the regret so prominent there.

Oh, the regret... that's what hurt.

"Talia, I... I never meant to... to force you to... do anything you didn't want... and I'm so... so sorry."

Force me?

Anything I didn't want?

OH! Oh, no...

"No, no... please..." I reached out instinctively, placing a hand on his shoulder. "How could you *think* that, Jase?"

As my words registered, I could see his shoulders drop slightly, his breathing ease incredibly even as two large tears fell down his face. "Are... you... sure?"

Was I sure? What the hell room had he been in?

"I... did want it, Jase. I wanted you, I wanted... it wasn't that I don't. It's just that I... me... I'm not ready."

As the words left me, I watched the confusion, followed oh so quickly by this... spark. There's no other word for it. It wasn't the look of the man who'd pushed me against that wall earlier. No, this was the look of the man who was... who was...

No, he couldn't be.

"Would..." He faltered slightly, his eyes so pained as he asked, "would you believe me if... if I said..."

He never finished his question. He could tell by my expression what my answer would be.

"I have a hard time believing right now."

He nodded, squeezing my hand as we sat there silently, another tentative truce in place. But this one, this time held so much more than just the wave of a white flag.

This one held hope.

JASE

"The condo's ready."

I put on my brave face, smiling up at Talli as she walked into the room. Her announcement had come as no surprise; I'd known this day was coming. I just wasn't as prepared as I thought I would be. Especially not after Groves Point, not after having her in my arms just a mere two weeks ago.

But she wasn't ready.

I was willing to wait.

She needed space.

So I was giving it to her.

"What's up with the cheesy grin, Warner?" she asked, taking a small handful of popcorn from the bowl as she passed, flopping down on the opposite end of the couch.

"What the hell?" I teased. "Did I say you could take my popcorn?" I ducked as she threw a kernel at me.

"Did I say you could pay my rent?" she asked, one eyebrow raised, poised to throw more popcorn at me. I thought for a moment before answering.

"Yes."

And that piece of popcorn hit me square between the eyes.

"Bitch."

"Queen of them," she corrected me. "And just when did I say you could pay my rent?"

"The day I promised you that you'd never have to worry, never go without."

She sighed then... not one of those annoyed smiles, not one of those 'fuck, here we go again' sighs, not even one of those sad sighs. It was the kind of sigh with that slight little smile as she leaned her head to the side that told me I was right.

I love this woman.

"I'm going to pay you back, you know."

"Not even if hell froze over."

"I have to! It's... Jase, it's too much."

No, this house all alone is too much. All the riches in the world mean nothing if I can't share it with you.

"I know ... well, okay, I eavesdropped," I admitted. "When you were in the hospital, I overheard you saying that you were having a hard time, and... and I know you. I know how stubborn you are. They're my kids, too. I just wanted to help."

"You've done so much already."

She reached out and held my hand, the first real contact since Groves Point, and my heart skipped a tiny beat. I closed my fingers around her hand, squeezing just slightly, wishing I would just listen to my heart and ask her to stay. My heart that was so happy for her, feeling such joy in watching her thrive, watching her find the spark that had been missing. But on the other hand, my heart was aching, watching her slip through my fingers, wishing that she needed me, thinking that maybe... maybe if she did, she would stay.

But I didn't want her to *need* to be here.

She was a strong, independent woman who had lost her way, and I had a big hand in that. I wanted her to find her passion again, and not the passion that happened in that room in Groves Point, per se, but the passion she'd had for life. She loved to live, and she'd been merely existing. So, no... the fact that she didn't need to be with me was not the problem.

I wanted… well, I wanted her to want to be here. And even in all of its Cheap Trick channeling, I wanted her to want me.

Not just wanting to make love or lose ourselves up against a wall.

Wanting it to be with me.

That was my wish.

Just as once upon a time my wish was for her to want the man and not the rock star.

I couldn't help but smile as I thought of how that wish had come true.

"Again with the grinning, Warner," she said, her head leaned against the back of the couch. "Care to share what's on your mind?"

"You."

I said it without a second thought, without worrying about consequences. I said it because I promised that I would be honest with her, I promised her that she'd be able to believe me someday.

"Me?" she asked, blinking a couple of times.

She was still holding my hand.

"Yeah," I replied. "You."

"What about me?" she asked slowly, her eyebrows drawing together. I recognized that quizzical look and I had to hold back to keep from placing a kiss right there, in the crease of her eyebrows.

"You've come a long way, Talli," I said softly. "It's nice seeing you again."

"I keep hearing that," she said, scrunching up her nose. "Call me just as oblivious as before, I suppose."

I smirked, shaking my head. "Liar. You know you see it, too."

She laughed softly causing my stomach to take a rollercoaster dive. "You know me so well."

I used to know her that well, for so long I'd misread her, or hadn't read her at all. But I was starting to, little by little. I know I was far too gun-shy now to make assumptions, try and second guess her feelings or the thoughts going on in her head. I'd made that mistake before, although I still wasn't sure I was that far off the mark. It wasn't something we'd really discussed, minus…

Well, minus Groves Point. In my Nan's house, no less.

When I'd actually blamed my infidelity on her indifference.
And that wasn't fair to her.

I stood with a heavy heart watching her put the few of their belongings they had in the back of the minivan. There were no tears, no hysterics, no screaming children. Instead, the house was permeated with a profound sadness, as if the cover was being closed on a chapter of our lives.

I wasn't ready for them to go.

This day wasn't supposed to come, see. I know I had said that I was only trying to help, and yes it was true; I had been trying to help. But I was also being selfish. And after all of the reassuring everyone that they were wrong, it turns out they had all been one hundred percent correct.

I wanted my family back.

I thought that maybe, just maybe, I could open Talli's eyes, make her see the good, see what we had before. Maybe I could jog her memory, be the man she'd loved, show her how wonderful our life really is when we're together.

And she'd remember.

She'd remember how we had turned this house into a home. Remember how good we were, how strong we were together. Remember the fun we used to have, remember the way we used to share everything.

Remember the love.

I thought... I really thought that some miracle would happen, and she'd fall in love with me again. But I blew it... I blew it in the worst way. I'd pulled away from her, I'd snapped at her when she went out with Paul, I'd spent more time with Kate than I had with Talli, and I'd done it not just out of spite, but out of self-preservation. Out of fear.

And then...

Then in Groves Point, when I couldn't take it anymore, I wasn't strong enough to walk away. Instead, I pushed her up against that wall and... and...

"I don't know what you want me to do with the clothes."

I jumped slightly at the sound of her voice. Glancing over my shoulder I saw her standing there, the clothes I'd bought for her on hangers in her hand and another small bag by her feet. "They're yours, Talli."

"Are you sure? I... I mean, I can pay you back for..."

"I'm sure."

Her cheeks were an adorable shade of pink as she seemed to stumble over her words. "They're really beautiful."

"They reminded me of you."

She had her mouth opened, as if she has something else to say, but was stunned silent, her eyes shining with unshed tears. For a brief moment I wondered if I'd said the wrong thing, then it kind of hit me-- she didn't know I was the one who'd bought them.

"I don't know what to say."

I smiled then, knowing it was all I could do to keep from crying. "You don't have to say anything, Talli."

Elizabeth walked into the entryway, carrying a small bag with her, her eyes missing that mischievous twinkle. She looked up at me, her lower lip trembling before she silently shuffled past, walking out to the minivan that was in the driveway.

Oh, that hurt.

"She's not handling this very well," Talli said, her eyes following our daughter's form.

Neither am I.

"She's doing better than last time," I commented, not ready for Talli to turn her eyes on me, not ready to see the pain, the hurt staring me in the face.

"Don't be so sure about that," was all she said. She walked slowly past me to the stairs, the smell of jasmine lingering behind her.

Don't do it, Warner. She's not ready.

So instead of following her up those stairs, I walked out to the minivan where Elizabeth was climbing in, pulling the straps of her booster seat over her shoulders. "Here," I said, reaching in. "Let me help you with that."

"Thank you, Daddy," she said softly with her wavering voice that broke my heart in two all over again.

"Hey..." I pushed her hair back, placing a soft kiss on her forehead.

"You don't have to cry, Baby Girl. It's going to be okay."

"But Daddy, you said you loved us and wanted us home. Why are you sending us away?"

Hold it together, hold it together, hold it together...

"I'm not sending any of you away, sweetheart. I know you're too young to understand, but..."

"My friend Lily, at school, she says her Mommy and Daddy got a divorce 'cause they don't love each other no more," she cut me off, her big blue eyes so troubled. "I thought you said you love Mommy."

"I do, very much," I replied, holding her little hand in mine. "I wish I had the answers for you, I wish I could tell you the future. Right now, all I can tell you is that we both love you, and Michael, and Em very much."

"What about Mommy's heart, Daddy?" she asked. "I thought they fixed it."

"They did, they did. And she's doing so much better. Doesn't she look better to you?"

"But Daddy... she said we had to go back so she could fix her."

It was my turn to be confused as I squeezed my daughter's hand ever so slightly. "What are you talking about, silly girl?" I asked with a soft laugh.

"I asked Mommy why we had to leave home again, Daddy. She said she had stuff to fix, and I didn't understand, and she said she had to fix herself."

My eyes opened wide with wonder as I turned to look back at the front door where Talli emerged, Emily on one arm, Michael close behind them.

Does she...

Could she...

"But Daddy, if her heart's not fixed, we're supposed to be here," Elizabeth said, capturing my attention once more.

"Baby Girl, I promise," I said as I worked with shaking hands to get her straps fastened, "that everything's okay. Mommy's fine, she's... it's..."

"Complicated," she finished for me with a sigh. "I know."

I chuckled softly and kissed her forehead again. "I love you, and I will be there Friday after you get out of school to pick you guys up, okay?"

"I want my story book, Daddy," she said, her sad eyes pleading with me.

"It's in your bag, isn't it?"

"No," she replied, placing her little hand on my cheek. "It's complicated," she continued, her expression solemn, "but some day you'll understand."

I shook my head as I grinned down at her, whispering how much I loved her before turning to help get the other children in the van.

"Thank you," Talli murmured, taking the bag from her shoulder and placing it in the front seat as I strapped Emily securely in her carseat.

"Not a problem," I replied, cursing in my head as I fumbled with the straps.

Damn it, Warner, don't lose it!

Even Emily looked sad as I waved goodbye, promising them all I'd be there in less than a week to pick them up. I held on to that handle, even after I'd pulled the door shut, telling myself over and over it was time to let go.

But I didn't want to.

"Hey."

My hands dropped to my sides as I turned to Talli, watching the wind catch her curls and lift them slightly. As much as I wanted to reach out, tuck her hair behind her ears, I stayed back.

"Thank you again," she said, taking a step closer. "For getting the kids back, for... for letting me stay here. You didn't have to do that."

"I wanted to," I said before I could stop myself, and she smiled.

"I know."

Just stay. Just take everything out of the van, just go back into that house. We've come so far, and it's been so wonderful having you here.

"I want you to know how much it means to me, not just that you took care of us, but... but that you continue to, and I'll make it up to you some day."

"Talli, you don't..."

"No, I... my thoughts are all jumbled, I'm sorry," she said, closing her eyes and shaking her head briefly. She took another step forward, looking straight up at me as she continued. "It was wrong of me to try and keep them from you, no matter the circumstances. It was spiteful of me to limit their time with you just because it hurt so badly to be replaced."

It was as if all the air had suddenly left my body as her words sunk in. "I would never replace,"

"But you did," she said, her words barely above a whisper, her shoulders lifting slightly. "You did. And I overreacted, and I'm sorry. I was wrong, and I promise you I'll never keep them from you again. You were right when you said they needed both of us, Jase. Any time you want to see them, you can."

I nodded, unable to speak without breaking down, without falling to my knees and begging her to stay.

To just… stay.

She turned from me then, her head bowed slightly as she walked to the driver's side of the minivan, away from me, away from this house, to… to… fix herself…

I remembered words that she'd said to me in anger, accusations she'd made in Groves Point, and it hit me it was really how she felt… or rather how she believed I felt.

"Talli," I called out to her, my voice much stronger than I thought it would be. She turned to me, her arms crossed in front of her as if she were trying to protect herself. "I never gave up." I watched as she took in a deep breath, knowing exactly when it registered what I was talking about. "I know it seems like I did, but I didn't."

Please believe me.

Her lips quivered slightly as she attempted to smile, and if that wasn't enough to make my heart sing, her next words were.

"I was never indifferent."

I didn't even know I was holding my breath until the moment I exhaled. I smiled as best I could as I watched her get into her van, waving slightly before she drove away.

I wish I could say her words put me in a jovial mood, but that wasn't meant to be. I stood and watched as the van grew smaller and smaller, finally disappearing as it turned the corner to make the rest of the twenty-two-minute drive back to the condo. Only then did I walk back into that big, empty house, the sound of the door shutting echoing in the hallway, echoing in my heart.

I stared at the lunch dishes, smiling wistfully as I held fast to those memories, knowing I was going to need to call on them in the long days to come. I was thankful for the busy work, cleaning up after the children, even with as heartsick as I was that they weren't there. Wiping the smudges off the table, around the island, cleaning up Emily's highchair tray kept me from going absolutely insane.

And their toys... their toys that were scattered around Talia's room, as if they'd dropped them haphazardly about on their way out the door made me smile. In just a few short days, they'd be back here, messing this room up all over again. But for now, I gathered them to distribute them in their rooms upstairs.

Michael's car bin was pretty much empty, meaning he'd dumped them elsewhere in this mess of a room. I set everything down, making his bed and placing his pillows on top, ready for him when he returned. I picked up his discarded dirty clothes, the knees green with grass stains from where we'd played out in the back yard, smiling to myself as I remembered that anytime I wanted to see them, I could.

The girls' room was much neater, thanks to Elizabeth's near-OCD cleaning and organizing. It reminded me so much of her mother that it warmed my heart even more. I straightened up the blankets in Emily's crib, where Elizabeth couldn't reach, and smoothed one tiny wrinkle in Elizabeth's blankets before returning her Barbies and Em's stuffed animals to the toy bins, missing the soft giggles that I always heard coming from this room.

Soon, Warner. Soon. Just a few short days and they'll be back. Hell, if you don't want to wait that long, just let Talli know and...

I paused in the hallway, looking down at what used to be Emily's room. The room where Talia had slept for weeks...

For months.

I was drawn to it, my feet moving of their own accord, as if I was going to find some hidden treasure behind that half-closed door. But of course, there was none. Only a neatly made bed, the throw pillow placed right in the center, angled just so. I stood beside that bed, staring down at the place she'd laid her head, standing in almost the same spot I'd find myself nearly every night, watching her.

There was no comfort in this room as there had been in the others. There was no assurance that she was coming back. There was only silence. Emptiness. A glaring reminder that now, more than ever, I was alone.

Don't break, Warner. Don't break. She needs time. She needs to fix herself. She's not indifferent.

I walked down the hallway, unlocking the door to my office, frowning at the guitar that sat collecting dust along the far wall. I hadn't played since she'd left the first time, I didn't want to. I looked at that guitar and I saw the reason I'd been pulled away from home, the reason my record company insisted I help young artists write material the way seasoned musicians had once helped me, the catalyst that set everything in motion, that sent her running as fast as she could.

Without her, I felt empty.

I picked up the guitar, staring at it as I sat on the couch, placing it on my lap. Slowly I began to tune it, cringing as I heard just how badly out of tune it was. I couldn't blame it all on lack of use; I could tell by the tiny fingerprints on the neck and body little hands had most definitely helped. One, two strums... a G followed by a D, and I was satisfied with the tuning.

With no real direction of what to play, I simply began putting chords together in no specific order. It was almost a comfort as the rust wore off and the music took over, carrying me through. I just needed some peace, some comfort, and it seemed I had found it, until I began to sing along...

"You're my everything, everything."

I stopped abruptly, feeling my heart begin to pound, my hands sweating as I set the guitar aside and began to pace.

Don't break, Warner. Don't break. Call in reinforcements...

I picked up the receiver, my hands shaking as I dialed the number, needing those reinforcements now more than ever. If I could just hold it together a little bit longer, I knew everything would be okay.

"Hello?"

But the moment I heard her voice, my resolve crumbled, the tears that I'd held away all day finding their way to the surface.

"What's wrong?"

"I just…" I took in a shuddering breath and said, "I've had the worst day."

CHAPTER 12

TALIA

"Home sweet home.

Mary Coffman was beside me in the parking lot, unloading her vehicle as I slowly unstrapped the children from their seats. I smiled tightly at her, trying to keep conversation to a minimum, not knowing how many prying ears or eyes were around.

"They said the tenth floor may still need airing out," she continued, and I winced inwardly. Like I need it announced to the world what floor I live on, thank you Mary.

"Thank you," I said softly, grabbing all of the bags that I could with Emily on my hip.

"Oh, you don't need to be carrying all of… Paul! Come over here and help!"

Of course Paul would be there, helping his sister move back in. "It really isn't necessary," I said to him as he walked up, a warm smile on his face.

"It is if you want my sister to shut the hell up," he muttered into my ear, and I couldn't help but laugh.

"Daddy would have helped," Elizabeth announced, dramatically pulling her bag alongside of her.

"I'm sure he would have," I replied without so much as a second thought, not wanting to correct her where it could end up in the tabloids. Besides, I knew it was true.

"You all right?" Paul asked, once we were on the elevator, just the two of us and my children. I sighed and nodded, drawing an understanding wink from him. The children had been through so much already, and I knew... oh, I knew, beyond a shadow of any doubt that today was more heartbreaking and confusing than ever.

The floor was bustling with activity as we finally disembarked from the elevator, the faint scent of smoke still lingering in the air. Elizabeth and Michael seemed to be dragging their feet, reluctant to even go back to our condo.

Kind of like me.

"Hello, Ms. Talli," my next-door neighbor said as she shuffled out in the hall. "It's good to see you back here, looking so healthy."

"Thank you," I murmured.

"It's a shame things didn't work out for you," she continued, placing her time-weathered hand on my arm. I swallowed over the lump in my throat, only managing to nod as I continued on.

Of course, Elizabeth just had to chime in.

"My mommy's just fixing herself now," she said defiantly, her eyes challenging me to correct or scold her in front of others.

"That's good, dear," she said with a warm smile and a pat to Elizabeth's head. "That's good."

Oh great. So now the little old lady next door thinks I'm some sort of loon. Or... perhaps not, judging by her knowing smile as she looked over her shoulder at me.

"That's Evelyn Truesdale," Paul said softly as I placed my key in the door.

"I know," I replied, looking at him like he had come from Mars. Hell, I was the one that lived next door to her for fucks sake.

"So, you know all about her running with the Rat Pack back in the day?" he asked, holding the door open as I ushered the younger children inside.

"Shut up!" I exclaimed, my eyes wide. I set Emily down to toddle away, turning my attention to getting some damn windows open. Mary wasn't kidding; this place really did need aired out.

"I'm sure she could tell some stories," he said with a laugh, still standing beside the door. "And…"

"Today is not a good day for a fishing expedition," I cut him off with a soft smile.

"Mommy!" Elizabeth exclaimed, running out to the living room. "Uncle Jackie moved Em's crib! She's in my room here, too!"

"Did he?" I asked, taking the note from her and looking it over.

"Uncle Jackie?" Paul asked, and I smiled at him.

"He's a friend, works with Jase."

And immediately my smile fell.

"Hey… I don't know everything that's been going on, but I want you to know that if you need someone to talk to I'm here."

He had somehow ended up right beside me, his arm around my shoulders, and I knew he meant for it to be comforting but it wasn't something I was quite prepared for. And the problem wasn't that he was bothering me, or even out of line because I knew he was being a friend.

The problem was with me.

The problem was with the fact that the arms I longed for… the strong arms that I adored, that collected tattoos over the years, that held me with such precision, making me feel alive… were twenty-two minutes away, attached to a man I didn't trust. I couldn't trust.

No matter how much I loved him.

"Need any help getting settled in?" he asked, and I shook my head, stepping away from him.

"No, I'm… I'm good. Thank you."

Good.

Wow, that was a lie.

I was far from good as I opened the refrigerator to see what I needed to pick up from the store, only to find it packed with all of my and the children's favorites.

I was far from good when I looked around and see my kitchen completely spotless, the way Linda knew I liked it, knowing she had to have been there too.

I was far from good as I unpacked, noticing I'd left all of my makeup and shower things at the house. I had some here as well, but it also meant he'd see I hadn't changed; I was still as absentminded as I had been, and I knew I'd never hear the end of it.

I was far from good when we all sat down to dinner in our condo, when it hit me how much I adored being with him, how wonderful it had been to be a family again, even temporarily. And when Emily started asking for him, I nearly came undone.

I was far from good as I bathed them, trying to console our youngest child as she cried for her 'Dase'.

I was far from good as I curled up in my papasan chair, holding that damn 'One Flew Over the Cuckoo's Nest' book that he'd slipped back into my bag, crying tears that I'd done my best to keep at bay. Which, of course, meant that when the phone rang, I was an absolute mess when I answered it.

"Hello?" I asked, saying a little prayer that the blocked call was from him.

"So the reports are true," Jeff said, his voice as flat as my heart. "You moved out again."

"Hi, how are you?" I asked sardonically through my tears, wiping my eyes hastily, angrily. "Gee, I know you're having a really hard time right now, I was just calling to see how you were doing."

"You're having a hard time? Give me a break. You had it fucking made, you're the dumb ass that walked away."

"You know what Jeff? Fuck you," I spat angrily. "Fuck you... and... and Shell, and Anna, and anyone else that thinks my only purpose on this Earth is to be kicked around by you. Because I've had enough."

"You know what, you little..."

"I might expect Lisa to be on the angry, bitter side," I cut him off. "She lost the only man she loved rather unexpectedly, and yet when she calls, it's not to demand that I do things to make her life better. And Eric... how often has he gotten laid off from his job? Not once has he asked for help... not once. But you know what? I'd give it to him. I'd give him anything I could, in a fucking heartbeat. Because he's been there for me when I've needed him the most, and he's apologized to me for treating me like scum on the bottom of his shoe."

"Hey, I walked your ass..."

"Down the aisle at my wedding, and you showed up at a function or two since then, but god forbid you treat me decently."

"You're nothing…"

"But a drug addict, right? Nothing but a home wrecker."

"Yeah, and you deserve what happened to you."

Oh.

Oh, that hurt.

"Fuck you, Jeff," I muttered, hanging up the phone, slamming it on the table beside me.

Thing was, he was probably right. When had I paid for what I'd done? And I mean honestly paid for it. It wasn't as if I'd sat down and had a heart to heart with Keith's now ex-wife. It wasn't as if she had the chance to rip my ass a new one. It wasn't as if I'd suffered the pain that she had, because when it came right down to it, I didn't love him. No, the only real love I'd had was with a man I'd sworn was out of my league. I'd sworn he would never be interested or stay interested in me with all these perfect girls out there throwing themselves at him.

And I'd been right.

I cringed as the phone rang again, wiping my eyes and taking a deep breath. I wasn't about to let Jeff know he'd bested me, nor was I going to give him the satisfaction of hearing me cry. I was going to answer that phone as pleasantly as you pleased and show him how a true mature adult acted.

"Hello?" I said, holding my head high even though I couldn't be seen.

There was a muffled sob on the other end of the phone, and I covered my mouth with my hand, my heart constricting as I heard my husband breaking on the other end of the line. Hearing him this way hurt more than any words he could say. Wasn't it supposed to comfort me? Wasn't it supposed to be some kind of vengeance, to know he was hurting? To know he may be feeling the same damn way that I felt?

It wasn't.

It was torture, it was hell. It was the longest two seconds of my life before I gathered my senses, knowing there was no way in hell I was hanging up that phone.

"What's wrong?" I finally managed to say, so afraid of his answer that I buried my face in my hand, holding my breath as I waited.

"I just..." he began, his breathing as erratic as mine, "I've had the worst day."

Oh, god...

"So have I, Not John," I sobbed, holding my knees up to my chest. "So have I."

"I feel like... like I lost my best friend."

I've felt that way for so very long.

"Have you?" I asked cautiously, chewing on my thumbnail.

"I don't know," he answered, his voice wavering. "I know that if I have, then I deserve it."

"Then I guess I'm in the same boat as you," I said, sinking down further into my chair, opening up the front cover to that book, running my fingertip over the inscription he'd written there when we were mere children ourselves.

For when you're lonely

~J

"God no, Not Telling," he breathed. "You didn't deserve that."

"When did you sign this?" I asked suddenly, ignoring his comment and gesturing towards the book as if he could see what I was holding. "I mean, I borrowed it, I told you I was keeping it. When did you put that in there?"

He chuckled softly, the sound like music to my ears. "Ah, the book. I actually signed it before I ever let you borrow it. I was just going to give it to you anyhow, thinking somehow that was going to be smooth enough to interest you."

"I was already interested, Dork."

"I didn't know that," he reminded me. "Hell, I damn near fell over when you dared me to kiss you."

I laughed at the memory, suddenly recalling with absolute clarity the look of shock on his face. "And... I was just trying... to be smooth," I added through my giggles.

"Hey, fuck you Not Telling."

"Whatever."

"Don't you whatever me, woman," he laughed.

"What are you gonna do about it, huh? You're all talk."

"Uh huh."

"No action... I can't even say that with a straight face." I threw my head back as laughter overtook me. "But... don't... just... keep your ego in check."

"My ego's pretty much in the toilet, if that helps any." Those were his words, but I could hear the smile in his voice. It was the same smile that was on my face, the one that felt so foreign to me that took less than two minutes for him to bring.

I just love this man.

"Of course it helps."

Which meant I wasn't above giving him ten kinds of hell.

"Wonderful. Fabulous. So now that my wounding meets your... whatever..."

"Expectations? Hopes?"

"Wow. I was going to say you're being harsh, but... yeah, you're right."

"Of course I am, duh," I said, feeling my body relax. "Say, you wouldn't mind flying out to Ohio to kick my brother's ass, would you?"

"What the hell did Eric do?" he asked, his tone nearly incredulous.

"No, no... my other brother."

"Other... brother..."

"Jeff, you know, the one you're always forgetting about? Damn. And you take shots at my memory."

"Well yeah, you're older than I am. So, what did Jeff do now?"

"Hey, fuck you! Six months isn't shit."

"Wow, watch your language ma'am, lest I remind you our children are within ear shot."

"They're not..." I glanced over to my right, seeing a pair of blue eyes twinkling as our oldest child peered around the corner. "Get back in bed young lady," I said to her before saying to Jase, "How did you do that? Did you have Jackie install cameras here or something?"

He laughed then, one of his big booming laughs that caused me to sigh, placing my hand over my heart. "If I were going to do that, the living room is the last place I'd have them."

"Oh!" It was my turn to laugh at his cheeky answer, knowing on top of everything else he was being honest about that. "Well, what do you know? Something out of your mouth I actually believe."

"Ohhhh, touché, Not Telling, touché."

"Thank you, thank you."

"Want something else to believe?"

Yes... yes. Anything. If only I could...

"Lay it on me, Warner."

"Uh... I... oh, hell, give me a minute. My mind just blanked."

"Oh you fucker, was Groves Point not enough?" I asked, then winced, mentally kicking myself.

"No," he replied, his tone serious. "No, it was not."

And I knew his libido, so I knew that was also true.

"Well, alrighty then. Two things I believe." I was chewing on my thumbnail, knowing I'd stepped over the line, unsure of how to bring the conversation back.

"Alrighty then?" he asked, and I could immediately tell he was mocking my mini meltdown shortly after I'd moved to California. *"Alrighty then?"*

"Hey, fuck you, I was pregnant and hormonal!"

"And really damn cute."

"Yeah, so cute you just had to laugh at me and make it worse."

"You were always adorable pregnant, you know? Always."

"An adorable beached whale, yay me."

"Talia Christine, don't... don't think that of yourself. Not at any time. Because you're beautiful."

I faltered then, at a loss for words, unable to tell him that I believed him.

"And I meant it, when I said you didn't deserve that... everything I did to you, Talli... you didn't deserve that."

My lower lip was trembling as I took in a deep breath, but I held it together. I was strong, resilient as I said to him, "You may be right."

"May be? What the fuck is that, Talli? What do you mean I may be right?"

"Please... I don't want to fight, this has been so nice."

"I'm not... it has been, hasn't it?"

"Yeah," I said, my eyes resting on the well-worn picture that Emily had left on the coffee table.

"So we're just going to ignore the obvious, and walk on eggshells?"

"Please, Jase, I just…" I pinched the bridge of my nose, willing myself to continue. "I just need a friend right now. I need… I need my best friend, the one who accepted me, the one… the one I feel I lost."

Not just today… I lost you so long ago…

He was silent for a while, his breathing heavy, uneven. Once again I felt I'd gone too far, and just as I opened my mouth to apologize, his words spoken so very softly cut straight through me.

"You've got me."

It wasn't the way I wished for, nor was it the way I longed for. But those five and a half hours we spent on the phone carried me through what would have been the longest night of my life. And as my eyes grew heavy, sleep threatening to overcome me, I tried to fight it.

"You sound so tired," he said, his voice soft, so reminiscent of years gone by.

"I'm exhausted," I finally admitted with a yawn I could no longer suppress.

"Go, get some sleep."

"No… I don't wanna."

"This isn't like it used to be," he said with a laugh. "You can't sleep as late as you want to, not with those children that are bound to stand and stare at you until you get up to get them cereal."

I laughed at his very accurate description of our son, ending it with a whine. "But I don't want to…"

"Silly girl," he scolded, his voice low. "We never say goodbye."

"No… no we don't," I replied, my hand on the side of my face, where my cheek ached from smiling. "You go first."

"I can handle that."

"I'm sure you can," I teased, and he laughed softly.

"Until later, Talli."

I sighed happily, contentedly for the first time in so long, a little piece of my heart mending.

"Until later."

JASE

"I know that you've been going through a rough time," Chris was saying through the strains of the speaker phone, "but you really should reconsider this sabbatical you've put yourself on."

I sighed as I leaned back in my office chair, bouncing one of Michael's small nerf balls off the wall. "There's nothing to reconsider, Chris."

"The storm has pretty much blown over, yes? The two of you are getting along much better, you've reached an agreement with the children, and yes the tabloids are having a field day with her moving back to the condo, but that doesn't seem to have affected your truce, or whatever it is."

"No it has not," I agreed with a smile, continuing to bounce that ball off the side wall. "But I'm just... I'm not feeling it."

"What do you mean, not feeling it? Or is this something I shouldn't ask?"

I laughed at his question, bouncing the ball a couple of times before I answered. "No inspiration, Chris. None."

"Inspiration."

"Did I stutter?" I asked, having to reach a bit out to the side to catch the ball that time.

"Have you even tried?"

"You know, I pick up that damn guitar and... and I play, but it's... it's like I'm forcing it. I'm just forcing it. Hell, who knows? Maybe it's all coming to an end."

"Is that really how you feel?" he asked slowly, and I knew then I'd said too much.

"I don't know," I admitted. "It's frightening to think about. I'm just in a funk, I suppose."

"You need to snap out of it."

"Can't I just take a break?" I asked, resuming throwing that ball, this time with a little more force. "The closest thing I've come to an actual break was when Elizabeth was born. Even when I got married, even when we were having the other children, I was always in the middle of something."

"Jase, I..."

"And look what it cost me, Chris."

"God, I know Jase. And you know I wouldn't ask if management wasn't clamoring to try and get this last record finished."

"Just set up some kind of meeting with everyone," I said, "and I'll lay it out on the line."

"So will they, you know."

I rolled my eyes at his statement, but I completely understood. "I'm sorry that I've put you in the middle of this."

"It's my job to be in the middle."

I grinned slightly, continuing to bounce that ball as a beep came through the speaker signaling another call. I sighed, catching the ball and turning my head towards the phone. "Hey,"

"Go ahead; get the other line. I'll call you when I have it all set up, okay?"

"Thanks, man. I appreciate it. I'll talk to you later."

"Of course," he said just before I hit that button switching over the call, throwing the ball at the wall once more.

"Talk to me."

"Hey, is this a bad time?"

I was stunned as Talli's voice filled the empty room, wincing as that damn ball that I forgot about came back and hit me in the forehead.

"Ow, fuck," I muttered, rubbing my forehead. "No, not a bad time at all," I added, the butterflies in my stomach taking off at full speed.

"What was…"

"You don't want to know."

"Hijacked one of Michael's nerf balls again?"

I smirked even though she couldn't see it. "Show off."

"Am I on speaker phone?" she asked, and my grin widened. I reached over, picking up the cordless receiver and hitting the button.

"Not anymore," I replied, still grinning like a schoolboy as I leaned back in the chair. "I know how much you hate it."

"Only with a burning, fiery passion. No big. But I think I forgot to tell you that Mary had apologized profusely for causing any problems."

"Mary?" I asked, a bit confused.

"Coffman, neighbor, night of fire? Any of that ringing a bell?"

"Ah, the bitch that made them keep the kids from me."

"Hey, easy there, Warner," Talli said with a short laugh. "She's apologized. Sort of, in her own way. She apologized for adding more stress, so there you go."

"Gee, thanks," I deadpanned. "Actually, no. Thank her, for real. It was an eye opener."

"For both of us," she said softly, and I was smiling again, or for a brief moment anyway. The last name was ringing all kinds of bells, although I wasn't quite sure if they were warning or not.

"Wait... Coffman?" I asked, my leg bouncing as I waited for her reply.

"Yeah, Paul's sister," she replied nonchalantly, as if it were no big deal. Sure, perhaps to her it wasn't a big deal, but damn it someone who was potential competition for my wife's attention had a family member on the inside? That just...

Wait a minute...

"Mary?" I asked, my mind in overdrive as I tried to suppress a sudden case of the giggles. "Do... do they have a brother named Peter?"

"What the hell is so funny?"

Refraining from whistling the tune of *Puff the Magic Dragon*, I merely asked, "Do they?"

"Yeah, I think so. Why?"

Oh. Dear. Lord.

I was howling with laughter as Talli continued asking why, and bless her heart she just didn't get it when I asked if their parents hated them.

"What is so wrong with those names?" she asked, still perplexed. "They are completely normal names."

"Sure," I said with a laugh, "alone, of course they're normal. Completely."

"Jason Michael Warner,"

"Oh, all three names even?" I asked as I slowly began to regain to control.

"What the hell is wrong with Peter, Paul, and Mary?"

Oh hell, she had to go there. I was laughing again, wiping a tear that was coming to my eye. "Nothing," I gasped, "you know, if they're... leaving on a... on a jet plane."

"If they're... oh hell."

She finally got it.

"You know you want to laugh. Admit it. It's funny."

"Damn it, Jase."

"Hey, easy there Woman."

"How am I supposed to look at them with a straight face now?" she asked and I could almost see the blush in her cheeks.

"You... don't?"

"Ugh, you are... you are..."

"Yeah, I love you too."

I didn't mean to say it, I swear I didn't. It just slipped, and left me silent, although not embarrassed—not embarrassed at all. Because it was true, whether or not she was ready or willing to believe it.

"Whatever," she said in her own soft, sweet way, both letting me know that no, she wasn't ready, but no, she also wasn't angry with me.

It was a start.

I could live with that.

"Anyhow, you're still picking up the kids tomorrow, right?" she asked.

"Oh yeah, of course."

"You're sure you can keep them all weekend?"

"No. Not at all. Really, Talli?"

"You're such a shit," she muttered with a laugh. "But too bad, too late, I'm already signed up for rounds and I don't have a sitter. So there."

"How old are you again?" I asked, grinning at my cheeky girl.

"Older than you, so you keep reminding me."

"Yeah, your old ass left some stuff here," I said. "Elizabeth said you were looking for some home movies, too."

She was quiet for a moment before she softly said, "I'm sorry."

"No! No, don't apologize, please. It's... no, wait. I'm sorry."

"What?"

"I'm sorry," I repeated. "I'm sorry that I was so hard on you, that I was such an ass. I shouldn't have made you feel that way, like... like you were anything less than... than perfect."

"I'm not perfect, Jase. No one is."

Fuck... fuck, she has to see...

"But thank you," she added. "It... it means a lot. More than you know, actually."

Bet me.

"I... I'll, um... I have this box." Great, now I'm tripping over my words. Smooth.

"Really?" she asked, almost teasingly.

"Funny, Talia. Real funny."

"You've rubbed off on me, what can I say?"

Not that. You shouldn't have said that. Because now I'm all beyond tongue tied.

"Jase?"

"I'm here, I'm here," I said quickly, silently scolding myself. "Um, I'll bring it over, okay? It has some home movies, and... and some more papers from your school. Just... stuff."

"Just stuff?"

I covered my blazing face even though she couldn't see me. "Yeah, just... stuff."

And she giggled. Damn it, why did that make me smile even more?

"I do have to go. I'm kind of at work."

"Just kind of? Tsk, tsk. Naughty girl, you're slacking off."

"Oh, you're one to talk! I hear that pen clicking in the background; I know that means you're not writing."

"Huh?" I asked, confused, before I looked over at my left hand that had apparently picked up a pen and started fidgeting with it unconsciously. I placed it down, a wistful smile on my face. "Huh," I repeated, this time not as a question.

"Yeah, huh. Snap to it, Warner."

And I tried, I really did. But even being on roughly cloud seven or so, I still couldn't get a single thought put together on that paper. And when Chris called, suggesting that maybe I consider writing with Raine or with Damien, with anyone, I asked him to wait.

Just wait.

Inspiration was sure to come.

I certainly felt a little bit of something stirring as Talia opened her door the next evening, the sweetest smile on her face as she welcomed me into the condo. She looked so beautiful, so... so happy as she gathered the children together, handing me a bag with the toys they just couldn't live without.

"Except Em's bath toys," she added.

"She has plenty at home, doesn't she?" I asked, bouncing Emily on my arm. Only when I heard Talli's breath catch in her throat did I realize what I'd said. "I'm..."

"Don't worry about it," she said softly as Elizabeth and Michael bounded into the room.

Don't worry about it?

And I'm trying so hard not to dwell on that one little sentence, trying not to read too much into it. So, she didn't correct me when I'd called this house their home... that didn't necessarily mean that she considered it their home, or hers... no, of course she didn't. She had the condo that looked so inviting to me with all of that furniture from Ohio, all the memories calling out to me of the simpler times.

Nope, not dwelling.

But the look of nostalgia on her face as she looked at the contents of the box that I'd brought... if I could bottle that up, keep it with me...

Who am I kidding?

I do carry her with me, everywhere I go.

Right here, in my heart.

And later that night, after I'd tucked our children in their beds, kissing them good night, I sat down in that overstuffed recliner in her room downstairs, pen and pad in hand, and began to write.

CHAPTER 13

TALIA

I knew the first test... the first true test... was going to be the first time I saw him. The first time we came face to face after I left the house, after we began to open up to each other. It was easy to open up to him over the phone, see. That has always been our safe zone. It was where the current version of us began. It was where we'd gotten to know each other, where I'd fallen so hard.

And I was falling again.

Not to say I wasn't in love with him already, because without a doubt I've always been. But I had become so jaded where he was concerned, so immune to his charm over the course of the past year. I know the arguments that we'd had, the silent treatment we'd used on each other had taken their toll and were the main cause of it.

There were still times, though, even with him on the other end of the phone that I wondered how many of these words, how much of this charm he'd used on Bree. And then I would wonder, especially with the tabloids and their constant hounding and harassment, if maybe they were right about Kate, too. I'd turned a blind eye, trusted Jase so implicitly when he'd sworn to me that nothing was going on. But there had been. And now...

Now I was so torn.

Torn between the man who had ripped my heart right out of my chest…

And the man who stood in my doorway, that lopsided grin on his face, who made my pulse quicken and had me smiling so warmly at him as I stepped aside to let him in.

"Are they about ready?"

"Hmm? Oh, yeah… yeah."

Shit, Talli. Keep it together. Quit staring at his… damn his ass looks good in those jeans. And oh hell, fire, brimstone, and all that other shit… this is one of those pairs of jeans where… where if he wore them on stage, his fans would aim their cameras right… there. Holy hell, I miss having him inside of me… Fuck! Quit staring!

"Elizabeth's school papers are on the coffee table," I said quickly, turning to go get them so he hopefully didn't see me blush. "And there's… um, there's this note, see?"

He picked up the note from her kindergarten teacher, grinning as he read about her being a bit bossy, but very bright. "Sounds like someone else I know."

"Yeah?" I asked nervously, rubbing my sweating palms on my yoga pants. "Who?"

His grin widened, his eyebrows disappearing below that shock of bangs that had fallen across his forehead when he set the small box he'd brought with him down. "You're kidding, right?"

"No…who… me?" I asked, placing a hand on my chest as if I were double checking his meaning.

"Very much so."

"You think I'm bossy?" It wasn't asked in a mean, spiteful way at all; in fact, he had me grinning as well.

"Must I dignify that question with an answer?"

I didn't have time to come back with a reply, which is probably a good thing. I don't think I could have formed a coherent sentence as I stared into those eyes that were the most beautiful color of green right then. Luckily for me, Michael ran out with a couple of his toys, placing them in the bag of their 'essentials' that they swore they couldn't live two days without. "Don't leave without me, Daddy!"

"Wouldn't dream of it," he said, handing Elizabeth's papers back to me.

"I'll be out in a minute too!" Elizabeth called out from her room.

"Should I feel insulted that they didn't come running right out?" he asked as he looked over towards the hallway. I wasn't sure if that question was really directed at me, or if it was more of his internal dialogue making its way to the surface, just like it used to.

"Well, you could," I replied, "or you could take comfort in knowing that they're... well, they know you're not going to disappear. At least not right away."

I watched as he swallowed hard, the corner of his mouth lifting up in a soft smile that faded before he turned his eyes to me. "I never disappeared."

"You know what I meant," I said with a wave of my hand, busying myself with looking through the box he'd brought over so that I didn't get caught staring at him in that t-shirt that fit just right, his arms looking absolutely phenomenal. They always looked phenomenal, especially when he was holding himself up with them as he hovered over me and...

"The tour."

I looked up as he said it.

"That's what you were talking about, right?"

"Of course," I said, confused a bit by his question. He grinned again, nodding slightly before he leaned down, scooping a squealing Emily up into his arms.

Oh, he was in such a good mood. He was... he was my Jase again, not that I could call him mine anymore but... but he looked so relaxed, so comfortable in these surroundings. It made me miss those times in Ohio a little, when he and I holed up in that apartment, curled up on that couch watching TV Land or making love, or making love with TV Land going on in the background. Hell, he looked almost as comfortable here as he did in our home...

Wait.

Our home? I did not just go there in my head. No, that's his house and this... is ... well, it's where I live, and...

"We're all set," Elizabeth announced.

"No, wait." I picked up the bag that they'd put the stuff the just couldn't live without and handed it to Jase, almost blushing at my thoughts even as he had our youngest child in his arms.

"Everything's in here?" he asked.

"All except Em's bath toys," I said.

He looked at our Princess, who was grinning and chewing on one of her fingers, her drool steadily pooling on her shirt. He bounced her up and down slightly and said, "She has plenty at home, doesn't she?"

And I felt my pulse quicken so fast I had to catch my breath. *Home. He... he still referred to it as their home. Did he... did he think of it as my home, too? Oh, shit. He's looking at me, and he looks... no... don't look sad, please. Please.*

"I'm..."

"Don't worry about it," I said with a smile as Michael and Elizabeth, who apparently had forgotten one last thing, came running into the room.

I didn't want to hear how he was sorry. Not yet. I wanted to hold on to that tiny stupid faux sliver of hope that someday... someday we'd get past everything. Someday I'd be enough for him, someday I wouldn't look at him and see...

Her.

Fuck.

I busied myself with going through that little box, noting that most of it were home movies that we'd made over the years. They seemed to go in order, all of them children related, from Elizabeth to Michael to Em...

Oh! To Emily!

It dawned on me as I held up the last four dvds that I still didn't remember all that much about the first few months of her life. I hadn't felt comfortable quite yet asking Jase to fill me in, as it also meant I would have to admit that there was so much that I didn't know. But here were some of the answers, on these discs that he'd labeled, his handwriting setting off even more butterflies in my stomach.

I popped myself a bowl of popcorn and grabbed a Diet Pepsi, curling up in the papasan chair after I put the first dvd in. I grimaced as the screen filled with my face, completely grossed out by how fat I looked.

"Say hi to our Princess, Momma," his voice rang loud and true, and with a shaking hand I hit the volume button to turn it down.

"I'll say hi to her when she stops putting me through hell," had been my reply. Oh...OH... I remember this. I was in labor with her when his smart ass decided he wanted to capture as much as he could. And my labor with her had been hard and fast, so fast I'd barely had time for the shot to kick in before I was pushing.

"You're doing wonderful."

Jaden had the camera at that point and thank goodness she was at my shoulder, so I wasn't about to view anything gross. Nope, nothing gross, just Jase running his fingers through my hair, kissing my forehead, and telling me he loved me. If I closed my eyes and just listened, I could almost feel it.

"She's almost here, baby."

I opened up my eyes as I heard myself cry to him that I couldn't do it anymore... I just couldn't do it.

"Of course you can." I could almost feel the kiss he left on my cheek, feel his hand holding mine. And I held my breath as I watched the next few seconds, as if I were there, pushing in real life, finally exhaling when I heard our daughter's first cry.

I watched with wonder as they laid her on my chest, watching mostly Jase's face this time, how he looked at Emily with such wonder, such love.

I thought briefly of the first time Jase had been to the condo to pick the children up, and how I had accused him of never being close with Emily. What was it he had said to me? Oh, right. That I had selective memory. And it had made me so damn angry, but now... now I could see.

That first dvd alone was mostly of Jase with Emily, from the moment she came into this world, where he kept saying he couldn't get over her and how beautiful she was, to when he sang her to sleep for the first time when she was a mere seven hours old.

"I'll keep it quiet," he promised, placing a kiss on her forehead and adjusting her hat just so before he began to sing *The First Time Ever I Saw Your Face.*

Oh God... this... this brought back a flood of memories, like tiny flashes going off in my mind. He did this... every night. Every night the first three months of her life he sang her to sleep with that song. Not once had I been the one to place her in her bed at night in that time. Not... once.

Through these discs I watched her first smile, when I'd been asleep in that damn recliner and she'd been in his lap. And I listened to her first laugh, which of course was at something Michael had done. I watched her bond with her big sister, who in spite of all of her meanness had always turned to goo around her baby sister. I watched how she would fuss and cry while in my arms and would smile when Jase would say something to her.

Wow.

She'd had him more wrapped then Elizabeth ever had.

And where was I?

The next to the last disc was shortly before he'd left, and I watched with wonder, with eyes wide open at how distant I had become with all of them. I'd still smile at Jase, and the children. I still told them all that I loved them. But I didn't show it as much. I didn't smile as much as I used to. I was in darker clothing, looser clothing. And even with as much as he had that camera trained on me, it was almost as if I was ignoring him.

And it had only gotten worse after he left.

"I'm so sorry," I whispered as I sat there for a moment, staring at the black screen.

The hour was late, and I was tired but there was one more to go. One that was simply titled "Birthday".

Oh, hell. This should be a train wreck.

I was curious, though. Curious to see what had been captured. I remembered many, many pictures being taken that day, but for the life of me didn't know who was shooting the video, or what they'd gotten.

I suppose it was time to find out.

"Hi Mommy," Elizabeth said with her big grin. Wait… this wasn't from Emily's birthday party. This was recent, or sort of recent, but… when?

"Daddy says we're doing a birthday video for you."

For me?

Oh, this was shot at the house, before we'd left. The furniture in the great room was the old stuff, and Michael was jumping on the sofa before Jase said sharply, "Little Man, don't let your Mommy catch you."

I had to laugh. Not… don't do that, you'll get hurt. Nope, it was don't let Mommy catch you. And he was right; I would have had a cow. Oh, but Michael... he looked so young, but this couldn't have been from... oh, and Emily! Look how little! She wasn't even walking yet.

Emily.

This was... a birthday video... for this year.

"We're supposed to tell you Happy Birthday even though it isn't yet," Michael said, choosing his words carefully. I could hear Jase trying to suppress his laughter... trying and failing miserably as Michael continued on about how he didn't get it.

"I don't get birthday presents til my birthday."

"That's when we're giving it to her."

Oh... oh he was going to give this to me for my birthday?

But my birthday had been ruined. My birthday was shortly after I'd caught him in bed with her. And he hadn't given this to me, not until today. He hadn't even wished me a happy birthday this year.

No one had.

But now... now here they were, all of my children, no matter how much Emily was protesting. Hell, at that point she was probably looking for me. Jase had been out of the picture and less than receptive to her clinginess with me when he returned. But he still told little anecdotes about each of them, making me smile and laugh over all of them. And it meant the world to me that he'd gone through that trouble just to give me something special for my birthday. It was so much better late than never.

I reached for the remote as I heard the children saying their goodbyes, expecting that to be the last of it, ready to call him and just thank him from the bottom of my heart.

But I stopped.

I stopped because after a small blip, I watched as he walked around to the front of the camera, that he'd obviously had set up on a tripod. Oh, he looked so tired... so tired and so defeated. I felt my lower lip begin to tremble at just the sight of him, cursing myself for being so blind.

"Now... now it's just you and me. Or me and this camera... but..." He pinched the bridge of his nose for a brief second as he looked away, like he always did when something was bothering him. His eyebrows were still furrowed, the lines between them slightly visible as he turned towards the camera again.

"Things are... they're different now."

Oh god...

"No matter how much I deny it, no matter how many times I put on my happy face, they're... they're different."

Was he really doing this, on a dvd that was supposed to be for my birthday? I felt a bit sick to my stomach but I kept it on, curiosity killing me almost as much as the sadness etched in his features.

"We... we don't talk anymore. Not like we used to."

How many times had I tried to tell him the same thing?

"And... and I'm sorry about... God, Talli, I miss you."

My hand covered my mouth as the first tear fell from my eyes.

His eyes were closed as he added, "So much."

"I miss you, too," I sobbed, curling up tight in that chair.

"Once upon... a time," he continued, his voice full of emotion, "there was... there was this girl." He grinned slightly, and I took that moment to grab a much-needed tissue before turning back. "And this girl got this... this crazy, insane... wonderful idea. She said that she wanted to fight. She wanted to fight for this boy."

Oh, I remember that conversation. And I remembered Colorado, the cabin, the hot spring...

"And she took the boy with her, away from... from all... this." His hands came up as he gestured around him. "And they found each other again. They were reminded, they knew why they loved each other, they remembered how wonderful it was, what a... what a team they were."

I sniffled as the tears flowed freely, wishing so badly I could turn back the clock to that exact moment, get home from work early, and just...

He thought of us as a team? Or... or he had, and...

"And I know," he continued, "that things are... well, they're different now. They're not the same as they were then, the circumstances are... they're different."

No. You think?

Stop. Stop it, Talli. You pushed him away. You may as well have handed Bree to him with a gaudy bow on top of her skanky head.

"But I feel... I feel that it's time. It's time for us to... to step back, and... and get away."

What?

"So this... this will be my birthday present to you. We will just... we'll just go. We'll get away. We'll get a sitter, or... or Nan, she'd take the kids in a heartbeat, and we wouldn't have to worry about them. And... and we'll find... each other again. I know we can, if we try."

But... but you were with Bree, I saw you with her. It was after this was shot, so it was obviously going on.

What was this going to be to you? The last hoorah? Was this to see if there was any spark before you left me for good? Or...

"Talli, I love you."

My mind seemed to go blank as those words fell from his lips, the only thing registering within me was the emotion behind them.

"I know we've had problems."

Yeah... one mental case of a wife and one whore.

"I know we're not communicating the way we should."

Isn't that the story of us?

"So let's get away. Just you and me."

Why hadn't we, huh? Why... why didn't you give this to me before? Oh.

Oh, because I caught you. With her.

I choked back another sob as he held up a brochure. Oh... Steamboat Springs...

"Here," he said with a half-hearted cheeky grin. "Or somewhere else. Anywhere. It doesn't matter where we go. Let's just get away, get back to where you and I are... are an *us* again."

"Could we?" I asked out loud, chewing on my thumbnail as I stared longingly at the screen.

"Because I love you," he said, and my chest tightened. "Happy birthday."

Oh, it would have been. It would have been.

Grief consumed me as the screen faded to black and I remembered how my birthday had been spent. If I'm not mistaken... no, no I'm not. My birthday was spent signing papers and paying the deposit on this condo I was in.

Why?

Why had he done this if he was with her?

If he truly loved me, then… why?

Suddenly, the conversation I'd had with Pete, no matter how short, hit me with absolute force. He had turned to Leah out of hurt, out of anger.

And I'd certainly done enough to hurt him.

I also remembered, with absolute clarity, coming home from work and bitching because the tripod had been left out, yelling about carelessness, and how someone could get hurt.

And I remembered his face. How stricken, how sad.

And yet… yet, he'd still taken the time to take what he'd recorded and make this for me.

Somehow, some way, I was going to make it up to him.

As I dialed his number, not even looking at the time, I recalled that full-scale fight, where it took him a whole hour to drag it out of me that one of the babies I'd delivered that night hadn't made it. And when he'd tried to console me, I told him he wouldn't understand, and I'd pushed him away. And it was just eating me up inside.

"Not Telling," his voice filled my heart as he answered, sounding far too happy and alert for this time of night. "What pray tell are you doing up?"

"I just…" I faltered through my tears, and I heard the concern in his voice as he replied to me when I couldn't speak. I couldn't bring up the dvd, the birthday wish that I so wanted to come true, not then.

"Hey… hey. What's wrong?"

"It's so… stupid. No, it's not stupid, it's…"

"Please don't cry. Just tell me, okay? If… if you want to. I'm here; I'll listen."

"That's just it. That's just… do you remember… that night… when I'd lost my first patient… my first baby, she was a baby."

"Ohhhh, oh, no, baby, tell me that didn't happen again."

"No, not… knock on wood… I just… I'm so sorry, Jase. I'm so sorry."

"For what?"

"For… for how I treated you that night. You didn't deserve that.

You... you just wanted to help, and I'm sorry."

He was silent for a moment, hurting my heart even more, but when he did speak, his voice was tight, his emotions raw. "I... I don't know what... no, yes I do. It's okay, Talli. I... I understand why, it was a really stressful night."

"But it's not okay, and... and I don't want your understanding right now. I... I don't want you to be nice to me. I don't deserve it."

"Yes, you do, baby. Yes, you do."

I choked back another sob at his words, hating myself for dragging him in on this pity train I was on. "I... I shouldn't have... bothered you with... I'm just... I'm sorry, Jase. I'm sorry."

"I was a pretty hateful bastard that night too, Talli," he said, and with a laugh I remembered just how hateful he had become. "Don't laugh, it wasn't funny."

"I know, I know."

"And I'm sorry, too."

"For that night," I said softly, and I heard him sigh.

"Yeah," he replied. "For that night."

And slowly, another piece of my heart fell back into place.

JASE

The minute October hit, I could feel this nervous energy coming over me. I was at peace with most things in my life, there were no major disruptions, the children were doing wonderful, and Talli and I... well, we were still getting along fairly well. Not to say that there weren't bumps in the road, but we weren't constantly fighting. We weren't always at each other's throats. And when she once again declined my offer of lunch, she didn't blow me off. She simply explained that they were short staffed, and she wasn't even taking a lunch that day. She even let out a nice little string of curse words when she realized she'd left her lunch back at the condo.

So, since I was the consummate gentleman, I decided I was going to pick something up for her, and just surprise her with it. I was going to be out and about anyhow; Chris had finally set up that meeting with myself, my management, as well as a couple representatives from the record label. Oh boy oh boy, was this ever going to be fun. So, first put on my resolve face and reiterate that I was in no, way, shape, or form going to be recording or performing for the next few months. Believe me, it took great effort to even drive to that meeting. But I did, knowing that at least I had something to look forward to afterwards.

"Jackie, my man," I said with a grin as I walked into the office building, "why the long face? You know you are a man of action, of peace, of love, and all that other shit."

"Yes, I am," he agreed, handing me over a cup of coffee and holding out his other hand which had two white pills in it.

"Thank you for the coffee, but what the hell are those for?" I asked, raising an eyebrow.

"Just… take the aspirin. Trust me. It might not even help."

"Oh, great, they're on the warpath?" I asked, taking both pills and swallowing them with a large gulp of coffee.

"Not… exactly."

"What do you mean not… oh, hell no."

I glared down the hallway where Bree Hamilton was emerging from one of the conference rooms dressed more like she was going to a night club then meeting with people who signed her damn paychecks.

"Hell no… fuck that." I took another drink of my coffee as I turned back towards the elevator but was stopped when Jackie placed a firm hand on my shoulder.

"You can't walk out of here, Jase," he said, his voice low. "She's part of the meeting too."

"Why?" I asked, a scowl firmly in place when I turned back around.

"Apparently the powers that be want to have a word with the both of you."

"They can do it separately."

"They will, but…" He sighed, shaking his head slowly. "I believe that they will have you both in the same room for at least part of it."

"Eavesdropping again, Alfred?"

"As always, for the good of the team."

"You're a good man, Jackie," I said softly. "A good man."

"Well, well, well… look what the cat dragged in," Bree said as she slinked her way up to us.

"I believe that phrase is reserved for use when the person it's in reference to looks a mess, or flustered, or perhaps bothered," Jackie said coolly, and I made a mental note to thank him later.

"Whatever," was all Bree would say to his comment. "Hey, I need to talk with Jase alone."

"Hey, it isn't happening," I replied, stepping around her and walking towards the conference room.

"We're here for a reprimand for our inappropriate relationship, you know," she drew out, rather loudly.

"So, let them reprimand away," I said, thankful that Jackie had stayed right on my heels. "It's a mistake that won't be made again."

"Oh, please," she scoffed. "Your wife is less than accommodating; you were bound to look elsewhere. And let's face it, she obviously hasn't changed, or you would have kept her around."

Keep your mouth shut, Warner. Shut. Very. Tight.

"Oh, and I've struck a nerve. So let's just make it clear right here, right now—just because your little reconciliation attempt with your wife didn't work out doesn't give you the right to be an asshole towards me."

"What the hell are you talking about?" I demanded.

"Oh, come on. I read the tabloids. I've been in them enough; I know how close to the truth they can actually get. Speaking of which, it must just kill you knowing she's been cozying up to that doctor."

"Let's make this clear," I said, trying my best to keep my temper in check. "The subject of my wife is off limits to you, got it? You don't speak of her, you don't try to contact her, you just forget,"

"That she exists?" she cut me off, her voice so falsely sweet I swear I almost threw up in my mouth. "Not a problem. It was easy enough for you to do."

"Hey, I don't know what the hell…"

"Enough," Chris said as he stepped in between us.

"It's so easy to villainize me, isn't it?" she said venomously. "So easy to pin the blame on me, to be an asshole to me, to leave me hanging out to dry just because you got caught with your pants down."

"I said enough," Chris reiterated, motioning for the doors to be closed. Oh, yippee. Apparently, the ass chewing was going to be first and I was going to be subjected to Bree for the next hour, and…

And wallow in even more guilt. And it wasn't necessarily because I agreed with Bree; I'd decided before Talli had ever walked in that my marriage was more important to me than whatever temporary gratification I was going to get from Bree, or anyone else for that matter.

"I was by your side for months while your wife couldn't be bothered," she hissed before sulking over to the opposite side of the table, where Chris had ordered her to sit.

"I suppose we all know why we're here today." I almost cringed at the sound in Mr. Albright's voice. When Mr. Albright was at your meeting, you knew you were in deep shit. Mr. Albright was one of those people from the record company, where Bree and I were both artists, who could snap his fingers and have you out the door with nothing left. He was one of those people who demanded respect, who demanded perfection.

This was not going to be pretty.

"Well," Bree spoke up, and I did cringe then, "my guess is you're going to give us a verbal lashing for getting caught screwing around. But sir, that was several months ago; if you had that big of a problem with it, you should have said something then."

"Is that so?" Mr. Albright drew the words out, and I could feel when his eyes turned to me. "Mr. Warner?"

"It's because of my refusal to work with her, because of the verbal sparring remarks in public," I said with a resigned sigh, knowing his demands that all artists on the label either get along, or at least put up the front that they do.

"Oh, well, yeah. That is a problem," Bree snapped, her hateful, icy stare trained on me.

"I didn't ask for your input this time, Ms. Hamilton," he said rather loudly, and she shrunk back just like I knew she would. "And Mr. Warner, you are correct. All of our artists are part of our family, and while families do not always get along, they must always respect one another. So, I am telling both of you, as well as your respective management teams, that it is time to make peace."

Fuck… fuck, fuck, fuck! Why? Not just why… why now?

"And, Mr. Warner, since you seem to be in such good health, I believe you have some upcoming appearances that you will be fulfilling."

"Mr. Albright, those appearances have been canceled," Chris said from his seat beside me.

"Oh, I'm sorry... perhaps I should clarify. Ms. Hamilton has appearances that Mr. Warner will also be attending, and these two artists from this family will perform together."

My eyes narrowed as Bree smiled in triumph from across the table. You were raised better, Warner. You do not want to smack the smirk off her face right now.

"Now, that we're all in agreement,"

"I'm sorry, Mr. Albright, but we're not."

Oh, fuck. Did those words just come from me?

"Come again, Mr. Warner? I'm not sure I heard you correctly."

"You did, sir, and with all due respect, I have to stand my ground on this one. I... I will continue to make sure all public comments are either non-existent or at least non-confrontational where Ms. Hamilton is concerned, but I will not perform with her."

"Again, I don't think..."

"If you want me to perform myself, then... then I will," I continued, praying that my offer of a compromise would help. "I'll... I'll even make sure I have something new to throw out there, but for the sake of... of not only our reputations, which in turn could hurt the company, but for the sake of..."

"What, your marriage?"

"Of my children," I said, my face flaming at Bree's comment. "Of my own peace of mind, of... of saving what could essentially be a PR nightmare for all sides, I am asking that you reconsider."

I saw a slight smile and a nod from Chris, which was directed at me so I knew he wasn't in on some major plot to try and screw me out of anything, wasn't trying to manipulate me back into performing. But I kept my eyes on Mr. Albright, gauging his reaction, praying he would see things through my eyes.

"I will consider it," he finally said, and I let out a sigh of relief.

"Wow. You are a real piece of work," Bree said, much to the chagrin of her manager.

"Ms. Hamilton, it would do you well to follow Mr. Warner's example. And when asked about your relationship, your answer here and forevermore will be 'no comment', do you understand?"

"Yes sir," she said, just like a pouting child.

What the hell had I ever saw in her?

"Well," Chris said as we emerged from the conference room, "one bullet dodged, and yet another meeting to go. Which is almost moot since you've practically committed yourself to performing and recording again."

"Don't remind me," I muttered. "Fuck... don't remind me."

So, needless to say, my mood was shot when I walked out of that office building, my head held high in case of any onlookers. I got into my SUV, turning on my cell phone about the time I started the vehicle, scowling at the radio that was playing Bree, of all fucking things. I quickly changed the station, settling in on a little bit of 80's before getting ready to pull out of my spot. Just as I was about to go, my phone began to ring, so I put the vehicle back in park and answered the private number.

"At least you still answer when I call," Bree said and I cringed at the sound of her voice.

"Because it's a blocked call and I don't want to miss..." I stopped, pinching the bridge of my nose before I continued, as nicely as I could. "Look, I'm not asking you to not call..."

"Good."

"No, not good. I'm telling you not to. I'm telling you that that there won't be any more communication between us. Got it?"

"Oh, unless I come up to you in public, and then you have to play nice. Right?"

I grimaced at the thought of that happening, what the consequences could potentially be, so I tried my best to just reason with her. "Listen... I'm trying to do the right thing here."

"She left you twice, Jase. Now either she's still a frumpy-ass prude, or she caught you with someone else again. Say, like... Kaitlyn Evans."

"You don't know what you're talking about, you don't have all the information, and you're not going to get it from me. So just please...

drop it. Move on."

"Oh, you are such an asshole, Warner."

"You're right; I am. And I'm sorry that you got pulled into the middle of it. I'm sorry if I did anything to make you think that there was going to be anything come out of... all this. Okay?"

"No, it's not okay."

I growled in frustration, so thankful that suddenly my phone was beeping. Hello, Tom, you are my savior.

"I have to get this," I said and clicked over without another word to her. "Talk to me."

"Where are you, dude?" he asked.

"Um... just leaving a meeting. Why?"

"Do me a favor and get your ass back to your house," he said. "Let me in, man, I have to piss."

"Holy shit," I said with the widest grin. "I am on my way."

I hightailed it back to my house, my sour mood forgotten as I pulled up next to his rental car. I was so damn excited I almost forgot to unbuckle my seatbelt, nearly choking myself before my dumb ass took the stupid thing off and bounded over to give my cousin a huge bear hug.

"To what do I owe this surprise?" I asked, my cheeks already aching from smiling.

"Let me piss and I'll tell you," he said, ushering me towards the door.

"Right... right, sorry." I had that door open as quickly as I could, grinning as he rushed past me while I was punching in the alarm code.

"Speaking of surprises," he called out on his way, and I was totally confused. Thrown for a loop, even. What the hell was he talking about? What...

Surprise...

He came back out, grinning from ear to ear as he approached me in the middle of that great room. "I washed my hands, I promise. Although I smell like flowers now."

"Yeah, Talli's soap on you does nothing for me. Sorry." I grinned as I bounced lightly on my heels. "Come ooonnnnn, Tommy!"

"What... you mean... this?" he asked, pulling a small envelope from his wallet. I reached for it, but he pulled it back, grinning down at me. "Huh uh, little shit. Say it."

"You are Spartacus, okay?" I replied, trying in vain to reach the envelope. "Oh, come on!"

"Here," he said with a laugh, practically shoving me backwards as he placed the envelope in my hand. It was so difficult to get it open, just to peek inside and...

Holy shit. Holy shit he did it.

"You are unbelievable, Tommy," I said softly, my fingertips tracing over the lettering.

"I try, I try," he said, laughing and turning towards the kitchen. "I am going to get a beer, grab a shower, and then a nap before we head out."

"Head out?" I asked. "Have I forgotten something else?"

"Nah, I just figure we're gonna need to celebrate," he replied with a wink. "Now get your ass to wherever Talli is and give her that damn surprise already."

I can't say I agreed with the celebrating. I mean, I was sure she'd love the surprise, but I hardly thought that I would be the one she'd share it with. Perhaps her sister, or her brother Eric. Or... or, as much as I hated to say it... Paul. The doctor. The one she had so much in common with.

But that... that would be okay. Because this wasn't about me, it was something I wanted to do... for her.

The small envelope was tucked in the side pocket of my leather jacket so the only thing she'd see was the bag with her favorite turkey sub from her favorite little deli. One glance at my watch and I knew either I was going to be her saving grace, or too late because someone else had swooped in and done the job. Someone like... like that suave doctor having a conversation with one of the M.As, a bag that surely contained some kind of food type substance in his hand.

Hell no, dude.

"Hey, sweetheart," I said to one of the front office girls with my best smile, "can I go take this back to Talli's office?"

"Sure," she replied with a smile, opening the door to let me in.

Take *that*, Dr. Paul Coffman.

My hands were trembling as I walked that hall back towards her office, knowing which one it was, wondering if she'd be in there or if I'd just have to leave the sandwich and envelope along with a little note.

No... no, if she wasn't there, I was going to wait. I would wait until she walked in, no matter how long it took, and Tom would just have to understand...

"Jase."

I jumped at the sound of her voice, the vision of her before me in the hallway taking my breath away. She looked so beautiful with those loose curls framing her face, her blouse a royal blue, setting off her eyes. I could only stare, grinning like a damn fool at her, which for some reason brought a smile to her face as well.

"Quit," she said with a laugh, opening her office door and motioning for me to follow her in.

"Quit what?" I asked innocently.

"Quit... that," she said, pointing at my face then her head tilted slightly to the side. "No, on second thought, don't."

Oh great. Now here I was blushing and sure to be a stammering fool, and...

She gasped as her eyes trailed down and for one brief second I was wondering if I was about to be mortified, wondering if she saw what she did to me, until...

"You brought lunch!" she exclaimed, and I grinned sheepishly, holding the bag out for her. "Oh, thank God, I'm starving! Here... here... sit."

"No, wait, I..."

"Why wait? I have just a few minutes and,"

"I have something for you," I said quickly, before I completely forgot, before she had to be pulled away.

"Something more than the best sandwich ever?" she asked playfully, and I nodded slowly. "What?"

I reached into my pocket as I began to speak. "I... I've wanted to do this for a while. I had Tommy working on it even."

"Oh, Tommy! How is he?"

"He's... he's great," I stammered, grinning as I realized just how much back to her old self she was becoming. Interrupting me now even... I could just... kiss her. "But, he was helping me and,"

"Helping you with what?"

"Damn, Woman, be quiet for two seconds and I can tell you!" I smiled as she giggled slightly.

"Sorry."

"Anyhow… It's just…well, it's just a surprise. For you. Um, a little late for birthday, a little early for Christmas…"

My voice trailed off as her face lit up, her eyes trained on the envelope in my hand.

"For my birthday?" she asked softly, then she looked back up into my eyes.

"Yeah… um… yeah," I stammered like the fool I was for her. "I… I hope you like it." I held my hand out, cursing at myself for being unable to stop the tremble, wondering… just wondering if she'd seen…

"I… I don't know what to say," she said, her voice wavering as she took the envelope from me.

"Just, you know, look." I gestured towards the envelope, trying to play it cool as she opened it up, pulling the tickets partially out before her eyes grew wide, a gasp leaving those beautiful lips.

"Michigan vs. Ohio… State… at… at the horseshoe…"

Only my girl.

"Oh… oh my… holy *shit*!" The squeak that left her was so damn cute, and then… oh then…

Then she launched herself straight into my arms, hers curling around my neck as she held me so… so tight…

"This is so incredible!" she was saying, her voice right in my ear. My eyes slid shut and slowly, cautiously, I wrapped my arms around her, cradling her to me, feeling as if I'd died and gone straight to the maker himself.

"Ohmygodohmygodohmygod…" Her words were all running together, and I had to stifle a laugh as I held her, breathing her in, never wanting to let her go.

The only thing I'd wanted was for her to enjoy her surprise, for her to get away the way she needed to so badly. To see her like this, to know that I could do this for her, was absolute…

"Oh fuck," she said, pulling back slightly, her next words equal parts shocking and euphoric, "what will we do with the children while we're gone?"

She… she wants… to take… me.

"Um… my… Nan?" I suggested, still not quite believing this was happening.

"Well… yeah, if she could come out here, but Elizabeth's in school, and… sit! Sit!" She gestured towards the chair. "Hell, if I don't sit down, I'm going to fall over."

"Me too," I replied, so softly I didn't know if she heard me as she continued chattering on excitedly. Maybe Linda would watch them, what day were we going to leave on, would we be coming straight back, did she have to go visit her family while we were there, or could we just stay in Columbus…

We.

We were going… to get away…

Just us. Just like I wanted.

I was going to have my chance…

"What do you think?" she asked excitedly, actually sitting with her legs crossed up in that chair of hers. She's so damn cute… "Jase, what do you think?"

"Just one thing," I said slowly.

"Really?" she asked, her eyebrow raised. "What's that?"

I smirked as I took in the glow of her cheeks, the smile that I could feel all the way down to my soul, knowing I couldn't tell her exactly what was on my mind at that moment, but there was one other stipulation.

"No air horn."

"Hmph," she said, reaching back into her refrigerator and pulling out a couple of drinks. She set the Dr. Pepper in front of me as she said, "Pussy."

"Whatever, Woman."

"Uh huh," she drew out, leaning back into her chair. "We'll see."

Mmm hmmm. We'll see indeed.

CHAPTER 14

TALIA

A *m I being presumptuous?*

"Yeah, I think Linda would love having the kids over," he said, after I threw out that suggestion.

"Good! Good, so that way Elizabeth doesn't miss school," I replied, my mind still going faster than my mouth.

Of course, I'm being presumptuous. I saw the DVD, he said birthday, he comes in with tickets. That doesn't necessarily mean he wanted to go with me.

"When will we leave? Oh! Can we be there early enough Friday to maybe… go to that one gym and see the pep rally?"

Oh, look at that smile on his face…

"Anything you want."

"Anything?" I asked, my eyebrows raised.

"Yep. Anything."

Wow. That was a loaded word. I'm going to have to simmer on that one.

"I'll remember that," I said, opening my sandwich, which by the way pretty much elevated him up to Hero of the Day status in my eyes. I was fucking starving. "Where's yours?"

"My what?" he asked.

Oh, he looks so yummy when he raises that eyebrow. I could easily eat him instead.

Wait... yummy? Seriously? UGH, Talia. Just... UGH.

"Your sandwich," I said. "Aren't we eating lunch together?"

Again with the smile. I'm dead. Seriously. Dead.

"Um, I... I didn't get one," he said, his cheeks turning a little pink.

"What do you mean, you didn't get one?" I asked as I pulled open my 'stash' drawer and retrieved a plastic knife. "Here... you're having some of mine."

"Talli, I can't..."

"Yes, you can, and you will. Besides, you know I can't eat all of this in one sitting, so..." I held out half the sandwich for him. "Here. Don't say I never did anything for you."

His laughter ringing in that little office made me the happiest girl on the face of this planet, and as he reached for the sandwich, our fingers inadvertently brushing, I could feel my pulse race.

"Talia, the next patient is about ready."

And the moment was over.

But I wasn't ready for it to be.

"Can you give me a few minutes?" I asked. "We're starving here. I swear it won't take long."

She smiled and nodded, pulling the door not quite closed, but at least a little more so as she exited the room. I turned my attention back to Jase, who was merely picking at his food.

"Oh, come on, there's no mustard on it. Eat!"

One corner of his mouth lifted up in a smile, his eyes trained on the half of a sandwich in front of him. "I had a meeting today," he said, picking at the turkey and placing some of it in his mouth.

"Oh? With your record company, or management?"

"Both," he said, still staring at his sandwich. He obviously wasn't going to elaborate, so once I was done with my bite and had swallowed, I tried to draw it out of him.

"What was it about?"

"They want my record finished," he said with a shrug.

"You're still not writing?" I asked, and he blushed slightly.

"I... I am now, actually." He grinned, looking almost shy, as he finally looked up at me.

I couldn't help but smile back at him. "That's wonderful! Who are you writing with?"

"Mostly just... me, but Damien said he'd like to work some with me."

"What, no big guns? Just the two of you?"

"You're mocking me," he said, a distinct twinkle in his eye. I shook my head, holding up one finger telling him I'd answer when I had chewed and swallowed.

"No, those are legitimate questions. But it's good that you're writing. It's... it's awesome, really."

"What about you?" he asked, his head tilted slightly over to the side.

"I don't write, dork," I said, and he rolled his eyes.

"Okay, smart ass, I know that. The... the therapy. How has it been going?"

It was my turn to blush, my turn to squirm just a little in my seat as I watched him finally take a bite of his sandwich, his cue that he wasn't about to continue until I answered.

"Frustrating but good," I said softly. "It's... I never realized how detached I had become. It didn't occur to me at all that I wasn't really living, just existing. Just existing, that's all. And everyone around me suffered, and I didn't catch on to the little things... like that, that twitch above your eye." I gestured and he rubbed his eyebrow absentmindedly. "What's up?"

"I told you."

"But not everything. Spill."

"They... um, they want me to do a few performances, too," he finally admitted, his eyes turning a stormy gray.

"What's wrong with that?"

As soon as I asked the question, as soon as his face flared red, I knew what was wrong with it, without him even answering.

"I'm just not too thrilled with some of the other people on the bill," he mumbled, looking up only when I hit him in the forehead with a torn piece of bacon.

"Snap out of it. We're having lunch."

He grinned at me, an almost wistful expression on his face. "I want you to know that I said no... initially."

"Oh, initially?" I teased, trying to keep the conversation light. "What did they do, threaten to hand you your balls in a sling?"

"Pretty much, yeah," he replied, his free hand scratching the back of his neck. "But hopefully they accept my compromise."

"Which is?"

He held my gaze as he said, "I promised them I would play the shows, if I played them myself. Not with anyone else. And I told them the new album would be done soon, new songs would be ready for the appearances. And... and that's important to me, that I can do this my way."

My smile was soft as I took stock in his words, letting them settle right around my heart that someday was bound to let him completely back in. This had to be a good thing, right? Agreeing only to play...

Wait...

"Oh!" I said suddenly, catching him a bit off guard. "I can finally take the kids to see you play! Or, again, but... but I wasn't able to for a while, and Elizabeth and Michael have been giving me all kinds of grief over it. Hopefully Em won't get sick again..." My voice trailed off as I tried to think of the number of things that could keep us away when I realized his head had dropped, his eyes trained on something on the ground. "Is... is it okay? Or would you rather that we,"

"It would be amazing," he said, his voice thick and full of emotion.

Oh...

"I'm so sorry we didn't make it out, the last tour."

He shook his head, seeming to gather his bearings as he sat back up. "It's water under the bridge, Talli," he said with a smile. "There's... always next time."

"Right."

We were silent, each of us picking at our sandwiches, taking sips of our drinks. I wasn't quite sure what was going through his mind, but I knew mine was still going a million miles a minute.

I had to know.

"Would things be different, if I'd gone?"

His eyes slid shut, and for a moment I regretted asking him the question no matter how much I wanted to know... no matter how much it... mattered. When he looked at me again, those beautiful eyes so full of pain, I could feel my heart begin to break. Especially when he said, "I don't know."

And suddenly I'd lost my appetite.

"I mean," he continued, "I... believe so, but... but our problems are... were... are... well, they're more than that."

What do you know? Something else I could believe.

"Talli...if... if you hadn't... would you have stayed?"

I thought back to how it had been between us, how strained, how distant. I remembered the biting remarks, the pressure to be absolutely perfect, the near anxiety attack I would feel if he found out that I'd forgotten something. I remembered the fights, the cold shoulders, the snarky comments, the icy glares...

"I...don't know, Jase. I don't know."

And with that answer from me, he set his sandwich on the desk with a sigh. But just when I expected him to get up and leave, he instead took a long drink of Dr. Pepper, raised his eyebrow and said, "Guess it's a good thing we're in a better place now, then, isn't it?"

Don't melt, don't melt, don't melt...

"Yeah," I replied. "Guess so."

"Besides," he drew the word out as he picked his sandwich back up, "you know, this Columbus thing... you still owe my five minutes."

"What?" I asked incredulously as he took a generous bite of his sandwich. He raised his eyebrows at my question, as if he was saying I should know. "You really think you haven't gotten your five minutes yet?" He shook his head. "No?! What do you mean no? I was at your house for fucks sake."

He swallowed his food and took a large drink of his Dr. Pepper before he answered. "I mean... no, I didn't. What are the rules?"

"It has to be five minutes."

"Five minutes what?"

"Alone."

"And?"

"Uninterrupted," I added.

"Correct, correct."

"Okay, so if you're saying we didn't get that at the house,"

"Hell no we didn't," he said.

"Um, two words. Groves Point."

His face flamed bright red, and for one brief moment I was going to tell him ha ha, too bad, so sad, your five minutes were up.

But first we were interrupted by my medical assistant asking me how much longer.

And then he said, "Hell, it probably didn't take five minutes anyway."

I yelped as I covered my mouth, laughing so hard that tears were forming in my eyes. "Oh hell," I gasped, still giggling as he merely sat there, one eyebrow raised, looking at me with the straightest face.

"It's not *that* funny."

"Yes, it is," I squeaked, wiping my eyes. "And... and yeah, it must have been more than five minutes. You and quickies don't mix. And then Michael,"

"Right!" he said. "We were interrupted! So there. You still owe me five minutes."

"And what the hell is this?"

"Interrupted many times, you're not eating the way you should, you have the audacity to argue with me after I brought this present to you..."

"I'm not arguing, shithead!"

"Talia?" The medical assistant was at my door again.

"I'm coming, I'm coming," I said with a sigh as I stood up, being sure to aim a swift kick at Jase's shin for the laugh he was unsuccessfully trying to stifle.

"I guess that's my cue to go," he said as he stood.

"Sorry I didn't have much time," I said, crinkling up my nose, and he laughed.

"It's all right." As his arms encircled me, I could feel any remote traces of stress dwindle away. I buried my face in his chest, breathing him in before reluctantly stepping back.

"Thank you, for everything."

His eyes clouded over a moment, just as I remembered the name of that song... that song I was so sure had been for...

"Don't believe everything you hear, okay? Please?"

....me.

"I'll try?" I grinned a little sheepishly, a shiver rushing through me as his lips brushed up against my hair.

"I'll see you."

"Huh? Oh... yeah... I'll s..."

Time stood still as his lips lightly touched mine.

And without another word, he turned and walked down the hall.

JASE

I've officially crossed the line into the 'playing dirty' field. Or... have I? I mean, technically she is my wife, regardless of the fact that our divorce hearing is scheduled the Thursday after that ball game. Still, I can't believe my fortune.

I wasn't born yesterday; I know that she had to have seen that DVD. I knew her curiosity would get the better of her eventually, but I'd also counted on her saying something to me about it. Now that I think about it, though, she kind of did. She remembered the no-holds-barred fight that ensued after she'd come home that same night, she'd called me to apologize for it. That fight had solidified my decision to go through with it, though... to finish the DVD, and to give it to her. I didn't think it would take this long, mind you, but I also hadn't taken into account all factors involved, my weakness being number one on that list.

But I did get it to her. On the sly even.

And it worked.

I wanted so badly to go with her, to see her face, to watch her as much as that game, regardless of the fact that I had done this for her. I knew how much of a fan she was, I knew she wanted to be in that stadium for that game someday, and I just wanted to be in her presence, to soak up that energy, that warmth that just radiates from her on days like... on days like...

Today.

But did I stop there? Hell no. I sweet talked the receptionist, or the medical secretary, or whoever she was into getting me back there before the slick doctor even knew I was in the area, before he could sweep in and save Talli's day. Did I expect it to evolve into a lunch date? Hell no, which also worked in my favor. My gentlemanly ways not only impressed her, but bought me more time to be there, be with her, to drink in all of that energy that surrounded her. And we talked, we really talked. Not all of it was pleasant, but... we talked. As I drove home, thinking about how excited she was to take the kids to one of the shows, my palms started sweating, and not out of nervousness either. Out of excitement, out of joy, out of holy shit I can't believe this is happening this day is too damn good to be true, minus the whole Bree part.

And then... then, as we were saying goodbye, when my peripheral vision caught sight of that doctor coming down that hallway...

I played dirty.

I still can't believe I did it. I can't believe I actually just... kissed her. I mean, what the hell was I thinking? Other than, mother fucker you need to step off she's mine. Oh, and damn she looks too beautiful for words. I'm sure the occasional I want to lock this door and have my way with her crossed my mind as well, but... but I just kissed her. Very soft, very fast.

And panicked.

Was I going to let ol slick doctor there know I had just potentially fucked up royally? Hell no. So I turned, as cool as you please, and walked out. Did I mention I was whistling *Puff the Magic Dragon* underneath my breath as I passed him? I'm so going to hell. But at least I have this stupid fucking grin on my face, and this song in my heart that's screaming to get out.

"Yo! Tommy!" I shouted as I entered the house, my voice echoing off the walls. What the hell, was he taking a nap or something? I grabbed a beer from my fridge, since I could have those in there now, and walked towards the stairs. "I said... Yo! Tommy!"

About that time, I heard the raucous laughter coming from the second floor, probably the game room if I wasn't mistaken. "Holy shit, just kill me and get it over with!" Damien said, his laughter loud along with an "Aw, dude, that was harsh."

"Hey, you told me to kill you," was Tommy's reply as I stuck my head in where the two of them, plus Jackie, were all playing something on the 360.

"Hey," I said, smiling so damn much my face hurt.

"Well?" Tommy asked, his attention taken away from the game long enough for Jackie to take advantage. "Ahhhh, man that's cheating!"

"Nah, that's playing the game," Jackie replied, and I had to laugh just watching him get all caught up in it.

"So, I take it that it went... well?" Tom asked as he kept his attention on the screen.

"Yeah... yeah it did. Hey Damien, can I borrow you for a bit?"

"Yeah, sure... what's up...dude... are you wearing lip gloss?" he asked slowly as he focused on my face.

Was I what?

I looked at him like he was off his damn rocker as I slowly ran the back of my hand over my lips...

Oh hell.

Remnants of that shiny, glittery gloss that she'd been wearing... seriously, she really had been, and now that I thought about it, it looked really fucking sexy on her, and...

They were all staring at me now, their video game forgotten.

"What?"

"How the hell did you get lip gloss on? Unless...." Tom's voice faded as his smile brightened.

"Wow. Never knew you had it in you, Jase," Jackie deadpanned.

"I did," Damien added, raising one hand. "Just for the record."

"Did you now?" Jackie asked teasingly, prompting Damien to flip him off.

"All of you can fuck off," I said, unable to contain that fucking smile anymore. "You coming, Damien?"

"Hell nah, you can't walk out of here!" Tom exclaimed, standing up and walking over. "So... surprise?"

"Um..." I bit my bottom lip and shrugged. "Awesome."

"So you're going with her?" he asked.

"Wait, what surprise?" Damien cut in.

"And going where?" Jackie added.

"Dude had me get her tickets to the holy grail of all Ohio State games."

"Isn't it blasphemous for a Penn State fan to do that shit?" Damien asked, and again I flipped him off.

"And you're going?" Jackie asked, smiling as he looked at me.

"Yup."

"I'm sorry, you're what?" Chris asked as he walked up behind me, causing me to nearly jump out of my skin.

"Fuck, Chris, don't do that! Damn, have you never heard of knocking?"

"We need to talk, Jase," he said, motioning towards the door down the hall.

"Great," I said with a roll of my eyes. "I finally get my parade and your ass comes to rain on it. Damien, give me a few, okay? I got this... thing in my head..."

"I ain't helping your ass with no 'thing' in your 'head'," he said smoothly, grinning as they started up another game.

"Ha ha very funny."

"Hey, Jase?" Tom said, and I turned towards him. His smile was warm as he said, "Congrats."

"I owe you," I replied, pointing at him. He laughed as I walked down the hallway, Chris on my heels, feeling as if I were going to the principal's office rather than my own. I unlocked the door, not giving a damn that the room was a mess when Chris entered behind me, although the first thing he noticed was...

"You've been playing." He pointed to my guitar that was lying across the sofa rather than in its perch. I picked it up, carefully setting it in its stand.

"Yeah. Quite a bit, actually." I knew he had shut the door by the drop in noise level, and I sat down in one of the chairs, swiveling to face him. "You don't look pleased."

"You agreed to appearances, and you're making plans for dates where you're supposed to be elsewhere," he said, handing a schedule to me.

"So I'll tell him I can't go to that one," I said with a shrug, placing the paper on my desk.

"Tell me exactly why."

Seriously? Was he deaf?

"I'm going to the Michigan, Ohio State game."

"You're... you're what?"

"This will be the third time you heard me. I said I'm going to the Michigan, Ohio State game."

"With Talli."

I smiled at the small, curt statement. "Yep. With Talli."

"The Saturday before your divorce."

And my smile fell. "Yeah, the Saturday before the divorce. So what, Chris?"

"Just tell me, Jase," he said, sitting in the chair in front of me. "What then? What are you going to do in Ohio with someone who's taking you to court just a few days later?"

"That's my own damn business," I muttered.

"Look... I know... you know, this isn't even coming from a professional point of view, okay? This is personal. I know that you're a bit short-sighted when it comes to her, a bit blinded."

"Fuck you, Chris."

"Damn it, would you listen? I know what it's like, to love someone that much. I would just hate to see you get your hopes up sky high that this weekend will change her mind when weeks living in this house with you didn't."

I scowled, picking at what was sure to be a hole in the knee of my jeans. "It's different, Chris," I said softly, a bit uncomfortable having this conversation with someone who wasn't exactly in Talli's corner.

"I hope so," he said with a sigh. "For you, for those kids... hell, even for her, I hope so."

I glanced up, eyeing him suspiciously. "What's that supposed to mean?"

"It means I know she loves you too."

She used to, Chris. She used to. And I can make it happen again. Instead of correcting him, though, I stayed silent, looking at him as if he'd grown another head.

"Hell, maybe you two just... rushed into..."

"Damn it, Chris,"

"The *divorce*, Jase. Let me finish, okay? I feel that maybe those papers were filed a bit too soon."

Now I really think he's lost it.

"But if you tell her I said that, I'll call you a liar."

"What should I tell her then?" I asked slowly, still waiting for the 180.

"Tell her..." He thought for a moment before his face broke out in a huge grin. "Tell her I said, 'Go Blue'."

"Dudes," Tom said a couple hours later, interrupting the song Damien and I were practicing, "I'm starving. Italian, anyone?"

"I think we both are. Damien, not so much," I commented, looking over at Damien who shook his head.

"Smart ass. Let's hit up that restaurant, the one T was raving about last Christmas."

"What... restaurant last Christmas? What the hell did I miss?" I asked, standing up and putting my guitar back in its stand.

"Everything. Last Christmas anyway," he said. I glared for a brief moment, then let out a resigned sigh.

"Yeah, you're right. So, which one is it?"

"I think," Jackie said as he fished his keys out of his pocket, "that it's the one on Melrose."

"The one she and Jaden always went to?" Damien asked, and Jackie nodded.

"What restaurant she and Jaden went to?" I demanded, following everyone as they made their way down the stairs.

"Just come with us," Jackie said. "I'll drive."

Which was probably a good thing, since I was introduced to an incredible red wine at said restaurant. That wine was flowing freely around most of the table, Jackie declining graciously. Damien, Tom, and I proceeded to partake of its goodness along with the most incredible fettuccine alfredo known to man.

"Holy shit, this place is amazing," I said, leaning back with my glass in hand. "Prefect ending to an almost perfect day."

"What do you mean almost?" Tom asked with a grin. "Dude, you are getting away with your woman for a weekend, what's not perfect about that?"

"She's... well..." I stammered a bit, so afraid to voice the fact that I hardly thought of her as mine at the time. "I was more referring to this morning."

"What... what was this morning?" Tom asked.

"The record company pretty much strong-armed him into doing some dates on the same bill as the one and only Ms. Hamilton," Jackie explained.

"And I'm not getting on stage with that bitch," I added, my words only slightly slurred

"You're in public," he reminded me, and I rolled my eyes.

"Yeah, I... I also have to behave myself where others can see and hear me. Can you believe that shit?"

"We need another bottle," Damien said as he emptied the rest of it into his glass.

"Damn straight we do," I agreed. "And... and Damien here said he's going with

me, for the... um, the..."

"Shows," Damien finished.

"Right, the shows."

"Awesome, so just like an acoustic thing, you two?" Tom asked.

"Maybe. Dunno. The rest of the band hasn't gotten... have they gotten back with us?" I asked Jackie, who grinned as he shook his head no. "So, maybe."

"So, back to this whole... game thing," Damien said, right about the time I heard a voice that was the equivalent of nails on a chalk board.

"Hi there, babies."

I groaned as Bree walked straight up behind me, giving me a hug from behind. "Would you go away? It's boy's night here."

"Temper, temper," she purred into my ear. "Do you need reminded of our meeting this morning?" I pulled away from her, shrugging her hands off my shoulders as she laughed.

"Is there something you need help with, Ms. Hamilton?" Jackie asked, his voice firm and authoritative. Thank God he was with us and hadn't been drinking.

"Nothing, he can't take care of Jackie," she replied, her hand back on my shoulder, and again I shook it off. "So, let me go get a chair, and..."

"No."

In surround sound stereo, all four of us men said it at the same time, causing more than one patron at the restaurant to turn our way. I turned in my chair, glancing up at her, keeping the look and my tone as nice as I could. "You're interrupting, Bree, and that's really not cool so... go back to your table or whatever."

"Ah, Jase... Jase..." she ran her fingers through my hair which I swear almost caused bile to come into my throat. "I already got what I wanted."

And in my inebriated state, I didn't know what the hell she was talking about.

Until the next morning, that is.

"What the hell?" I groaned, wanting to vomit at the shit that I was bombarded with in my email, my twitter, and on the front page of *Celebrity Gossip*. Tommy was muttering something about how Bree must have set it up, must have had someone waiting with a photographer to make it look like a hell of a lot more than it was.

"You need," he said as he handed me two ibuprofens and a sports drink that my ass had forgotten the night before, "to just give that bitch a verbal beat down."

"I can't," I said, exasperated. "Not in public, anyway, and she knows it." I grabbed my phone, scrolling through the numbers as quickly as I could.

"So you're calling her to cuss her ass out?" he asked.

"No," I replied, hitting the send button. "Something much more important."

"Hello?" her soft voice floated through the line.

"Talli," I began, my nerves causing my voice to shake, "I'm so sorry... I just... it's not what it looks like, okay? I swear."

She was quiet for the longest moment before she took in a deep breath and said, "Jackie already called me, Jase. About an hour ago."

"He did? I... well, I just woke up to this shit, I... I wanted to call you. Myself."

"Thank you. I appreciate that."

Wow, she sounded really calm. Almost too calm. No mention of our kiss, either. This could go either way.

"And here I thought," she continued, "that you were calling to cancel on me."

"Are you fucking kidding me?" I asked with a laugh, still a bundle of nerves regardless of what she was saying. "I... um, I was going to call today, start setting everything up."

"Good luck with that," she replied with a soft laugh. "Getting rooms this close to the game is a bitch."

And as she said that, I thought to myself... not rooms baby, just room. Just one. And it's going to be wonderful, magical. I won't push her into anything she isn't ready for; hell, I'll even take the couch so she can have the bed, or the floor if I can't get a big enough room.

And we'll talk. I'll lay it all out on the line for her, tell her exactly what she means to me, tell her how much I love her. I'll get those five minutes and I will use every single second to beg for one more chance.

Just one more chance.

But even with all of these elaborate plans, even with her acting as if the previous night was no big deal, even if every single detail fell into place...

Would Bree still be in between us, even when we were all alone?

CHAPTER 15

TALIA

S ometimes we see things we don't want to see, aren't intended to see. Sometimes... sometimes those things hurt more than words can ever describe.

Like walking in on the man you love hovering over someone else, someone who is moaning, someone he is kissing. Someone who is naked in your bed, fucking your husband. And your husband is a very, very willing participant, when he hasn't touched you in months.

It rips your heart out. It changes you. It distorts your way of thinking. And sometimes, no matter how far in the distance that memory is, it creeps up. It haunts you. It dangles itself in front of your face just when you feel you can move past it.

And sometimes...

Sometimes the things you witness, that you were never intended to...

Sometimes they give you hope. Sometimes they strengthen your resolve.

Sometimes they make you question the bad and wonder... was it really what it seemed?

Okay, so I'm not making sense here. Let me rewind a bit. Let me start with the cloud twelve million I was on after Jase left, and how it all crashed down around me within a few short minutes.

"So," Paul said as he walked up to me, his eyebrows high, "what was that about?"

"A game." No, not just a game, *the* game, but I didn't expect Paul to understand.

"Yeah, you can say that again."

"What the hell is that supposed to mean?" I asked with a laugh, grabbing my lab coat on my way to see my next patient.

"We'll talk later," was all he said, placing a kiss on my cheek before taking the same route Jase had and heading out of the office.

I couldn't help but wonder what the hell he was talking about, which kept me just a little distracted while I did my next patient's 20 week checkup, going over her ultrasound report with her and congratulating her on keeping her pregnancy weight under control. I really knew I was distracted when I called her husband Jase, and apologized all over myself on my way out.

"I have November's schedule finished," Dr. Stewart was saying as I passed her in the hallway, and I cringed.

"About that…"

"Oh boy. Come to my office after your next patient," she said with a laugh.

And that went bad. Well, not so bad that I couldn't shake it off, and I got the time off with the promise that I would be straight in that Monday morning, no questions and no extensions. It was the interrogation, the look of confusion on her face as she slowly digested my words.

"I… I'm just a little confused here," she said as I told myself to just keep smiling, it would all be all right.

"If it makes you feel any better, so am I," I muttered, rubbing my temple.

"So, you're going away for the weekend with your soon to be ex-husband? Just a few days before your divorce?"

I blushed, shuffling my feet. "Yeah," I said softly.

"So he just asked you to go away with him? Really?"

"Not… exactly."

Her eyebrow shot up at my words. "If you don't mind my asking…"

"He just got the tickets for me," I said, shrugging. "And… and I asked him to come with."

"Instead of your boyfriend."

"My *what*?" I asked with a laugh.

"Paul," she explained. "Dr. Coffman."

"He's not my... I don't have a boyfriend, Alicia, I'm married." I bit the inside of my lip after the words tumbled from my lips, my eyes instantly averting to my folded hands.

My rings were still there.

How could I possibly consider myself being married? I was in the middle... no, not even the middle... I was in the end stages of divorce, merely waiting for that hearing date to roll around to make it official. And it was a divorce that I had wanted, that I had initiated, that I had pursued.

And I didn't have to ask myself why.

Because suddenly, there it was in front of me. Those images, all over again. The sounds, the candles, the roses-- oh, how I *hate* roses now! And he'd done all of that for her.

For the bitch whose voice was coming through the speakers of our office radio, singing with my husband, singing the song she announced on television was for her.

What was I doing?

But back to the Paul being considered my boyfriend thing... see, that was really irking me, to the point where I had to talk to the one person who wouldn't bullshit me in the least.

"Jaden, am I dating Paul?"

"Well, yeah. Duh," her voice went straight through that phone line and to my heart.

"I am?" I asked, nearly squeaking. "But... but we're just friends."

"Friends that you have lunch with, go to dinner with..."

"I haven't been out to dinner with him since the whole paparazzi thing," I cut her off.

"Friends that you spend all your waking time with, friends that you're constantly on the phone with..."

And the more she went on and on, the more I was beginning to see a pattern. And not just for myself, either.

"That... asshole!"

"How does this make Paul an asshole?" she asked, and I sighed.

"No, not... not him. Jase. Jase was... he was *dating* Bree, right in front of me!"

"Which you knew, in your own way. Which was why you gave him all kinds of hell no matter how much he denied it."

"Yeah, but..." I sighed, sinking back into my chair. "I need a drink."

"Can't help you there, sweetheart."

"I know, I know. Jaden, what do I do?"

"Well, you talk to Paul, for starters. Because if you're not dating him, he should be on that list of 'need to know'."

"Yeah, and he's really not going to understand about the game."

"Game?"

"Yeeeeah," I said, dragging the word out. "Um... can I say long story and leave it at that?"

"Hell no. Ethan's sleeping, you have my full attention, and your ass needs to spill."

"I didn't mention this to you?" I asked, stalling.

"Damn it Talli..."

"Oh, all right, all *right*. Jase got me tickets to the OSU game with... that team up North," I said, unable to contain my smile as I looked down at that little envelope.

"Holy shit, he pulled it off?"

"Hey, you bitch, you knew about this?" I asked, and she laughed.

"Damn straight I did! Soooooooo?"

"So, he's... well, he's kinda coming with me," I said, my voice growing softer with every word, shaking my head as she began to cheer.

"Well, hot damn!" she finally said. "Good news at last."

"We're going to Columbus that weekend," I continued. "He... well, he's supposed to be handling the transportation and the rooms."

"Rooms? Plural? No. No, that won't do."

"It has to do."

"Why? You afraid he's going to screw you into submission so you drop this farce of a divorce?"

"Hey... fuck you! You're supposed to be my best friend!" I exclaimed, my face on absolute fire.

"I am your best friend and admit it. Just... admit it. It's crossed your mind."

You know what I hate about having Jaden as a best friend? The same damn thing I love about having her as my best friend. Because she knows me so well.

Of course, I'd thought about it. And the more I thought about it, weighing the pros and cons, the more confused it made me. If I didn't love him, this wouldn't be a problem. But I do. And every time I think about how much I love him, how much I want him, how much I am going into absolute withdrawals without his arms around me, my mind goes back to her.

I was getting cabin fever, too, if it could be called that. I was itching to get out of the condo, out for an evening, and after my little discussions with Dr. Stewart and Jaden, the last person I needed to call was Paul. No, that just wasn't going to do... so imagine my surprise when I saw Sondra's name on my caller id.

"What," she began, "is this about you and Jase going to Ohio in November?"

"How the hell did you know?" I asked.

"Puh-lease. Chris is up in arms trying to rearrange his schedule so he can go."

"Yeah? Good."

And then I stopped, fumbling over myself. He had plans, as in a schedule, as in stuff for his music... and he said no... to be with me?

I sank down into my chair, my fingertips touching my lips as Sondra continued on, relaying how pissed off people from the record company were, all the while thinking... I was that important?

Me?

"So, I was thinking," Sondra continued, "and I talked to Linda about it already, please don't hate me."

"Not... not hating," I said, still reeling.

"We need to go out, even if it's just for dinner. What about that Italian restaurant, that one on Melrose?"

"Oh, I haven't been there in forever!" I said, snapped out of my daze. "That would... you know what? Yeah, that would be wonderful."

Wonderful. Needed. Perhaps deserved, even. So as I got myself ready, explaining to Elizabeth that I was going out to dinner and no they absolutely were not coming with, I could find my spirits lifting.

It was going to be a good night.

I could feel it.

So with the two of us tucked in a back corner of the restaurant, we began the wine and gossip fest that we had denied ourselves since before I'd even moved out of that house. Some topics were off limits, in their own way, but Sondra... yeah, she's always been pretty good about saying things without actually... *saying* anything.

"So Chris is completely up in arms," she said, her eyes twinkling with mischief.

"Isn't he always?"

"So true, so true. Dude needs to lighten up. Anyhow, the record company demanded that Jase make these appearances, but apparently Jase's chosen to finally put his big boy pants on and make demands of his own."

I let out a short laugh, my hand covering my mouth to keep from spitting my sip of wine out. "Oh, Sondra, that's hilarious. But seriously... now?"

"Oh yeah, now. As far as I know, it will be just Jase and Damien, just a handful of shows, but you didn't..."

"Hear that from you," I said with a nod, taking another sip of wine to suppress my grin. I could only imagine what the record company was demanding.

"So, they give Chris the schedule, and *bam!* Right off Jase can't make two of them, and he's *refusing* to budge."

I blushed, a smile tugging at the corners of my mouth.

"And I asked Chris why, and all he would say was 'Go Blue'."

"What?!" I asked quickly. "Hmph. Rat bastard."

"See, but I didn't know what he was talking about, until I Googled that phrase, right? Don't laugh. I've never been a fan of football."

"I know, I know. I've forgiven you."

"So, I cornered Chris about it in the middle of his big rant after he gets his ass reamed by the record label, right?" she continued on, a commotion from the other end of the room interrupting us. We glanced over and I could feel a combination of excitement and annoyance.

What the hell were the boys doing here?

"Did you tell them we were coming here?" I hissed quietly, and she shook her head no.

"Do you want to..."

"No," I said quickly, positioning myself to where I couldn't easily be seen. "Damn it, he would bring Tommy here."

"You know you want to say 'hi'," she teased.

"Not now, not now." I turned and took another drink of my wine. "Fucking men, always interrupting."

"Tell me about it. Anyhow... where was I?"

"Chris getting his ass reamed by the record company," I replied, thanking the waiter when our food was brought to us.

"Right, so... so I asked him about the game, and he just went off about how Jase was going to Ohio with you, about how he was going to get pummeled into little pieces, whatever that meant, and how you couldn't even bother to ask your boyfriend..."

"Oh for fucks sake, I don't *have* a boyfriend," I said for what seemed like the millionth time that day. "Paul and I are *just* friends, and I'm going by *my* definition, not Jase's."

"Meee-ow," she purred with a wink.

"Thank you. I try."

"Rumor has it a certain rock star is determined to keep it that way," she said, a smug grin on her lips as she took another sip of wine.

"Oh yeah? Who is he to..."

I cringed as the bitch from hell's voice was audible all the way over at our table. My voice trailed off as I watched a slight scene unfold.

Did he just push her hands off of him?

"Hey, I know for a fact it was just the boys today," Sondra said quietly, leaning over the table a bit. I know she was trying to distract me, trying to take my attention away from...

Whoa. That was one mean ass look he shot her.

"You set this up," I said, my voice barely above a whisper as I turned back to Sondra.

"Oh hell no I didn't," she replied, and I could tell that she was being honest. "We're just in the wrong place at the wrong..."

"NO!"

That in stereo reply from all of the boys caused us to collapse in a fit of giggles that we were trying oh so desperately to keep quiet. The last thing I wanted right at that moment was to be seen by anyone. Not any potential tabloid squealers, not Jase, and most definitely not...

"Okay, she's leaving."

I licked my lips before taking another sip of wine, again trying to stifle my giggles.

"Wow," someone from the next table spoke up. "What a tramp."

Sondra raised her eyebrows along with her glass. I slightly tapped her glass with mine, saying a very soft, "Cheers," before we took a drink.

We actually managed to eat, pay, and make our way out to catch a cab without being seen by a single member of his well-inebriated party. Minus Jackie, it seemed he had been designated as the sober person for the evening. I was still smiling the next morning, even when that phone call that I knew was coming arrived. Bless Sondra's heart, she hadn't said a word to them about us being there, just like she'd promised. And as I thanked Jackie, I almost felt guilty about not telling him we'd already seen it. I almost felt guilty about not saying a word to Linda about where we'd went.

I just wasn't ready to.

See, I had too much to process right at that moment.

I had seen him publicly just... shrug her off. Practically push her away. Give her the look of death. And I didn't know what it meant. It certainly didn't mean what the damn tabloids were making it out to be, but I was beginning to see how they twisted everything, even if some of the information they had was the truth.

And I had the knowledge that he was demanding that weekend off, the weekend of the game. I also knew that his record company was threatening him if he didn't go, so I was half expecting him to cancel on me anyhow.

And damn it, Paul is *not* my boyfriend!

The children were actually up, playing in their rooms and not pestering me when my phone rang about an hour after Jackie had called. I knew who it was; there was no question who it would be. He'd promised me full disclosure, right?

But I'd heard the excuses before. And the moment I heard his voice, I could see him.... Not from the night before, but then. Then when he'd been right in my face yelling at me about how Bree was nothing more than a friend, and how he was sick and tired of my accusations. I calmly explained to him that Jackie had called, and I waited.

I waited for him to cancel.

But he didn't.

And I told him that getting rooms was a bitch, and he told me not to worry about it. He could handle it. He didn't correct me, though; he'd left it at rooms. Plural.

Just a few short days before our divorce, I will be halfway across the country with him. I will be sitting beside him in the freezing cold, as close as I could not just for body heat but because I miss him. That much. And I'll fight off these memories that keep haunting me... the ones from before, and the ones from last night. I will try and keep the negativity at bay and try to tell my heart to just shut up.

Just. Shut. Up.

Because last night, that wasn't the look he'd had on his face the night he'd been with her.

Was it?

Because in that bedroom, he was kissing her back, not trying to pull away.

Right?

And when Jaden called with a sigh, saying "I see Scooby Douche is at it again," all I could do was sigh.

"What should I do, Jaden? I don't know what to do."

"Sure you do," she replied, her voice soft and kind. "Just follow your heart."

So I will.

JASE

At least one good thing had come from my record company's demands... I was far too busy for the time to creep by. Damien and I finished up three new songs, had them demoed and ready to go, and had several different acoustic sets ready for the shows lined up. All that, *plus* I'd had a lot of time with the children, not one single argument with Talia, and one short but sweet phone call from my sister in law.

Oh yeah.

Talli's *not* dating Paul.

So I couldn't help but smile a little wider, stand a little taller.

And I couldn't help myself. When she asked me to take care of the rooms for our trip to Columbus, I did.

Ish.

I mean, they're *rooms*... they're just a connected. You know, as in... a suite. With only one bed. But it has a couch, too, just in case, but if that five minutes works...

"We're home, Mommy!" Michael announced as Talli held that door opened up for us the Wednesday before that trip.

"You think?" she asked with a laugh, her expression softening even more when she saw Emily fast asleep in my arms.

"Sorry," I said, crinkling my nose up. "Thanks for letting me keep them later, though."

"What can I say? I'm a sucker when you beg," she teased, taking Emily from my arms as I turned several shades of red.

Is that so?

So I suppose she won't mind this weekend, now, will she?

"Oh yeah, I know when you say nothing, I've won," she called out as she walked down the hallway.

"We'll both win," I mumbled, a smile tugging at the corners of my lips when... when...

She turned the opposite way. She's not going to her bedroom.

Where is she taking Em?

"We'll play in Michael's room," Elizabeth stated, and Talli quickly said no.

"You have school, they have daycare," I heard her say. "And then after that..."

"We go to Linda's!" Michael exclaimed before running out and throwing his arms around me. "Night Daddy. Tuck me in?"

"Yeah... yeah, sure," I said, picking him up and heading towards his bedroom. And I totally wasn't doing this to spy, to see what the hell was going on. I'd made that decision that if Talli wanted me to know something, she'd tell me.

Just as I'd told her nearly everything.

There were some things I was saving, though, for that five minutes.

When we were alone, when we would be uninterrupted. When I could take the time, stretch it out as long as I had to, and tell her the truth. All of the truth. And hope that she believed me.

"Okay, we'll get you... dude, your shirt's backwards," I said to Michael, setting him on his bed and helping him fix it.

"Mommy says you're not raising a dude, you're raising a man."

I had to smile at his words. That was something that Talia had stated from the beginning, that she would not be raising him to be some random guy. He was going to have manners, he was going to have values and morals, and he was going to know how to treat a woman.

I faltered momentarily, knowing I'd been far from a perfect example.

"Hey."

I jumped slightly at the sound of Talli's voice and I glanced over my shoulder, smiling at her.

"Just helping Little Man here." I adjusted his shirt, giving him one last kiss and hug before I laid him down, pulling his covers up.

"And no getting up in the middle of the night," Talli said as she walked over, leaning down to give him his good night kiss.

Oh hell, she looks good bent over like...

Damn it, Warner, stop! She's leaning over our son's bed!

I turned to try and keep her from seeing the blush that was sure to have crept up into my cheeks, and also -- if I must admit it-- to keep from staring at her ass any longer. Besides, in two more sleepless nights I would be picking her up.

For our weekend.

Together.

"I want a kiss, too!" Elizabeth pouted from her bedroom.

"Sssh," Talli said, walking with me towards Elizabeth's room. "You'll wake your sister."

I stood in that doorway, trying desperately to swallow over that lump in my throat as I took in the darkened scene before me. Talli had walked in, glancing down into Emily's crib where she was sleeping straight through, and then she'd leaned beside Elizabeth, kissing her cheek.

Our girls...

Emily was sharing a room with Elizabeth, just as she has been at my house.

With her sister.

Not her mother.

"Daddy!" Elizabeth whined, and I pushed myself off the door frame and walked straight over to her.

"Good night, Baby Girl," I said, kissing her temple, willing the tears to stay away. Talli was pulling a blanket over Emily as I walked past, my hands trembling, suddenly at a complete loss for words. What was I supposed to say? And this… this makes me so very happy, and yet at the same time my heart ached so badly.

"Thank you, by the way."

I nodded as her voice washed over me.

"That was an ingenious move, having the two of them together. It really does help, you know?"

I nodded again, my eyes sliding shut as her hand came to rest on my arm.

"And I'm sorry."

My eyes opened and I couldn't stop myself from looking over at her, the sincerity in her features fighting off that chill that was trying so hard to creep in.

"I'm so sorry that I didn't listen… that I didn't even try."

I shrugged, doing my best to smile. "Live and learn," was all I could say, then instantly wanted to kick my own ass. "But… it's…"

I couldn't say it was okay. Because it wasn't okay, because right on the tip of my tongue was the 'why' and the 'what if' and…

My thoughts scattered off in the wind as she wrapped her arms around my waist in a quick hug, and as she began to pull away I finally snapped out of my daze.

And I held her.

And it felt so good.

"We can do this," I heard her murmur, and as I drove away that night all kinds of confused, I began to think over the million different definitions of 'this' that she could possibly be talking about.

"Linda!" I called out in a panic. "Linda, I can't find…"

"The airline tickets are in the top drawer of your desk in the office, right where you told me you put them," she cut me off, and I couldn't help but smile. I stuck my head around the corner, grinning at her while she straightened up Talli's room that the children had all but destroyed the night before.

"You're an angel."

"So you keep telling me." She grinned back as she asked, "So…"

"That's a loaded word there, Linda," I said as my doorbell rang. "Crap, am I expecting somebody?"

"Not that I'm aware of," she replied as I walked down the hallway. I spied Kate's little red sports car through my window and my smile widened instantly. Whoops. I had been expecting somebody.

And she may not be very happy with me.

"Evans!" I exclaimed, pulling her in and swinging her around.

"Holy hell, Warner," she giggled, "I missed you, too!"

"Come in, come in… not that you're not here already," I said, dragging her by her hand to that front room, where the black and white pictures of the children now adorned the walls.

"Oh, those are gorgeous!"

"Aren't they?" I agreed, smiling up at them, my eyes resting on an empty spot.

I knew exactly which picture I wanted to go there.

"Sooooo the east coast was lovely, as I was telling you on the phone, and I am in for some serious work ahead of me this week."

"Don't you have three more weddings out here?"

"Yes," she said with a sigh, sinking back into her chair. "But… I have tonight free, so get your shit together and come with me."

I felt my face grow hot as I stammered slightly. "I… I can't, Kate."

She frowned as she asked, "Why the hell not? We made plans, remember?"

"I… I know, and I'm so sorry, but…" I began fidgeting with my shirt, shrugging with one shoulder. "There's a lot going on right now."

"The upcoming tour, you and Damien working together, you already said you wouldn't be in the studio today or tonight, so… I don't get it. What's the problem?"

"I… well, I'm leaving first thing in the morning," I said, smiling shyly.

"So? When has that ever stopped us?"

"Kate, I have so much to tell you," I said quickly. "And right now… right now I'm so fucking happy… cautiously, but happy, you know? And… just trust me. I can't, not now."

Her eyes narrowed as her eyes moved up and down, her expression softening slightly. "Look, I know this coming week is going to be really hard on you, but you don't have to put on a brave front for me."

"I'm not!" I insisted, bouncing slightly in my seat. "I'm going to Columbus tomorrow… with… with Talli."

Her eyes widened in surprise, and it was her turn to begin tripping over her words. "You're what? I mean… well, that's good, I suppose, but… you're *what*?"

"I didn't want to… to worry you or anything," I continued, "because I love you, Kate, but you do worry, sometimes about things that you shouldn't worry about. But, just… just trust me on this, okay? That surprise…"

"The tickets."

"Right! The tickets, to the Ohio State game! Tommy got them, and when I gave them to her, she asked me to go with her."

"Oh, Jase…"

I did not like the sound of pity in her voice.

"So, we're going and…"

"Jase, stop."

"And it's going to be wonderful, see? And… and then this week… it might not be so bad…"

"Are you listening to yourself?" she asked, placing a hand on my knee. "You know I want whatever makes you happy, but don't you think if she didn't want this divorce, she would have said something by now?"

"I don't know, Kate. How… how am I supposed to know that?"

"She's dating a friend of my ex husband's, that's how."

"No she's not," I said, smiling with confidence. "She told Jaden she wasn't dating him, and…"

"And you told everyone that you weren't messing around with Bree, when you obviously were."

Ouch.

"Listen, I'm... I'm not trying to downplay everything, because maybe you're right."

"I know I am," I said, with much less conviction than I'd had before.

"I'm just... well, I want you to go into this with your eyes wide open. She has been a part of your life, of your family's lives for years now, and she sees how everyone is... well, still *together*, even when they're not."

I opened my mouth to protest, but suddenly remembered every Thanksgiving, and how we spent it in Illinois with my family before my mom had moved back to Groves Point. All of my family. Both of my parents and their new spouses, everyone under the same roof. Everyone getting along.

Oh, God.

What if that's what Talli had meant, when she said we could 'do this'?

"I'm not saying that... that if you don't want this divorce that you shouldn't tell her, because you *absolutely* should. I'm just... well, coming from someone who's been there for you every time she's broken your heart, I just... I want you to be ready."

"I have to believe," I said, my voice so very small. "You... you haven't seen the difference, Kate, you haven't seen the changes."

"No, you're right, I haven't. But I can see you're already closing yourself off, shutting out..."

"I'm not shutting you out."

"You're changing your plans, you're... canceling your plans with me, and we're supposed to be friends. We are friends, right?"

"Yes," I said, taking her hand in mine. "You know we are; we've always been friends. It's just..."

"She doesn't trust you."

And again, I could feel myself blush. "No. No, she doesn't. But... I can't blame her, Kate. And I can't give her anymore reason not to."

Kate merely nodded, pulling her hand from mine as she stood.

"Please don't be mad."

She sighed heavily, pushing her dark brown hair back. "I'm more disappointed, Jase, that's all. I would have hoped after all these years you wouldn't continue to turn your back on me because whomever you're interested in doesn't approve."

"Damn it, Kate, this… she's my…"

"Wife, I know. And I'll get over it; I always do." She gave me a brief hug, pulling back as I tried to hold her closer. "Just know, that if I'm right… no, I can't say I won't be there for you. Because I will."

"Kate…"

"Don't." She held up her hand, shaking her head. "I can see myself out, okay?"

"Kate, would you…" My voice trailed off as she made her way out the door, and I flinched slightly as it clicked shut.

Oh, the memories this brought back.

I wandered back into the great room, a long sigh escaping as I sunk down into the chair she'd just occupied, remembering that lunch we'd shared all those years ago.

"You look so tired," she said softly, her hand reaching out to caress my cheek, a frown on her face as I pulled away.

"I… I'm sorry," I mumbled, my brow furrowed.

"Are you feeling all right? You've barely touched your food."

"I'm not that hungry," I admitted.

"Then why did you ask me to lunch?" she asked with a laugh.

She was so happy.

And it hurt my heart, knowing I was going to hurt her.

"I wanted to talk with you," I replied, and her smile was a little too radiant.

"Good, because I wanted to see you, to talk with you too," she continued. "The phone is just… it's so impersonal."

"Not always," I said softly.

"I'm sorry, that was insensitive of me."

She sounded so sincere when she said that.

"And it isn't my place to pry, but… but I know that you've been so upset, and I know you'd mentioned that you weren't speaking with Talli anymore."

*"No, I said we weren't **talking**," I corrected her. "We… speak almost every day."*

She blinked several times as she set her fork down, her chocolate brown eyes locked with mine. "I know that you're hurt. But you can get past this."

"I don't think I want to," I said slowly.

"I... well, I know that I've been going back and forth, and I'm sorry that I seem to be so indecisive," she continued on. "But I've missed you. And... and we've found each other again, and..."

"Have we?"

Her eyes lowered at my question, and I knew it was time.

*"Kate, we're not... we're not **dating** or anything, we've just been... we've just been talking about the past."*

"And how much it meant to us," she added. "Both of us."

*"And it **does**," I said, "but it's... it's the **past**."*

"You're just hurt right now. I know the drill, Jase. I know because I've been the one to pick up the pieces for years."

"But I don't want my pieces picked up." I shrugged slightly, my voice soft, wavering. "I don't want them swept away; I don't want them thrown away. I don't..." My voice faltered and I took a moment to compose myself, remembering Talli's words that I'd carried with me every day. "I don't want to walk away from my future for my past, Kate. I can't do that."

"'I'm... sorry, what?"

"We're friends... right?"

I needed that reassurance, just as I always did. She nodded briefly, even with the tears in her eyes.

"Because... please understand. I can't try to save my heart or try to give it to someone else. Not... not when it belongs to her."

"Jase?"

There was something in the tone of Linda's voice that made me turn to look in her direction, where she stood with the phone receiver in her hand, her face stark white.

"Hey... hey what's wrong?" I asked, moving quickly towards her.

"This... is for you," she said, holding the receiver out. "It's your mother."

"Oh fuck, what happened?" I asked in a rush, taking the phone from her and putting it up to my ear as Linda gave me a quick hug before turning and walking out of the room. "Mom? Mom, what's..."

"Oh, honey."

Oh, fuck, she's been crying.

"Mom, what's wrong? What happened?"

"I... just got off the phone with your dad... he... he's so beside himself."

"What happened?" I asked, the panic setting in, my breathing becoming erratic almost instantly.

"Honey, there's been an accident."

I sunk into the nearest chair, gripping the arm with my free hand. "Who... and... and are they okay?"

"It... was a head on collision, and..."

Head on... oh, fuck...

"Mom, please," I sobbed, shaking. "Who's hurt?"

"Tommy..."

"Tommy?" I asked, and for some strange reason a sense of calm washed over me.

"Tommy was... was on his way to Nan's house."

"Hell, Mom, Tom... he's... he's been shot at in Afghanistan, he's been hit by shrapnel from a roadside bomb, he's..."

"He's gone, Jase."

Gone?

I covered my mouth, shaking my head even though she couldn't see.

Tommy... he was... he was a rock. He was invincible.

"They said it was instant..."

No...

"...and that he felt no pain."

Not Tom.

Not my Tommy.

He was... he can't be...

"And... and I know what he did for you, and for Talli," she continued as my first sob broke free. "Jase, he'd want you to..."

"No... no, I can't do that," I said, shaking my head.

"Baby, this is..."

"She'll understand," I said through my tears, instantly thinking of Jack and how she'd dropped everything to be there.

She would understand.

"I… tell everyone I'll be there as soon as I can, okay?"

"Jase, Tommy would want…"

"He was like a…" I took in a deep shuddering breath, feeling Linda's hand on my arm. "He's like a brother to me, Mom. I… I have to be there."

I have to be there…

I don't know how long I sat there in that chair, holding onto that receiver long after I'd hung up with Mom, just stunned.

Shattered.

"I just got off the phone with Jackie," Linda said softly. "He's booking a flight, too."

"My flight…"

"He's calling Sondra to have her change it."

"Oh, God, Talli," I said, suddenly snapping out of my daze. I dialed her cell phone, knowing she was at work, and not the least bit surprised when it went to voicemail.

This was the last thing she should hear like that.

"Talli, it's… it's me," I said, sniffling slightly, trying to mask the fact that I'd been crying. "I need you to call me right away, okay? Please, this is really important."

And I left the same message on the voicemail of her office phone.

And I left the same message with the receptionist, who informed me she was in Labor and Delivery, and that they were very busy.

"Jase," Sondra said as she breezed in with my e-ticket information, "you've got to get going if you're going to make your flight."

I don't know if I can do this…

"Thank you," I murmured, my hands shaking as I shoved the paper in my pocket. "Linda?"

"I have all of the information for Talli," she said softly. "The… tickets, the hotel reservations, and I promise when she drops the children off tonight I will tell her everything."

I nodded, my bottom lip trembling.

"And I'll tell her that… that you said she could take whomever she wants to. And that you said it's… it's what Tommy would want," she added. "Are you sure that's what you want me to do?"

"I wish she could be there, in Groves Point" I admitted, trying in vain to keep my emotions in check. "Her... and... and our babies. I just need..." I crossed my arms in front of myself even as Linda pulled me into a warm embrace.

"I know, sweetheart, I know."

So instead of the most wonderful weekend of my life, I found myself sitting on a plane, alone, cold, heartbroken.

And just like that, my hope was gone.

CHAPTER 16

TALIA

"*Talli, it's... it's me.*"

Oh, this can't be good.

"*I need you to call me right away, okay? Please, this is really important.*"

Apparently it was important enough to have left the exact same message on my cell phone as well as my office phone, almost causing me to giggle. He'd definitely become the master of attempting to do the same thing each 'take'.

"Talli, I have this message for you," Nicole, our new receptionist, said as she handed me the pink slip of paper that held the exact same message.

"Thank you," I murmured, pulling out my cell phone as I hurried towards the daycare center to pick up the kids. They tended to be very cranky if I was late.

Shit.

It went straight to voicemail.

"I just got your message; I am so sorry. I have been up to my elbows in babies today, and that…well, that just sounded wrong. But I'm trying to reach you now. I'm getting the kids and taking them to Linda's, so when you get this message call me. And no backing out!" I laughed softly, then added, "I'm kidding, I'm kidding. But if something's come up, let me know."

I bit the inside of my bottom lip as I closed my phone, placing it in my purse.

Oh no… what if he **is** backing out?

"Mommy, you *has* to hurry!" Michael exclaimed as I stepped in the daycare.

"I know, I know… Linda said she'd have dinner ready by 6:30," I said, holding my hands up. "Let me sign you kids out."

"They are so excited," one of the teachers was saying. "They say it's an adventure weekend."

I smiled softly. "It kind of is."

"You know," she continued, "rumor has it…"

"And we'll just leave it at that, shall we?" I said with a wink, gathering Emily into my arms. "I have Linda's name on my contacts list, she'll be the one dropping them off and picking them up tomorrow, okay?"

"Absolutely. Oh, and Mrs. Warner?"

I turned back towards the woman, my eyebrows raised slightly.

"Good luck."

I don't think my smile could have gotten any bigger when I murmured my thanks and ushered the children out the door.

With all of the excitement that had continued to build over the passing weeks, I had honestly been looking for that shoe that was bound to drop. Seriously, it had to. We had been doing so well, getting along famously. He had been such a big help to me, taking the children when I was called in, or picking them up from daycare when I had to stay late. He had even smiled and gave me the sweetest little one-armed hug when I had forgotten my purse at work. No admonishing me, no cruel words, nothing of that sort. Something was bound to give.

I just never dreamed it would be *this*.

I was clutching the note Jase had scribbled, understanding exactly why he hadn't left the message on my voice mail.

We'd always agreed if it was something… bad, something just…

horrible it would *never* be left on voice mail.

Talli,

I'm so sorry I couldn't reach you. I swear I tried. And I hate that this is in a note, and that I wasn't there to tell you myself.

And I just don't know how else to say it.

Tommy's gone.

He was killed in a head on collision in Groves Point this morning.

I have to be there. I know you above everyone will understand. Please don't hate me. You know how much I wanted this, how much I wanted to go with you. But Tommy, he would want this for you. I've left everything with Linda... the tickets, the hotel information, and they know it will be you checking in. Go. Have a wonderful time, for all of us. Take whomever you want. Grab an airhorn.

Tommy would want this for you.

And I know you don't believe me, and I don't blame you, but I swear with everything in me that it's true.

I love you.

~J

Tommy's gone?

How the hell is this possible?

"Mommy, why are you crying?" Michael asked, but I just wasn't ready to explain it.

"Mommy's okay, baby," I lied, wiping my eyes hastily.

"I don't know what all's in the note," Linda was saying as she rubbed my back.

He loves me, Linda. He loves me! Or... or he's saying it out of grief or...

But Tommy?

"...but he went over all the instructions of what I was to say to you about a million times."

I laughed softly through my tears, leaning into her. "I think... everything's in the note."

Everything.

Does he really love me?

I just... I can't believe Tommy's gone, and I want to kick my own ass, up and down this entire town. Why didn't I go up to him, give him that big hug in that restaurant when I saw him? I mean, sure I'd called him and thanked him a million times over for getting the tickets, but… but I wouldn't get another chance now.

No more Tommy hugs that would lift me off the ground.

No more watching him play with the children, no more laughing at him practically melting whenever they walked in the room.

No more Tommy at… Thanksgiving…

"I… I can't reach Jase," I finally managed to say with a shrug.

"I know his phone was close to dying before he ever left," Jackie added, walking into the kitchen with his duffel bag on his shoulder.

"Where are you going?" I asked him, my heart aching at the tears in that big man's eyes.

"Groves Point," he answered, and I nodded, staring at the tickets in my hand.

The tickets that would take me to Ohio.

And now… now that was the last place I wanted to go.

"Oh, baby, go," Linda said, as if she could read my mind. "Have some fun, you need it."

"I'm not much in the mood for fun," I mumbled. "Not without…" My voice trailed off before I could voice what was truly on my mind.

This weekend wasn't about the game, not at all. This weekend was about Jase, about us, about how much I miss him and how much I just want to talk with him.

Honestly.

"Perhaps you could talk to that doctor friend of yours," Linda suggested, and I shook my head.

"No. No, this was…"

"I know, sweetheart. But Jase wants you to go, baby."

"He said that?" I asked, looking over at her.

"Well… no," she said, pushing my curls back. "No, he said he wished that you and the kids would be there with him. But he's thinking about *you* and…"

Wait, what?

"He wants me there?" I asked, my voice small.

"Yes, baby, he does."

He… wants me there?

"So you just go have some fun, I've got the kids, and…"

"We have to go."

I stood up, holding those tickets in my hand, brushing the tears away as Linda placed her fingertips on her lips, just like I knew she would.

"We… we have to go," I repeated, pulling out my cell phone and my wallet, my debit card securely in my hand. I made a mental note to thank Jase for paying my rent as I dialed the number to the airline, knowing I should be able to change my flight as well as adding the kids.

"It's pepperoni macaroni night!" Elizabeth was saying, jumping up and down.

"Make sure you all have enough time to eat before you go," Jackie said, giving me a quick one-armed hug. "My flight leaves about 10 tonight, see if you can get on that one. And if they say no, I'll get Sondra on their asses."

"Thank you, Jackie," I said softly.

Turns out I didn't need Sondra's help getting us on that flight, but I did enlist her help in getting the Buckeye tickets sent to Lisa overnight. Lisa, who was just beside herself and all kinds of giddy when I called her, telling me that she was calling Eric as soon as she got off the phone with me. And Jaden was calling me just as I told Lisa about Tommy, so I didn't have to listen to how sorry she was, or have her compare it to Jack because I just didn't have the time.

"Hi, baby," I said to Jaden as I clicked over. "I am so sorry."

"It's just… it's so awful," she said, sniffling. "I can't believe it."

"Mommy, why are we getting on a plane?" Michael asked, tugging on my pant leg. "Aren't we staying with Linda?"

"You're… you're coming?" Jaden asked.

"Yes… but… but can you… not say anything, please?" I asked quickly. "I can't reach Jase, and I want to tell him myself."

"Pete and I are waiting for him here, at the airport. His flight has been delayed."

"Okay, so that explains why I can't get ahold of him. Seriously, though… don't say anything."

"Nothing. I promise. Except to Gayle, and probably John so they can make sure all of you have a place to stay. Or Nan's. Our place is already full. I'm so sorry."

"I didn't even think of that," I groaned. "Thank you, Jaden, and don't worry about it. Give that baby a kiss for me, okay? I'll see you tomorrow."

"I will... and... Talli, thank you. This is going to mean so much."

I thought back to the wedding reception, when Tommy had my feet a good 10 inches off the ground as he called out to Jase, telling him *that* was how he swept someone off their feet.

And I remembered him throwing Michael up in the air, only laughing when Michael spit up all over his face.

Then there was the phone call...

"T, let me tell you... I know how you feel, okay?"

"Yeah, the game... it's... it's going to be amazing, Tommy. Absolutely amazing."

"No, I mean... about Jase, about him being with someone else."

I couldn't say another word as I remembered that he and I had essentially gone through the same thing.

"But he loves you, Talli. And you don't have to say anything to me, you don't have to agree or disagree, just... you asked him to go with you for a reason."

Damn straight I had.

"If nothing else, T, just... hear him out, okay? Just hear him out. Give him those five minutes. Would you do that for me?"

I was going to do that anyhow, but now...

I looked up at the night sky as Jackie helped put the luggage in the back of the van.

"I'll do this for you," I whispered, somehow knowing he was listening. "For you... and... for us too."

JASE

This was not how this weekend was supposed to be.

"Why don't you try and get some sleep?" Mom had said to me as I sat in that chair by the window, an old photo album in my hand. I looked up at her briefly before shaking my head and returning my attention to the pictures. I felt her soft kiss on my temple before I heard her exit the room.

See, I wasn't supposed to be sitting in this chair in Groves Point right now.

I was supposed to be pacing the halls of my house, checking my watch, going over to that condo early to pick Talli up for breakfast under the guise that I was running late and was starving. And I would promise her a double shot caramel macchiato from Starbucks if she would come with me. And she would, because I know her, and she would have been packed by at least the night before.

But I'm here.

And I'm looking at these pictures of scrawny little Tommy Warner taken when he stayed with us in Illinois. And I'm remembering.

Tommy and I ran away from the creek, knowing we'd just been the one place we were forbidden to go, giggling like a couple of girls the entire way. He had our treasure in a baggie in his hand, holding it out in front of him as we ran, dodging trees and hiding behind bushes to keep from getting caught.

"Do you think," he asked, half out of breath, "they'd notice if we brought the tadpoles in?"

"Nah," I answered in all my naivety. "We'll just put them in Pete's room, say he did it if they get all... weirded out or anything."

Which, of course they did. And they never believed that Pete hadn't gone to the creek after we'd all been strictly forbidden to, because Tommy... he was a good kid, and me? I could charm my way out of anything.

My how things have changed.

I turned the page, letting out a short laugh at the pictures from summer camp. Ah, the time we set up the rival cabin, putting buckets of water, paint, whatever we could get our hands on over each of their doors. We couldn't even blame that one on Pete if we'd gotten caught, but lucky for us that time we hadn't. Almost, though. Almost...

"You boys seem to be in an awfully good mood this morning," Mr. Taylor, one of the camp counselors, said to us as he took a seat at our otherwise deserted table.

"We just had a good night sleep, sir," I replied with a grin, kicking

Tom's shin underneath the table when he began to laugh. He covered with a cough, straightening up when Mr. Taylor turned his eyes to him.

"Coming down with something, son?"

"Aller... allergies," Tom finally managed to say, covering yet another laugh with a cough. Oh hell, it was so hard to keep from just burying my face in my hands and laughing hysterically, especially seeing Joshua Rose, the asshole who'd been harassing Tom forever, walking by with his hair still an odd shade of blue.

"His allergies are horrible," I chimed in, as convincingly as I could.

"Hmmm, perhaps you should make a trip to the nurse then, after breakfast wraps up."

And once Mr. Taylor walked away, we both began snickering into our bowls of what they were trying to pass as oatmeal.

"You know he's going to come after me, right?" Tom asked.

"Don't sweat it, Tommy. I got your back."

Tommy looked up at me, his face completely serious. "One of these days, I'm going to be the defender. I'm going to be the one who makes sure people don't get pushed around."

I smirked at his scrawny ass, nodding slightly. "Sure you are, Tom," I said, merely to appease him. "Sure you are."

I glanced over at the window where the scenery was lightening with the impending sunrise. I hadn't even been to sleep yet. My mind was still in a whirlwind, still unable to process it all, still debating why I'd said yes when Aunt Gayle had asked me to speak at the funeral.

No, I knew why.

Because Tom was someone I admired, someone I was proud not just to have known, but to be related to. He was a man of honor, a man who lived his life just as he said he would-- defending others. And he did so without batting an eyelash, without questioning whether or not it was right, without fear.

One turn of the page of that album, and there they were... the pictures from that party, the night before he left for basic.

"Scrawny little Tommy Warner... going into the Marines," I'd teased, smiling up at his lanky self.

"I won't be scrawny forever," he replied with a grin of his own. *"And when I get back, all huge and buff, you'll be all settled down and married to Kate."*

I scowled at the prospect of having my future all wrapped up in a bow like that. *"Nah. Too young."* I glanced across the lawn where Kate stood talking to my mom, her hair blowing in the soft breeze, my heart skipping a little beat like it always did. *"Someday, though."*

"Yeah, someday you're going to be saddled down to a hot wife with a bunch of little rugrats that will have you eating out of the palm of your hand."

"Really?" I asked with a laugh. *"And what the hell are you gonna be doing?"*

He stood a little taller, an intensity in his eyes that I'd never seen before. *"I'll be protecting you."*

And protect us he did.

Through tours in Afghanistan and Iraq, through being shot at, injured in a roadside bomb, through helping take down some of the baddest of the bad...

Little Tommy Warner became a man.

He became a *giant* of a man, one who not just towered over me but could probably bench press my ass without breaking into a sweat. But his heart... his heart was even bigger, probably bigger than this entire state. He loved with everything in him... I suppose that's just a family trait. And he'd seen his share of heartaches, his share of hard times, but never once did he ever sit around feeling sorry for himself.

I looked down at a picture taken that Thanksgiving, the year he'd come home to his wife being with someone else. I smiled wistfully as my fingertips traced that picture, his hand protective, loving against the side of Talli's baby bump, where our Elizabeth was. Even with everything he'd been through, even with everything he'd seen, when the circle came to him... what he was thankful for... he didn't even miss a beat.

"Life."

And he said it every single year, no matter what.

Pete and Jaden were passing by, walking towards the room they were sharing here, and my heart sank just a little. My arms felt so empty, more so than they had in months. What I wouldn't give to have my family here. Keeping Elizabeth and Michael from fighting would remind me of all the times Tom would step in between Pete and me. And Emily... I just want to hold my little princess right here, in my arms, let her fall asleep on me like she used to, and I would protect her...

And Talli. I would tell her that I love her, and I wouldn't care if she didn't believe me. Okay, that's not true. Of course I would care. But I need to tell her, and I need to hold her in my arms and just... and just...

Cry.

If only she would let me.

I glanced out the window again, remembering the last time I'd spoken with him, a single tear making its way down my cheek.

"Now listen," he said, *"and listen good, because I wont be there to remind you. Once you're there, in Columbus, it's all on you."*

"On me. Right. Got it."

"Wow, you really are nervous, aren't you?"

"I'm scared out of my fucking mind," I admitted, chewing on my non-existent thumb nail.

"Just remember, Jase. That's all you need to do. Remember that feeling, the first time you saw her. Remember the moment you knew you were in love with her. Remember... remember when you asked her to marry you, remember that day, your first dance. Remember... the first fight you had, remember how you worked it out. Remember the look on her face when she told you she loved you for the first time..."

"That wasn't so sweet," I said with a laugh, wiping a tear away.

"But it was, because it's part of you, part of the two of you and who you are. And you need to remember the good, you need to let that cancel out every single fear you have. Just... go for it. Because if you're going to be timid or shy, if you're going to worry about rejection the way your ass always does, then you're never going to know. And you will miss out on spending the rest of your life with the woman you are meant to be with... and all you'll have left are the memories. Memories and regrets. Got it?"

"Maybe?" I admitted, still fidgeting in my chair.

"Out with the bad, in with the good."

"Yeah, got that. And the whole 'no fear' thing."

"Jase, I'm being serious."

"What about you?" I asked suddenly, and he was silent for a moment.

"I went for it," he finally said.

"But it didn't work."

"No... no it didn't," he replied. *"But I have no regrets, Jase. I did everything I could. It's time for you to man up and do the same."*

He was right.

He was always right.

That was Tommy Warner, the man. Always looking out for others. Always fearless.

And I miss him like crazy already.

I heard the front door open, Jackie's voice greeting whomever it was that answered, and I sighed. We were one step closer to the hardest day I'd ever faced. And I know... I know they were going to ask Jackie, just like they asked me and Pete, to be one of the pallbearers, to carry one of our own to the place where they were going to lower him into the ground. And I just... I just didn't know if I had the strength to do this. I didn't know if I was ready to say goodbye, on the weekend he'd helped set up for me no less.

"Sorry, dude," I said softly, looking at the morning sky. "I had to be here. You're just going to have to understand."

I stood, stretching, muscles aching from sitting in that chair for so long. The commotion coming from down the hall let me know that luggage was being brought in, small voices making their way towards the bedrooms this way, and...

Small...voices...

"Daddy!"

They're... here?

Elizabeth and Michael entered the room, filling my heart with so much love it overflowed. With a sob I dropped to my knees, my babies rushing into my arms, and I held them. I just... held them. And I left little kisses in their hair and on their faces, and I just... held them.

"Why you crying, Daddy?" Elizabeth asked.

"I'm just happy to see you," was all I could say, not wanting to burden their little hearts with everything I was holding in mine.

"Daddy, where did Tommy go?" Michael asked, and I choked back another sob, holding them just a little closer. "They said he…he left, that he's gone."

"Yeah, he's gone, Little Man," I replied, trying to pull myself together, the added shock of their presence flooring me. I couldn't break any more in front of them.

"He just doesn't understand, Daddy," Elizabeth said with a sniffle, and it broke my heart just a little more to know that she did. I placed another soft kiss in her hair.

"It's okay, Baby Girl," I murmured as I heard another sob leave her.

"Dase."

With that one little squeak, I looked up, my eyes swimming with tears at the sight of my little Princess, her eyes heavy as she looked down at me from her perch on Talli's hip.

Talli…

My angel.

Just like they always did, Elizabeth and Michael stepped back, only this time Michael patted Elizabeth's arm as if to tell her it was okay, and I found myself choking back another sob as I stood to walk over to their mother.

And Talli… she held out her hand to me.

I walked straight into her arms, holding her and our Princess close to me, breathing them in, unable to stop my tears any longer. Emily squeaked again, this time in protest, and I kissed her temple before Talli set her down, leaving her other arm still around me, tears of her own on her cheeks. I could hear our children making their way out of the room, looking for their Nana, as I stood transfixed, looking into Talli's eyes, questioning my own sanity, thinking I must have fallen asleep in that chair.

Wasn't she supposed to be in… in Ohio, or going to Ohio? I know she had the tickets; I know she would have the note because Linda would give it to her. And Tommy, he would have wanted…

Well, he would have wanted us together, no matter where we were.

But…

This had to be a dream. This… this wasn't happening…

My eyes slid shut as her fingertips lightly brushed my tears away before she wrapped her arms around me once more, her ear resting above my hammering heart. Slowly, so unsure, I wrapped my arms around her... the feel of her there holding me together, letting me know it was real. She was there. She was comforting me, consoling me.

And I just held her.

In my mind, the words were swimming around, bumping into each other, battling for control.

I love you, I love you so very much. That's what I was going to tell you this weekend, when I had you alone in our room. That's what I was going to show you all weekend long. And I'm sorry... I'm so sorry for everything I've done, for everything I failed to do. I'm sorry I wasn't the man you needed me to be, I wasn't the husband or the father I should have been.

But now... now wasn't the time.

Not when I couldn't speak. Not when I couldn't breathe. Not when all I could do was just... hold her.

And cry.

CHAPTER 17

TALIA

Jealousy is at sometimes a complex emotion, well hidden in the midst of one's mind, contained, controlled. And suddenly, out of the blue, it rears its ugly green-eyed head, comes roaring to life. The results can be devastating, heart breaking.

And loud.

Very, very loud.

"Emily Danielle, you know better than to screech like that," I scolded my youngest child as she stood at my feet, her lower lip firmly out, tears clinging to her lashes as she glared up at me.

"NnnnnOOOO!" she screamed yet again, huffing and puffing as she glared at her baby cousin that was nestled in my arms. Ethan was merely staring at me, completely unfazed by Emily's cries.

Oh, but Emily wasn't done.

She inhaled sharply, threw her head back, and let out her 'my life is over' wail, most of her relatives saying their sympathetic "awwwwww"'s as she fell to the ground. And just as I was ready to hand Ethan back over to his mother, around the corner came Emily's knight in torn jeans and a t-shirt.

"Heeeey, Princess," Jase crooned as he stooped down, scooping our daughter into his arms. "Why are you trying to wake the neighborhood?" He stood, cradling her to him, where she buried her face, her tears still falling. I was getting ready to say something to him, some sort of explanation of what was going on, when I saw his face, his eyes, the dark circles underneath them.

"Have you been to sleep yet?" I asked softly, and he turned to me.

He didn't even have to answer.

"I'm fine," he said with a sleepy smile.

"What, don't worry about you?" I asked, and he shook his head.

"That's your line," he replied. "I'll take her back, get her changed."

"You need changed yourself," I reminded him as he made his way down the hall, knowing the viewing was less than an hour away.

"Yes, Mother," he quipped, and I couldn't help but smile, looking down at my little nephew.

"Wow," I said softly, sitting down in a rocker recliner. "You're getting so big!"

"Isn't he?" Jaden asked as she passed by. "I'm sorry, I'll be ready soon."

"Oh, take your time, take your time," I said reassuringly, smiling as Ethan squirmed in my arms, perhaps looking for his mother. The older he got, the more he looked just like Jaden, and his dark eyes were every bit as expressive, giving me something to focus on, to take my mind off the sadness that was permeating the air.

"So happy that you're here, love," Gayle whispered in my ear as she passed.

And that.

It's so hard to be around his family, even though there's nowhere else I'd rather be. With so much love here, not just for Tommy but for each other, it's a reminder of everything that I had lost. Not just with Jase, either—our impending divorce only entered my mind when Gayle had mistakenly, heartbreakingly, thought that we were back together— but with my family. The divisiveness, the backbiting, the bitterness that occurred any time my immediate family had attempted almost anything, including my mother's funeral, none of it was visible here. Ever. Not just with the reason everyone was together, but *anytime*, and my heart ached with a longing I'd pushed aside.

See, I wasn't just going to lose Jase.

I was losing *this*.

I was losing the mass of people comforting each other, laughing with each other, crying with each other. I was losing that sense of completeness, that sense of being a part of something... bigger. Better.

Oh, my therapist was just going to love me when I got back.

"What's a viewing, Mommy?" Elizabeth picked the imperfect time to ask. And while I had this whole monologue written out in my head, one that I'd gone over when I wasn't quite sleeping on the plane, it just wasn't coming to me at that moment. Thing was, I wasn't going to be put on the spot by this precocious child in the middle of Tom's mother's living room, with all of her relatives suddenly paying attention.

"Is it a movie?"

Add her little brother in to that mix, and I found myself at a complete loss for words, other than to stammer that no, it most definitely was not a movie.

"But I wanna watch a movie," he said so matter-of-factly.

"I'll take the laptop, Little Man," Jase once again saved the day as he walked down the hall. "Pick your movie. And... where are her wipes?"

"Not in her bag?" I asked, and he shook his head. "Oh, yay... um..."

"I got him," Jaden said as she walked up, kissing my cheek. "He needs to eat, and your boobs are on sabbatical."

Ethan apparently enjoys being in the arms of someone who's laughing, which I couldn't help but do after my darling best friend's comment. "I love you, Jaden," I said to her, kissing her cheek as well after she took her son from my arms.

"Hey, Talli?"

"Yeah?"

She leaned in just a little closer, her voice soft. "It means the world to him that you're here. I know he looks like hell, but... but he's so much better with you and the kids here."

I swallowed as I glanced down the hall, where Michael had followed Jase, asking him again what we were supposed to be doing when we left.

"Really?" I asked, my heart aching, thinking how could it have been worse than *this*?

"Yeah... really." I felt her push my shoulder slightly. "Go, seriously. He really needs you right now."

And I really understood that feeling, all too well. I remembered needing him in Ohio... not once, but twice. The second time he didn't make it... and the more I think about it, the more I understand. The first time, though, when I'd lost my mother... he was a true godsend. While he hadn't made it for the services, he'd shown up when I really needed him. He'd just held me while I cried, while I let out every pent-up emotion that had been building inside of me, just as I had done for him earlier. I'd nearly lost it myself, when I'd started to pull away, and he'd just sobbed, holding me closer. What was it he'd said?

"Don't let go... please, don't let go."

And I'd just held him to me, letting him cry it all out until he wasn't able to cry anymore, promising me he'd sleep.

Behold his success with that.

I stood in the doorway, holding the bag of wipes that I'd retrieved from the room that the children were sharing here, where one of them had obviously taken it since I knew that I'd had them in here last. I was about to speak up, to get his attention, to stop him from looking any more for the wipes while our children were firing off a million questions a minute.

Until Michael's latest question stopped Jase in his tracks.

"When are we gonna see Uncle Tom, Daddy? I wanna play with him."

"Hey," I finally said, coming in and pulling the door shut behind me, knowing it was time for us to try and explain what was happening.

"He won't be playing with us no more," Elizabeth said, even as I saw Jase's hands begin to tremble.

"But I want him to play with me," Michael whined. "Doesn't he love us no more?"

"It's not... he's not here anymore, Little Man," I tried my best to explain, sitting down beside him on the bed, tousling his hair slightly.

"But you said we're gonna go see him, Daddy," Michael said, his little lip sticking out as he looked up at Jase, who knelt down in front of our two older children.

"I know it's a lot for you to take in," he began, putting on his brave Daddy face like he was so wonderful at doing, "but it's just... Uncle Tom's spirit is gone." His eyes narrowed, as if he was trying to decipher if what he said would make sense.

"What's a spirit?" Michael asked.

"Is that what makes your heart beep?" Elizabeth asked, and the corner of Jase's mouth lifted in a smile.

"My heart beeps?" Michael had to ask, excitedly, and Jase shook his head.

"It's heart*beat*," I corrected softly, not wanting to set Elizabeth off, not knowing how sensitive she was going to be with everything going on. "And... kind of?" I directed the question at Jase, who met my gaze with a slight nod.

"Yeah, it's... it's the part of you that's alive," Jase continued, shaking his head. "Wow, this is hard. Um... do you understand what we're trying to say?"

"So his heart don't beat no more," Michael said, and Elizabeth let out a little sob.

"Come here, Baby Girl," Jase said softly, placing one arm around her and kissing the top of her head. "It's okay to cry, and it's okay to miss him."

"But Daddy, he's not old like Gram or Nana."

"Oh, baby, I don't think you want Gram or Nana to hear you call them old," Jase said with a laugh.

"So old people's hearts stop beating?" Michael asked, his eyes on me with this question. "Are you old, Mommy?"

"Relatively speaking?" I said, my tone more of a question, which of course Michael didn't understand.

"You're not old," Jase scolded.

"Oh, now..."

"Older than me," he added quickly. "But not old."

"There you go."

"What?" he asked, none too innocently.

"Your heart, Mommy... will it stop beating?" Michael asked, pulling us back to the discussion at hand. "You... you said you were dead when you had Lizbeth."

And for not quite the first time, I felt a twinge of guilt over the joke I'd made. Not just from the tears swimming in my son's eyes, but the way the color drained from Jase's face, and I knew... I *knew* what was going through his mind.

"Baby... I... well, I was sick."

"Both times?"

"Yeah, I was."

Elizabeth wiped her face, taking a deep breath before she added, "But you work at a hospital, Mommy. They fix people all the time."

"Was Uncle Tom sick?" Michael asked, and Jase's eyes welled up as he shook his head.

"No, buddy, Uncle Tom was in an accident."

"But didn't... didn't they call somebody?" Elizabeth added her question. "The doctors in the trucks?"

"The..."

"EMT's, and yes, I'm sure they did Baby Girl," I finished, when Jase took a little bit to process what she'd said. He smiled at her phrasing, and I felt rather than saw him take my hand in his, giving it a light squeeze.

"They said that he was gone right away," he added. "So he didn't suffer any."

"Did you suffer, Mommy?" Michael asked, little tears on his cheeks.

"Hey... hey, sweetheart, Mommy is fine, see?" I placed him on my lap, scooting a little closer to Elizabeth, so now Jase's hand was resting on my thigh, his thumb moving back and forth slowly.

"But... Daddy, Uncle Tom's not old," Elizabeth tried to reiterate her last point. "Only old people die, right?"

"No, Baby Girl. Not just older people," Jase answered her. "Uncle Tom was right about my age... unless you're saying I'm old,"

"No," she replied with a soft giggle, turning to mush around her Daddy just the same way he did around her... around all of them, really, including...

"Dase."

"Yeah, yeah, you get up here, too," he said, hoisting Emily up on the bed beside her sister, whose ponytail she immediately yanked on. "Be nice."

"She's never nice, Daddy."

"Do babies die?" Michael asked suddenly, his stormy eyes on me. Tears instantly touched my eyes, just as I heard Jase inhale sharply, and again I knew our minds were on the same thing.

Our Angel.

And although we'd talked to them about their sister (no matter how many times Jase tried to add 'or brother' in there) that wasn't with us, I didn't expect Michael to really relate to that, having never met her, never speaking with her, never playing with her the way he had with Tommy.

"You work with... with babies, right Mommy?" he asked, bringing me back to the present.

"Yes... and... and as sad as it is to say, yes. Babies die, too."

"Their hearts stop beating?" he asked.

"Yes, but... but it's really only if they're sick, or if they've been in an accident," I added, trying to shield him from some of the harsher parts of reality without misleading him.

"But I get sick."

"Little Man, you are such a worrier," Jase said softly, leaning in to kiss his head softly, and that's when it hit me.

The five of us, together, in this room... all huddled in a small circle... we were a family.

A real family.

One that pulled together, one that was held together by a bond so strong that no piece of paper was going to make it or break it. One that rallied together, young and old, to take care of their own, to ensure that within this family they would always be safe. Secure.

Loved.

Even with what the week ahead held for us, no matter how much I...

Jase's arms reached around me, and around Emily who sat beside Elizabeth, holding all of us to him, and instinctively, I rested my head in the crook of his neck, breathing him in, letting his presence wash over me, filling me with a sense of calm.

That calmness was still with me as we entered that funeral home as one, our hands joined, our children beside us.

Elizabeth sad.

Michael frightened.

Emily indifferent.

Jase… and me… a team.

A team that took turns with the children, calming fears the best we could, drying tears when we needed to, chasing our youngest when she thought playing hide and seek would be a blast.

A team that thanked his mother, almost in unison, when she offered to look after the children so we could go into the room to see Tommy, to say our goodbyes.

A team that held hands tightly when we saw that giant of a man lying so peacefully in his coffin, waiting for someone to jump out and shout that we'd been punk'd, knowing that no one would.

A team that cried silently for a life lost too soon, a piece of our lives that would forever be altered by his silence.

A team that held each other in the privacy of the funeral director's office, faces buried, consoling one another even as we both cried.

"I… I just…"

"I know," I said softly when he wasn't able to finish what he was saying, and my hands instinctively ran through his hair.

"Thank you, Talli. I know… it sounds…"

"Trite?"

"Yeah," he said with a half-laugh, half-sob. "That's ten."

"Ten?" I asked, pulling back, searching his eyes even as I brushed his tears away.

"Sentences of mine you've finished since we got here," he answered with a grin, kissing my fingertips as they passed his lips.

"Really? You're keeping track?"

"It's keeping me sane," he said, lifting one shoulder. "You… the kids… you're keeping me sane right now."

I was silent as I stared into those eyes that I knew oh so well, too well, and my heart soared. "What do you know?" I said, my voice full of wonder. "Something else from you that I believe."

And that brought out another laugh from him.

And a kiss, so very soft, across my lips before he held me to him again.

A kiss I passed on to Tommy, leaning in and placing my lips against his ice-cold forehead. "I love you, Tommy," I whispered to him before we left that evening. "Thank you, so much, for everything."

And with those words, I turned, placing my hand in Jase's before we turned to leave, knowing tomorrow would be even harder than today. But that was okay, because we could face this.

All of this.

Because we... we were once again, even if for that brief moment in time... a team.

JASE

Insomnia is not my friend. And not just because this is one of the hardest weekends I've ever had to face, not just because in just a couple hours we're going to be saying our final goodbyes to Tom. No, it's because my mind kept wandering down that hallway, two doors down to be exact. Two doors away on a little twin bed, Talli slept peacefully, looking so angelic, so beautiful.

How do I know this, you ask? Well, I could easily say by memory, and that wouldn't exactly be a lie. But the truth was, earlier I'd found myself standing just inside the doorway, at the foot of that bed, watching her sleep. I could say I don't know why I did it, but that would be a lie. It was the same reason I'd stood by that bed she slept in those few short weeks she was back at the house.

Because I miss her.

Because having her so close to me was torturous.

And not because I wanted to lie on top of her, skin to skin, sinking deep inside of her. Okay, not *just* because of that.

Because I want to hold her. I want to wrap my arms around her, curl myself into her just like I used to, breathe in that soft, sweet jasmine scent, and just *be*.

But, no.

Instead I'm lying here, two doors down, my eyes closed tight begging for sleep to come. Begging for just a little bit of a reprieve from...

"Daddy?"

I jumped at the sound of Michael's voice, blinking my eyes to adjust to the darkness as I turned towards him.

"What are you doing up, Little Man?" I asked, reaching out for him. Normally he'd crawl right up in bed with me, or he'd be asking me for cereal, but not then. No, he chose that moment to tug on my hand, his words causing an icy chill to creep up my spine.

"Daddy, she won't wake up."

And he was crying.

"She who?" I asked, sitting up and swinging my legs over the side of the bed.

"Mommy… Mommy won't… she won't wake up."

No… no, she's just tired. The powers that be surely wouldn't play such a cruel joke on me, having her so close for me to lose her… to really lose her…

Keep it together. Calm. For Michael.

"She's probably just really tired," I reassured him, even as I stood and made my way out of that room, two doors down, and straight for Talli. I'm sure she looked completely normal, sleeping just as peacefully as before, but all I could see were those damn white hospital sheets, and her so pale with those dark streaks under her eyes and those tubes and wires and…

And I dropped to my knees beside that bed, my hand on her arm, shaking her as I had so many times before.

"Talli?"

Baby, please wake up…

"See?" Michael whined, but I tried to play it off all cool, acting like the big bad Daddy that I am.

"She's tired, Little Man," I said as convincingly as I could, even though I was still shaking her, just a little more forcefully. And she's lucky I love her so much, or I probably would have let a nice string of curse words fly as I saw one corner of her mouth lift, even though she was keeping her eyes closed.

Just because I wasn't going to cuss her ass out though, didn't mean…

"I'm awake!" she screeched as I reached in the covers, poking her side, in that one little spot that always had her collapsing in a fit of giggles. She jumped, moving just a little back on the mattress and giggling slightly, and damn it I couldn't help myself. I can blame nostalgia, or... or... habit, there I can blame habit for the way I tangled my fingers in her curls before I leaned down, leaving a light kiss on her lips.

"Don't scare me like that, Mommy," Michael whined, crawling in between us and burying his face in Talli's chest, his little body shaking as he cried.

"Oh hell, he really *is* a little you, isn't he?" she asked, a twinkle in her eye for just a brief moment, before her smile fell, and I felt her take my hand, tugging slightly as she scooted further back on the bed. I had to catch my breath at that small gesture from her, but again... I played it cool. For Michael. I don't think our three-year-old would take too kindly to me pushing him out of the way to press myself up against her, especially not when he is apparently having issues.

I sat on the edge of that little bed, biting the inside of my lip as I felt her hand brush up against my chest, almost looking straight up at the ceiling and cursing at Tommy, who had to be up there scheming his heart out. Instead, though, I smiled at Talli, who pushed herself to a sitting position beside me.

"Now, are you going to tell me why you kept waking me up?" she asked Michael, who wiped his eyes with the back of his hand.

"No," he answered honestly, and I coughed slightly to cover my laugh, biting back a grin as Talli nudged me.

"Have you slept?" she asked, and he shook his head vigorously. "Damn, he *is* just like you," she said, her words obviously meant for me.

"I don't know what you're talking about," I replied smoothly, my eyes sliding shut as she adjusted herself, leaning her head against my chest, right above my heart.

Just like she used to.

I wrapped my arm around her, holding her to me as she snuggled in, with Michael eyeing us as if we'd come from another planet. "So," she said to him, "are you gonna go lay back down now?"

"No, I want..."

And before the word 'cereal' could come from him, he heard my mom's voice and was bounding out of the room looking for his Gram, leaving us alone, and me wishing he'd shut the door behind him.

"I was just pretending, you know," she said, rubbing my back as her voice had chills springing up all over me. "To be asleep, I mean. I was hoping if he couldn't wake me up, he'd just go back to bed." She pushed herself up, scrunching up her nose so adorably before she said, "Sorry."

"Don't sweat it," I managed to say, my eyes taking in every detail of her beautiful face.

"I... I didn't mean to frighten you."

"Me?" I shrugged, flashing my half grin at her. "I'm a big boy, I'm all right."

And that was all I could say, all other words leaving me as her eyes flickered down to my lips before rising to meet mine once more. I wanted to kiss her, right then and there, more than I'd wanted almost anything else in my entire life. But life itself had other plans.

"Oh, there you are," Aunt Gayle said as she poked her head into the room. "I'm letting all of you boys know that Tom's First Sergeant called, and they're going to have the almost the whole Honor Guard there, so you can stay with your family. They're going to act as pallbearers, okay?"

I could only nod, holding Talli just a little closer as the tears threatened again.

"I didn't know you were going to be one of the pallbearers," Talli said to me after Aunt Gayle had walked down the hallway.

"Yeah," I replied, sniffling slightly. "That and she asked me to say something today."

Talli lifted up again, her troubled blue eyes meeting mine. "Are you going to be okay with that?"

"Hell, I do public speaking all the time," I quipped with a shrug and a half-hearted smile.

"Ha ha, very funny. You know what I'm talking about, Jase." Gently, so sweetly she placed her palm on the side of my face as she continued. "I know how much he means to you."

And again I smiled. Only my Talli would know to keep on using present tense.

"Do you know what you're going to say?"

"Not a clue," I admitted with a short laugh, one tear escaping. "But it will come to me."

So I kept telling myself that morning as I took my shower, slipping into the suit that I'd had cleaned for this coming Thursday, my heart still set on somehow changing her mind.

And I continued telling myself it would come to me as I helped Talli with the children, her heartfelt "Thank you" bringing yet another tear to my eye.

And I began to worry about it as I followed Mom's car to the funeral home, my wife beside me, our children in their seats in the back. Until, that is, we were at a stop light, my turn signal on, my arm on the rest between the two front seats.

That's when she slipped her hand in mine.

That's when my heart skipped a little beat.

That's when the clouds parted and the sun shone brightly, and I couldn't help but smile. Just softly, and no it didn't stay with me, especially not when we pulled into that parking lot, or when we walked through those doors. It also wasn't there as the parlor began to fill, as the parking lot became too full to hold all the cars, as the men and women in dress uniform filed by Tom one by one, saying their goodbyes.

But it stayed in my heart.

When she mouthed the words "Are you okay" from across the room, where she held Michael, who was beyond cranky, I placed my hand over my heart, and her expression softened. And instead of silence, instead of the cold shoulder, instead of the indifference that I'd endured, she said "I know".

Not "me too".

But "I know" would do, that would give me enough lift, enough hope to get through this.

"Ma'am," a familiar voice caused me to turn my head towards my Aunt Gayle where a familiar face in a dress uniform was addressing her, his last name displayed prominently.

Rose

"Well, hello sir," she said, smiling through her tears, as she did at everyone who'd approached her. She held out her hand for him, and instead of shaking it, he held it between his.

"I've known Sergeant Warner for years, long before we ever served together. And we weren't the best of friends, not back then. But I fought side by side with him in Iraq, and I've never been prouder, more honored than I was to do so. He told me one hell of a story before he covered to get us out of that building, that same building that was blown sky high not thirty seconds after we'd cleared it. He's the only reason I am still standing here... that many of us in our battalion are still standing here today."

"That's... thank you," she stammered, a bit choked up, but I couldn't stop my smile.

"Would that story have anything to do with buckets of water and paint?" I asked.

"And blue hair," Joshua Rose replied with a grin, holding out his hand which I shook. "Scrawny Tommy turned into one hell of a man."

"Not to condone any... um... behavior," I said, my head slightly to the side, "but that day... that day, Tommy made up his mind what he wanted to do with his life. That was the day he said he wanted to be the one who protected others."

And with those words, Joshua Rose teared up, nodding his head before he turned to walk away, pausing only to turn around and say, "Thank you."

"Thank you," I repeated back to him, chuckling to myself at the thought of Tommy standing there telling him what we'd done in the midst of all that horror they were facing.

Only Tommy.

"Oh, there she is," I heard Gayle say, and I looked up, half expecting to see his ex wife standing there.

"She who?" I asked.

"The lady in the minivan. The... the vehicle he swerved in front of."

"What?" I was a bit confused, only knowing that Tom had been in a head-on collision.

"She had a van full of children, wasn't really paying much attention to the road. She said she was talking to one of the kids in the back, when she heard a car horn, and Tommy swerved in front of her. She had to slam on her brakes, but...but he took the crash. The other car was headed straight for her."

Oh hell.

I felt the tears well up once more, and I smiled at that coffin where his body laid, thinking to myself... only Tommy.

If only there were more Tommys in this world.

They began to clear the parlor about 15 minutes before the service was scheduled to begin. I knew this was going to happen... Aunt Gayle had insisted that the coffin be closed before services, so that we could celebrate his life, so that people could stare at the picture boards instead of his lifeless body, and let those images be what everyone would remember as their last goodbye. I watched my father guide her away from the coffin, to the back room where she finally broke down in his arms, and I had to step out for a moment.

Besides... I had a thing or two to say to Tommy. In private.

But when I entered that room, that nearly deserted room, I wasn't quite prepared to see this.

To see his ex-wife standing above him, sobbing.

"I... I love you," she stammered out, gently touching the side of his face. "I was so wrong... I never deserved you, you know. You... you were always so loving, so forgiving, and... and I never appreciated it, or you, or everything you did for us... for me. No... no, I had to throw it all away, and I couldn't see... and I was going to tell you. I was going to call you and tell you, and I kept putting it off. And it's too late... too... too late. And you'll never know."

I wanted to scream at her. I wanted... hell, I wanted to cuss her up one side and back down the other, ask her why.

Why would she hurt someone like him?

How could she do that to him?

But that would have been rather hypocritical of me.

So I merely nodded in her direction as she walked out, not even staying for the services but heading straight outside, to her car, perhaps too ashamed to face his family.

I understood, though. I understood how she felt, why she was running away.

And there was no way in hell I was going to make the same mistake.

"Did you catch that?" I asked softly as I wandered up beside his casket. "She was here. And you'd be proud of me; I didn't call her out. I wasn't an asshole. Yeah, yeah… I don't have much room, I know."

I took a deep breath, the memories, the emotions washing over me. "Ah hell, Tom… for the first time *ever* I'm half tempted to be angry with you, you know that? Angry over that damn heart of yours, the one that refused to stand aside and watch others get hurt. I'm angry because… because now you're not *here*. And that's really fucking selfish of me. But you know what you made me promise? I'm doing it. I'm going to do it. I… I'm not going to let her walk into that courtroom, even… it's not going to happen. I don't know how yet; I'll just have to figure that shit out on my own. But a little divine intervention wouldn't hurt. Just sayin."

I adjusted his tie, laughing softly as I did so. "You hated these things, but you know your mom. She always said how handsome you looked all dressed up. She loved seeing you in your dress uniform, too. Oh, hell Tom… you should see how many of them are here today. Even Joshua Rose. I had no idea, you know? No idea you'd told him the prank we'd pulled. And your timing? Classic. Pure… classic. And knowing you… and I think I do… you probably did it to help calm him, remind him there was a life outside of there that he had to fight to get back to. Because that's just you, Tom. That's… that's you.

"The kids… Elizabeth and Michael, they miss you. Em's too young, but I promise she's going to know all about you. And some day, when they're old enough, I'm going to tell them how you pushed me in the right direction, how I owed it to you to be brave, be strong, be the father to them, the husband to Talli that I should be, to… be more like *you*. And I… I'm going to miss you, too."

"Mr. Warner?"

It was the funeral director, standing beside me, his hand on my shoulder.

"I have to go now," I whispered to Tommy, turning and walking out of the parlor, towards the hall, flinching as I heard the casket being closed.

"Jase?"

And I was ever so thankful that Talia was there, taking my hand, holding it as we were led into the room, seated in our chairs. She held it as the rest of the guests all came in behind us, only letting go when Michael insisted on being in her arms. One glance to my right, and there they were-- Talli, with Michael, Elizabeth, then Pete with Emily on his lap, and Jaden beside him, holding Ethan, and... oh, I could kiss Aunt Gayle... Jackie sat beside Jaden, his face solemn, his eyes rimmed red as he stared straight forward.

We were all there, pulled together, held by the strongest bond ever.

Love.

Love for Tom. Love for each other.

And I knew... oh I knew exactly what to say, and not just as I stood before the standing-room-only crowd, the sea of people there to pay their final respects. Because the words, I felt them deep in my heart. And I would carry them with me the whole day, sometimes even having them replay over and over in my mind.

At the cemetery, where my family and I sat in the second row, staring at that flag-draped coffin, the sounds of the bagpipes playing Amazing Grace, muffling Aunt Gayle's soft crying, the words began to echo. I felt Talli's fingers lace with mine, and I held on with everything in me, trembling from more than just the cold.

"The first word that pops into my head when I think about Tom is 'fearless'. And maybe it wasn't an accurate description, but 'brave' just didn't seem to cover it. It wasn't just his approach with others, it wasn't just that protective side of him. It... it was the fact that the phrases 'should have', 'could have', and 'would have' were never part of his vocabulary."

At the signal of their commander, the 21-gun salute rang out, each of the rounds seeming to pierce straight through my heart.

"Take responsibility, and not just for what you've done wrong, but for everything you've done right as well."

A lone bugle began to play that sad, somber tune, and I knew I'd never hear 'Taps' again without weeping openly.

"If there's something that needs done, do it. If there's something that needs said, say it. And he did... he always did."

Slowly, precisely the flag was folded, its corners crisp, perfect, into the triangle that was presented with love, with respect to Aunt Gayle, who held it up to her heart.

"The world... the world needs more people like Tom. And I know when I grow up, I want to be just like him."

"I do too, Daddy," Elizabeth said as we finally stood to go.

"Hmm?" I asked, more than a bit distracted.

"I wanna grow up to be like Uncle Tommy."

I couldn't help but smile at her, and even more when Michael piped up with, "You not grow'd up, Daddy?"

"Not even close," I replied as I lifted him. "Just ask Mommy."

Talli's laughter was like music to my ears, warming me on that cold fall day. She was still smiling--even with her red-rimmed eyes-- as we worked together to get the children strapped into their seats, with promises of lots of goodies and time on the X-box when we got back to Gayle's house. And her smile only grew as she pulled out her cell phone, checking her messages as I maneuvered the car through traffic.

"Eric and Lisa are already having a wonderful time," she commented, pushing a few buttons to reply.

"Good," I said, grinning back, happy that Lisa had taken Eric with her. For all of his flaws—who doesn't have them?—I genuinely liked him, and I knew he could use the reprieve.

"Oh...oh!" Talli continued as the next text came through. "The guy sitting next to them told Eric to call him on Monday, see about possibly getting a... a job with his company."

I smiled again, looking up at the clouds and wondering how much divine intervention had taken place.

"Oh... get it, girl," Talli said with a giggle.

"What?" I asked, my interest piqued.

"Some guy behind her asked for her phone number, and... WOO! Buckeyes score!" Her smile, the one I'd missed so badly, could have lit up that entire stadium.

And I still got to see it.

"Wha's that stuff, Daddy?" Michael asked, his voice full of wonder as tiny white flakes began to float down from the sky.

"It's snowing!" Elizabeth exclaimed, her excitement bubbling over. She reminded Michael he must have been too young to remember, but yes he had most certainly played in the white stuff, and she continued on, asking in a rush if they could go outside and play, catch snowflakes on their tongues, and if we thought there would be enough to make a snowman.

But my mind was, once again, elsewhere as I stole another glance at Talli.   I could tell by her expression that she had something she wanted to say, but was hesitating as she read and re-read the latest text message from her sister.

And I knew exactly what it was about.

"Yes," I said, my eyes straight forward, focused on the road.

"Yes what?"

"Yes, I only booked one suite."   I stole another sideways glance, smirking slightly.   "Technically it was more than one room.   Nice big couch in the living room, or that's what they told me."

"But just one bed."

I took a deep breath, calming myself before I said, "Yes."   I pulled up to the red light, bringing the car to a full stop, my heart hammering in my chest because I knew…. I *knew* the next question.

"Why?"

And it hurt.   It hurt like a sonofabitch, not going to lie.   But she'd asked, and I'd promised full disclosure.   All I had to do now was be fearless.

"Jase…"

"Because I miss you," I said, looking over at her.   And just as I'd done when I told Kate, and Linda, and everyone who'd listened, I crossed my arms in front of me, adding, "Right here."

I watched as the words sunk in, her beautiful blue eyes filling with tears.   She shifted in her seat, facing just a little more my way, causing the nerves to really take hold.   I knew I was laying it out there, no matter how small the 'it' was, and with everything we'd been through I was waiting for the shoe to drop.   For the reprimand.   For the rejection.   For anything that told me I was in the wrong.

It never came.

Instead, she reached out, taking my right hand in hers, the trembling of her fingers ceasing as she squeezed.   And softly, sweetly, full of an emotion I was still too hesitant to name, she said four words that sent my heart soaring.

"I miss you, too."

CHAPTER 18

TALIA

How many chances had we been given to talk? How many golden opportunities had we just let slip through our fingers, leaving it to some other day, some other time? As we continually were dragged in opposite directions by a house full of family, I firmly gave up trying to count. Instead of the nagging anxiety that would have filled me on any other day, though, I felt calm. Serene, even. Minus one tiny little detail in the form of an extremely tired and cranky three-year-old, that is, but we handled it as best we could.

Jase's father, bless his heart, made sure the Buckeyes game was on in the family room, so every chance I could when I wasn't chasing after the children or helping in the kitchen, I caught a glimpse, sometimes even a play. And, of course, would hear, "Thank the lord there are no air horns here."

"You think I can't yell that loud?" I asked Pete with a wink.

"She can," Jase added as he walked into the room, his jacket and tie off, the top two buttons of his shirt undone. "Trust me."

"I'm sure it was nothing you didn't deserve," Pete replied, batting his eyelashes as Jase had to refrain from flipping him off with the children running past. "Ha! Wuss."

"I think," Elizabeth said, walking up to Pete, "that he was going to do this." And she flipped him the bird, as calmly as you please, before walking out of the room, leaving Jase and me gaping after her and his father trying to stifle his laughter.

"That… that's so not funny," Jase said to his father, and Pete who was now cracking up.

"What the…"

"I'll handle this one," Jase cut me off, placing a soft kiss on my temple. "I'm sure it's my fault."

"No, I didn't…"

"Seriously," he interrupted me again, shrugging. "You were always the one censoring yourself around them, where I failed miserably. I got this."

And again, I was speechless.

Until…

"Mooooooooommmmmyyyyyyy!"

The monster had woke from his five minute nap howling because I wasn't in the room with him.

"Ah, a mother's work is never done," Pete said from his perch in the recliner, where he was gently rocking his son to sleep.

"Mmm hmm, and neither is yours," I replied, making my way through the sea of people back to the room that Elizabeth and Michael had been sharing. He was already in the hallway, his tear-streaked face showing his state of near-panic. "I'm here, I'm here," I said as I lifted him, rubbing his back as I walked us back to that room.

"I… I'm not sleeping," he stammered, wiping his eyes and sitting straight up on my lap as I lowered myself onto the bed.

"But you need to."

"Not… I'll sleep later, okay?"

"Are you afraid to be in here by yourself?" I asked, and he nodded, his lower lip trembling. "Would it make you feel better if I was in here until you fell asleep?"

"I… I'm hungry."

"Hungry?" I asked with a laugh. "You ate every single pickle in this house, many little pinwheel sandwiches, and about three helpings of chips."

"With dip."

"With dip, I stand corrected. You're hungry?"

"I'm growing, Mommy."

And he looked so sweet, so earnest, that I fell for it, just like I always did with his father. Or, I used to. Yeah, used to.

"Hey," Jase stuck his head in the door just as Michael ran out. "Sorry about that, with Elizabeth. I'll watch myself more closely around them, I promise."

If you have something to say...

"You're a good father," I said, stopping him as he began to walk down the hall. He looked over his shoulder, his expression unreadable for only a moment. "A wonderful father, actually," I added, my head leaned to the side slightly. "And I'm sorry if I ever made you doubt that."

He shook his head, so slightly I almost didn't catch it, but his eyes were shining, the unshed tears held in check for the moment. "I'm the one who should apologize, Talli. I was... so wrong..."

"Hey, sweetheart," Gayle's voice sounded in the hall, interrupting us yet again, "could you give me a hand out here for a sec?"

I nodded at him, and he winked before he followed her, leaving me with a heart so heavy and yet... not. But the one thing that had been lacking all day, that nagging anxiety, suddenly began to creep in.

Slowly I stood, making my way out into the masses of people, being led to the family room so I could see the end of the game, but my mind... my mind was firmly elsewhere. It was back in that room... no, no it wasn't. It was back in Los Angeles, back in that house that had once been our home, back in that little bed I'd slept on, wishing for the strength to go down that hall, crawl in bed with him.

Why hadn't I?

And it wasn't just Bree. Sure, she was a big part of the answer, but... that wasn't it.

I was afraid. Terrified. For months he'd been disinterested—or had I just missed it?—and he'd confirmed every fear I had.

I wasn't Hollywood gorgeous. I wasn't the thin Barbie doll. I wasn't perfect. Why... why would he want me? And if he'd told me no...

That was it.

Pure, complete fear of rejection. So true, so consuming, so...

So reminiscent.

Of Cleveland.

Of that hotel room, where he would look across the room at me, just the way he was doing now. Where he would touch me softly, even if it was just a hand to the small of my back as he leaned around, shaking the hand of someone who was leaving, just like he did then. A short gasp left me as I suddenly remembered, with extreme clarity, when he'd said goodbye to Chris Webber that night, the exact same way. I looked over my shoulder at Jase, his expression wistful, nostalgic, and I knew... I just *knew* he'd been thinking the same thing.

But the moment passed us by, someone else wanting to talk with Jase before they left dragged him away, leaving me there watching him.

Again.

And he glanced over at me and smiled.

Again.

"Here you go, Spunky." Jackie was suddenly beside me, handing me a cup with a steam rising. "Careful there, it's kinda hot."

I stared down at the contents, my lower lip trembling slightly.

"Apple cinnamon tea, with a touch of honey," he said. "Just the way you like it."

And with that, after holding myself together all day long, I burst into tears.

"I feel so stupid," I muttered, placing the cold washrag on my face before lying back on that full-size bed the kids had been sharing, having been led back there to get away from the absolute chaos.

"Don't feel stupid," Jaden scolded, stretching out beside me. "It's been a..."

"And I feel guilty!"

"Why the hell would you feel guilty? Because you cried the day of the funeral?"

"It wasn't over Tommy," I mumbled, my voice muffled by the washrag.

"Huh?"

"It wasn't over Tommy," I repeated, pulling the washrag down. "It was… it was stupid."

"What happened?" she asked, turning towards me. "Did my douche bag brother-in-law do something? Or something *else* I should say?"

"No," I said, sniffling slightly. "Jackie made me tea."

Her eyebrow raised as she looked at me as, just as I'd suspected, as if I'd lost my mind. "You're crying because Jackie made you tea?"

"Apple cinnamon tea," I replied. "With honey. Just like…"

"Cleveland," she said with a wistful sigh.

I nodded, tears filling my eyes once more. "And… and remember when I told you… about when everyone was leaving, after you'd already made your getaway with your future hubby?"

"How your future hubby kept looking over at you, and… just little…"

"Touches," I finished for her. "I'm driving myself insane, you know?"

"Do you love him?"

"Well, *yeah*, duh." I sniffled again, thanking her when she handed me a tissue.

"Do you want this divorce?"

I couldn't even speak as I began to cry again, shaking my head no.

No.

Absolutely not.

"Then why…"

"What else am I supposed to do?" I sobbed, wiping my tears with the back of my hand. "Love isn't… it isn't enough, Jaden. It isn't trust, and it isn't forgiveness. And I just… I don't know if I could forgive him."

"Do you trust him?"

With another sob, again I shook my head 'no'.

"Oh, baby… I just… I don't know what to say." She held my hand, giving it a big squeeze. "No… no, wait. Do you remember Leah?"

"Ugh… Hurricane Leah? Yes," I said, holding my tongue before I told her about the conversation I'd had with Pete.

"Duh, I know Pete brought her up when he was bringing you to the hospital. Sorry." She shook her head slightly, then continued. "But… you're right, trust is a tough thing. I… I did but didn't have the forgiveness issue, because he and I weren't together, but I had to trust him, trust that he wasn't going to run out every time things got tough."

"He told you what we talked about?" I asked.

"Well, yeah. He tells me everything."

"Everything," I said softly. "What the hell is that like? Hell, my husband... he doesn't tell me half of what's going on, and the other half is... well, I don't know if it's the truth or not."

She growled in near frustration, covering her face with her hands before she looked over at me. "Couples counseling."

"I tried. He said no."

"Try again! Seriously, Talli, try again. Do something, do *anything*, just not this. Not if it isn't what you want."

"But he... Jaden, I was right. I knew he couldn't stay away from those little Barbie dolls and... and what will..."

"If you even say one word about 'what will other people think'..."

"Oh, hell no. I've never given a shit about that," I said with a wave of my hand.

"Good, good. Just... talk to him."

I nodded, sitting up and wiping my eyes again, knowing my nose was probably bright red and glowing. "I'm going to. I... I'm really going to."

"For real, for real? Not just saying you will?"

"For real," I replied, resting my head on her shoulder when she pulled me into a hug. "I'm so happy you're here, I've missed you like crazy."

"I've missed you, too."

"I hate when life gets in the way," I mumbled, and she laughed softly.

"We're coming in for Elizabeth's birthday," she said, and I sat back, smiling.

"For real, for real? Not just saying you will?"

"Okay, smart ass," she said, nudging me as I laughed. We paused as a knock came at the door, very softly, just before Jase walked in, holding a finally sleeping Michael in his arms.

"Sorry," I said, scooting off the bed as Jaden stood up, giving room for Jase to lay our son down.

"No, no... it's... good." He pulled Michael's shoes off, placing them to the side as I gently covered him up. "What about you? Are you okay? Did I..." He looked so sad as he looked over at me. "Are you upset with me?"

But I couldn't answer him. Not without breaking down.

So I did the only thing I could think of.

I walked straight into his arms, burying my face in his chest, inhaling deeply as his arms slowly circled around me. I could feel myself relax against him, feel the tension leave my limbs, feel the soft smile touch my lips.

"Talli?"

"Hmm?"

I heard his heart pick up pace slightly, his arms tightening around me. "Can... can we talk now?"

"I don't know, can we?" I asked automatically, cringing at my mom-like question. "Sorry, sorry. Yes."

Yes. Finally. We could...

"Mmmooooooooooommmmmyyyyyyyyy..." Michael woke up wailing, his bottom lip quivering, the circles under his eyes almost as dark as Jase's. Both of us turned to him instantly, his tears a far greater concern for that moment in time.

"Hey, hey..." I said as I laid beside him, nodding at Jase as he crawled in on the other side. "What is the matter, Little Man?"

He sat up, his sobs exaggerated by his exhaustion. "No sleep, Mommy, okay?"

"No, not okay."

"Come on, bud, what's up? Why do you not want to sleep?" Jase asked, and his tone... that one he always used with them... could have easily made my ovaries ache if I wasn't so adamant that Emily was my last.

"I... I won't... Daddy, Uncle Tommy didn't wake up."

We exchanged a knowing glance from our spots on either side of him, even as Jase easily laid him back against the pillows.

"I... I don't think you quite understand, not the way we thought you did," he began, gently brushing away our son's tears.

"But he..."

"Tommy isn't sleeping," I tried to explain, taking Michael's hand in mine.

"But they said... resting, and... and... then they closed the box, and he couldn't get out and..."

"Baby, he's gone. He wasn't in the box," I said.

"Like a magic trick?"

"No," Jase replied, laughing softly. "No, it's... it's not a magic trick, and it's not sleeping. It's... it's final. It's..."

"But Mommy says that babies die too, and I'm just a baby kinda sorta, right?"

"Going to sleep doesn't mean you're going to die, Michael," I said as calmly as I could. "It means you're tired and you need to rest, and you'll feel so much better when you do."

"But Daddy doesn't sleep, do you Daddy? Daddy, you're in your office all the time, you don't even use your bed no more."

I looked over at Jase, whose cheeks were a soft shade of pink. "That's... well, Daddy needs to sleep too."

"Mommy don't sleep so good either. She cries a lot. Sorry, Mommy."

"No... it's okay, it's okay," I said, caressing the back of his hand.

"But... Em, she can't sleep without Lizbeth. Maybe you an' Daddy should sleep in da same room 'gain, cause you slept a *lot* then."

For a moment, I could have blushed at his comment, until it hit me: he wasn't speaking about way back when Jase and I spent every moment we could in each other's arms. No, he had to have been too young to remember that. He was thinking about after Emily was born, when sleeping seemed to be the *only* thing I did.

And I was so ashamed that it was bad enough, prominent enough, for our children to have noticed.

I felt the light touch of calloused fingers on my arm, and my eyes met Jase's over our son, who was chattering about everything he could to stay awake. And in those eyes... oh, in those eyes, I could see. Not the bad parts, not the damage we had done to one another, but all of the good, all of the love we'd shared, all of the nights we'd woke up in each other's arms and had shown each other just how deep that love flowed.

"...and I don't want the girls in...my room, not all da time. Lizbeth is a bed hog anyways."

"Am not," she said as she entered the room, crawling up on the bed in between Michael and Jase, who smiled over at me. "Em's asleep with her butt in the air. Nana took pictures and said she's gonna blackmail her when she gets older. Daddy, I want a story. Like you do when I'm home with you."

Michael was yawning as I nodded to Jase... yes, yes he most definitely should tell a story.

"What story do you want to hear, Baby Girl?" he asked, his body relaxed as he laid on his side.

She grinned impishly, a giggle escaping as she said, "Sleeping Beauty."

"Elizabeth Christine," I said, trying to cover my laughter even as she giggled uncontrollably, with Michael following right behind.

"You... you made a funny," Michael said.

"I did," she agreed, and I watched Jase's expression soften even more as he watched them giggle before they settled down, Elizabeth turning her eyes to her Daddy. "Please?"

"Oh, all right, if you insist."

"Which one you gonna tell, Daddy?" Michael asked, and one side of Jase's mouth lifted.

"I guess I'll just have to make one up."

And then, his eyes were on me.

"Once upon a time... there was this girl."

"Does it always hafta be about a girl?" Michael whined.

"It's my story," Elizabeth said, nudging him. "Is she a princess, Daddy?"

"She... was the most beautiful girl in the world," he continued, his eyes still locked with mine, causing my heart to race. "And not just... not just because of her eyes, or her smile, but because she had a heart that was pure, so full of love. And this boy, he never thought he would be good enough for her."

"Why not?" I found myself asking as laid my arm across the top of the bed, my hand automatically reaching into his hair, gently playing with it. His eyes began to droop slightly as I did so, but he still answered.

"Because he was a fool."

"What's a fool, Daddy?" Michael asked.

"Someone... who... who screws up royally, sometimes on a regular... basis," Jase replied, his voice beginning to trail off.

"Did she love him anyway?" Elizabeth asked excitedly.

"He... he really wanted her to."

"Did they have babies?"

"Ew," Michael interjected.

"Why are you ew-ing?" Elizabeth asked. "You're a baby, aren't you?"

"They had three of them," Jase continued. "And they loved them all... very, very much. And they wanted to do everything for them, everything they could to make them happy."

"But were *they* happy?" Elizabeth asked, even as I heard Michael's light snoring beside me.

"He... wanted to make her happy," Jase said, his eyes so heavy. "And... once upon a time... they were."

"They were?" Elizabeth added another question as Jase struggled to keep his eyes open, his breathing more and more steady as my fingers gently played with his hair.

"Very much so," I added, and Jase's eyes met mine one last time, the sweetest smile on his lips before sleep claimed him as well.

"What happened, Mommy?" Elizabeth asked with a yawn.

"They lost their way," I said with a soft sigh. "But... but they were determined to find it. And that boy? He was wrong. It was the girl that wasn't good enough for him."

"That's... that's not true." I faltered briefly as those words left Jase's lips, wondering if he'd even remember saying them.

"Did she love him Mommy?" Elizabeth asked, her eyes drooping as well.

"Beyond the telling of it," I said, smiling down at 3/5 of my family, all of them now sound asleep. Listening to the light breathing, and sometimes light snoring, held my heart captive, and I laid there for a moment to savor it, never meaning to close my eyes as well. My body, though, had other plans as sleep overcame me, my dreams oh so sweet. There was giggling, and child voices, one complaining about a bed hog. And Nan... when did she get into my dream? But suddenly, the room was very cold as the small voices trailed away while the children left the room. There was a rush of wind, and a little warmth, but I was searching... searching...

And strong arms reached for me, pulling me in, holding me, making me feel safe.

Loved.

And I never wanted to wake from this dream, its feelings and sensations so calm, so soothing, but with the click of the furnace kicking on some time in the night, I did. I opened my eyes, taking in the surroundings of the darkened room, gathering my bearings as I shifted back into…

Oh…

Oh…

He was holding me. Really… holding me, just like I missed him doing, just like I'd longed for, wished for through all of those lonely nights.

He was… holding me.

Jase's arms tightened around me, holding my back to his chest, the position we'd slept in most often, the one that brought back the most memories of all the mornings we'd woke up together. I bit the inside of my lip to keep myself from letting out a sob, tears touching my eyes as his fingers laced with mine, just like they used to. His breath was hot against my neck, setting every nerve ending on fire, making my body tremble. As if on instinct, he pulled me closer, perhaps thinking I was cold, his lips searing my skin as he placed a soft kiss on my neck. A tremor passed through me at the touch, a sigh escaping my lips before I could stop myself.

If I wanted to stop myself.

But I felt him freeze, his body tense up at my reaction and I knew that hadn't been some random act done from memory. He was awake. He was holding me because…

I couldn't answer that one. Perhaps I was too afraid to. But…

If something needs done, do it…

I turned in his arms, one lone tear escaping as my eyes met his in that darkened room, the only illumination coming from the streetlight thorough the small separation of the curtains. We were face to face, our eyes locked, my arms now between us, but pressed straight up against him. I…I could see him… perfectly *see* him, the raw emotion in those eyes making my body ache in a way that was almost foreign to me now.

He was so close, his lips only a fraction of an inch from mine as he leaned in, moving at the last possible moment to kiss away the tear that lingered behind. Instinctively I pressed closer to him, one arm snaking around and holding him closer, my eyes sliding shut at the contact of his lips on my cheek. They fluttered open as he pulled back, only slightly, still so close that his eyes were all I could see, our chests rising and falling simultaneously as our labored breathing fell in unison. All I wanted, right then, was to kiss him. To just... kiss him, and...

His lips brushed across mine softly, just a whisper of a kiss, hovering above mine as he waited, for reaction, or rejection, but my mind... oh, it was not cooperating as my heart wanted to beat its way straight out of my chest. Again, his lips lightly touched mine, this time just a little more pressure as I responded to him, his shuddering sigh against me spreading chills across my skin.

Slowly, with each touch of our lips, that wall I'd had around me, protecting me began to crumble, leaving my heart vulnerable, raw, in his hands. His *expert* hands that held me, caressed me as if I were the most precious thing on this Earth. His open-mouthed kisses had me sighing, whimpering, pressing myself up against him, wanting just a little more of *anything*. I wanted us closer, I wanted... oh, I wanted that damn shirt of his out of the way. I brought my hands to the buttons of his shirt, popping them open one by one until his strong hand gripped my wrist, pulling it away. He pinned my wrist to the bed, rolling us to where he was half lying on me, the sensations sending a ripple of pleasure so intense I squirmed up against him, needing that warmth, that heat, that weight on top of me, crushing me into the mattress. And as I opened my mouth to beg, to plead, to say anything, my eyes met his.

And my heart ached.

It ached for the pain, the confusion, the longing in his expression as he stared down at me, perhaps waging that same internal war that I'd given up. Or... or maybe he was remembering our last time here, and how it all fell apart. Maybe... maybe he thought I didn't want this. Or... maybe... he didn't want *me*.

Oh, that just... it just... hurt.

But damn it, I wasn't going to let him get up, let him walk away. Not again. If... if it was someone else he wanted, then he could have her, but not... not without a reminder of what he was leaving behind. And maybe that was wrong of me—no, I know it was—but it was what drove me to push myself up, covering his lips with mine, kissing him boldly, then deeply as he opened up to our first touch of tongues. The kiss deepened even more as I turned us, straddling him as I resumed my task, popping those buttons open one by one, moaning against his lips as my fingertips came in contact with his skin. His hands... oh, his hands were all over, cupping my ass, gripping my hips, tangling in my hair as my trail of kisses led down to his neck. His responses were pure, raw, his soft moans and labored breathing pushing me on, and as I shifted... oh...*fuck*, I could really feel what this was doing to him. He was rock hard, hot through the fabric of his slacks as I pressed up against him again... and again... and again.

I tangled my hands in his shirtfront as I sat up, pulling him with me so I could push that damn shirt off his... shoulders, oh hell... I forgot how fucking sexy they were. And his... his arms, and his chest, and... and all I could do was kiss him. Kiss him and run my hands over his skin, soft whimpers leaving me as he gripped my ass, pulling my hips to his.

And we began to move.

As if there were no articles of clothing between us, as if he were buried deep inside of me, we moved, my legs circling around him as our hips began to grind and rock. The heat, the friction, the pleasure was almost too much to bear, a light sheen of sweat covering me as his hands began to pull at my shirt, working it up my torso, our lips parting as he pulled it over my head and tossed it aside. I moved in to cover his lips with mine once more, but the look on his face stopped me.

Again, I felt tears spring up as his eyes took in every inch, his gaze one of wonder, one of adoration, one of... of...

Does he really mean it?

His hands were trembling slightly against my skin, the fabric of my lace bra tightening before it loosened completely, its straps falling down my shoulders. His calloused fingers felt like heaven against my skin as he finished pushing the straps down, pulling the lace away from my body setting my breasts free, my nipples hard, sensitive even before his thumbs brushed across them. A moan escaped from me as his lips and tongue explored my breasts, his arms securely around me, holding me to him as if... as if I were precious. And instead... instead of the vulnerability, instead of embarrassment, once again he made me feel...beautiful. Desirable.

Just like he used to.

My head fell back, my fingers entwining in his hair as he continued his exploration of every inch of my chest, my neck, my jaw line, before his lips reached mine once more. The edges of his hair were becoming damp with sweat, and that part of me, the one that had craved to see him hovering over me took over, my hands my hands trailing down his sides before reaching between us, tugging at his belt as if my very existence depended on him being buried deep inside of me. As if he sensed my urgency, his arms circled around my waist, holding me to him as he laid us down as one, the mattress soft beneath me, his weight welcomed.

Needed.

A soft moan of protest left me as he lifted up, our hands working together on his belt, his button, his zipper, my fingers gripping his bare hips as he pulled his pants and boxer briefs down together. And slowly, surely, even as his hands worked my pants and underwear down my legs, my fingertips brushed the underside of his cock, circling around and giving a light squeeze as it twitched against me. Something between a growl, a moan, and a slight hint of a whimper left his lips as I began to stroke him, my legs dropping apart as they were finally free from the confines of the clothing. And his hand... his fingers... oh, so slowly he traced the curve of my hip, my thigh, before turning, those calloused fingertips against my inner thigh making me moan, twist, writhe, lift my hips until...

Oh, sweet... sweet relief...

He moaned against my mouth as he found me slick, hot, wet, oh so ready to have him thrusting harder and harder inside of me. But first... first his fingers teased my clit, spreading my juices around my folds as my hand held him tighter, my thumb circling the head of his cock with every stroke. We continued bringing each other closer to that edge, closer to falling over, closer to complete ecstasy, but this... this wasn't going to be enough, not for me.

I pulled his hand away, pushing him onto his back and straddling him, his cock nestled between my thighs, not inside of me but still... Oh... skin to skin...

Completely, totally, *finally* skin to skin as our tongues battled for control, our breathing erratic, our bodies moving closer and closer to that final union. His hands gripped my hips, holding me steady, keeping me from lowering myself onto his erection, stopping me from taking him inside of me, and I moaned again in protest, trying to break free.

I needed him.

I... I wanted him.

Wordlessly, with soft kisses, with whimpers I began to plead with him, gasping as he turned us as one, his weight completely on me, his tip... just slightly...

I gasped, arching my back, trying to draw him further in. As he left feather light kisses on the tip of my nose, on my eyelids, I opened my eyes, a tear once again escaping from me. His hand reached up, covering mine, interlacing our fingers, our foreheads resting together as he slowly, surely, deliberately filled me completely.

And I was in heaven.

It was pure bliss to be lying beneath him, connected in every way, my body adjusting to him as much as it could before he began to move. Slowly, surely, every stroke measured, even, we moved together, eyes locked, hands clasped tightly. In the complete silence of that house, the sounds of our breathing, our soft kisses, our bodies moving together seemed to echo, adding to the intense amount of pleasure he was giving me, and... and... oh, there went his eyes, rolling back slightly before they slid shut... yeah, pleasure he was receiving as well.

We were as close as two people could possibly be, our kisses light, our limbs intertwined even as he shifted, lifting one of my legs slightly with his free hand. I gasped, arching up against him as each stroke now hit that one spot, my muscles tightening as the pressure began to build. I could tell by that look, that pure concentration in his features he was trying to hold on, trying to hold back, and I knew the exact words that would leave him at this point.

"I don't want to hurt you..."

I locked my legs around his waist, moving against him with more urgency as I felt my orgasm build, silently begging for more... harder...

faster... and he obliged, his hips surging against mine with a force that tore a cry from my throat, one he muffled with his lips, his tongue. The kiss deepened, capturing every whimper, every moan as he again pushed harder, chills spreading across his skin.

Oh... oh... he was going to come. He was going to come so hard, and it was going to fill me, and... and...

And I arched sharply, burying my face in his neck as I cried out in ecstasy, my muscles holding him in a vice grip as wave after wave after... oh hell... it was building again...

His face was buried in the pillow as he thrust his hips against mine, his moans getting louder, and louder, and suddenly my eyes clamped shut, stars bursting behind them, my nails digging into the soft flesh of his back as I came again, harder, oh so hard... and he was with me, intensifying the sensations, our bodies slowing down little by little, never stopping until every drop was spent.

And I couldn't breathe.

I... I was... I wasn't just satisfied. I wasn't just sated. I was...

I was in love.

I was so in love with him.

And it filled my heart, overflowing as our lips joined in soft, sweet kisses, our tears mixing together as we held one another. And... and he smiled at me, his fingertips gently pushing my curls out of my face.

Oh, I knew... I knew that look.

That was the same soft look he had on his face for a brief moment in Cleveland.

It was the same look in my bedroom in Ohio a few days later.

It was the look in Vegas.

It was the look on our wedding night.

It was the look I wanted to see for the rest of my life.

We stayed that way, our bodies joined, sometimes kissing, sometimes not. Sometimes we just smiled, sometimes we sighed contentedly, until we drifted off into sleep-- a deep, peaceful sleep-- without ever saying a word.

JASE

I'd had big hopes for this weekend, big *dreams* even. I'd wanted to see her face light up the way it always did when her team scored. I wanted time together, away from the chaos, just her and me. I wanted to talk with her, tell her how much I love her, tell her the truth regardless of whether or not she believed me. And I wanted to hold her, breathe her in, maybe even sweet talk her into letting me sleep in that huge bed in that suite that I'd booked, completely platonic, just so I could hold her.

Like this. Um... ish.

But those hopes, those dreams-- while they never included losing Tommy or being surrounded by my family... they paled in comparison to my reality that Sunday morning. As I opened my eyes, taking in my surroundings, smelling that sweet scent of jasmine, I couldn't help but smile. And it wasn't just because my body was so relaxed, or because I felt so well-rested. The reason was in my arms, skin to skin, a faint smile on her lips. I didn't want to move, didn't want to disturb her. I wanted to watch her, hold her to me, never... *never* let her go. I was content, happy even, not a trace of anxiety present.

And then she began to stir.

And I waited. I waited for her to pull away, waited for the morning regret to settle in with her, the look to cross her face saying it all: she'd never meant to kiss me, or to finish what we had started, or...

Instead, though... instead she turned, snuggling in, placing a small kiss on that tattoo on my chest.

Speak, Warner. Say something. Anything.

"Good morning."

And I winced inwardly at my insanely un-witty morning banter.

"Mmmm," she said with a sleepy smile, "good morning to you, too."

Oh, great. Of course Little Jase would spring to life now. Control. More control than last night.

"How did you sleep?" I asked.

*Really? This is the first time you and your wife have woke up in the same bed in over a year and **that's** the best you can do?*

As one lone curl fell across her cheek, I couldn't stop myself. I softly, lifted the curl, tucking it behind her ear, letting my fingertips linger against her skin just a hint too long. My heart rate picked up at an alarming race with her reply.

"Amazing," she breathed, her arm snaking around my waist. "You?"

I couldn't stop my lips from brushing across hers before I whispered against them, "The best."

"Jase…"

"Fuck, Talli, don't say my name like that," I moaned, burying my head in her neck, shaking my head as she began to laugh. "It's not funny."

"Awww, what's the matter? Having a… *hard* time?"

I lifted myself, one eyebrow raised as I looked down at her. "Now listen, woman…"

"Oh, I missed you calling me that."

I blinked a couple times, a wistful smile touching my lips as I shifted, holding her body close to mine. "I…" I licked my lips that seemed suddenly dry. "I… Talli, I want my five minutes," I blurted out, my heart hammering so loud I swear I could hear it in my ears. "And I know, um… last night…"

"That was mine," she interrupted me, like she always used to, only this time I faltered, my eyes sliding shut as she again snaked her arm around me, tightening momentarily, in… in a hug. The sweetest little hug, and I could have cried it made me so damn happy, but…

"Ours," I corrected her, kissing the tip of her nose lightly. "But… yeah, five… five minutes, because there's so much I want to say to you. No… no, I *have* to, Talli. I *have* to."

Those blue eyes were swimming with tears as she slowly, surely nodded, letting me know it was okay, it was time. Scratch that, it was past time. I should have done this months ago. Months. Hell, I should have done this before it ever got to the point where I'd ended up in that bed with Bree, where I never should have been to begin with.

"Has the time started?"

"Give me a second," I said, holding up one finger before leaning in and giving her a light kiss on the lips, saying a little prayer that this worked. "Okay, I'm ready."

"Hmm? Oh. Oh, um… what…"

"Five minutes," I whispered, smirking at her stammering. *Oh, yeah.*

I'm good.

"Right, and time... starts... now."

"I love you."

A lone tear dropped from her eyes and I caught it with my fingertips, holding her gaze steady as I continued.

"Talli, with everything in me... I just... love you, and..."

We jumped as a loud banging on the bedroom door sounded, and she let out the cutest little shriek, just like she used to. I chuckled softly, holding her to me.

"Talli," Jackie's booming voice sounded from the other side of the door, "I am so sorry, Spunky, we must have all overslept. We have to leave in about 15 minutes."

Talli's big blue eyes widened slightly and she pushed herself up, the covers falling away before she could hold them to her. "Did... can you see..."

"There's nothing else available before tomorrow afternoon," he interrupted her.

And I laughed.

"This is *not* funny," she said as she scrambled over me, searching for her clothing.

"More typical than funny," I admitted, still smiling even as I pushed back the covers. She stopped short, her eyes raking over me before she shook her head slightly.

"I have to get back, I'm so sorry. I promised, and it's really important, especially with two doctors out on maternity leave."

"You'd think given their line of work they'd know how to prevent that."

"Ha ha, you're so funny," she deadpanned before turning to me. "The kids."

"I got em, I got em," I said with a lazy smile, pulling my boxer briefs up, handing her shirt to her. "Are you sure you have to put this on?"

"I have to... I have to shower, and pack, and..."

"Did you ever unpack?"

"Not really, and..."

"You're so damn cute when you panic."

She stopped briefly, a light pink color in her cheeks as she looked at me, scrunching up her nose. "Really?"

"Yeah, really. Clocks ticking; I'll bring your stuff to the washroom."

"Thank you, thank you. When are you coming home?"

Home. She… she asked when I'm coming… home…

"Are you coming in tonight?"

"No, actually I was going to stay until Tuesday morning, try to help out some around here before I go back."

"Oh, that's so sweet."

And she meant it.

I could tell she meant it, especially with that smile even as she rushed to the washroom. "You know…"

"No, not on the phone, Talli."

"Right. Right… Tuesday, then?"

"Talli." I opened the door to the washroom and pointed. "Shower. You're running out of time."

So once again, I was without my five minutes, although this time… this time it didn't really seem to bother me. Not after last night. Not now that I knew I was going to get that time, and not now that I believed, I really believed I had a shot.

No, I had more than a shot.

And being the fantabulous team that we are, Talli was ready--minus a ton of makeup, which she didn't need to begin with--and so were the children. The bags were in the rental car that Jackie would be handing over at the counter in the airport and I was kissing my family goodbye, promising them I would see them in a few short days.

"I wish I didn't have to rush out like this," Talli was saying, looking so sweetly frazzled that I had to kiss her, just a soft, gentle kiss on the lips.

"Thank you, so very much for coming out here," I said softly. "It means more to me than you'll ever know."

"I had to come, Jase," she replied. "Not just for Tommy, but for you."

I blushed slightly at her words, my eyes dropping before I met her gaze once more. "You thought of me?"

"Yeah, duh," she said, lightly pushing my shoulder. "I mean… you were a godsend when I lost my mother. And Jack… I… I know how much I needed you there when he passed away."

She... what?

"And I understand why you said no, why you couldn't make it."

"Said... no?" I managed to ask, my mind racing, trying to recollect exactly when I'd... no, I hadn't, so how...

"Bree told me, when she took the call. I just... I understand. Lisa and Jack were divorced so we weren't *technically* related to him anymore, and you were hardly a fan of his. But, yeah, like I said... I understand, and I just wanted you to know that."

My mouth had to be hanging wide open at this point, but I was stunned beyond any explanation of the word.

She had wanted me there?

In Ohio?

When...

And then, Bree...

"I have to go," she said with a soft smile, giving my hand one last squeeze before she turned and walked to the car.

Find your voice, damn it! Say something!

"Talli, wait."

"We'll talk when you get back," she said, before covering her heart with her hand. "I promise."

She was damn straight we would.

But Tuesday... Tuesday just wasn't going to be good enough. Gayle completely understood when I got on that phone, rearranging my flight. Jackie was right, nothing was available that day, but I would be touching down in Los Angeles about three in the afternoon tomorrow. That would give me just enough time to have everything done, and be completely ready for my five minutes.

Because we needed this.

But first... first I needed answers.

And I knew exactly who I had to get them from.

"Well, hello baby."

I swear my skin literally crawled at just the sight, let alone the sound of her. And the last damn place I wanted to be was at her apartment complex, standing out in the blazing sun even with my damn sunglasses on, but still out in the open where anyone passing by could see her throw her arms around me.

"Remember," she cooed in my ear, "we're in public. You have to behave."

"We're not about to be in public."

"Oooo, even better." She stood back, crooking her finger at me. "It's about damn time you came crawling back."

I pushed the front security door firmly shut as I stepped inside, pulling my sunglasses off. "Keep dreaming, Breeann. You should know why I'm here, and…"

"Temper, temper…"

"We're not in…"

"We're in public until you're in my apartment," she said softly, her icy stare so different from the way she'd once looked at me.

How could I have been so blind?

I stepped through the door of her apartment on that first floor, rolling my eyes at the stench of smoke that hung in the air. "Have a seat, baby."

"I won't be here long enough to have a seat, Bree."

"You know…"

"When the fuck did you make it a habit to answer my phone?" I asked between my teeth.

"You know I took your messages…"

"From the front desk, whenever they called or brought them by. But my *cellphone*?"

"Well, what, was I supposed to let it go to voicemail?" she whined.

"Yes!" I started to take a step towards her but knew I shouldn't. "Yes, damn it, my personal calls… those were none of your fucking business."

"Oh, what is *your wife*…"

"How many times did she call about Em being at the doctors… or… or…"

"I told you."

"Or in the fucking hospital, Bree? The *hospital*."

"Once or twice, okay?"

I threw my hands up in frustration before running them through my hair, pulling at the ends of it.

"But come on, Jase," she continued, her voice that shrill whine that caused me to inwardly cringe. "We were writing and recording, you had performances that you couldn't just cancel over... some... coughing thing, or some ear infections, or..."

"Seriously?!" I shouted, feeling my pulse throbbing in the vein on the side of my head. "You even knew *why* she was in the hospital, and all you could tell me was she was sick again so Talli wasn't coming?"

"What were you going to do, just pack up and head back there? She handled it just fine without you there doing, what? Sitting there?"

"Supporting my wife, being there for my children, everything I should have been doing the whole damn time."

"Oh, what*ever*. You were perfectly fine where you were, and you rather enjoyed the company, or did you forget?"

"I wouldn't have been there if..."

"If what?" she asked, stepping closer and flipping her blonde hair back over her shoulder. "If that frumpy, dull, boring thing you married..."

"Do *not* speak about my wife," I said through clenched teeth. "She has more class in her little finger than you have in your entire body."

"Oh, class is it?"

"The last thing she would do is manipulate someone into..."

"You think she's not manipulative?"

"At least you're not denying that you are."

"Oh, come on, Jase, I..."

"Jack's death," I cut her off, my nostrils flaring as I inhaled sharply over her laughter.

"So I forgot to mention that. Oops."

"You not only failed to mention that Jack died, but that Talli wanted me there."

"Oh no, I think the exact word was *needed*, hello pathetic much?"
It is unethical to hit a woman... it is unethical to hit a woman, it is...
Holy shit.

"You set me up."

"What?" she asked, her bravado faltering slightly.

"You... how did know when she was coming back? Because you

did. You know exactly when she would be there."

She rolled her eyes. "Oh, please…"

I pulled out my cell, waving it slightly. "One phone call and I'll know."

"All right, fine. I called your house and Linda let it slip."

"And then you… you fucking bitch, you set me up." I ran my hands through my hair again, inhaling, exhaling, trying to control my anger. "You heard her, didn't you?"

I glared at her as she sat in her chair, picking up her nail file and going back to her primping. "I don't know what you're talking about."

"Hey… HEY, fucking tell me!

She sighed, rolling her eyes as she looked up at me. "Look, Jase, I told you what I wanted. I told you I would go to any lengths to get it. It's not my fault you didn't listen."

"Fuck!" I yelled in frustration.

"We may as well have," she replied with an uninterested shrug. "No one would believe we didn't."

"No, they… they're going to believe, because *you* are going to tell them."

"Oh!" she let out a short laugh. "Oh, that was… that was a good one. Emphatically not, okay? Not even if hell froze over. Even you knowing all this? It doesn't change anything."

I shook my head, my breathing erratic, my mind racing over everything… everything…

"You're wrong," I said, full of conviction. "This changes… everything."

"Really?" she looked up from her nails. "So you and Talli are… back together? And… and this sudden revelation is the miracle fix? Funny, I haven't heard anything about the divorce being called off, and…" She glanced up at me, her eyebrow raised. "My new buddy, Mary Coffman? Yeah, she tells me that her brother Paul has a hot date with *his girlfriend*, none other than one Talia Warner. Name sound familiar?"

No… no she wouldn't. They're not dating, she told… no, Jaden told me… and…

"Kind of… ironic? Is that the word I'm looking for? That here you are thinking you've had some epiphany, that your marriage can be salvaged after some damn football game, and guess what? The weekend was her goodbye to you."

"Not… even close," I said with much more conviction than I felt.

"Really? That lovely little restaurant, the one that I saw you at when you were out with… with the boys? That's where they're going. Go on. See for yourself."

And I had to.

Damn it, I had to. I had to see it with my own eyes, see how Bree was lying again. Because she had to be. Because this weekend, it wasn't goodbye. No, this weekend, it was a… a reconnection. A recommitment.

And yet…

Yet I sat there, staring at her back, where her shoulders shook with laughter at whatever that damn doctor was saying.

And I saw her place her hand over his, just as she had with mine.

And I saw him lean in and… and kiss her.

And the air left the room…

And so did I.

I walked brusquely, trying to hide my face, my tears from people entering the establishment, pushing my sunglasses back on my face even in the dark of night as my phone began to buzz.

Damien.

"Talk to me."

"Dude… are you okay?"

No. No, not in any way, shape, or form. I couldn't breathe…

"I… fuck. No. No, not even…"

"Timmy's band, Opium Den. Meet me there in five."

I nodded, even though he couldn't see. "Make it ten." I wiped my eyes, unlocking my car and sliding into the driver's seat. "And be ready to call a cab. I need to get my drink on."

CHAPTER 19

TALIA

It almost seemed fitting that the temperature was so unseasonably warm, even for California. Everything about that Monday seemed just a little off, and if I didn't know better, I could have sworn that the little hairs kept sticking up on the back of my neck, telling me something was terribly wrong. But I had no way of even seeing the back of my neck, since my hair had decided to be one damn frizz ball that day. Even my clothes were sticking to me, making me feel absolutely gross.

Work was insanely busy, to the point where they talked me into taking a beeper home in case they needed 'full-moon' back up, so I needed an all-night babysitter, which luckily wasn't too hard to find. And she'd even agreed to take them from the moment I left work, so that I could go out to dinner with Paul...

Yeah.

But I had to. He just... well, he was my friend. But that was all he was to me, and somehow, some way he'd gotten the impression that perhaps we were something more. Perhaps we were actually a... a *we*, and we weren't. That was something that had to be remedied immediately.

"So I'll pick you up..."

"Oh, no," I interrupted him, holding up my hand and shaking my head slightly. "I'm dropping off the kids and I can meet you there."

"Seriously, I..." His voice trailed off as I held up the beeper.

"Just in case," I said with a grin and a shrug.

"I could always... okay, okay, that look on your face says it all. I'm overstepping, I know."

Did he know? Because I was beginning to wonder. Hell, he'd even assumed that I was dropping the kids off with Mary for her to watch them, and that was so far from my mind that words couldn't begin to describe it. There was just something a little off about her as well, something I couldn't quite place but... but every time I saw her, there were little questions she would ask that I found... intrusive. There. That's what it was. She seemed intrusive, as if she were fishing for information, and if she was going to do that with me, what questions would she ask my children? Not that she would get very far with Elizabeth, who would tell her to mind her own 'beeswax'. Michael, though, might say something, tell a little snippet of our private lives to her without even being aware of what was happening.

Hell, I didn't even know what was happening.

Especially not after a cryptic message Jase had left on my voice mail while I was in with a patient.

"I hope you have some time tonight. To talk, I mean... to talk, because we really need to, okay?"

He'd left that message rather early in the morning and his phone had been going straight to voicemail all day long. Again, this was another one of those 'oh this can't be good' things, but I couldn't listen to that, not right at that moment. I know he had things to say, but so did I.

How exactly does one say that they made a rash decision, that they're not so sure that divorce is the answer?

"What is on your mind?" Evelyn Truesdale asked as I brought the children to her condo, where her niece would be watching them.

"So very much," I admitted, smiling over at Lila, the twenty-three-year-old wonder who my children had instantly adored from the moment we met her. "Thank you for doing this, both of you."

"Not a problem, it's my pleasure," Lila replied. "I do have a few questions for you, though."

"Oh, of course."

"I have this… ugh, this *huge* paper that I have to do, as part of my final project for Early Childhood Education," she began, "and I promise I won't use names, or I'll change them if need be, but I would love to use your children as… well, inspiration, and examples."

"Oohhh, can I read it?" Elizabeth asked excitedly, looking up from her coloring book that Lila had out and ready for them, and I couldn't help but laugh.

"I don't think you'll understand it, munchkin," I said to her, before turning to Lila. "Of course, of course. It's the least I can do, with all the help you've given me ever since this building opened back up. And Evelyn, I can't believe you were holding out on me!" I have my neighbor a one-armed hug.

"Not holding out, dear, just waiting for you to be ready."

"Whatcha wanna do when you're out of school?" Elizabeth was asking as I wrote down my cell phone number along with the number of the restaurant.

"Well, *this*," Lila replied, and I looked up from my paper.

"Really? Not teaching in an actual school setting?"

"I'm really leaning more towards being a nanny, having more hands-on with the children, being there for children whose parents…well, aren't so much *absent* as they are busy." She scrunched up her nose as she tilted her head over to the side. "Did that make sense?"

"Total sense," I replied, feeling my heart sink. Of course, she'd want to be a nanny, and she'd make a wonderful one, but damn my kids would miss her. I pasted my smile back on, though, and continued on with my laundry list of instructions.

"You're on call this evening?" Evelyn asked, gesturing towards my beeper.

"Yeah," I said, still grinning. "It's full moon night and I promised I'd help."

"So it's not an old wives' tale?" Lila asked and I shook my head.

"No, that extra gravity pull definitely increases the number of babies that want to make their appearance." I pulled out my extra key, leaving it on the counter beside my note. "I apologize if I've forgotten anything, but there's the key, just in case. Just… oh, the place is such a mess right now."

And in my eyes it was, although to someone else it probably wouldn't be. This wasn't the reason, though, that I was so reluctant to have someone I didn't completely know watch the children in my home. I'd learned my lesson from Hurricane Leah about strangers being in my house, and even if I wasn't with Jase anymore I still had to protect our children.

"I'm sure you thought of everything," Lila said with her easygoing smile.

"I'm actually rather known for being forgetful," I admitted, chewing on my bottom lip. "But... that's why I'm leaving the key. And... and I know they'll be good for you. I know it."

"Off to dinner with your doctor?" Evelyn asked, and I sighed.

"He's not my doctor, no matter how much... no, just..."

"Ah, I see. I see." She smiled up at me, placing a trembling hand on my arm. "And now you do as well."

Wow, sometimes she was confusing.

But I said my goodbyes, with a promise that Lila would bring the children home in the morning, when my on-call stint would be over. And she'd also promised to call if anything came up, if there was any emergency, if Elizabeth lost another tooth, or if she got a text from me saying I needed a call to get me away from an uncomfortable situation. Yes, I most definitely liked this girl, almost as much as my children did.

My cellphone was securely in my pocket as I walked into that restaurant and let the hostess know my 'party' was already there. Paul smiled and waved slightly at me, and I could feel the nerves begin to take over.

I despise hurting people.

"You look beautiful," he murmured as he took my hand in his, kissing the top of it softly. I pulled my hand away, shaking my head slightly.

"I... I am so sorry," I stammered.

"Over, what? Being late?"

"Pardon?" I glanced at my watch, frowning. "Five minutes, right. Yeah, I'm... I'm sorry about that, too."

"I took the liberty of ordering our wine. I hope you don't mind."

I did mind. I minded a lot.

"I can't drink, Paul, I'm on call tonight."

"Oh, right, right. Sorry." He grinned, shrugging. "And here I thought I could…"

"Please don't finish that sentence," I said quickly, keeping my voice low.

"Are you ever going to loosen up around me, Talia?"

I opened my mouth to reply, but was interrupted when a salad was placed in front of me, the waiter gone before I could ask what in the world he thought he was doing.

"Just a Caesar salad, to get you started," Paul said with a wink. "I know how much you…"

"You don't know as much about me as you think you do," I interrupted him, tears of frustration in my eyes already. "And this… this…"

"Something obviously has you upset."

Nah, you think?

"I tried telling you that going to that football game with Jase was a bad…"

"I didn't go to the football game, Paul," I interrupted him yet again. "I was in Groves Point, for Tommy's funeral."

His eyes showed his surprise, which he quickly covered. "Tommy, the one who got the tickets?"

"Yeah," I said softly, picking at my salad, my appetite completely nonexistent.

"But he's *Jase's* cousin?"

"He's family, Paul. He's family."

"Who, Tommy? Or Jase?"

I lifted my eyes to his, my gaze and voice unwavering as I replied. "Both."

"Ah."

"And… and I feel… well, I feel that everything being left unsaid is… well, it's confusing, in more ways than one."

"Well, going off with him the weekend before your divorce is bound to be confusing."

"Wow, I'm not really making myself clear, am I?" I took a deep breath, placing my fork down on my plate. "Paul, we're friends, you and

I. That was all I'd seen us as from day one. I wasn't ready for anything more with you, or anyone else for that matter, and now... now that I... Paul, I'm sorry. I'm sorry for anything I've ever said or... or done that made you think otherwise."

His eyes narrowed slightly as he took in my appearance, my expression, my trembling hands. "What did he say to you?"

"What are you talking about?"

"Because you... you're a bundle of nerves."

"Well, I... I dislike hurting people."

"And Jase... how does *he* feel about how much he's hurt you?"

"Paul, I... I am going to ask that you please respect me, and... and my decisions."

"I wasn't aware you'd called off the divorce, Talia."

I blinked back my tears, shaking my head slightly. "No... I... I haven't. Not... not yet."

He ran one hand through his hair, taking a deep breath before he continued. "So you've forgiven him? For... for everything, for his treatment of you, for his affair, for his flaunting it for the whole world, including your children to see?"

And the blood immediately rushed to my cheeks, because I knew the answer to that.

No.

No I hadn't forgiven him. And I wasn't even sure if I could. There was one thing, though, that I was one hundred percent certain of.

"I love him, Paul. And even if he and I can't make this work, I... I can't be with anyone else, not with the way I feel about him. It wouldn't be fair, not to me, not to... well, not to anyone, actually."

He nodded, his frown lines still showing prominently.

"I... I'm sorry, I can go..."

"Nonsense," he said, flashing his smile. "Nonsense. We're friends, right? We're friends having dinner."

"Right," I said, my shoulders dropping slightly with a bit of relief. "So you don't hate me?"

"I could never hate you." He took a sip of his wine, still taking in my expression. "And I'll be here for you, whenever you need a friend."

I knew what he was suggesting. I knew he was saying that it was going to happen again, that Jase was bound to cheat again. He'd said that about his ex-wife, about all cheaters actually. He'd said it was only a matter of time, especially if they'd gotten away with it before. The worst part about his observation, or his opinion, was I actually believed it, in one tiny part of my heart, the part that kept arguing with me, telling me I was making a huge mistake.

But I wasn't going to say any of that to Paul. No, all I was going to say was, "Thank you."

He smiled warmly over at me, replying with, "Don't mention it."

Dinner seemed a bit more relaxed after that, even when Lila called to let me know that Elizabeth was upset.

"I'm sorry," I murmured to Paul before returning my attention to the phone call. "Did she say what was wrong?"

"She said something about you and… and her father fighting."

"Really?" I asked, blinking back my surprise. "We haven't in quite some time."

"Oh, she's rather adamant that the two of you were fighting during the night in Indiana, before you came back here."

"What would make her think that?" I asked, confused.

"She said something about… she thought she heard him yelling at you, and you crying."

"What? She's imagining…"

And I stopped.

I stopped and my face flamed bright red as I remembered *exactly* what had happened the night before we left.

"Oh… oh, no we… we weren't… um, can I… no, I don't know what to… can you just tell her that I said we weren't… um, fighting?" I asked as embarrassment along with a strong case of the giggles began to consume me.

"Oh… OH! Oh, I'm so…"

And the fact that she *got* it caused me to giggle even more uncontrollably, as if I needed that in the middle of the restaurant. I apologized profusely to Paul, and to Lila who was giggling herself.

"No need to apologize, ma…er, Talli."

"I was about to say," I said through my laughter. "Call me back if you need anything else, all right?"

I could still feel the heat radiating off my face as I placed my phone down on the table. Wow, this certainly was going to make the rest of dinner a bit awkward.

"So, um… Elizabeth heard you… arguing?"

And with that question I began to giggle again, trying to keep it as silent as I could, my shoulders shaking slightly.

"I'm sorry, I'm sorry… um…" I reached over placing my hand over his. "How about let's change the subject?"

And that's when the mood changed.

That's when he leaned across the table, missing my lips only because I turned my head slightly to the side.

"What the hell do you think you're doing?" I hissed as quietly as I could.

"What I should have done weeks ago," he replied, his arm still around the back of my chair.

"No… no, I'm sorry, Paul, but I have to go." I stood abruptly, reaching into my bag and pulling out money that I placed on the table. "That should cover my half."

"Talia, wait. Have a seat."

I took a deep breath as I glared at him. "I don't know what the hell game you're playing, what you're trying to prove, or who you're trying to prove it to. I love my husband, and I thought I made that perfectly clear. Until you can accept that, until you can *respect* that, you need to stay the hell away from me."

I didn't wait for his reply, nor was I interested in it at the time. My head was down low, looking at my beeper that was going off as I stepped out into the warm breeze.

Damn it.

Here I was in a shitty mood, needing to go the hell off and vent, and instead I was going to have to put on my happy face and be professional and…

Did I just hear Jase's voice?

I shook it off, reminding myself that Jase wasn't coming back until the next day, my heels clicking loudly on the sidewalk as I made my way to my vehicle.

Fuck, it was going to be a long night.

"Thank you so much for all of your help," Dr. Stewart said with a smile as I walked out of the locker room early the next morning, changed back into my civilian clothing, my damp curls pulled up in a messy bun.

"That's what I'm here for, right?" I glanced at my cellphone, smiling as I saw the missed call from Jase. *He's thinking about me.*

"Guess it's a good thing you're not coming in until later."

"Right," I said with a laugh. "But believe me, I'll be taking advantage of the daycare today so I can get some sleep."

It was nearly four a.m. when I finally pulled into the parking lot of my condo, still in desperate need of unwinding despite my extreme exhaustion. I grabbed my purse, leaving my duffel bag with my change of clothing in the vehicle, and made my way towards the front door, keys in hand. I know I should have been paying better attention, but I was staring at my call log, still grinning like a fool that he'd called me, even if I missed it when...

"Oh, shit!" I screeched as I ran into someone. "I'm so sorry, I... I..."

And my voice trailed off as I looked up into Jase's stormy eyes. There was something in the way he looked at me, a profound sadness crying out, that could either be shielded or enhanced by the alcohol that I could smell on him.

Oh fuck... oh, fuck he... he really wasn't dealing well with Tommy's death...

"What are you doing, Talli?" he asked, his voice low, raspy, sending shivers through me despite of the slight slur in his speech.

"When did you get here?" I asked, inhaling sharply as his fingertips lightly touched my face before lifting a damp curl. His eyes slid shut before he leaned down, resting his forehead on mine.

"God, Talli, what are you doing?" he breathed.

"I... I'm just getting back from work," I stammered, my hands on his chest even as his right arm circled around my waist, holding me to him.

"Damien, he told me... he told me I needed to be here. *Here*... with you, because... because..."

"Jase, what happened?"

"This... the clothes, the hair, the..." I could almost swear I heard a sob come from him. "This isn't you."

Oh, he really wasn't making any sense, and I'm sure the obvious extreme amounts of alcohol he'd consumed had something to do with it. But curiosity, wondering what he meant, had me asking, "Then what is me?"

"This," he said, his fingertips lifting my chin slightly, his lips hovering above mine. "*This* is you."

Softly, gently he placed his lips on mine, sighing as his tongue swept in my mouth. His kiss was a heady mixture of passion and sweetness, the taste of his tears mingling in with the Jaeger that lingered behind on his lips. I was trembling in his arms, responding with everything in me, my heart hammering behind my ribcage. This... this was the last thing I'd expected tonight, and damn it if he was sober... if he was sober, I would be pulling him up to my room, stripping him down, and making love with him, just as we had back in Indiana.

He pulled away, his hands still on my shoulders, his thumbs caressing lightly as he spoke again.

"That's you, Talli."

And I was so confused... confused by the extreme hurt in his features, confused by his tears, because this... this wasn't fitting in with what I thought was wrong at all.

He dropped his hands, pushing one into his pocket and pulling out his keys. "I... have to..."

"No... no, no, no," I said quickly, reaching out and taking his keys from him, and holding his other hand in mine. "Come on up, okay? Let me make some coffee, and... and we can talk, all right?"

He had no choice but to follow me into the building, since he couldn't go anywhere without his keys... well, it was either come with me, or wait outside for a cab. He was silent, though, the entire ride up in the elevator, but his eyes... oh, his eyes were so intense as he stared at me, my clothing, my face. I made it a point to thank him when he was sober for making me even more self-conscious, but right at that moment I had to get him up there, have him crash until he sobered up.

"I'm sorry it's such a mess," I said, pushing my door open, and motioning for him to go inside. He let out a short laugh as he looked around. "What?"

"Only you, Talli," he said, stumbling slightly as he stepped further inside. "Only you."

"Is this a good or a bad thing?" I asked, kicking off my shoes, but didn't wait for him to answer. "Come on, to the kitchen."

"I don't want coffee," he said softly, his eyes following me as I walked past.

"Not coffee," I said, pulling down the ibuprofen and reaching into the refrigerator for a small bottle of Gatorade. "Before you go to sleep, you need this."

I jumped as I turned around to find him directly behind me, staring down at me, his eyes a dark gray. "Your hair... it's..."

"Yeah, I had to shower before I left work," I said with a shudder. "I was a mess."

A muscle in his jaw twitched as he contemplated my words, his eyes focused on my hands that I held out, the ibuprofen and Gatorade there for him to take. He murmured his thanks, tossing the pills into his mouth and chasing them with a long drink.

"Jase, I... well, we need to talk, okay?"

He let out something between a laugh and a sob before he shook his head. "I... I don't think I could take it right now."

"I really need to..."

His arms were around me, holding me to him so I couldn't see his face. "Please not yet. Just lie to me, okay? Please? Just for tonight."

But I wasn't lying.

I wasn't lying when I kissed him. I wasn't lying when I sighed against his lips as his hands peeled away every piece of clothing I had on. I wasn't lying when I wrapped my legs around his waist, begging him to not make me wait any longer. I wasn't lying when he took me to my bedroom, placing me so tenderly on that bed that I could have cried. I wasn't lying when I pulled that t-shirt off of him, or when I helped with his pants, or when I pulled him on top of me. I wasn't lying when he asked me what I wanted, and I told him...

"You... I... I want... you."

And maybe it was wrong, maybe it was taking advantage of his vulnerable state of mind, or maybe... maybe it was meant to be as he thrust into me, harder and harder, his fingers digging into my hips. There was no masking the moans or cries, no holding back the words that tumbled from our lips.

"This… *fuck*, Talli… this is… is you…"

"Yes," I moaned, my head falling back as I arched up against him.

"And no one… *no one* else can make you feel this way…"

Tears touched my eyes as the scene of roses and candles flashed in my mind. "Jase…"

"Just say it… just… just lie to me."

"I love you," I breathed, holding him to me until the last shudder and sigh.

But I wasn't lying.

And that's the part that hurt so… *so* very much as I stood in the doorway of my bedroom, watching him sleep on that bed that we'd shared in Ohio, with *Celebrity Gossip's* report of his visit with Bree playing in my living room.

I loved him.

But I would never be enough for him.

And all the lies in the world couldn't change that.

JASE

Do I know how to fuck up royally, or what?

"Damn it," I muttered as I pushed the covers off of me, staring down at my naked form in the middle of Talli's bed.

Alone.

I could hear the banging of dishes in the kitchen, and I knew she was pissed. Half of me wanted to kick my own ass for what had happened, half of me wanted to kick Damien's ass for telling me I should go to Talli, and then the other half… no, wait. That's three halves.

"Fuck.

Her muttered curse came after the sound of glass breaking.

Oh, this was going to be bad.

Of course it was going to be bad. I'd come over here to confront her, to ask her why… just… why. I don't know how long I'd waited for her to pull in, but there was no mistaking the wet hair, the different set of clothes. She didn't even have her bag with her, the one she used for work. Fuck, did she just have clothes over at his house now?

But then…

Could I blame it on the Jaeger?

I couldn't stop myself from kissing her, and as I pulled my boxer briefs up I reminded myself that I should have known better. I suppose I'd asked for it though… I was the one who told her to lie to me.

And she lied so very well.

I finished dressing and shuffled my way to the bathroom, rolling my eyes as I glanced down at the packaged toothbrush and short note from her. Did she think she was being courteous? Of course, she did, she was always doing little things like this for people who stayed over. Hell, had she done this for *him*? Had he spent the night over here before?

And where the hell were my kids?

I was simmering just below the surface as I made my way into the living room area, glancing over at her from her seat in her throne, aka the papasan chair. She had the nerve to glare at *me*? Just… rich.

"When did you get back?"

Sure. Now that I have my shoes on and I'm ready to walk out the door she speaks.

"Yesterday."

"*When*?"

I glared at her, telling myself to just calm down… just calm down…

"Where are the kids?"

"Here, let me help you," she said, ignoring my question as she hit a couple buttons, bring up whatever she had DVR'd.

"So here we have Jase Warner," a familiar voice came through the speakers, "here at… yep, there she is… Breeann Hamilton's place."

"You've got to be fucking kidding me," I said with a roll of my eyes.

"Even after this weekend," she said, standing up and walking towards me, "the first damn thing you did, aside from lying to me about when you were coming back, was going to see your whore."

"Jeezus, Talli, you think you know every fucking thing, don't you?" I snapped. "Go on. Ask me what I was doing there."

"Well, let's see…" She hit another button and the damn thing began to play again.

"Rumor has it that Ms. Hamilton was pissed that he had some

supposed rendezvous with his wife this weekend, and she ended their relationship."

And she hit the pause button again.

"Does that ring any bells, Jase?"

I didn't mean to lose my temper, but damn it... *damn it*, she should know. She should know that I love her, how many times have I told her? And a relationship with Bree? Fucking, seriously?

"That's what I..."

"*Fuck* you, Talli!" I snapped. "I have... I have tried over and over for... for weeks, for *months* now to make it up to you! I told you I love you, I *showed* you how I felt, and you don't fucking believe me! What am I supposed to do?"

"And you're back to blaming this on *me*! I didn't put a gun to your head and make you..."

"*I didn't sleep with her!* Not... not then, not *ever*, okay? But no, you're not going to believe that because..."

"I *saw* you!"

"You don't know what you saw," I yelled back. "And you... you're a fucking hypocrite, you know that?"

Her blue eyes widened before she glared at me once more. "How am I a hypocrite?"

"You..." I stepped in closer, my eyes looking at her flushed cheeks, trying to suppress the memories from the night before. "How was dinner, Talia? Your date with the doctor?"

And her cheeks turned an even deeper shade of pink.

"Work my *ass*. I watched him kiss you, Talli. And then... then you don't..."

"You what?!"

"...then you don't get back until, what, going on five in the morning?"

"I was on call... I... you were spying on me?"

"Hey, at least you took a shower in between us, got to give you that..." I caught her wrist before her hand made contact with my face.

"Did you stay for the finale?" she asked, her eyes full of unshed tears. "Did... did you see the part where I left, where I told him to stay the hell away from me? Did you bother to catch that?"

I let go of her wrist, stepping back and shaking my head at her.

"You *should* know better, Jase, because I'm not like..."

"Like what?" I snapped when she stopped. "Like *what?*"

"I'm not like you! Okay? I'm not like you!"

I nodded slowly, not saying a word as I swallowed over that lump in my throat, over the tears in my eyes.

Now I knew exactly what she thought of me.

And there was nothing more to say, was there?

"Just go," she said, turning her back to me. "Just... just go. Get out of this condo, get... get out of my life. Just... go."

"Fine," I said, pulling the door opened, glancing over at her back that was still turned. "See you Thursday."

Thursday.

At our divorce hearing.

And I started to walk out of that condo, I swear I did, but damn it...

I ... I wasn't done.

And I slammed that door as hard as I could as I turned back around, ready to give her a piece of my mind, ready to scream at the top of my lungs at her, but... but I stopped.

I stopped.

Because at the sound of that slamming door she... broke.

And she dropped to her knees, her back still to that door.

"I didn't mean it," she sobbed, her face buried in her hands as her body began to shake. "I didn't mean it, I swear, please... please don't go... please don't leave me."

The room began to blur, my heart splintering as she continued to cry.

"Why? What... what have I done? What... did I do... that was so... wrong?"

Slowly I walked forward, my own tears falling before I made it across the room.

"Whatever... it was, I'm so... so sorry. Just don't go... just don't go."

I knelt beside her, reaching out but so afraid to touch her, afraid... of... of...

No, I couldn't be afraid. Not now.

"Talli?"

And she froze.

She held back her sobs as I placed my hands on her shoulders, giving a light squeeze. *Please don't pull away... please... please don't pull away from me...*

"I'm right here. I'm... I'm right here, and I'm not going any..."

I stopped as she turned suddenly, her arms so strong as she held on to me, her tears soaking the front of my shirt. "Why?" she sobbed to me.

And I knew what she was asking.

And my heart broke right along with hers, as I finally saw... as she finally let me see... how badly I had hurt her. I could see it, I could feel it, I... I could hear it as over and over she just kept repeating that one loaded, painful word.

"Why?"

"I... I don't know, Talli, I don't know why. I just... I just know I was wrong." I held her to me, my fingers tangled in her hair as she shook in my arms. "It's time, okay? It's time."

"Time for..."

"Before we... before this is over, okay?" I leaned back, my hands cupping her face, my thumbs brushing away her still-falling tears. "I... I want my five minutes. Now."

Please say yes, Talli...

She nodded briefly, taking my hand and standing as I led her over to the couch, that same couch we'd spent so many hours on all those years ago.

"Sit down, baby, okay?"

She lowered herself down on the couch, her back stiff and straight, her hands twisting in her lap. Her tears-- those large tears were still dropping from her eyes, each one taking another piece of my heart. She took a deep breath as she looked up at me, her eyes watching as I sunk to my knees in front of her.

And I knew.

I just... *knew.*

"Jase, what..."

"I love you," I cut her off, placing my hands over hers. "I... love you so much, with everything in me. I just love you."

Her lips were parted slightly as a sob broke through, her hands trembling as I pulled them apart, caressing them.

"I... I know," I continued, trying to steady my voice, "that love isn't always enough. I know it doesn't fix everything. And... and I didn't show you, for the longest time I didn't show you. That was so wrong, and I can't take it back, I can't erase it. But I can show you now. I... I can be the man I should have been this whole time, if... if you just let me."

Her lower lip quivered as she inhaled again, looking down at our hands.

"No... no, look at me, Talli. Look up... look up at me."

I waited for her eyes to lock with mine before I continued. "I'm sorry for... for everything. I'm sorry for being such an asshole, for... for being so short with you. I'm sorry that I was harsh, I'm sorry that I... that I gave you so much hell, that I argued with you over every little thing. I'm sorry I made you so anxious, I'm sorry I wasn't supportive, I'm... I'm sorry I went on that fucking tour, because I should have *seen*. I should have known something was wrong. And I know you don't believe me, but maybe... maybe someday you will. I didn't sleep with her. I couldn't sleep with her. And I could never love her, Talli, because I... I love *you*."

"She wasn't some random girl, Jase," Talli finally seemed to find her voice. "She was someone you... you brought into our home. She's someone you had a *relationship* with, someone you lied to me about repeatedly, purposefully. How am I supposed to get past that? How am I supposed to forgive that?"

"I ... I don't have that answer," I said, squeezing her hands, the guilt threatening to consume me. "I can tell you... I can tell you that I know how wrong I was. I can tell you that I should have turned to you, that I can see that now. I can't find what I need or what I'm looking for elsewhere, because they're not you. I... I let petty bullshit get in the way, I wasn't honest with *you*. Hell, I wasn't even honest with myself. I know now, I see now I... I should have fought for you, for us. I should have been the man you needed, the man you once loved."

"Once?"

"I... I..." I felt my face growing hot as I stammered over my words. "Talli, this... this isn't about the kids. Not anymore. We've proven we can do that; we can be a team; we can do what's best for them no matter what. And... and this isn't about our friends, or our extended families, or... or about Bree, or Paul either. This is about you... and... and me. This is about *us*. We..." I held her hands so tightly, praying with everything she would just listen, just believe.

"We didn't *try*. Not when things went from bad to worse, not when they blew up in our faces, not when we were handed that opportunity on a tarnished platter. I didn't just let you walk away once, Talli... *twice*. Twice I let you walk out that door. Twice I wasn't man enough to... to do *this*. I wasn't man enough to get on my knees in front of you and... and... oh, sssshhhh, please don't cry..." I wiped her tears away, then caressed her beautiful face, my hands tangling in her hair at the nape of her neck, recalling the words I'd said to her so long ago in the pouring rain, the words I'd repeated over the years. "I love you, do you hear me? *I love you*. Above all others."

"Please don't..."

"I love you like there's no tomorrow," I went on, ignoring her whispered plea. "Please let there be a tomorrow."

She closed her eyes as the sobs shook her shoulders, and I wanted so badly to take her in my arms, hold her to me, never let her go... but I wasn't done. Not yet.

"Open your eyes, baby," I said as softly as I could, feeling the shiver pass through her. I leaned forward, so close I could feel her shortened breaths on my face. "Talli... I love you like it's never going to hurt, never going to rip my heart to shreds, never going to make me wish the hurt away, never going to..." My voice trailed off at the pain in her eyes, and I just had to know.

"One more shot, Talli. One more shot, okay? Give me a chance to make this right. Not just your friend, not just a voice on the phone. And maybe... maybe you can find it right here, in your heart, to let me back in, to love me again."

"I never stopped."

It was my turn to be silent as her words sunk in, as I searched her eyes looking for a sign-- any sign, either way.

Was this really happening?

"Talli?"

"It wouldn't hurt... *so much*... if I didn't love you."

I took the deepest breath I could as that weight, that soul-crushing weight I'd been carrying, lifted from my chest.

She loves me

"I just... don't know if I can..."

"Say it," I cut her off, my voice a muffled sob as I rested my forehead against hers, my eyes shut tight against the stinging tears. And just as she had so many times before when I'd asked, she complied.

"I love you."

Oh God... it's real...

"Jase, I just..."

I silenced her the only way I wanted to, covering her lips with mine. So much heartache, so much love flowed through that one soft kiss, and I was reluctant to end it, especially... oh, especially when I felt her fingertips on my face, that one sweet gesture healing just a little piece of my heart.

I kept my hands tangled in her hair as I pulled back, searching her eyes. "You once said that I was the only man who'd broken your heart that you could forgive. You'd said that... that I didn't have to say I was sorry, because that's what forgiveness is for."

"That's not fair," she whispered, and I knew it wasn't. The circumstances had been so different, but the threatened consequences had been the same.

"Just... one more shot," I said. "Just... a continuance, okay? We get a continuance, and we... and we *try*. Really try. No more avoiding the subject, nor more skirting around the issues, no more walking on eggshells. All... or... or nothing. And if we can't fix this, if you can't forgive me, I'll... I'll walk away. But not... not now."

She was silent, tears clinging to her lashes as we held each other's gaze. And when she spoke, her voice was so very soft, so unsure. "If I say okay... what do we do then?"

"Whatever it takes," I replied. I kissed her softly once more, reveling in the feel of her lips against mine, sighing contentedly as she leaned forward.

"What..." She shrugged slightly. "What do we do?"

"We... we call our lawyers." I pushed her curls back and kissed the tip of her nose. "And then, we... we go to... breakfast? Or... or lunch. And we... we decide where to go from there."

"Lunch? Like a... like a... date?"

And I couldn't help myself, I couldn't stop the laugh that escaped my lips, I couldn't stop myself from kissing her again, I couldn't stop myself from holding her so, so close to me.

"If that's what you want it to be, Spunky," I whispered in her ear. "I'd sweep you off those pretty little feet if you... if you just let me."

I heard another sob leave her as her arms snaked around me, her face buried in my neck.

"I love you so much," I said, "and someday... someday you'll believe me. Just... just say yes."

Another sob left her, but this time... this time I felt her move. I pulled back slightly, searching her eyes, watching as... as her head moved...

North and South. North and South...

That... that meant...

"Talli?"

And with one soft word, my world was one step closer to being whole.

"Yes."

COMING MARCH 2, 2022
THE CONCLUSION TO THE TIME STANDS STILL SERIES

My Happy Ending Part 3
Time Stands Still Book 5

Authors (especially indie!) rely on your reviews. Please take a moment to review this novel on the platform that it was purchased from. It is appreciated more than you will ever know!

ABOUT THE AUTHOR

Carlie Yates (That One Writer Chick) has been writing stories since she was in the fifth grade, convinced that if she didn't get her thoughts and characters down on paper, her head would 'plode; it could be ex- or im-, but either way, it wouldn't be pretty. Inspired by S.E. Hinton, she always said when she grew up that she would be a published author. This Midwest mom of boys has addictions to reading, road trips, hair dye, and the Oxford comma, and is thoroughly convinced at any given time the theme track to *My Three Sons* will start playing in the background of her home. She is currently renouncing her pledge to grow up.

ACKNOWLEDGEMENTS AND THANK YOUS

Rose Thank you for reminding me that being me is my greatest asset.

Kayla My business bestie for keeping me on track and my ego in check.

Tami The T to my J for the name and so much more.

Nellie For showing me that I deserve to succeed.

Zach, Marcus, and Jake Without whom I am nothing.

My Visions et al Loves For yelling at me for over a year to fix it.

Jon and Amy For being your awesome selves and for a kickass song. Until Later…

Cody For showing me that life is happening NOW.

Rich Words are never adequate!

Jeri Without whom Rebecca St. John would never have existed. You are The Queen!

Christa For your belief that I could do this and showing my what true friendship is.

Stephanie For you editing skills and for showing me that loyalty really does exist.

Carlie's Crew Because you're all AWESOME.

My Readers You. Yes YOU. Thank you for giving this indie chick a chance!

ALL NOVELS BY CARLIE YATES

<u>The Entangled Series</u>
Entitled
Entrapped
Enlightened

<u>Time Stands Still</u>
Wrong Number
Right Reasons
My Happy Ending Part 1
My Happy Ending Part 2
My Happy Ending Part 3 (March 2022)

<u>Standalones</u>
Everly's Hope
Broken (July 2022)

<u>Anthologies</u>
"Perfect" in Shattered Illusions (The Authors' Table)

www.ingramcontent.com/pod-product-compliance
Lightning Source LLC
Chambersburg PA
CBHW032139270626
47172CB00009B/471